1 January 2016, 9.02 a.m.

NY RESOLUTIONS
Delete Tim's number
Get job IN LONDON
Make money
Exercise 5 times a week
Have sex at least once a month
Find my G spot
Make more fun friends
Take a course in design
Give up carbs and sugar mon-fri
Rebrand personal style – less high st
Move out of home TO LONDON

Sara-Ella Ozbek is a London-bred author of South African and Turkish descent. After graduating from the University of Exeter with a BA in English Literature, she interned at *Vogue* magazine and subsequently fell into a job as an assistant at a modelling agency.

After six exciting, if somewhat draining, years as an agent, she left to pursue a career in writing. She attended the New York Film Academy screenwriting programme then went to Los Angeles where she joined the hustle of the screenwriters. Out of the frustration and misery came her first novel, *The High Moments*.

Aside from the novel, she has written non-fiction for titles including *Because* Magazine, *Suitcase*, *Tatler*, *Drugstore Culture*, *Voyage D'Etudes* and *Soho House Notes*, covering stories on fashion, travel, culture and – when she's allowed to – feminism.

THE HIGH MOMENTS

SARA-ELLA OZBEK

**SIMON &
SCHUSTER**

London · New York · Sydney · Toronto · New Delhi

A CBS COMPANY

First published in Great Britain by Simon & Schuster UK Ltd, 2020
A CBS COMPANY

1 3 5 7 9 10 8 6 4 2

Simon & Schuster UK Ltd
1st Floor
222 Gray's Inn Road
London WC1X 8HB

Simon & Schuster Australia, Sydney
Simon & Schuster India, New Delhi

www.simonandschuster.co.uk
www.simonandschuster.com.au
www.simonandschuster.co.in

A CIP catalogue record for this book
is available from the British Library

Paperback ISBN: 978-1-4711-8797-1
eBook ISBN: 978-1-4711-8798-8
Audio ISBN: 978-1-4711-9170-1

Typeset in the UK by M Rules
Printed and bound in Great Britain by CPI Group (UK) Ltd, Croydon, CR0 4YY

CHAPTER 1

Whenever the first of January came round, I had a habit of imagining myself a year on, as someone who had enigmatically outgrown the person I was in that moment. But year after year, it was like déjà vu – and it was starting to get old.

I had always thought of my life in Topsham as a sort of drawn-out prelude to the life I planned on eventually living. I'd expected that once I'd done all the things you're supposed to do – like finish school and university – I'd float naturally into a job for some London-based fashion designer, who would be blown away by a talent that even I'd been uncertain I possessed. I'd live in a flat with palm-printed wallpaper and a free-standing bath, wear embroidered kimonos and get a blue tick by my name on Instagram. I hadn't accounted for being sucked back into the arse-end-of-nowhere to pull pints and wait for a call from the recruiters who had sounded so eager when I was fresh out of the graduate oven back in June. And I certainly hadn't accounted for spending New Year's Day on yet another bathroom floor I didn't recognise, in England's tiniest town.

'You're not still looking for it, are you?' Billie called out from the other side of the door.

I cradled the toilet basin. 'Looking for what?' I said, moving my mouth as little as possible in case it put pressure on my stomach, which was at that very moment threatening to expel the contents of the night before.

The door opened a crack and Billie looked down at me, her blood-red, boy-short hair standing up in all directions. 'Your G spot? Last night you were worried you didn't have one.'

It was then that I winced – not because of what she'd said, but because it reminded me that I'd sent an unsolicited selfie, at three in the morning, to Tim, the on-off fling who hadn't been ready for anything serious throughout the three years we were at university, whom I hadn't seen since graduating and whom I had been known – after a few drinks – to refer to as 'my first love'.

Please.

'Shit,' I muttered.

'Still missing then?' she said.

I wriggled my hand around the floor for my iPhone and braved a peek at the damage: an aerial shot of myself on the loo, captioned, 'Miss me?', as if murky urine framed by average thighs was a truly irresistible thing. Seeing it in the cold light of day, I had a vision of myself shrinking in size and morphing into the screaming face emoji.

I held the phone up to show Billie and moaned. 'This is a disaster!'

I never sent messages like that to Tim, or anyone I was seeing, in the daytime. I was very much Cool Girl in the daytime. That was my safe spot, even if it got me nowhere closer to the discovery of my G spot. That was what he'd always liked about me. No pressure, no strings. Nothing in it for me, basically.

Billie looked at the photo, shrugged, and said, 'At least your piss looks good,' because she knew it would make me laugh. She always knew how to make me laugh.

Billie and I met at school. She was in the year above me,

where she had earned herself the uncreative nickname 'Dyke', owing to the fact that she was the only girl in her year who wasn't a walking blow job charity, and, to be fair, looked a lot like Ant or Dec. We came across each other on a tree-lined hill near school that was called 'the smoker's slope', and its function was self-explanatory. One day, when it was just the two of us, she said to me, 'Can I tell you something, as a friend? I don't think you know how to inhale a fag properly.' I looked at her, amazed that she'd taken notice of some girl in the year below. And it was true. I just took little bird-like sucks on the end of my Lucky Strikes, which was why my cigarettes took longer than everyone else's to burn down, though sometimes I'd blow into them to speed up the process. So Billie kindly taught me how it was done and we'd been best friends ever since. I'd been addicted to cigarettes ever since, too.

'Where are we?' I asked, unsticking my tongue from the roof of my mouth several times in a row.

She shook her head and gave me a look that said, 'You don't want to know.' Billie was my only fun friend and I was hers, so the people we ended up mingling with on nights out were usually unpalatable before the sixth tequila or when you were on their bathroom floor the next day, dying of alcohol poisoning.

'Can we Irish?' I asked hopefully, not in the mood to be polite to anyone.

Billie held her finger to her lips, reaching out with her other hand to haul me up off the ground. I caught a glimpse of myself in the mirror, looking like the grim reaper in a blonde wig – or, rather, an orange-tinged wig, thanks to the home-dye job. As I followed her out, I realized – or remembered – that we were on a boat. I had a fleeting vision of looking out the small window to find that we were halfway to France, but thankfully, or maybe disappointingly, we had not drifted from the sleepy quayside of the town that I'd spent my whole life waiting to leave.

Billie handed me my raincoat as she threw on the bomber jacket that I'd customized with patches and sequins for her when we were sixteen (I'd hardly seen her wear anything else since) and we made a beeline for the exit.

'Can I come back to yours?' I asked as we tumbled out onto the path and started walking.

'I love you, but I need a few more hours' kip before my shift,' she said. 'And you'll want to talk my ear off.'

I got it. She needed her space. Something that I found I had way too much of. Too much space was bad. Too much space led to boredom, and if you let boredom happen, it often mutated into something much gloomier.

'Can I come for a drink later, while you're working?' I asked.

'I'll kill you if you don't.'

With that we parted ways, and my mind began spinning with a faux-methodical reverie detailing exactly what I'd do from that moment on: walk briskly home, prepare a cheese and mayonnaise sandwich, boil the kettle, eat the sandwich while listening to some podcast that would likely instruct me how to be a better human, make coffee, run a bath, soak in said bath while drinking coffee, get into pyjamas, get into bed and take out my long-suffering sketchbook to draw for the rest of the day. I hoped that the familiarity of drawing would be comforting. More than that, I hoped that I'd feel resourceful by feeding the burgeoning fantasy of becoming a fashion designer, which was still loitering in the back of my mind, like something on a hypothetical to-do list.

When I reached the end of my road, I put the whole plan on pause and sat down on someone's doorstep to light a cigarette.

My mother would probably be up and she didn't know that I was a smoker. You'd think as a fully-fledged adult, I'd be able to admit to it, take the disapproving headshake on the chin and move on with life. But, not so.

I took out my phone and opened the Notes application to do what you were meant to do at the start of the year, but what I probably should have done six months earlier.

1 January 2016, 9.02 a.m.

NY RESOLUTIONS
Delete Tim's number
Get job IN LONDON
Make money
Exercise 5 times a week
Have sex at least once a month
Find my G spot
Make more fun friends
Take a course in design
Give up carbs and sugar mon-fri
Rebrand personal style – less high st
Move out of home TO LONDON

'That's not how you chop onions,' said my mother. She took the knife away from me and started slicing them horizontally.

I sank down into one of the mint-green kitchen chairs and opened Instagram on my iPhone, resigned to the fact that I couldn't even chop an onion, let alone get a job, move to London or tick off anything else on the list of New Year's resolutions I'd only just made. I scrolled through the anecdotal squares as the smell of those onions filled the small kitchen, prickling my eyes. There was something so mindlessly captivating about the holidays of people I'd never met, the poached eggs drizzled with green sauce I'd never tasted, the £5 vouchers for a clothing brand I'd never heard of, the fitness videos and makeup tutorials that I always meant to emulate. I stopped on some supermodel I followed who had taken a mirror selfie in a fancy-looking room. She was wearing sunglasses and dangling a pair of high heels from her fingers. The shot was simply captioned, '@KurtGeiger 👠', tempting all of her impressionable followers onto the shoe brand's Instagram page. I clicked right through. Kurt Geiger's profile bio was a one-liner, promising anyone who clicked on the link to their shopping page a chance to feature on their Instagram. Again, through I went.

'What can you possibly still be looking at on that virulent device?' my mother's voice came cascading over my shoulder.

'I like these shoes,' I said, showing her a pair of metallic silver heels.

She glanced briefly then let out a small laugh that I would describe as a chortle. 'When would you wear those? You never go anywhere but the pub!'

'Where else am I supposed to go around here?' I muttered.

The doorbell rang before she could answer, though I'm not sure she had an answer to that question. Her friend Philip had arrived for dinner, like Friday-night clockwork. He was virtually her only friend and she was in love with him, although he was almost certainly gay. They were both lecturers at the University of Exeter, the reason I had been uprooted from an exciting South London life, at the age of four, and dumped into seaside monotony. My mother had taken the job when my father – 'a Dutch immigrant' as the locals now referred to him – left her for a buxom blonde. I'd always imagined she looked like Ursula Andress, but now I think about it, that is highly unlikely. It wasn't something my mother and I spoke about.

My mother and Philip were both reading some book about Russia's cultural elite, which sounded so depressing that I could have slit my wrists just listening to them unpack it over spaghetti bolognaise. The conversation then mutated into Brexit chat, as it always did, which seemed pointless given that we were all set on voting Remain, so what was there to really talk about?

And then Philip asked me the question that I so dreaded to hear, especially around my mother: 'So, Scarl, what are you doing with your life?'

I would've taken the Russian elite or Brexit over that conversation topic.

'I'm trying to find a job, but the recruiter says there's nothing at the moment,' I said, opening my mouth to allow a greedily large forkful of spaghetti to enter.

'The recruiter's been saying that for six months now,' said my mother, without looking at me, which was her way of saying, 'She's a lazy cow.'

'Can't be easy the way things are at the moment,' said Philip, no doubt hoping to open another riveting conversation about the state of our country.

'Yes, but we can't always rely on other people, like recruiters, to do everything for us, can we?' said my mother.

She liked to make comments like that when other people were around, so that I was forced to curb my natural reaction. Instead of welling up with tears of frustration and storming out of the room, as I might have done in her company alone, I just muttered, 'When you live in Topsham you can.'

I couldn't bring myself to tell her that I'd sent off nearly a hundred job applications – to fashion houses, retailers, textile studios; to be a PA, to be a copywriter, to be a goddamn personal shopper; whatever came up on Indeed.co.uk when you typed in 'jobs in fashion London' – and had either been rejected or plain ghosted by every single one of them.

'She wants to work in fashion, you see,' said my mother, with a subtly mocking half-smile at Philip.

'Sounds ever so glamorous,' he said, brightly.

'Glamorous, maybe. Stable or lucrative, absolutely not,' she said, and that was settled.

After dinner, the two of them sat in the living room drinking Pinot Noir and jizzing over a Radio 4 podcast. When I popped my head in, Philip was sitting slim and dainty by the arm of the sofa and my mother was sitting unnecessarily close to him, twirling the ends of her long, silver-streaked hair around her fingers.

'I'm going to the pub,' I said, a sentence I knew she was bored of hearing.

'Are you working?' she asked.

'Nope.' (Couldn't even claim that excuse.) 'Just going to see Billie.'

She gave me something between a nod and an eye roll before holding up her hand dramatically, evidently anxious that she was missing some particularly arousing soundbite of condescending intellectual bullshit.

When I arrived at the pub, Billie was busy serving a couple of battered kids who had come down to crawl the Topsham Ten, like the university students loved to do during term time. It had always baffled me – the idea of escaping the shackles of home and entering the freedom of uni life, and thinking the best you could do was a pub crawl in a town with a population of five thousand. But hey, each to their own.

While I waited, propped up at the bar, I re-read my New Year's resolutions, hoping they would seep into me by osmosis, and that a light bulb would miraculously appear above my head, or a rocket would force its way up my arse. Finally the kids staggered off, pints of dark lager in hand. It was the fifth pub on the trail and it was standard that they'd all be sick by the seventh, but who was I to judge, given my own track record with vomit?

Billie slid a vodka tonic over to me and tapped her long, acrylic nails against the bar top.

'No money,' I said, guiltily.

'What a surprise,' she said, and started rubbing a pint glass with a dirty tea towel.

'What am I gonna do?' I whined. She was better at coming up with solutions than I was.

'Just work more shifts here. It adds up,' she said.

'I need a proper job.'

'You mean a *Landan* job?' she said. She'd been teasing me about being London-beguiled ever since I'd gone to see the Alexander McQueen exhibition at the V&A museum the year before and had come back banging on about how the city had given me life.

'I don't know how I'm going to make it happen,' I said, and rested my head on the bar to show just how hard I was finding life.

'Why don't you shut up talking about it, pack your stuff up and just bloody go?' she said.

'Yeah, that's realistic,' I said, looking up.

'Why not? Just walk into one of these wank-arse fashion places you want to work for and tell them they'd be mad not to hire you. You've got nothing to lose.'

Nope, just my dignity, I thought, and returned my head to the sticky wooden bar top, where it belonged.

'You're so fucking hard to pity when you do nothing to fix your problems, Scizzle,' she said, which pissed me off, because I knew it was true. And also, 'Scizzle' was a nickname from school, and I was growing to hate what a stupid word it was.

Over the next few weeks, I continued sketching, scrolling, creating Pinterest boards and making lists of all my favourite designers and fashion icons in preparation for the job interview that I was becoming less and less confident was coming. I even started going on runs, adhering to at least one of my resolutions, in an attempt to prepare myself for the lifestyle that I still believed was ahead of me, though the route into it was nowhere in sight. I'd never been the sportiest of types, having opted for the smoker's slope or the art room rather than the lacrosse field at school, and was rather regretting those years as I rasped along the quay with a splitting pain from throat to abdomen.

It was towards the end of January, when I returned from one of my runs looking like a sweaty beetroot, that my mother announced, 'I've got you a job at the university.'

I reached over to pluck a digestive biscuit from the packet she was holding (runs meant that I could eat whatever I wanted, obviously) and asked, 'What kind of job?'

'Assisting one of the history professors with faculty research.'

'That sounds bleak,' I said, flatly, and bit into the biscuit, letting crumbs fall down my chin.

'It's not bleak, actually. It's very interesting,' she said defensively.

'I doubt *I* will find it interesting!' I retorted, amazed that she was still imposing her interests – which, clearly, were not mine – onto me. 'There's no way I'm doing that job.'

'Well what, may I ask, are you going to do instead?' she said.

'Not your problem!' I replied, though it probably was, given that I was living with her. 'Just leave me alone.'

Then she used her go-to weapon: 'God, you are so like your father.'

At one time, tears would have been my response to that remark, but I'd grown so used to hearing it that I simply snapped a sardonic 'Thanks!' back.

She carried on: 'You're never going to get a job sitting in the pub waiting for a recruiter to call. You have to be proactive, you have to—'

'I've applied for about a million jobs. No one fucking wants me!' It bubbled out of me unexpectedly, like a carbonated liquid that had been shaken too hard. Immediately, I felt embarrassed that I'd admitted to what I suspected she already thought: no one wanted me. Her cryptic silence prompted a creeping pain in the base of my throat, so I muttered, 'Just leave me alone,' and flounced away from her.

As I was slamming my bedroom door, I heard her call out my name, which I knew always reminded her of my father. He'd given me that name, after Scarlett O'Hara. I assumed it was because he was hoping I'd turn out to be a charming belle, but he'd not stuck around long enough to find out. There had been the odd visit in the early years after he left, but they had become more and more infrequent, until, finally, they were nothing but a memory. I didn't even know he'd married Ursula Andress until years after. I wondered if he'd be disappointed to see me now, the girl who was always 'too' something: too loud, too messy, too promiscuous, too bold.

The thought of his hypothetical disappointment made me angry. I was done. I was done being the 'too-something' girl with that very clever mother, who had somehow turned out to be so useless. *Somehow.* 'Somehow' meant that it was my fault. It didn't mean that my mother had been so engaged with her students and her writing that there had been nothing left for the child drowning in the room with her.

I heard Billie's voice in my head — *'Why don't you shut up talking about it, pack your stuff up and just bloody go?'* — and, without even thinking, I took out a suitcase and started packing.

If I wasn't in a bad enough mood already, the crinkled mound of clothes that were on offer to me really sent me raging. All of a sudden, I hated my Topshop jeans, my well-worn Dunlop trainers, the River Island boots that I'd begged my mother to buy me on a shopping trip to Exeter, and I particularly hated the collection of thrift-store dresses that she'd bought me over the years. But I packed them all anyway, because I had nothing else.

And then I saw a familiar bell-sleeve hauled up against the mound of disappointing garb. Momentarily forgetting about my packing stress, I pulled out Henrietta, the dress I'd crafted for my A Level final and named after my dead dog. As dresses went, it was pretty heinous, with its overly pointed collar, messy line of buttons and poor choice of Aztec fabric, but it still made me smile. I'll never forget the feeling of stepping back after the eight hours spent draping and stitching the patterns that my art teacher had helped me pre-prepare, and seeing the finished piece, which was offbeat compared to the country landscapes that the other students had gone for. My mother had barely acknowledged Henrietta, even on results day, when the only A grade on the page was for art, just as she'd never shown any interest in the paper dolls I'd spent all the hours of my childhood drawing, cutting and colouring whole wardrobes of outfits for.

I rolled Henrietta into a cylinder and stuffed her into

the corner of my suitcase. Last, I added a collection of what I thought were my favourite books, because they'd been so heavily Instagrammed – Joan Didion, Zadie Smith, Jay McInerney – and my actual favourites – Caitlin Moran, Jilly Cooper, Tina Fey – and then I texted Billie to tell her I'd made a major life decision and that she was responsible for it.

When I went downstairs, my mother was sitting at her desk, marking essays. She was totally immersed, oblivious to the sound of my suitcase rolling over the wooden floors. Even when I planted myself right in front of her, she didn't lift her eyes from the paper. It was a familiar sight. In fact, this was exactly how my mother materialized in my head whenever I thought about her.

'I'm moving to London,' I said.

Her eyes flickered towards me for a millisecond, but she still didn't look directly at me. 'Don't be ridiculous.'

'Okay, bye, then,' I said in an infantile manner, and whirled away.

'Scarlett, you are *not* going to London,' she said imperiously.

'Yes, I am.'

She stood up and pressed her palms over her eyebrows, like I'd just given her a terrible migraine. 'I cannot afford to bankroll your zeitgeist millennial fantasy.'

'You don't have to bankroll it. I'll be bankrolling it!'

'Let's see how long you last in London before you're on the phone, crying to me because you've hit the bottom of your overdraft and you're at some obscure train station or airport, completely alone, and I'll have no choice but to bail you out, or let you starve.'

To be fair, it sounded like a plausible scenario. Or, rather, something that had actually happened the last time I'd gone to London . . .

'Maybe I'll let you starve this time!' she added, and even in the dimness of the room, I could see that she was at the end of her tether.

'Great, I could do with the fucking weight loss!' I shouted angrily. I turned around and headed towards the door.

'Scarlett! Come back here!'

But I didn't. I slammed the front door like a teenager in a sulk and headed for the station.

CHAPTER 2

It wasn't until I was on the train that I had the real, *what the fuck am I doing?* moment. I wasn't so blinded by the bright lights that I didn't care about having three meals a day, central heating and a roof over my head. I took out my iPhone to look up 'cheap flats to rent in London', which was futile given that I only had a few quid to my name. Each and every one of them was – *quelle surprise* – extortionate. What was London, the third priciest city in the world? I decided to Google it. It was the first.

Say goodbye to that wardrobe rebrand or a student-debt-free existence, Scarlett.

I did have a friend from university who had moved there, but every time I'd suggested coming to see her she'd seemed less than enthused, so I'd given up. But since I didn't even have enough money to take the train back to Topsham, I picked up the phone.

She answered after a few rings with a somewhat suspicious 'Hello?'

'Liz! How are you?' I said, trying to sound both easy-going and responsible – like someone you'd want on your sofa. We did the small talk, the niceties, she made her excuses for being out of touch, and then I went for it and said, 'So, I'm on my way to London.'

'Oh, cool.' Her voice faded before she reached the 'L' in 'cool'.

Don't get too excited, I thought, *that rod might fall out of your arse.*

'I'm coming for a job interview,' I said, which I figured was only half a lie, since I did plan on getting at least one job interview. 'I wondered if I could stay for a couple of nights?'

I heard a sigh down the phone, and then: 'Scarlett, you can stay, but . . .'

'But what?'

'I live with . . .'

'Hello?'

'I live with Tim.'

Silence filled the phone line for a few seconds, which is all it took for me to compute that Tim was not her flatmate. Suddenly, her efforts to keep me at arm's length made perfect sense. I even took some comfort in knowing that it hadn't been anything to do with how much she liked me. She probably didn't really want to push me away from her; she just wanted to fuck and live with my 'first love'. The thought of seeing Liz and Tim together was all too strange. Liz was a straight-A student, with a degree in economics, a job in the city, a burgeoning savings account and perfect hair. And Tim had once stolen the light bulb from my bedroom after I'd slept with him because he couldn't be bothered to buy his own. He was, frankly, not good enough for her.

'Scarlett?'

But I had nowhere to go.

'Shall we talk about this?' she asked softly.

I cleared my throat. 'Sorry, the line broke up. Can I come stay anyway?'

'It's only temporary,' I promised my friend and ex-boyfriend – her new boyfriend – who, I was sure, had no idea that he'd taken my virginity.

'It's cool, any time,' said Tim uncertainly, looking anywhere but directly at me as he held out a fleece blanket. For someone who had spent the years of university looking like he'd bought all of his clothes at Dubai Airport, he appeared awfully sensible in his white collared shirt and badly fitting suit pants.

Liz hovered awkwardly in the open-plan kitchen. 'Let us know if you need anything.'

Us.

I looked at the perfectly clean and hard-looking leather cushions on the sofa. 'Could I maybe have a pillow?'

'Of course,' said Liz, eagerly hurrying off into the bedroom.

I smiled at Tim, a slightly humorous smile in the hope of making light of the situation, but he wouldn't meet my eyes. In fact, he even started humming through his teeth – some football tune, I believe. As he came round to the second verse, I was suddenly amazed that he'd ever been able to arouse me, sexually or emotionally.

Liz came back with a plush white pillow from their bed and he stopped the silly little tune self-consciously. I wondered if the pillow was hers or his and if it meant they'd now be sharing one.

'Thank you so much,' I said, an image of his face buried in her glossy hair loitering in my mind.

'Good luck with the job interview,' said Tim, hanging onto that thing we both knew was not really happening.

'Thanks so much again, guys. Sleep well,' I said pleasantly.

They disappeared down a corridor – together, into their bedroom – together. I wondered what they would do once they'd shut the door. Probably look at each other with rounded eyes and let out a long-held breath while mouthing things like, 'What is she thinking?' and 'Mega awks!' Would they have sex on the other side of the wall, making every effort to be quiet? Did they even have sex? I couldn't imagine Liz standing for his 'in-out, me-me-me' attitude towards love-making. Had she trained that out of him? Or had he been different with her from the start?

I opened a kitchen cupboard. I was feeling too hyper and on edge to think about sleep. My usual solution was to eat an entire packet of fizzy sweets or chocolate buttons, which would send me flying on a sugar high followed unfailingly by a crash into heavy, sticky sleep. But I only had oats and almonds to contend with in that perfectly organized new-build kitchen.

I settled into the sofa that was clearly made for perching, not slouching, and definitely not for sleeping. Much to my annoyance, I had a Find My Friends request from my mother, whose calls I had not been answering. Was she crazy? Who allows their mother to install a tracking device on their phone that gives them the ability to virtually follow them around?

I ignored the request and opened the Notes application.

25 January 2016, 11.12 p.m.

Fuck my life right now

The next morning I went to a local internet café to print out my flimsy-looking CV, one hundred times over. Then I embarked on a public transport tour of anywhere that could possibly hire me: Vogue House, Sunbeam Studios, Harrods, Selfridges, Harvey Nichols, Net-a-Porter, Matches, Farfetch, LN-CC, Fenwick, Erdem, Michael Kors, Burberry, Alexander McQueen, Alice Temperley, Louis Vuitton. I even tried every store on Bond Street that might have needed a sales assistant, for God's sakes. Every time I was met with a vacant smile and a look of 'Are you fucking serious?' from some receptionist or store manager. Desperate for hard cash, I also dropped my CV into a heap of restaurants and cafés, but even they were unresponsive. You'd have never known from my Insta-montage of city streets, museum lobbies and artisan bakeries, with captions like 'This'll do 👌', that my days were nothing but a broken record of rejection.

During this time, Liz kept mentioning people we'd been to university with who lived in London. And even though they were people I'd barely known, I got in touch to suggest a drink, because we both knew that the situation at the flat was fucking dire. The problem was, apparently there was something called 'dry January', which hermitized the population for an entire month. Most evenings I slipped into bars or pubs to spend a few hours browsing memes and sending the funniest ones to Billie while sipping orange juice – because I knew that getting drunk alone was never a good sign (or a good look, for that matter). Then I'd return to the domesticity of Liz and Tim's coupled-up life claiming to have had a fabulously fun night out.

I was finally in the metropolis where I'd thought I would feel endlessly invigorated, but it turned out that there were only so many times you could walk the streets solo and get a kick out of the heaving pavement of drinkers and Soho sex shops and tube station saxophonists. I'd never understood the concept of the lonely city dweller, but I was starting to. London, it turned out, wasn't the easiest place to make friends. Everyone existed in tightly sewn-out pockets, and I didn't know how or when I would find mine. I knew I should be going on Tinder dates, or something. But what would I tell a stranger? That I was a homeless, jobless and, frankly, prospect-less addition to the city?

Lock up your sons, London.

*

It was three weeks into my overstay at Liz and Tim's that an email finally appeared in my inbox, like a shining beacon of hope. A current went through me when I saw the subject line: 'Assistant job'. I opened it eagerly. A 'creative stylist' – whatever that was – called Pawel Dyk – no joke – needed a 'second assistant'. The email came from his first assistant, who had been given my CV by another company.

This is it, I thought. *My misery is about to end.* I responded immediately and an interview was scheduled for the following day. I went online to research Pawel Dyk. He certainly seemed to be a big deal, given that he had a blue tick, 70K Instagram followers, and there were hundreds of Google pages about him. The most recent picture on his Instagram was a model reclining on what looked like a hospital bed, dressed in an evening gown, with one nipple hanging out and her legs splayed open. Pawel's caption read, 'created by me'. The next was a pastiche of a 1950s housewife, vacantly drinking vodka from the bottle with a straw, also with one nipple on show. The next was a 'business-woman' in her office, handcuffed to the chair with a gag ball in her mouth and, yet again, the exposed nipple. I suddenly had a vision of my mother looking through the images of these slightly dead-looking (or at least drugged) women when I told her the name of my new boss.

But however uncomfortable the images made me, I wasn't hesitant about the interview. I needed the job. And anyway, there were countless articles calling Pawel a genius, so what did I know? Maybe I was taking it all too literally. There was probably an irony to these images that I had totally missed. Pawel could be depicting a powerful feminist message, one that only a true creative could decipher. Perhaps he was an advocate of 'free the nipple'. Or maybe I had just become oversensitive as a result of all the virtuous podcasts I listened to and needed to open my mind.

When I arrived at Pawel's studio the next day, the first assistant who had emailed me opened the door. I couldn't help but think she looked more like a cadaver than a woman. Obviously I kept that little observation to myself, however.

'Hi. Come in,' she said, the suggestion of a smile trying to break its way through her seriousness.

In total silence, I followed her down a concrete corridor of strip lighting with blue doors along the walls. There was a horror film vibe to the place and I wondered if I was about to walk into a dungeon lined with handcuffs and gag balls and the carcasses of the women in Pawel's Instagram photos. When we entered the unit, though, I was relieved to see that it was a legitimate fashion studio, the first I'd ever been into, which gave me a millisecond of excitement before I felt sick with nerves. There were rails of clothes, floor-to-ceiling pin boards of magazine cuttings, and a long table covered in a mound of thick, expensive coffee-table books.

Pawel sat at one end of the table, delicately leafing through a book. He had black hair, cut short at the back, with a side fringe hanging halfway down his face. He wore a variation of a white shirt, with an Indian-style collar and a phantom bow tie. I couldn't see what the bottom half of the ensemble was, because he didn't get up from his desk, or even look at me.

'Sit down,' said the cadaver woman, gesturing to the chair furthest from Pawel. She placed herself next to him. 'So, where did you go to fashion school?' she asked.

Fashion school?

Had they even read my CV?

'I went to university,' I answered dumbly. 'Loughborough.'

There was no suggestion that Pawel even knew I was in the room.

'Okay. What did you study?' asked cadaver-lady.

'Sociology.'

It finally became clear that Pawel was not in fact deaf when the two of them exchanged a tiny, complicit glance.

'But I did art at A level. And I've always, *always* wanted to be a designer,' I added.

'So, why don't you go work for a designer?' said Pawel, monotonously, still not looking up from the book.

Because no one wants me.

'Because I really admire your work,' I tried, desperate, but unconvincing.

Pawel looked up. His eyes swept over me, evaluating me like a product. And I thought my mother was judgmental!

'I feel I could learn a lot,' I continued, to fill the silence.

'Why do you admire my work?' he said.

Because I think you might be trying to do more for women's rights than the suffragette movement itself, but I can't be sure.

'It's very bold,' I said instead.

He shifted his eyes towards the cadaver and I thought I saw the minutest of eye rolls. He sighed, and asked with an intonation of boredom, 'So, what do you want to design?'

Finally, something I could answer. 'I want to make clothes that redefine the term power dressing.' I'd practised that one the night before.

'What does that mean?' Pawel almost scoffed.

'Clothes that are designed to make women feel confident,' I said. And then, 'Clothes for real women.'

They both stared at me and I suddenly thought that maybe I'd insulted him. The cadaver spoke next. 'Have you got a portfolio?'

'Um ... sort of,' I reached into my bag and pulled out Henrietta, whom I'd ironed and folded that morning. I stood up and let the full length of the dress fall to the floor. 'I made it on my own,' I said proudly. 'It's not the fabric I would have chosen, but it's all I could get in Topsham, where I'm from. I taught myself how to sew.'

Pawel glanced at the cadaver again and this time it was not a snarky eye roll – it was something darker.

She stood up and said, 'I think that's all we have time for today.'

'I also have a sketchbook—' I tried.

'We'll be in touch,' she said, and briskly walked off to open the door for me. The message was clear: I was to get the fuck out of there and never come back.

I walked down the creepy industrial corridors alone, feeling almost suffocated by those strip lights, and out into the street. I sunk down onto the doorstep and hung my head in my hands like the failure I was. How could I have been stupid enough to think that I could waltz into a job like that? Why would the fashion industry, who could cherry pick the best of the best, give some random sociology student from the arse-end-of-Fucksville a chance?

I had obviously been way ahead of myself. Fashion school was what I needed to do. *That* was the stepping stone. University had been a total waste of time. But how was I supposed to make fashion school happen? There was no way I could pay for it, and my mother certainly wouldn't help. I didn't even know if there was a fashion school that would want me, considering no one else seemed to.

I took out my iPhone and attempted to make a plan.

19 February 2016, 3.22 p.m.

TO DO
Research fashion schools
Start portfolio
Make a new friend who will have me to live for free
Become an escort????
Fuck cfuck fuck fuckckjsflksfjl

Then the door opened. The cadaver nearly tripped over me on her way out and looked down at me with what I translated as disdain. Then that ambiguous smile as she lit a cigarette. 'Number one rule in fashion: no one wants to hear about "real women",' she said after taking a drag.

'He asked me a question and I answered it honestly,' I snapped.

'We're not selling honesty. We construct fantasy.'

'Right,' I said, with little patience for pretentious rhetoric when all my dreams were crumbling around me.

The cadaver tucked her free hand under the opposite elbow and eyed me for an unsettlingly long time. Then she took out her phone, to distract herself, I assumed, so that she didn't have to talk to me anymore. But she carried on: 'They're looking for a women's division assistant over at Pure. I'm going to put you in touch. Think it might suit you better than this.'

I frowned. Was she trying to help me? I had no idea what Pure was and thought that a 'women's division assistant' sounded like a role at a female prison, but at that point, I would've taken it.

'You got Instagram?' she said, without looking up.

'Yeah, I do.'

'Check your DMs,' she said, and then turned her back on me, ambling away to enjoy the rest of her cigarette in peace.

Within a few moments, she had put me in touch with someone called Steph Conway, suggesting me for the role of 'asst'. Steph replied, almost immediately, asking me to come in for a trial day on Monday. That was in three days' time. I thought it was strange to go for a trial day before you'd had an interview, and even stranger when you had no idea what the job was, but I was not about to complain. I replied that, of course, I'd come in on Monday. Then I delved into Steph Conway's Instagram to try and put the pieces together.

Her feed was filled with magazine covers and fashion shows, interspersed with pictures of the London skyline and fancy-looking cocktails. Not a bad sign. I clicked on an image of a model on a catwalk captioned, 'You go girl! @PureModelsWorldwide #newface'.

I clicked through to the Pure Models Worldwide Instagram and read their bio: 'Leading global agency, representing women, men and special talents.'

Pure was a modelling agency.

CHAPTER 3

I can say with confidence that I have never felt more out of my depth than I did perched on the cow-skin sofa that was on a diagonal angle in the reception of the Pure Models agency in Covent Garden. I was staring up at a wall of framed magazine covers, meticulously spaced out and inhabited by women who looked as if they had grown from the ground, like perfectly formed trees.

I had no idea what a model agent did, but I had a sense that it meant you were on the cusp of being relevant.

The receptionist, a thin-faced boy in gold-rimmed spectacles, glanced up from his computer screen. 'You said you're here for a trial day?'

'That's right,' I said, too loud, dragging the palms of my sweaty hands along the faux-leather skirt that I'd bought especially the day before and decided for some God-known reason to wear with knee-high boots and, worse, star-printed tights.

The receptionist closed one eye and scrutinized me through the remaining open slit. 'It's not in the system. Did you get an email confirmation?'

'It was done through Instagram,' I said, realizing that it was a sentence that pretty much defined my existence.

'Oh, you're from Pawel's?' he said, with inevitability rather than surprise.

I guessed he'd heard the tragic tale of Pawel & Henrietta.

'That's me!' I smiled, suddenly conscious about my jagged teeth, which I'd refused to let anyone put braces on, screaming that they gave me 'character' at the age of twelve.

The receptionist stood up to his full height of six-foot-four, and my eyes swooped to the ankle-length denim skirt he was wearing. 'Come with me.'

I stood up and clopped along behind him – my knee-highs beating against the hard floor like hooves – into what he called 'the booking room'. It was entirely white, like a large rectangular igloo, its walls lined with models faces gazing out of bordered cards and tight rows of magazines. Clean and sharp but, disappointingly, nothing too fancy. The main feature of the room was a long table, on which stood twelve desktop computers. Two faces bobbed up from behind the screens, both of them male, one so tanned and shiny that it looked like plastic, and the other a pigmentation of pale and rosy skin. It was a Monday morning and they were the only people in, it seemed.

'Morning, Worm!' said the tanned one, with a heavy Australian accent. 'Heard you went bareback riding at the public toilets on Friday.'

'The prospective is here,' said the receptionist (*Worm?*), sounding bored.

'What fucking *prospective*?' said pale and rosy. He sounded like he had a problem with his vocal cords and was not exactly the person who came to mind when you envisioned someone who worked in the fashion industry.

'The Instagram girl from Pawel,' said the receptionist, a title I sincerely hoped wouldn't stick. 'Prospective assistant.'

'I don't know anything about it,' said the man with the vocal cords, who turned to the Australian. 'Do you know anything about this?'

The Australian shrugged. I'd expected a model agency to be a place swarming with twenty-somethings who spent their evenings on the rooftops of East London members' clubs and went home to flatmates who worked at magazines, or maybe to their aspiring photographer boyfriends and blog-writing girlfriends. But these two were both much older than me. They were proper grown-ups.

'Steph organized it,' said the receptionist.

'Oh, you'll have to wait for that hot mess to get in,' said the vocal cords, getting up to open a window.

'No, Drew, it's cold!' the Australian barked at him.

I took note of Drew's name, so that I could stop feeling like I was in the opening of a bad – and probably offensive – joke, as he whined, 'I'm sweating!'

'That's because you're overweight!' said the Australian, and I stifled a sputter of laughter, wondering how I would take it if someone ever said something so cutting to me.

Drew just rolled his eyes and said, 'Oh, you're so cruel!'

'It's not cruel,' said the Australian. 'There are chubby-chasers out there. It's a big scene!'

'You would know, honey. You're no twink!' said Drew, giving him an exaggerated look up and down.

'Do I wanna be a twink aged nearly fucking forty?' the Australian snapped, and finally I could hold in the laughter no more. It was all too ridiculous. They both turned to me, amused that they'd amused me. I could see them sizing up the carefully considered combination of fast fashion, which I gathered was over the top, given that they were wearing jeans and trainers.

'D'you wanna sit down?' said Drew, nodding at a lone desk at the corner of the igloo. 'You can get started on tear sheets, since you're a *prospective*.' He stood up and traipsed around the table holding a pile of magazines, which he dropped in front of me with an aggressive thud. 'Go through these magazines and tag any pages that have our models on them. Then you'll order two more copies and tear out the relevant pages for their portfolios.'

'How will I know which ones are your models?'

He looked a bit irritated with me then, but how was I meant to know? 'The names are in the credits, at the end of the fashion stories. Check on our website if you're not sure.'

And with that, he left me. I sat down at the little corner desk and picked up one of the magazines, nearly dropping it, given its unexpected weight. It was the kind of magazine that I usually flipped through at the newsagent's but couldn't afford to buy. I didn't think there was anything more luxurious than one of those perfectly A4 glossy titles. The paper felt thick between my fingers, not flimsy like the weeklies, and had a distinct smell, almost like perfume. Every page, whether it was an advert, a fashion story or an article, was a visual sensation. There was a fantastical element to the photography, the images depicting something incredible but wholly unreal. I stopped at a black-and-white double-page spread, captured on a beach. The model was reclining sideways against the sand, adorned in nakedness, not a muffin top in sight. When I checked the credits for the model's name, I found that it matched a name on Pure's website. I tagged the page, as I'd been told to do, finding it surreal that this otherworldly creature must have passed through the very room that I was sitting in.

Over the hour, more and more people came tripping in, each with a groan and a different metaphor to describe how they were feeling: 'Hanging out my arse', 'Like my organs are slowly disintegrating', and 'Still sneezing Columbia', among others. It was towards the end of the hour that the 'hot mess' called Steph dragged herself in sporting the homeless-chic look: beanie hat, oversized coat, a small backpack slung over one shoulder. She, at least, was younger than the others, mid-twenties maybe, and looked like someone you'd see at the back of one of the weeklies, like *Grazia* or *Now*, talking about her favourite coffee shops and why she loved her job at Urban Outfitters.

'Good afternoon, sunshine,' said the Australian, whose name I still didn't know.

'Lilah is having an absolute shit fit,' said Steph. 'Crazy booked her on another shoot with Damien Stern. Last time he photographed her, he made her take off her knickers and stand on a mirror.'

'That sounds about right,' said Drew, with a slightly uncomfortable pursing of the lips. 'Not surprised Lilah's in a rage.'

'Yeah, well, Crazy and Damien were getting on it together at Tramp the other night and organized it without telling me,' said Steph. 'Now I have to do damage control.'

'And I suppose you forgot that you ordered an assistant on Instagram?' said Drew, looking over at me.

Steph whirled around. 'Yes, I did. But I'm so happy you're here!' I detected a Northern accent. Mancunian, perhaps. 'What's your name, darling?'

I'd soon learn that when you worked in fashion, you could call anyone 'darling', regardless of how many seconds you'd known them for.

'Scarlett,' I said, with a smile that must have looked either fake or pained. And then, for some reason, I gave her a stupid wave of the hand and a high-pitched 'Heya!'

'Scarlett. Leave the magazines, you can do those later. Take this—' she handed me a credit card. 'Go to Gail's. Get a turmeric latte with oat milk and something delicious-looking, like a cake ... No, wait, she's dieting. Um ... Get the latte and then maybe a bunch of flowers from somewhere else.'

I'd already forgotten what kind of latte she'd said.

'Then I need you to take it to Lilah at the shoot. I'll give you the address.'

'Okay. Who's Lilah?' I asked.

'She's a big up-and-coming model, darling,' she said, sounding quite impatient.

I did wonder how a model could be both up and coming and big, but didn't think it was the time to question semantics.

'You really think it's a good idea to send a prospective you've not even had a conversation with?' said the Australian, as if I wasn't sitting right there – as if I hadn't just told them my name.

'Literally, *je* cannot right now,' said Steph, which he seemed to understand, as did everyone – even, weirdly, me. 'Turmeric latte. Bunch of flowers for about fifty quid.'

I groped around the desk for a pen and jotted it on my hand that time. I'd never heard of a turmeric latte, but imagined it was the new-age, less basic version of a pumpkin spiced latte.

The address she gave me was in north-west London. I took the Bakerloo line, as instructed by Citymapper, and then walked to Gail's, a charming local bakery (or so I thought). As I ordered the elusive turmeric latte, I felt a small sense of triumph. Sure, it was just coffee, but still, I had been given a task and I was doing it. When it was handed to me, I took a tiny sip, just to see if I could believably pull off being the kind of person who casually ordered a turmeric latte of a Monday morning. I decided that I most definitely could. Next, I went to a flower shop down the road where I purchased an expensive bouquet of peonies. It turned out to be rather small and probably not spectacular enough for the big, up-and-coming model, or worth the fifty quid. Clearly, I'd been ripped off, but what could I do?

Damien Stern's studio was at the top of a red-brick building. On the way up the stairs, I heard loud dance music and suddenly realized that I wasn't just getting coffee and flowers. I was about to walk onto a fashion shoot: I was about to be at ground zero of the glossy magazines I'd been thumbing through less than an hour before. As I reached for the door handle, I told myself to play it cool, but that immediately went to shit as I was hit by a gust of cold air that made me gasp.

'Chill out, it's only the wind machine,' a voice said. I turned to see a very bored-looking girl dressed all in black, much like the thin woman at Pawel's. I tried to laugh off my clear out-of-placeness and she coldly asked, 'Can I help you?'

'I'm looking for Lilah,' I said, with faux-confidence.

The girl, presumably an assistant, threw her arm out unenthusiastically, and I turned in the direction of the flop.

I was expecting to meet a raging diva in sunglasses, refusing to get out of her robe and throwing hard objects at anyone who came near her. But the only person who looked like a model was the gangly, nonchalant figure lounging on the floor with a cigarette hanging from her plump lips. I remember thinking that someone who chose to sit on the floor rather than in a chair (of which there were many), and to smoke inside rather than out in the cold, was bound to be a kindred spirit.

I approached her with a little more caution than I did most people, wondering if she really wanted her quiet moment interrupted by a plant-based hot drink and a second-rate bunch of peonies, and said, 'Are you Lilah?'

She looked up curiously, no doubt wondering whose idea it was to send a badly dressed, bottle-dyed blonde, who didn't even know who she was, to make up for having shoved her helplessly into the hands of an alleged molester. She had that rock-and-roll dishevelled look that I'd always wanted: a messy brown tangle of hair hanging by the collarbone and a fringe brushing the eye line in a partially blinding way, like Chrissie Hynde in her Pretenders days. Her lips curled up into a smile, revealing a wide and oddly inviting gap between her front teeth. Another thing we had in common.

Sitting on floors, smoking indoors – and imperfect teeth.

I knew she was expecting me to say something else, but all I managed was, 'You all right?', far too loudly, and I think I even slurred a little. I lowered into a half squat and my skirt tightened, the bulge of my lower abdomen pressing so hard at the pleather that I expected it to burst open as I thrust the flowers and the turmeric latte towards her. She sort of laughed, stubbing her cigarette out in a mug. I would've laughed too, if it weren't for the precarious skirt seam.

'I'm from the agency,' I explained, as she took the gifts.

'Thank you! Steph knows the way to my heart,' she said. I had expected her to talk like Marianne Faithfull – melodic and whimsical – but she had a coarse Essex accent. She took a sip of the latte. 'Is this oat milk?'

For a second, I thought about lying, having completely forgotten the milk specification. Turmeric *and* oat was all a bit too much to remember. She obviously read my expression before I could say anything, because she laughed. That time, I laughed too.

'Sorry about that,' I said.

'Babe, it's fine. I'm not allergic or anything.'

Apparently 'babe' was also an acceptable term for addressing strangers. I kind of loved all this pet-namery.

'So, how are you liking the agency?' she asked.

Do I tell her I'm just a prospective?

'I just started, less than an hour ago,' I said, planting myself on the floor next to her, tucking the knee-highs out of sight behind me.

'No way! What were you doing before?'

Waitressing at a pub in Shitsville and trawling around London begging someone to hire me.

I couldn't bring myself to tell her that.

'I was working for a stylist.'

'Oh, cool, who?' she asked, taking the lid off her non-oat-milk turmeric latte and licking the froth, without the decency to take her eyes off me and give me some privacy to formulate another lie. I felt a little panic flutter in my chest. I only knew the names of really famous stylists and imagined that she knew them all personally.

'Someone in Paris,' I said, racking my brain for another conversation topic to cut this one short, because I'd never even been to Paris.

'And you wanna be an agent now?' asked Lilah, her lips golden-yellow with turmeric.

'Actually, I want to be a designer,' I said, with a tiny sigh of relief that I was finally telling the truth about something. 'I'm just doing this until I start fashion school.'

It wasn't a total lie. If I got the job at Pure it would only be a stepping stone towards fashion school. That's what I was thinking, at least.

'How did you end up at the mad house?' said Lilah, and I assumed she meant Pure, given how my morning had gone so far.

'Friend of my mum's,' I muttered. I still don't know where that one came from, but sometimes I just can't stop myself from embellishing the truth. Or in that case, just lying.

'Madeleine?' said Lilah, and I nodded dumbly, not even knowing who Madeleine was. 'Love Madeleine!'

At that point I managed to move the conversation on by commenting on her trainers. They had been custom-made for her, she told me, by a friend who was an aspiring designer, and then she reminded herself that she needed to post them on Instagram. *Maybe I could make her an item of clothing to post on Instagram*, I thought.

We chatted away easily about how much we preferred trainers to high heels and straight cigarettes to roll-ups. That conversation, that first time, her attention was so fully on me, so complete, that for a few minutes I felt like I was literally the most important person in her world. It was such a welcome contrast to how I felt in the flat with Liz and Tim, to how I felt at home with my mother – to how, in fact, I'd felt with most people.

When she was called to wardrobe, she placed her slender hand over my less slender wrist and whispered, 'Can I ask you a favour? Could you stay until I've finished shooting? I just think he might behave better if an agent is here.'

The thought that I could be called an agent, given the unemployable state I'd been in only a few days before, seemed mind-boggling, but of course I was delighted to stay. I wondered if the agency would be as delighted, given that I was only a prospective, but Steph sounded relieved when I called her and told me to stay the whole day if Lilah wanted me to. I sat on a folding chair next to the catering table, invisible to all intents and purposes, but for once oddly content in being so.

Damien Stern finally appeared, swinging two large cameras

around his neck like weapons, and he really was the shortest man I'd ever seen. I felt a swell of disgust watching him shamelessly saunter over to Lilah, and thought that, as her surrogate agent, I should be protecting her in some way. But Lilah seemed totally unfazed and greeted him like an old friend. After a brief exchange, Damien lifted his camera and suddenly everyone was ready to go.

Lilah took her place at the centre of the studio roll, like a Barbie in her box. She was dressed in a heavily embellished angular jacket that – I overheard the stylist say – was Balmain, and a pair of ripped jeans. I'd never seen a Balmain jacket in real life. It sparkled under the bright shooting lights, the hundreds of throbbing jewels shooting rays onto the ceiling, like a disco ball. I had an urge to walk up and touch it, but thankfully not an uncontrollable urge, because that would have been quite something. Lilah looked fiercely into the camera, flirting with the lens in a way that I imagined she flirted with men (or women?). She kept making sharp, cat-like movements, changing position for each shot. The song 'Le Freak' was blaring out over her and I was aimlessly bobbing my head to the beat. Hearing that song will forever remind me of how I felt in that moment: awestruck.

Lilah looked like a supermodel who'd stepped right out of a black-and-white photograph from the sixties. If we weren't living in an era where anyone with an iPhone and an Instagram account could become a celebrity, she would have been an icon, I thought, like Brigitte Bardot.

When Damien lowered his camera, Lilah dropped her pose and went over to the clothes rack. She took off the jacket and stood there, naked on the top half, the minimal bust she had completely exposed to the eyes of the room. I glanced at Damien, but he was busy with his camera and had no interest – it seemed – in looking at Lilah's tits. She changed into a long black dress that was swampy until the stylist belted it with a *Fifty Shades*-esque contraption. When she returned to the studio roll there was a long wooden bench waiting for her, and I thought, *What the hell is that for?* Without hesitation, Lilah, clearly the professional, mounted it, placing one leg either side and spreading the front of her body across it.

'Very nice,' said Damien, and I think I actually turned my nose up in disgust. Luckily, no one seemed to notice, most probably because no one was looking at me.

I hoped that she would shake off the persona, having done the job she'd been forced to do. Instead she arched her back even more and gazed over one shoulder, mouth open, as if waiting for someone to come and fuck her, looking so different to the timid animal I'd pictured when Steph had told the mirror story.

Damien captured her several times, then said, 'Now, show me your orgasm face.'

Please don't, I thought. But she was going for it already, contorting her body so that it looked like it was in some sort of pain, thrusting her throat towards the camera and shutting her eyes to form a small crease between her eyebrows. I'd never had an orgasm, but imagined that if I ever did – and I hoped I would – it wouldn't look anything like that.

'Thank you, darling,' said Damien, sounding sickeningly triumphant, and lowered his camera.

Lilah let her body relax and laughed, instantly killing whatever she – or Damien, or myself – had been feeling before.

The shoot went on for hours. There were outfit changes, makeup touch-ups and lighting tests. I observed everything, more silent than I'd ever been in my life, almost completely still apart from the occasional stealthy grab of a shortbread biscuit from the catering table. I wondered if I could sneak a quick picture for Instagram, to show my 113 followers just how high I was flying that day. I sensed it wouldn't go down well if anyone in the room noticed, however.

Steph texted me throughout the day, asking how it was going and sending thumbs up emojis whenever I told her that it all seemed fine. When the shoot ended, everyone clapped, and I joined in. The team started to pack up their equipment and Lilah changed into jeans and a polo neck that had 'SEX' spelt out across the bust in loud pink letters, her eyes and one thumb glued to an iPhone.

I approached her and said, 'Anything else I can do for you . . . babe?'

She shook her head without looking up and muttered, 'My Uber's outside,' seemingly to herself. Her sudden aloofness was such a change from the charismatic friendliness she'd shown me before that I was sure it was to do with my awkward use of the word 'babe'. Something inside me felt embarrassingly desperate to claw back an inkling of that close-girlfriend-ish interaction, so I told her I'd walk her to the car.

On the way out, she took an apple from the catering table and bit into it with a loud crunch. The juice of the apple ran down her chin and she didn't bother to wipe it. We stepped onto the pavement together. Lilah turned and pulled me into a fast, warm hug. I felt a pathetic sigh of relief inside me, taking the hug to mean that she hadn't lost interest in me.

She said, 'Thanks, babe. You are literally the best.'

Literally. The best.

And with no more than that, she was gone.

I took out my phone to call Steph, as she'd asked me to do at the end of the day.

'Hi, darling,' she said, as soon as she answered. 'Sorry about today. Basically, I've interviewed so many people for this assistant role and it's impossible to tell how someone's going to do. Madeleine's fired everyone we've hired so far. So I thought a trial day would work better, but I know that throwing you straight onto set was a bit much.'

'Honestly, it was fine,' I said. 'She seemed calm.'

'Really?' said Steph, brightly. 'That's good! Lilah calm is good.'

I couldn't imagine Lilah anything but calm, given how easy-going she seemed.

'Listen, you obviously did a great job, because she would've complained by now if you hadn't,' said Steph. 'I need you to meet Madeleine, our agency director. Can you come in tomorrow?'

'Of course,' I said.

I gathered that Madeleine – my mother's imaginary friend – was the one they referred to as 'Crazy'. The nickname made me nervous, given that my future was entirely in her hands.

I returned to the flat with the warm feeling of a girl crush settling over me. From my nook on the sofa, I googled *Lilah Fox*. I found out that Lilah was twenty years old and was originally from the East End. She had 200K followers on Instagram. She'd been modelling since she was sixteen. She'd been shot for top fashion magazines, like *Vogue, Dazed & Confused, Love, i-D* and *AnOther*. She was the face of Valentino's diffusion line. She had a gaggle of fit model friends. She loved to party and was always photographed coming out of The Box and the Chiltern Firehouse, or a central London townhouse at dawn, looking a glamorous mess. There were pictures of her sunbathing topless on Roberto Cavalli's boat in Cannes, so no wonder she hadn't been bothered about exposing herself in front of an entire shoot crew. She smoked a lot. *Vice* magazine described her as 'a good old-fashioned rock 'n' roll gal'.

Basically, Lilah was the real-life version of myself in my wildest dreams.

When I arrived at the agency the following morning, Steph seemed less of a hot mess than she had the previous day. She sat me down and explained that Madeleine was on her way in from the airport, having just returned from a press trip with Yulia Kuznetsova, who was apparently the agency's biggest model, though I'd never heard of her, so clearly not the most famous. Madeleine's arrival worked like a cup of Bulletproof Coffee, in that everyone suddenly looked more alive than before. She strode in, brisk, stick-thin, wearing a utilitarian Burberry trench coat and cat-eye Miu Miu sunglasses. When she grabbed one of the model's set cards off the wall, I immediately understood the nickname.

'A 35-inch hip?' she said sharply, in a heavy New York accent, waving the card above her head.

Was thirty-five inches too big or too small?

'Whose girl is this?' she said, whipping her mane of glossy black hair out of the way.

All eyes rolled towards Steph, who stood up with an anxious expression on her face. 'She's mine. I know the hips are big. But look at the cheekbones.'

'Who's gonna care about her cheekbones if she can't even fit through the door?'

Too big, apparently. How many inches were my hips?

'Reprint the card to say she's got a 33-inch hip,' said Madeleine, tossing the card onto Steph's desk.

'Clients get angry when the girls aren't the size we say they are,' said Steph, with the look of someone who'd been through this conversation before.

'Just tell them she got her period and swelled up!' said Madeleine, as if it were the most obvious thing. She peeled the trench away from bare, rippled arms, like she was skinning herself alive, and sat down at the centre of the booking table. 'I've confirmed Lilah for a Gucci video. I need someone to go to the fitting with her now.'

'I'll go,' said Steph.

'You are not going anywhere until you change that goddamn hip size.'

'I can go.' The words just slipped out of my mouth.

Madeleine turned to look at me, still wearing sunglasses, clearly wondering who the fuck I was.

Steph shifted her blue eyes over to me, silently letting me know that I'd spoken out of turn.

Drew jumped in. 'Have you met Scarlett yet? Our prospective assistant?'

Madeleine whipped off her sunglasses. 'No, I haven't.'

'Sorry, I should've introduced you,' said Steph, now in a flap. 'This is Scarlett.'

I'd never thought of myself as a particularly shy person, but I have to admit, my neck was burning.

'Why are you wearing a hat?' was the first thing Madeleine Schwartz said to me.

It took a second for me to realize that I was, indeed, wearing the baker boy hat I'd bought at a stall on Oxford Street, thinking I could pull it off like I was Gigi fucking Hadid. I removed it, shamefully, and flattened my bad blonde hair with my hand. Everyone was looking at me.

Steph started speaking, 'Scarlett did a great job on the shoot with Lilah yesterday—'

'You sent a prospective on a shoot?' said Madeleine, twisting around in her chair to face Steph.

'I had so much work to do here—'

'You mean you were out all weekend,' said Madeleine, with finality, and switched her computer on.

Now it was Steph's turn to burn hot, and I felt my stomach drop for her.

Madeleine picked up the phone. 'I'm going to ask Lilah who she wants with her.'

'She'll want me,' said Steph, and I could tell how important it was to her that that was true.

I returned to my desk, determined not to let my embarrassment show, and continued with the duty I'd been given: searching Models.com for any new editorials or campaigns featuring Pure's models and sending the links to the entire agency. Apparently it had to be done every morning.

As I listened to Madeleine on the phone, a small part of me thought that Lilah might ask for 'that lovely blonde girl who'd been on the shoot yesterday' to accompany her to her Gucci fitting. But, of course, she requested Steph. Why wouldn't she? Steph had been there for five years – according to her Instagram feed – and I'd been there for five seconds. Lilah probably didn't even remember I existed.

As Steph got ready to go, Madeleine gave her a ranting lecture about not spending too long out of the agency and keeping on top of her emails. Steph walked past me, swathed in her great sack of a coat, which she'd told me that morning was from Cos but looked 'very Celine'. She gave me a loaded smile as she walked out.

Sink or swim, I felt she was saying.

'Serena!' squawked Madeleine.

'Scarlett,' Drew corrected her.

I jumped up from my chair and turned to face her.

She was standing too, having swapped her sunglasses for bulky Tom Ford spectacles. Her brows were knitted into a frown above the frame as she craned to look at my desk. 'God, your desk is a mess. I hope your pussy doesn't look like that!'

I actually stopped breathing for a few seconds while everyone else shrieked with laughter.

Then Madeleine spoke at me with a light smile, 'I need an espresso and a list of models in town. Ten seconds from now!'

My life had officially become a movie.

After the espresso and list of models in town – which Drew kindly printed off and slipped me – Madeleine paid me very little attention. No one was giving me any jobs to do, but I was wary of looking idle, so I acted very busy by retagging the magazines that I'd done the morning before. When Steph returned, she came straight over to me and I waited for her to tell me that Lilah had been singing my praises, but instead she asked me to organize the stationary cupboard.

Towards five o'clock, Madeleine left, complaining about jetlag, and I felt a little sink in my stomach as I realized she obviously wasn't going to offer me the job. I didn't know whether it was the hat or my misguided volunteering, but that was that.

Steph walked Madeleine to her car, which I thought was a strange and intimate thing to do with your boss. When she came back, however, she crouched by my desk and spoke in a hushed tone. 'Okay, so she's happy to give you the job,' she said, in a voice that was more foreboding than congratulatory.

'What?' I said, genuinely confused.

Steph looked fearful. 'Do you not want it?'

'I do,' I said quickly. 'Of course I do. I'm just surprised. She barely spoke to me.'

'Trust me, the less she speaks to you, the better,' she said. 'She told me to tell you that we can do fifteen grand a year, which is a grand more than reception, so don't say anything to Worm.'

My heart started thumping fast, even though I knew that fifteen grand a year wasn't exactly something for most people to pop a cork over.

'Can you start tomorrow?'

'Yeah, I'd love to,' I replied, without hesitation.

'Amazing!' she sung, and lurched over for a hug, surprising me.

Did a hug mean that we were friends now, or was it the same as being called 'darling' or 'babe'? And was it okay to be friends with your colleagues? I just didn't know all the etiquette surrounding London work life.

I got my first lesson, however, when, after the hug, she casually said, 'We're going to a party tonight if you want to come?'

If I hadn't fallen in love with Steph when she ended my eternal unemployment, I fell in love with her then. But rather than kiss her glossy lips with tears in my eyes at the thought of a night of real human interaction over drinks and music, I smiled, gave a little shrug, and said, 'Sure, why not?', proud that I had successfully contained myself.

'Great! We're going straight after work.'

My face fell. 'I don't have anything to wear,' I said, like a millennial Cinderella.

'I'm literally going like this,' said Steph, holding her arms out to display the *à la mode* hoodie, sport luxe silk trousers and Reebok trainers. Then she looked at me in my rather dated skinny jeans, dirty old Converse and stained jumper – my clothes were always stained for some reason – and said, 'Let's find you something in the fashion cupboard.'

Again, I had to keep a lid on my civilian excitement at the thought of a fashion cupboard. I imagined it to be a long corridor lined with rails of luxury clothing and a wall of high-heeled shoes and handbags, and maybe even a sunglass chandelier hanging from above. I have to admit that I was disappointed when Steph took me into a room no bigger than the average disabled toilet, which was stacked with boxes and crammed full of hanging garments, seemingly in no particular order. As she pushed her way through the mess, she explained that it was a mish-mash of gifts that had been sent for models, items that had been borrowed from PR companies and never returned, and 'staple clothing for digitals' (whatever that meant).

Eventually she pulled out a yellow and grey plaid skirt, which I assumed must have been a high street number until she handed it over and I noticed the weight; it screamed quality. I glanced inside the waistband to read the label: Prada. Steph had just handed me a Prada skirt and casually told me to try it on with my old T-shirt. Knowing that she meant then and there, I peeled the jeans away from my legs and a lawn of sprouting black hairs came into view. Even more horrifying were the fuzzy patches on the tops of my feet and my toes. Had anyone so unkempt ever been allowed to step into a Prada skirt before? I knew that I really should be in the habit of shaving my legs, feet and toes on the regular, but I just wasn't expecting them to be seen. The next scare was the struggle I went through to close it around my middle. I had never had trouble getting into clothes before. I was a comfortable size ten, sometimes a twelve, but apparently not sample size. The important thing to remember is that the skirt did, eventually, close. I tucked my T-shirt in, all the way, then Steph pulled at it, so that it was half-tucked, half-untucked. I made a mental note of how a T-shirt should be worn. Then she handed me a black crinkled PVC jacket – McQ by Alexander McQueen – that cinched in at the waist, a pair of tights and six-inch Charlotte Olympia heels.

'We don't have any flat shoes in here,' she said. 'You're not too tall, so you'll be fine in heels.'

'Love a heel,' I said.

Have never, ever loved a heel.

I forced my trotter into one of the elegant structures, and there I was, fully dressed. Steph fluffed up my hair with the end of her fingertips, and again I wondered if this was the gesture of a friend or a fashion person. She turned me towards the full-length mirror on the wardrobe door. I looked like something in between a high-school student in a nineties rom-com and a female Bond villain. On the plus side, my legs looked longer than I'd ever known they could be, though the heels forced me to stand at an angle that drove my pelvis out in front of me like I was getting ready to limbo.

Cinderella, eat your heart out.

With difficulty, I tottered down the pavement alongside Steph, Drew and Patrick (I'd finally learnt the Australian's name), having to take double the steps to keep up with them. It seemed unfair that I was the only one in heels.

We were on our way to a party that was being held to launch a collection of printed scarves. A well-known editor was hosting it for the designer, who was her good friend. I couldn't quite comprehend a world where scarves warranted whole parties to celebrate their existence, or where well-known editors hosted events for their good friends. I was secretly hoping Lilah would be there and was preparing a self-deprecating gag about the high heels I'd been forced to wear after we'd bonded over being trainer girls.

A queue of people stood outside, waiting to be admitted into the bar by a very serious girl with an iPad. My unit immediately recognized individuals and dived into hugs, kisses and 'darlings', while I stood behind them with an idle grin, waiting to be introduced, but no one did the honours.

Eventually, we reached iPad girl.

'Patrick Land, Steph Conway and big fat PIGGIEEEEE,' said Patrick, wrapping his arm around Drew.

The iPad girl burst out of her serious face into a fit of laughter. 'Come on in, guys,' she said, appropriately well spoken.

'Oh, and we have a plus one,' said Patrick, tugging at my hand and drawing me closer.

'Sorry, guys, we're actually guest list only tonight,' she said in the most inauthentic apologetic voice I'd ever heard.

My abdomen grew tight at the thought that I'd have to turn around in my heels and go back to Liz and Tim and their rock-hard sofa.

'She works at the agency,' Steph muttered, with little confidence.

'Shauna's actually approved everyone personally tonight, so I can't really do anything, I'm afraid,' said iPad girl.

'Oh, for God's sakes, let me talk to her,' said Patrick. He sashayed inside dramatically and Drew followed without a backward glance. Steph stayed behind, looking apprehensive. She was obviously eager to get inside.

'You don't have to wait,' I said, though I didn't know what I'd do if I had to stand alone out there, because I didn't really believe that Patrick was coming back.

Steph forced a smile and shook her head, as if to say, 'I won't for much longer.'

A few minutes later, and to my amazement, Patrick reappeared, followed by a bone-thin blonde with perfect skin and an icy manner. This, I imagined, was Shauna, the well-known editor.

Patrick pointed at me. 'There, see, she's half a fucking person,' he said, hopefully not referring to my personality.

Shauna made eye contact with iPad girl and gave a small nod, her expression unchanging. I felt a tad embarrassed that the well-known editor had been dragged away from her own party to get me in, but also a tad important.

As I stepped inside, I was met by every urban cocktail bar visual imaginable: open brick walls, brass ceilings, soft lighting, copper cups, bottles of St. Germain and even a full-sized vintage air streamer that I spent a good deal of time wondering how they'd got through the door. A female DJ with hot-pink hair, whom I recognized from Instagram, was elevated above the crowd in a small booth by the air streamer, scratching her decks with the concentration of a heart surgeon.

'Let's get a drink,' said Steph, pushing her way to the bar – a girl after my own heart. I followed rambunctiously, almost salivating at the thought of a drink, given that I'd been gagging to get pissed ever since I moved to London. I reached for an ice-cold copper cup with mint sprouting from the top. Taking a sip of what I recognized as a mojito (I'd had mojitos before, but never any quite so strong, or quite so cold), I turned around and absorbed the ultra-hip scene, feeling like I was watching it on a screen.

The first thing I noticed was how carefully curated everyone seemed to be. Each person looked like they were shining a spotlight on a known style or particular look. Handbags, shoes and jewellery had been selected for a reason, not thrown on haphazardly. Even Steph, whose clothes I'd previously associated with her being a 'hot mess', I now understood, had established a signature style. I shrank under the realization that I wasn't quite the fashion connoisseur I'd fancied myself, just because I could name a few top designers and mainstream fashion icons, had read the odd design book and crafted a frock called Henrietta. But I hadn't studied and identified trends. I didn't know that style was an expression of one's personality, or understand the self-awareness that came with putting together a look.

Suddenly, I realized that I was standing alone, gawking like the overimpressed idiot I was. I spotted Patrick and Drew seated on low sofas among a group of men who looked like rappers, and headed over. As I got closer, I noticed Steph a level below them. She was squatting, crow style, next to a caramel-skinned man, who was possibly one of the most beautiful men I'd ever seen. He was older than me, but not too old. Thirties, I guessed. I crouched beside Steph so that the two of us were gazing up at him, like titillated penguins.

'This is Scarlett, our little assistant,' she said, nudging me.

The beautiful man smiled. He had a smattering of freckles across his face, almond-shaped green eyes that literally glowed, and inches of dreadlocked hair standing up like a crown. He said, 'Hi, Scarlett,' and I melted at the sound of my name dripping off his tongue. I barely even heard him introduce himself with, 'I'm Zack.'

'My feet are killing me,' was apparently the most interesting thing I had to say at that moment. It was true though – the crease between my toes and the balls of my feet were stinging from the damn heels.

Steph placed a silver-ringed hand on Zack's knee to balance herself and I wondered if they were together. 'Doll, you have to go to this new hypnotherapist I found. She's, like, three hundred quid, but so worth it.'

'What did you go for?' he asked, closing his full lips around the metal straw in his drink.

'Gak!' she said.

'Really? Are you off the gak now?' he said, raising a sceptical eyebrow.

I had never heard the word 'gak' before, but had a fairly good idea of what it was.

'Not completely,' said Steph, her voice croaking up. She cleared her throat. 'But it's changed my attitude towards it. So, when I do it now, I'm doing it because I *want* to do it. Not because I need to stay up, or because everyone else is doing it.'

I gathered from the way they were speaking to each other that they weren't, in fact, fucking, and breathed a little sigh of relief. As if that meant I had a chance.

'Think I'll give it a miss,' said Zack, his mouth turning up at the corners. 'I already *want* to do it too much!'

She laughed. 'I gave up fags for a week too, but now I'm back to, like, ten a day.'

My knees were aching in the crow-penguin squat.

'Money well spent, Steph,' said Zack, flashing a line of straight white teeth.

Oh, why did I say no to those braces?

Zack lifted his drink and the sleeve of his sharply cut maroon blazer rolled above the elbow. I fixed my eyes on a geometric pattern that was tattooed all the way along his forearm. A tattoo was something that I'd always wanted, but my mother had told me I'd regret it. Staring at Zack's, I promised myself that the next time I got paid, the tattoo parlour was first on the agenda. And then, in the next second – I don't even know how it happened – I toppled backwards, the copper cup sliding through my fingers.

I lay there for what felt like a long time, feet on the ground, knees up, practically immobilized from embarrassment, knowing that everyone was going to think I was some lightweight rural girl, pissed as a fart after a mere few sips of a mojito. And then the divine picture of Zack came into view between the frame of my thighs and, mortifyingly, we made eye contact. All I could think about was that I must have had about five chins from that angle, as if that was a bigger problem than the fact that I was supine on the concrete floor. For a fleeting moment, I thought that Zack was going to help me up, even though he hadn't moved from the sofa. Then there was a heavily braceleted hand on his shoulder and a mane of sumptuous auburn hair falling by his face. A skinny girl in a voluptuous puff-sleeved dress was leaning over to hug him. Her Chanel handbag swung in my eye line, and I felt like those double Cs were cackling at me.

Having been similarly eclipsed by the woman, Steph finally noticed me there and quickly helped me up.

Back to the bar it was.

23 February 2016, 11.51 p.m.

It's all happening. So stop falling around like an idiot and be cool.

CHAPTER 4

I was allocated the same lone corner desk that I'd inhabited as a prospective. My title was 'Women's Division Assistant'. That meant I was only to assist the agents on the women's division. I was warned about being manipulated into helping agents on the men's division, the digital influencer and talent division, the press officer, or the accounts team. The agency budget didn't allow them to employ their own assistants.

Patrick, Drew and Steph were the women's division agents. Patrick and Drew were responsible for developing the new face models, and Steph looked after the established faces, along with Madeleine.

Liz practically gasped with excitement when I told her, and I could see by the way she pressed the tips of her fingers over her lips that she was literally having to stop herself from asking my move-out date. Tim had the unexpected decency to pretend to be disappointed to lose their 'roomie', even though he'd gone to such lengths to leave for work in a silent dash, every single morning, while I pretended to be asleep, so we didn't have to interact.

I made my way into work for the first time, my first day as a Londoner who worked in fashion. I smoked a cigarette and called my mother to tell her the news.

'A model agency, Scarlett?' she sighed down the phone. 'A model agent?'

'Look, it's a job in fashion. It's a stepping stone to design,' I said, though I wasn't sure if that was true yet. 'And they've offered me twenty grand a year.'

She almost laughed. 'That will hardly get you a boiled egg in London!'

Thank God I didn't tell you what I'm really on, then.

'You wanted me to get a job, and now I've got a job, you're not happy. What a surprise!'

'I want you to get a *real* job!'

'This *is* a real job, Mum.'

That time, she did laugh. 'It's a ridiculous excuse for a profession, with a low-rate salary to prove it!'

I hung up the phone, a knee-jerk reaction prompted by anger. Of course she couldn't just be happy for me, and God forbid proud. She hated the fact that I'd done something on my own, without her help or guidance. I sucked on the last of my cigarette and chucked it aside. Then I lifted my head and sashayed into the agency proudly, because I was making things happen.

After a few days, Liz could hold back no more and flat out asked me when I was leaving, so I plucked up the courage to speak to the office manager, who seemed to be in charge of all things financial. I asked for an advance payment so that I could move off of the sofa from hell. I rented a room on spareroom.com that was advertised as a charming flat in the heart of Seven Sisters, which, being on the Victoria line, had fantastic transport links. In reality, the underground station was a twenty-minute bus ride away and the flat was in a council building that felt a stone's throw from criminality, which prompted me to begrudgingly accept my mother's Find My Friends request. My room was eggshell blue, with venetian blinds that must have been twenty years old, a single bed, a black IKEA wardrobe and a small chest of drawers. I tried to cosy it up in a way that I knew some people had a natural aptitude for: fairy lights over the bed head, a black-and-white print of Kate Moss that I'd bought at a street stall, my books lining the one tiny shelf.

As for my new flatmate, I'd hoped that someone who lived in the cheapest flat in London would be a struggling artist or musician who made her own clothes and milked almonds. Instead, I got a newly divorced ceramicist of about fifty who'd just suffered her fourth heart attack and was easily alarmed by sudden loud noises. When I brought up the online misrepresentation of the flat, her response was, 'Princess Diana, are we?'

I sensed we were not going to become friends, which was upsetting, because the two friends I thought I had made since moving – Steph and Lilah – seemed to be misjudged. Steph was always friendly to me at work, but since the scarf party she hadn't invited me out again, even though she rolled in day after day like the hot mess she was and bragged – I thought it was bragging, at least – about nights out painting the town. Of course, I inevitably thought her not inviting me was to do with my unbecoming tumble, rather than the fact that I'd never asked to come.

And Lilah, it seemed, had disappeared into thin air. I held onto the hope that she might come into the agency, given that my girl crush had, like any crush, flourished into fantasy. In the same way that I'd known myself to plan my wedding to a guy I'd yet to kiss, I had a scenario at play in my head in which Lilah and I were the closest of friends, and I very much believed that idea to be a premonition.

I eventually learnt that I could, in fact, track her movements via the chart system.

Every model had a chart. Each chart was kept up to date with that model's specific castings, job details, client meetings, as well as time blocked off for personal arrangements. As far as the agents were concerned, if it wasn't on the chart, it wasn't happening. The chart was also the keeper of all personal information about the models, including their contact details. Ever since I'd found out about the charts, I'd wanted to open Lilah's and discover her email address, her phone number and where she lived. I realized it was stalkerish and I didn't know what I'd do with any of the information – call her up and just plain ask her if we could be best friends? – but I still wanted it.

About a week into the job, I went for it, and opened that chart.

Lilah lived in Primrose Hill. I'd heard of the 'Primrose Hill set' and knew that it was a trendy place to live. I wondered what her house was like. I imagined an ultra-modern kitchen, with glass doors that opened up onto a pebble-lined garden, where she held summer parties for her famous friends. I wondered if she lived alone, or with friends, or a boyfriend maybe? She probably went through boyfriends too fast to live with any of them. Maybe I could move in?

My eyes travelled down to her email address: LilahFox@gmail. com – that's all it was. No alias, no frills, just her name in all its simple glory.

My first pay slip arrived in the mail on 25 March 2016. I looked at my name, Scarlett Willems, and the London address on the front of the slip, and I suddenly felt like a resourceful imposter. Something dawned on me: I was fully capable of looking after myself. As I gently tore off the edges of the slip, as instructed by the small letters, I thought about the wardrobe rebrand I'd committed to in that New Year's resolutions list, a Marc Jacobs handbag like Liz's and the tattoo I'd promised myself. And then I saw the net pay.

After tax, I was making £1,123 a month. The ceramicist took

the first wedge of that generous total for rent, gas and electricity bills, council tax, and sometimes for a contribution to cleaning products, even though the flat always smelt like a rotting dead animal. The sum I was left with, hardly – as my mother had so poetically put it – got me a boiled egg in London.

That's why I quickly became the last person to leave work. Even when I'd finished my duties for the day, I'd find extra. There was always some magazine to be tagged or some portfolio that needed updating. When the agency emptied out and I was alone with Venus, the Jamaican cleaner – who was truly wonderful – I'd slip into the kitchen and use whatever food supplies were left to prepare some sort of meal for us both. It was usually a ham sandwich, or grapes and cheese, or somebody's leftover sushi. Venus was always pissed off if it was sushi. I was starting to regret that I'd never learnt to cook. Cooking was a necessity for my mother – my childhood was slopping with macaroni cheese, baked beans and fish fingers – not a pleasure, and she usually did it alone and rapidly, so whose fault was it that I couldn't even chop an onion?

Sometimes, I'd slip into the fashion cupboard to arouse myself with garment porn. I'd tried on all of the clothes. The agents often borrowed pieces for the weekend, or for personal engagements, like weddings. Sometimes, on a Friday – which the agents called 'Prosexy Friday', owing to the afternoon bottle of Prosecco they treated themselves to – there would be a gathering of people outside the cupboard trying on various pieces, telling each other what looked good and what didn't, always brutally honest. Occasionally, if I was passing by, someone would ask my opinion and I'd say, 'You look a ten out of ten ... babe.'

I wished that I had a personal engagement to borrow clothes for.

Eight p.m. was normally the time I left the agency. The ceramicist was usually conked out in bed and didn't like me to use the washing machine at night, so I was constantly turning crusty and, sometimes, period-stained knickers inside out. I wondered how I was supposed to make it to fashion school when I couldn't even afford hand-wash detergent.

My routine – and my world – was rattled, six weeks into the job, the night that Patrick hung around late. I was using Photoshop, which Steph had spent an afternoon patiently teaching me to use, to retouch images of Breje, a 16-year-old model who had just arrived from Poland and was sent straight to a shoot with the lovely Damien Stern. The agents had nicknamed Breje 'the scarecrow' after someone had pointed out that she was the spitting image of the character in *The Wizard of Oz*. She had patchy, short, ice-blonde hair, pale skin, and was the size of a twiglet. Drew's notes on the images I'd taken earlier that day were, 'Stretch legs, eye bags – get rid, fix bingo wings!!'

The girl barely had arms, let alone bingo wings.

It got to almost eight o'clock and my stomach started rumbling loudly, but I knew it was not chic to eat agency leftovers for dinner and I did not want Patrick to know that I did.

'What you doing tonight?' he asked suddenly, putting emphasis on the end of the sentence, in his Australian way.

'Nothing.'

As per fucking usual.

'Great. Come to the Louis Vuitton party with me.'

'Love to, but I'm not on the list,' I said, keen to go to a party, not keen to repeat the Shauna scenario.

'You can use Steph's name. She's not coming.' He stretched his leathery neck to see what I was wearing: frayed jeans (eBay purchase), mustard shirt (Topshop and *guilty*) and trainers (the old Dunlops). Then he said, 'Put some heels on. We're leaving in ten.'

I headed to the fashion cupboard, excited that I finally had an opportunity to adorn myself in its most spectacular items, but when I got there, the choice was too much to handle. What would actually look good on me and what was going to make me look like an arsehole? In the end, I just went for the Charlotte Olympia heels I'd worn to the scarf party and an understated Alexander Wang bomber jacket over what I was already wearing. *Typical.*

The event was at the Louis Vuitton apartment, above their flagship store on Bond Street. What they needed an apartment for, I had no idea. We travelled up a long, futuristic escalator, surrounded by mirrors, like we were ascending towards fashion heaven. I managed a clandestine video of the whole thing for Instagram while Patrick was buried in his own iPhone. I could already see the caption in which I'd thank @LouisVuitton, even though they thought I was Steph Conway. When we entered the apartment, we were greeted by a row of Ken dolls – probably out-of-work male models – holding trays of glistening champagne flutes. I went straight in for one (the champagne, not the man), feeling like I needed to down the whole thing in order to brave a conversation with one of the shiny people around me. Everyone, I noticed, had a small bit of Louis Vuitton stuck somewhere to them, like it was important to show off their ability to conform to surroundings. I suddenly wondered if it was a huge *faux pas* to wear an Alexander Wang jacket to a Louis Vuitton event. Probably.

Nailed it, Scizzle.

And then something unexpected happened: someone said my name.

I turned around and saw Zack, the beautiful man from the scarf party, sitting on a sofa, just like he had been the first time I'd seen him. How did he remember my name? I'd only muttered it briefly while gaping at him from below. He stood up, smiling, and kissed me on the cheek. It was simple. Nothing more than the way you'd kiss an acquaintance. But everything – the way he smiled, the way he pressed his finger into the centre of my spine as his lips touched my cheekbone, the fact that he remembered me at all – made me think that there was so much in that greeting.

'All right?' he said.

'All right,' I repeated, dumbly.

Say something interesting.

'How are you?' I added.

Ground-breaking.

'Better for seeing you,' he said, and I felt as if my whole body was breaking into a smile.

'Scarlett, this way,' Patrick interrupted, jabbing his finger urgently towards the other room, where, surely, there could be nothing more exhilarating than this deity.

Zack stepped back, as if giving me permission to leave. I smiled, and wandered off with a lingering thrill. Then Patrick led me into the main room and quashed my smile by heading straight over to my favourite five-foot-tall perverted photographer.

'Hi, Damien, how are you?' said Patrick, bowing his shoulders, shrinking himself as much as possible owing to Damien's status as a top photographer, whereas he was just a lowly model agent.

'You sent me that awful girl to shoot,' said Damien.

'You didn't like Breje?' said Patrick, looking genuinely distressed. 'I thought you'd love her! She has that cool nineties vibe, you know?'

'She's bald and doesn't get a period,' said Damien matter-of-factly.

I wondered how he knew whether or not Breje got a period, or if it was a figure of speech.

'Isn't that usually your type?' said Patrick, attempting to

make a joke, but Damien looked very serious. 'Madeleine loves her!' he added.

'And Madeleine's always right?' scoffed Damien.

'Well, she does *think* she knows everything,' said Patrick.

That, finally, melted the ice off Damien's expression. He laughed.

Patrick laughed too, with relief, and he continued the joke: 'She's like a crocodile. Sleeps with half the brain. That's the only way she can know so much.'

Damien laughed even harder at that, and even I joined in, though I knew it wasn't really my place to mock Madeleine.

'Gotta love her though,' said Patrick. 'At least she's got some spice. Fashion is so boring these days! Remember shoots in the nineties? Everyone was passed out in a cocaine coma!'

'The good old days,' said Damien.

'Now everyone's AA, NA, SLAA, Fuck-knows-what-A!'

'Have you been an agent since the nineties?' I asked, simply because I felt I needed to speak, and they both turned to look at me.

'Agent?' said Patrick. 'I was a model, darling!'

'Really?' I almost shrieked.

'Don't sound so surprised!' he said, and Damien guffawed. 'I used to be a looker before I got old! I'd go to gay clubs every night and take my shirt off on the dancefloor and they'd all start climbing me like a tree.'

I giggled at the image of Patrick, as he was then, topless in a throng of sweaty men. Then a petite brunette, who was a famous actress, passed by and touched Damien on the arm. He gave a tight-lipped smile, narrowing his eyes. When she was out of earshot, he leaned in towards us and said, 'She wants me to shoot her, but I hate short people.'

I laughed again because I thought Damien was making a joke about himself, but he was actually serious. He hated short people. *Other* short people. Once I realized that, I felt an inexplicable thrill that Damien, the revered photographer, was sharing his innermost prejudices with me. What was that about?

'Why are actors so small?' asked Damien, staring after the girl, truly and utterly confused.

'So that they can fit in the TV,' said Patrick.

I lost concentration then when I noticed Zack standing a few clusters of people away from us. I muttered an excuse about needing the loo and shoved my way through the glittering idiots, with no plan as to what I'd say when I arrived at my destination. Luckily, as soon as I planted myself next to him, he placed his large hand on my shoulder and said, 'Can I get you a drink?'

'I think they're free,' I said, hoping that I was being cute and cheeky. 'But sure.'

'Yeah, but you have to fight for them,' he said. It was true. The champagne flutes were being snatched off by skinny vulture hands within seconds, and you had to practically chase one of the Ken dolls around the room to get a look in. But they seemed to know Zack and he got us two glasses, no problemo. Then he said, 'You coming to the bathroom?'

I nodded vigorously – there was nothing I loved more than an inappropriate suggestion – and followed him to the front of a long queue for the loo, where two of his friends, whom he introduced as Johnny and Lolly, were already waiting.

After a few moments of small talk, the bathroom door opened and two girls slipped out, smiling – apologetic, but not embarrassed. Then the four of us stepped into the large, luxurious bathroom. I'd read enough McInerney novels to know that we were about to do cocaine. I'd done it once before, when Billie

Sara-Ella Ozbek

found a little bag in the bathroom of the pub we worked at. It did nothing but dehydrate us and I didn't understand the hype, at all, but decided it was something that I should get into if I wanted a gregarious life in London.

Johnny and Lolly stood at the sink, fiddling with a little bag of white powder and a credit card, making jokes about 'packet' that I didn't understand one bit. I leant against the bathtub and crossed one ankle over the other, to give my poor heeled feet a rest. Zack perched next to me.

'Do you work in fashion?' I asked, thinking that it was a very grown-up way of starting a conversation.

'Music. I'm in A&R,' he said, which I later Googled to discover meant 'artists and repertoire'.

I wanted him to ask what I did, but he was distracted by the little plastic bag and credit card that Lolly was handing him. He slipped the corner of the card into the mouth of the bag and heaped it with powder. Then he carefully held it up to my nose. I took a big old sniff, but most of the cocaine went into my lap, because I didn't cover my free nostril, which put me into a bit of a fluster. Zack pinched a white flake from my jeans and held his finger up to my nose and I took cocaine directly off his beguiling finger. Perhaps this was how all great city romances began: an invitation to the bog and a finger up your nostril. He fed himself, after that. Then me again. That time I covered the other side of my nose and felt the cocaine drip bitterly down my throat, which made me want to gag, but I didn't.

'We'll leave you two alone,' said Johnny, with raised eyebrows, and he left with Lolly.

I thought that if we were going to kiss, that would be the moment. Instead, Zack smiled, or perhaps gritted his teeth, and asked if I was done. We left the bathroom seconds later, and I felt an inner blush, embarrassed with myself for thinking he was into me. How stupid could I be?

I returned to the safety of good old homosexual, definitely-not-into-me Patrick. Suddenly I started to freak out that he would know I'd taken drugs at what was, essentially, a work event. Was that okay? Probably not. I rubbed my knuckle against my nose several times to get rid of any possible remnants. My mouth started to numb and no amount of champagne seemed to dampen it. Perhaps London cocaine was a bit stronger than the stuff found lying around in Topsham pub loos. It seemed to bring me into a state of heightened awareness, and I mentally tagged Zack, even though I'd decided, for sure, that he wasn't after me. I watched him from a distance as he worked the room. All the women were touching him, on the arm, on the face, or squeezing themselves into his embrace.

When I saw him put his coat on, I knew that he was leaving, and felt this sudden sense of urgency. I wanted him to see me, to remember that I was there, to remember that I existed and that he'd pinched a flake of cocaine from my leg and fed it up my nose. I slipped into the entrance hall ahead of him. There was a small bathroom by the front door that no one seemed to have discovered. I shut myself inside and stood with my ear at the crack of the door, like a total lunatic. When I heard his voice, I opened it, as if I'd just happened to be coming out at that very moment. How convenient!

His green eyes settled on me and he said, 'We're going to Johnny's. Come.'

Needless to say, I didn't need much convincing. None in fact. I could text Patrick and tell him I'd had to run off for tampon-related reasons. I followed Zack straight out of the apartment, nervously over-chatting about the height of the escalator as we descended into the real world, or a version of it.

There was a kerfuffle going on at the front door, which – would you believe it? – was my fault. Steph had arrived and was trying to get into the party, but I'd already used her name. Embarrassingly, I had to explain the situation to the iPad girl, who looked miffed, but not interested enough to argue. Zack told Steph we were going to Johnny's and asked if she wanted to come. She declined the invitation, not so politely, and gave me something of a warning look as she headed towards the escalators, which I thought was a little too judgmental, given that *she* was the hot mess more often than not.

We took a taxi to Johnny's place in Kentish Town, which Zack paid for in full. It was a maisonette above a restaurant and very clearly a bachelor pad. We all stood around in the narrow kitchen as Johnny emptied out the fridge. Two almost finished bottles of vodka and a bottle of tonic water was all he had.

Cheers, Johnny, great invite.

'We should've gone to the offy,' he said, looking in the dishwasher for glasses.

'You don't even have ice,' said Lolly, who I'd decided was his girlfriend.

Johnny turned to Zack. 'You two don't wanna walk to the off-licence, do you?'

'Yeah, we'll go,' said Zack, and that was settled.

I don't know if it had been planned, or if Johnny was just an intuitive being, but either way, I could have kissed him in that moment.

Zack and I stepped out into the dark and headed down the pavement, side by side.

The street was silent. I looked up into the sky, navy with a smoggy auburn swirl of pollution painted through it. Tiny rain-drops were spitting at us, and I thought, *Am I in a rom-com?*

Zack took off his coat and draped it over my shoulders. No one had ever offered me their coat before.

'Thank you,' I said silkily, so very girlishly. After that I couldn't think of anything to say. That's what always happened when I was alone with a member of the opposite sex. It was like I couldn't come to terms with the fact that they were real people, just like me – people I could connect with in the way that I did with other women. I was split over what my position was, as a woman, in relation to men. The part of me that read Caitlin Moran and lis-tened to every woke podcast targeted at my demographic made me feel superior to them, but then there was this other part of me that was overcome by an overwhelming pressure to say the right thing, be hilarious, make them think that I was the most impressive person in the world, who belonged on the highest of pedestals. In simple terms, I always felt like I needed to please them, like it was my duty or something.

We turned a corner and the illuminated sign of the off-licence appeared in the distance. He stopped, suddenly, with purpose, turned to me and took hold of my shoulders. The next few seconds happened in clichéd slow motion. I remember seeing the outline of his facial hair, overgrown at the time, as he pulled me towards him. He closed his lips softly around mine. I opened my mouth, expecting him to ram his tongue inside, but he didn't. He parted his lips again and used them to gently shut mine, pressing his hands firmly into the dip between my jawline and my neck.

I'd never been kissed like that before. Tim had never kissed me like that. Nor had any of the pint-chugging, hockey-playing sixth formers that I'd worked my way through at school. Nor any of the louts I'd shared saliva with on nights out in Loughborough. The way Zack kissed me was, I imagined, what kissing *should* feel like. When he ended it, we continued walking, silent for a few long steps.

This is it, I thought. *I'm going to have good sex for the first time in my life. I am going to have an orgasm.*

Then, he said, 'I'm in a bit of a weird situation.'

'What situation?' I asked, trying not to allow any dread into my voice.

'With my girlfriend.'

And the fantasy disintegrated around me.

He continued. 'We're sort of ... half together, half not. We may stay together, or we may break up.'

I said nothing as the dust settled.

'I probably should have told you before,' he said.

'It's okay. I won't tell anyone,' I said, like an idiot.

'Don't say that,' he said, taking my hand.

What did he want me to say?

'Steph knows my girlfriend quite well,' he said, turning to look at me sheepishly.

'I won't tell her,' I said, now understanding the warning look she gave me as I left the party. If only she'd used *words*.

We arrived at the shop and his demeanour changed back to that of the self-assured person he'd been before we stepped out of the house together. He chatted to the shop assistant like he was an old friend, discussing brands of tobacco and the different types of beer they sold. It kind of made me sad because it made me think of what a great couple we'd be – I also liked to talk to random people about random stuff – even though there was nothing to say that coupledom would have been on the cards if there wasn't some elusive girlfriend in the picture. Then we walked back to

Johnny's, in silence, weighed down by cans of beer and a burdensome bag of ice.

'We've broken up a couple of times,' he said, out of the blue, when we were nearly there. 'She's wicked. She's my best friend. But there are some things . . . We both travel a lot.'

I wondered what she was like, this nameless girlfriend, who travelled a lot and whom Steph knew quite well. I also wondered what, exactly, his motive had been, flirting with me, kissing me and then telling me he had a fucking girlfriend. What was the point?

Again, all I said was, 'I won't tell anyone.'

And that wasn't the end, would you believe it? Outside Johnny's place, he turned me towards him and kissed me again. I have to admit, the idea that he just couldn't resist one more kiss made me swell with delight, though I knew that it was a totally arrogant thought to have. The beers and ice dropped to the floor and my shoulders sighed with relief. I stepped back, flattening myself against the front door. He curled his hand around my throat and pressed into it with his fingers. He must have felt my racing pulse because, much to my own surprise, the mild strangulation was turning me on.

'I'm going to fuck you,' he whispered.

But I knew that he wouldn't. Not then, anyway.

14 April 2016, 11.52 p.m.

I know it's not exactly fourth wave feminism to want to sleep with someone else's boyfriend but I can't stop wishing I had.

CHAPTER 5

Go-sees were fast becoming the goddamn bane of my life.

Go-sees, I'd figured out, were basically appointments that agents made for models to 'go see' photographers, casting directors and fashion houses, even when they had no potential work for the model and zero interest in seeing them. The only purpose of go-sees was to make the models believe that the agents were doing something useful for them. Madeleine kept a miniature horn in her desk drawer, which she called 'the go-see siren'. Every once in a while, if she noticed agents on their iPhones, or if there were too many non-work-related conversations happening at the booking table, she'd take out the horn and blast it, which meant, 'Stop being so lazy and get some fucking go-sees!'

The worst part about go-sees was that they actually had nothing to do with me. The agents were the ones who had relationships with the clients and they were the ones who were supposed to arrange the go-sees. But for some reason they hated calling these clients that they had so-called great relationships with, in the middle of the work day, in the absence of champagne and cocaine, so the onus fell on me. If Madeleine noticed that a model had no go-sees on her chart, she would rip that model's agent a new arsehole and then that agent would look at me like, 'Thanks a lot,' because I hadn't done their job for them. But I wanted them to like me, so I never complained.

Madeleine was blowing that aggressive go-see siren the day that Lilah finally came into the agency. I'd been working there for months and she hadn't been in once, despite numerous appointments on her chart saying, 'Meeting in the agency'. I'd pretty much given up on the idea of our fantastical friendship, until I saw her saunter through the door – tall, spindly, wearing a black crop top with 'MOSCHINO' written all over it in bubble letters, black shiny jeans sharply cut off at the ankle and Gucci trainers with a green and red worm embellished in a slither along the side. My eyes settled on her tiny middle, which was like a marble floor.

She pulled a face and said, 'What the fuck is that noise?', her voice as crass and gritty as I remembered it.

Madeleine stopped blowing the horn and laughed, but she also looked a little embarrassed. 'Just waking everyone up!'

Within a split second, Steph was up and flinging her arms around Lilah, while Patrick and Drew seemed to shrink, their usual confidence thrown off track by their lack of involvement in the situation.

'You look banging, girl!' said Madeleine, walking over to pinch Lilah's protruding hip bone.

'Thanks. I'm fully loaded up with cum,' she said, bending at the knees, symbolically I guessed.

I wondered what that had to do with how 'banging' she looked, but loved her for being so wildly unrefined. Patrick and Drew shared a look of mutual disgust, which was odd considering their usual crude exchanges.

'I'm jealous! Whose cum?' said Madeleine, distinctly overanimated.

I was jealous, too.

'Guess!' said Lilah.

'Oh my God, you're back with him again?' Madeleine

69

stretched her long fingers out in front of her like she was about to perform a piano concerto.

Lilah shrugged – *guilty, not guilty!*

'It's like the never-ending fuck story!' shrieked Madeleine.

I was dying to know who the elusive 'him' of the fuck-story was, so I got up from my desk and wandered over. Lilah turned to me and for a split second I'm pretty sure she had no fucking clue who I was, so I quickly said, 'Hey! Haven't seen you since my first day.'

Her face fell into a smile and she pulled me into an over-familiar hug, which I had no problem with. I could feel Madeleine's eyes all over me and noticed a subtle twitch in Steph's jaw.

After the hug, I went into the art department to set up the camera and shooting lights because I knew that I'd have to take digitals of her, like I did of every model who walked through the door. Digitals were something I was told I had to be good at because they were a huge part of my job, but as it happened, I was very bad at them. In the old days, they'd been called 'polaroids', which is what most of the agents still called them, because they were old-school and had trouble moving with the times. I could've been a lot better at 'polaroids' had I been using a vintage polaroid camera, but a digital one made everyone look a stone heavier and five inches shorter, which was not ideal when your job was literally to be tall and thin.

I'd been warned that Lilah wasn't easy to take digitals of. Steph said that she 'over-modelled', which I didn't believe was a thing, but turns out, it is. Digitals had to be simple, and it was hard to get a fresh, clean shot of a model who was squatting, twirling, pouting and just about climbing the walls the way Lilah was. Eventually I gave up and asked her to change into lingerie. Not in a creepy way, just because that's what I was supposed to do.

'Not today, babe, I'm not feeling it,' she said.

Fair enough.

Who would feel like stripping down to their underwear in a busy office space to be photographed from every possible angle? I knew that I wouldn't. But I also knew that I was supposed to force the girls into having their lingerie digitals taken, even when they weren't 'feeling it'. With Lilah, for some reason, I couldn't bring myself to be anything but compliant.

'No problem. Is it okay if I measure you?' I said, thinking how weird my job was.

'Oh, I suppose so,' she said, like it was a real old drag, which made me feel bad for asking.

I retrieved the measuring tape from its home – my pocket – and reached my arms around the sides of her body, pulling the tape against her buttocks and then tightening it as much as I could around her hips. I repeated halfway up her torso. She measured 34 inches on the hip and 24 inches on the waist – a hell of a lot smaller than any normal person, but still, I knew the agents would say that she was meant to be an inch narrower in both areas. I didn't mention anything.

It was the end of the day and most of the agents had cleared out, so technically I was free to leave. I didn't want to go home to the grimness of the flat and spend another night fantasizing about having sex with Zack (yes, I knew he had a girlfriend), whom I'd pretty much gathered I'd never see again, given that I'd slipped him my number that night and hadn't heard from him. I really was becoming the expert on bad life choices. So, as Lilah gathered her belongings, I went for it: 'Feel like a drink after work?'

I felt like I was asking her on a date.

'I'm actually going to Annabel's house, to see my girls,' she said.

It almost made me laugh that she referred to her friend by name, as if I knew her. The funniest part about it was that I did know all about Annabel Weber, the youngest daughter in a rock-and-roll dynasty, the type of client that the agents referred to as a 'model-ebrity'. Technically speaking, she shouldn't have been a model at five-foot-six (the industry standard was apparently five-foot-nine), but being the daughter of coveted rock stars meant that even the top-tier clients made exceptions for Her Rock and Royal Highness.

Lilah continued: 'I've been away so much the past few months, I literally can't remember when I last just chilled with my friends.'

'No problem,' I said, though I don't think she thought it was a problem. 'We can do drinks another time.'

'Why don't you come with?' she said – so casually, so lightly, as if it was nothing – and for a second I wondered if I was imagining it.

Could this friendship really be going to line up with my fantasy so quickly and easily?

'Sure,' I said, with a shrug and a smile. 'Sure, why not?'

We took a black taxi to Annabel Weber's Camden pad. Lilah spent most of the journey looking at pictures of herself from the night before on the *Mail* online, spitting rage about the bitter and, frankly, offensive comments that had been left by the 'GP' (general public).

'*Lilah is a wannabe member of the twenty-seven club waiting to happen!*' she read aloud.

My phone started vibrating and a picture of Billie from way

back when flashed up at me from the screen. I rejected the call, because I knew I wouldn't talk freely to her in front of Lilah, and being Billie, she'd definitely call me out on it.

'What the fuck do you know, Shelley from Bexhill?' Lilah shouted at her own screen. 'Sounds like a basic bitch,' she muttered.

My heart rose to my throat, because it felt like she was saying it to me. I'd been the invisible person at the end of a *Daily Mail* comment at points in my life. Was 'Shelley from Bexhill' so far off 'Scizzle from Topsham'?

My phone vibrated again, this time with a message.

> Billie:
> Dude call me. Had a shocker of a day
> need to talk

I hardly took it in, still feeling apprehensive that Lilah – or anyone – thought I was a basic bitch.

'We're here,' said Lilah, as we pulled up outside a modern-looking structure tucked away in a mews.

Another vibration in my hand. Billie was calling again. I held my finger down on the side button of the iPhone and switched it off, feeling a twinge of guilt.

'Do you have any cash?' said Lilah, still ninety-nine per cent buried in *Daily Mail* world.

I guessed that she was expecting me to pay and expense it to the agency. I didn't want her to know that I wasn't senior enough to do that, but neither did I want to look cheap, so I handed the driver the last twenty quid I had for that month, feeling a flutter of panic about how many days were left until payday.

Obviously I knew who all of Lilah's friends were from my

incessant social media stalking, but the thought of meeting them face to face made my stomach swirl. However friendly Lilah was, her sporadic moments of aloofness combined with her total confidence in saying things like 'I'm fully loaded up with cum' meant that she was undeniably intimidating, and I imagined her friends to unfold out of her like clones.

The bottom half of the house was built out of beige bricks, like a council building, but the top half was entirely glass-fronted. Lilah rang the bell three times, and I thought, *There's a girl who's certain that people want her around.* It opened in one fanning motion, and Annabel Weber stood there, raw-boned, in a loosely hung tank top, braless, her platinum blonde hair falling dead straight from beneath a baker boy hat. Unlike me, she could pull it off.

'Hey, babe,' she said in a gravelly voice, looking at Lilah through glassy eyes. They hugged, and Annabel's skinny red hand fluttered up like a tired butterfly to rest limply on Lilah's shoulder blade.

'This is Scarlett. My new friend,' said Lilah, and my organs leapt into my throat at the idea that my plan had gone so well. We were now friends. Not *best* friends – not yet – but friends. It reassured me that she didn't, in fact, see me as she saw Shelley from Bexhill. Did she?

Annabel turned to me and smiled coldly. 'Hi.'

We stepped into an open-plan space which was everything I would have imagined the home of the youngest daughter of a rock-and-roll dynasty to be: eclectic art hanging from the walls, a cactus in almost every corner and a neon light sign inexplicably spelling out the word 'cunt'. A large brown leather sofa was the main feature of the room, which surprised me, because Annabel sold herself as an environmental activist. On the sofa, among

Union Jack pillows, sat a girl who I knew – from Instagram – was called Moffie Dunn (maybe 'Scizzle' wasn't such a stupid name after all). Moffie had her own fashion PR company and a lot of quasi-famous friends.

'There you are, you fucking slut!' she said, opening her arms to Lilah. 'Where in Christ's arsehole have you been?'

Moffie was a posh girl gone street. I knew that from Instagram, too. I'd been pretty far back on all of their feeds, which I had to sternly remind myself not to let onto.

'White wine, or vodka?' asked Annabel, with one of her alarmingly red hands on the Smeg fridge. She was looking at Lilah, so I didn't answer, but Lilah and Moffie were in a tight embrace that showed no sign of ending. Annabel repeated the question.

'Vodka soda, babe,' said Lilah, finally releasing the grip on her friend.

With bitchy reluctance, Annabel turned her eyes on me, and said nothing.

I gathered that I was being invited to answer the same question and said, 'Wine, please!' with the same kind of cringey exclamation that I'd heard my mother use.

'I've just been talking about the party I'm doing for Sunglass Emporium, in fashion week,' said Moffie, returning to the sofa. 'Big celeby do. Gonna go old school and do it at some cool underground place like Dance Tunnel, or maybe the roof of Shoreditch House.'

I remembered something she'd posted about a new place called Sexy Fish, so just to make it sound like I was in the know and had something to offer, I said, 'Or Sexy Fish.'

She frowned at me and blinked several times. I guessed that Sexy Fish was not the kind of place you had a party, or, worse, that she realized I was regurgitating her Instagram and therefore that I was a stalker freak. She carried on without acknowledging me. 'Moet-splashed Moscow Mules all night. Might get Stormzy to do a set. You know. The usual.'

'Why do you always do it in fashion week?' said Lilah, helping herself to one of Moffie's Marlboro Lights, something Billie was always shouting at me for doing. I suddenly thought of her shocker of a day and made a mental note to call her as soon as I got home. Lilah continued, 'Everyone's so tired!'

'You models!' scoffed Moffie. 'Always so tired from doing nothing.'

'You know how stressful fashion week is for me!' said Lilah defensively.

Moffie laughed, but she backed down. 'I'm only joking.'

'I'm not walking shows this season,' said Annabel, and I noticed that she, too, had a West London drawl slipping through her blue-collar words. 'But I will have to do front rows,' she added. 'Can't get out of that one.'

Do front rows? I had a lot to learn.

The doorbell rang and the last of the flock arrived. She strolled in blithely, long-limbed and sinewy. I didn't need to be told that this was Jade Deress: the face of Calvin Klein, a *Vogue* cover star and the top-ranked black model on the oracle that was Models.com. I'd read a profile about her that very morning – of Ethiopian descent, born and raised in New Orleans, addicted to buying expensive vintage T-shirts – and there she was in front of me, carrying her mixed-blooded beauty like a crown. Her tightly braided hair was pulled up carelessly in a bun. A metal ring looped one of her nostrils to the other. She wore jeans and a vintage T-shirt, of course. She always wore jeans and a vintage T-shirt. Then she spoke. 'What the fuck is this music?'

'It's Unknown T!' said Moffie, looking appalled.

'Sounds like rape music,' said Jade.

'I didn't know rapists provided a playlist,' said Lilah. I laughed. She caught my eye and laughed as well. The joke, it seemed, had been lost on the others and I felt like we were sharing a moment.

Jade swaggered over to the iPhone speakers and replaced the heavy grime beats with the more euphonious Alabama Shakes. She sat down, legs open wide, with admirable disregard for any notions of feminine behaviour. *Easy to do when you look like that*, I thought. Then she caught sight of me, a stranger in the mix, and stared with curiosity. I smiled. She smiled back, warmer than I'd have expected, given the rather aggressive picture that the fashion media painted of her.

'Anyone for some wonky donkey?' said Moffie, which I didn't understand.

'Oh, go on then!' said Lilah. 'Twist my rubbery arm.'

Moffie pulled a folded piece of paper from a battered and dirty Saint Laurent wallet. She emptied a heap of white powder onto the coffee table and I guessed that 'wonky donkey' was yet another London slang term for cocaine. I couldn't help but wonder how much such a huge amount of drugs would cost.

'I'm seriously considering a boob job,' said Jade, yawning, which confused me; I'd pegged her as someone who had zero shits to give about the male gaze.

'Like you need to change anything about yourself,' muttered Annabel, sounding almost bitter about it.

'I've been working flat out for no money. I'm over this editorial career,' said Jade. 'If I bought a pair of double Ds, I could make a shit load as a swimwear model and never do a motherfucking show again.'

'Well, I need to get my fanny snipped. It's nearly on the floor,' said Moffie, before leaning over to snort one of the lines she'd drawn out on the table.

We all laughed at that one. Moffie handed me a rolled up twenty because I was the closest person to her. I got down on my knees, hovering over the table like I was about to perform a sexual favour on it, and lifted the note to my nostril. I exhaled out of my mouth so that I didn't blow the powder everywhere, and lowered myself further.

'Babe?' said Lilah.

I covered one nostril and inhaled the substance through the other, chuffed with what a pro I seemed, then looked up at her.

'Babe, you do know that's K, right?' she said, with a light smile.

I nodded, though I hadn't, in fact, known that I was ingesting a fucking horse tranquilizer. I'd heard horror stories about ket-amine. One particular tale had gone around Topsham High of a boy who'd scratched half the skin off his arms, thinking that they were made of wax. I tried to stay calm, but in my head I got into a total flap about suddenly morphing into a figure of Madame Tussauds. I passed the note to Jade. She shook her head, in an almost disapproving way, and reached into her pocket for all the components of a joint, which made me even more anx-ious, because the one time I'd ever smoked a joint had ended in vomit. What if the ketamine made me vomit too?

And then I heard a voice in my head that could have been me, or could have been the horse tranquilizer, telling me to calm the fuck down. *People do this because it's fun, not because it's shit*, the rational voice said. *Relax and enjoy it like a normal person.* And then a languid feeling came over me, and my hands and feet, to all intents and purposes, detached from the rest of my body. It felt great.

'God, I love K!' said Moffie, slumped on the sofa, her legs spread wide – a stance she couldn't carry quite like Jade, which was a thought I was ashamed of having.

Jade, suddenly the most decorous of the group, lit her joint and muttered, 'You gnarly Brits.'

'We are gnarly, aren't we?' I said, happy that there was something as simple as being British that put me in the same bracket as the rest of them (though, technically, I was half Dutch).

Jade reached towards me, from what felt like another world, and held a joint in front of my eyes. 'Can you pass that to Annabel, sugar?'

I took it carefully, focusing on the task at hand. Where was Annabel sitting again? I followed the direction of Jade's gaze and turned to the left. There she was, next to me, with her eyes closed. I thought she might have been asleep, and wondered how I was meant to get the joint to her if that was so. But I'd been given a task that I strongly felt a need to complete. I looked down at her hand, resting on her thigh, and slid the joint between her knuckles. She came to, looked up slowly, and took a toke of the joint. *Mission accomplished.*

Somewhere in the distance, the doorbell rang. I didn't think it was real and didn't particularly care, because I was in a faraway world, musing over Britishness, and things like doorbells didn't matter. I only started to care when I saw Steph standing above me. She looked like a figment of my imagination, though I knew that she wasn't. I tried to picture what I might look like to her, but my thoughts seemed very far away, and I couldn't quite access the image. The eclectic art started rotating in a dizzying way. The neon 'cunt' sign rolled over my head. Then Steph was handing me more drugs. Cocaine this time, she told me, heaped onto the corner of her credit card. I shook my head, but she was very insistent that I take it. After a few bumps, the eclectic art came to a standstill and clarity slapped me across the face.

'Water?' said Steph, in a way that told me she was in full control of the situation.

'I'll get it,' I said, trying to feign some composure, unnerved that my colleague had just found me on the edge of a K hole with our client. Who was the hot mess now?

Steph shook her head and indicated that I should stay where I was. She brought me a tall glass of cold water and I drank it ravenously.

The doorbell rang again. How many times could one doorbell ring?

'That's him,' said Lilah.

Steph glanced at me strangely.

The front door opened. I looked up and saw the spectacular line of white teeth, the sleeves rolled up and the geometric tattoo glaring at me. Then Lilah was directly in front of him, almost his height, her arms around his neck, her face so very close to his. He slid his hands around her back, pressing his fingers into the base of her spine, like he'd done to me, then slipped both large, capable hands into the back pockets of her jeans. My eyes rested on the AG logo bulging on top of his knuckles and I thought, *Just my bloody luck.*

'You guys are too much,' said Jade, barely looking up from the joint she was rolling.

I thought he would pretend that he didn't know me, but he greeted me like an old friend, totally unfazed. I stood up, for some reason, and gave him a hug, like I was totally comfortable with the whole situation, though I was having a minor panic attack.

Lilah didn't ask how we knew each other. No one did.

But when I turned around, Steph was looking at me, and I knew that she knew.

Steph ripped a piece of naan bread and dipped it into a bowl of mango chutney. 'Tell me everything that happened.'

The small Indian restaurant was the only place open at midnight, but for once, I wasn't hungry. We'd left Annabel's house when the others decided they were going out clubbing.

'It's a school night,' Steph had said, grabbing my elbow.

'The staff are leaving!' Moffie had chimed, making the others laugh.

Zack had given me a huge hug to say goodbye.

I told Steph everything that had happened after the Louis Vuitton party, which was a relief. We were on the way to becoming, sort of, friends. She listened attentively, sipping beer, her expression giving away nothing.

When I finished, she said, 'Well, at least you didn't bang him!'

'Yeah, thank God.'

Still wish I had, though.

'Are you going to tell her?' I asked, dreading the answer. Even though I didn't think I'd really done anything wrong, I knew that my burgeoning friendship with Lilah would be over quicker than it started if she knew what had happened with Zack.

'Am I fuck, darl!' said Steph.

'Should I tell her?' I asked, uncertainly. A rhetorical question, really.

'Are you crazy?' she said. 'She would literally rip you apart.'

'Me?' I cried, eager to quash any notion Steph had that this was *my* fault. 'I didn't know! He didn't tell me he had a girlfriend until after we'd kissed. I was in it by then! If I'd have known it was her, I'd have obviously left, immediately!'

'Would you?' said Steph, teasingly, which I knew was an indication that we were becoming friends – but still, I was not in the mood for being teased. She set her beer down and leant towards me. 'Listen to me. Do *not* tell her. She's been on and off with Zack for years. She keeps going back to him, no matter what he does, and she will find a way to make excuses for him. So, don't do it to yourself.'

The waiter arrived with a chicken tikka masala and a bowl of rice for us to share. As he rearranged the table, Steph asked, 'How did you end up at Annabel's place, by the way?'

'Lilah invited me,' I said.

Steph looked at me like she was trying to suss something out. She spoke with unsettling hesitance. 'Listen, sweetheart –' (sweetheart was a new one!) '– no one gets it more than I do. This job is fucking confusing. And there's no right way to do it, by the way – we all wing it! But the more senior you get, the more confusing it becomes. One minute you're on private jets and red carpets, the next you're on the Bakerloo line at rush hour, nuzzling an old man's armpit.'

All I heard was private jets and red carpets.

'But you'll find life a lot easier if you understand boundaries,' she said. 'We're here to do a job, not to be friends with the models.'

'You're friends with them,' I said defensively.

'I'm not saying that you can't be friends with them. But put yourself and your career first. And know your place. People will pretend to want us, but in the end it's always them they want. Not us.'

I pinched a small piece of poppadum from the white table-cloth and crumbled it between my fingers. I knew she was talking about Zack.

'I don't get it,' I said. 'He's got the most beautiful girlfriend in the world. Why would he bother with me?'

Steph shrugged. 'When you get caviar every night, sometimes you just want fish and chips.'

I laughed, because I had to, but really, the last thing I needed was to be told that I was fish and chips.

21 April 2016, 12.49 a.m.

You knew it was too good to be true, so why are you
surprised? At least he liked you. Means maybe others will too

I woke up the next morning in a state of emotional mayhem, to say the least. There was excitement, probably because I was, technically, friends with Lilah, even if I had been tongue-fucking her boyfriend the week before. Demoralization because, truthfully, I'd felt a little out of place in her set. And then there was disappointment. Disappointment because I'd never get to sleep with Zack. On top of that, a wave of remorse came over me when I remembered that I hadn't called Billie back. And it didn't help matters that I had a sticky nasal passage and a brain that felt like it was swelling to the size of my skull, thanks to the ketamine fiasco.

I dialled Billie's number, but after two rings it went to voicemail, which meant she'd rejected the call, just like I'd done to her. I wrote a message:

Me:
So so so sorry I didn't call yesterday. Was
having a work emergency. Talk later? xxx

I knew that she wouldn't think anything fashion-related could warrant a status of emergency, but I couldn't think of another excuse. I got out of bed, splashed my face with cold water and got dressed. As I was leaving the flat, I remembered that I didn't have a fucking penny to my name, or my wallet, having splashed out on the most expensive form of transport in London. There was only one person I could ask.

I knocked on the ceramicist's bedroom door. She opened it, looking like she'd just been electrocuted, and squinted at me. I asked, in my sweetest voice, if I could possibly borrow some money, promising to pay her back as soon as payday came around. Being the generous soul that she was, she asked how many days that would be. I looked at the date on my phone, 24 May, unfolded three fingers to count the days to the 27th, and waved them in her face. She sighed and disappeared into her bedroom. Seconds later, she returned with a ten-pound note. Three pounds and thirty pence per day.

Lifestyles of the rich and famous.

I rushed off to work, thinking of frugal ways to stretch it out. I guessed a Starbucks latte wasn't on the cards that morning. As I was waiting for the tube, refreshing Instagram to see how many people had liked my throwback video of the Louis Vuitton escalator journey, I got a reply from Billie.

> Billie:
> Yesterday I needed to talk. Today I don't
> feel like it.

There was something undoubtedly alarming about that message. I wrote back immediately asking if she was all right before getting on the tube. When I got off the other end, she had responded.

Billie:
Yeah fine, apart from my ovaries are fucked
and can't have kids. But whatevs. Never
wanted them anyway.

I called her then and there, and that time she picked up. It meant
I would be late for work, but I didn't care.

When Madeleine came into the agency that morning, she was in
one of her upbeat moods, which meant you weren't sure if she
was actually about to erupt with volcanic rage. 'You,' she said,
eyes on me, strutting across the room. 'Get me an espresso and
meet me in my office.'

I felt the blood in my hands go thin as I realized that I was
about to be fired. *Some friend Steph was!* I thought. Without
looking at anyone, I got up and walked to the kitchen. I could've
fainted, had I been a fainter. I wondered what I was going to be
fired for – kissing our client's boyfriend, or engaging in illegal
substance abuse with said client? My hands were shaking, most
likely from the hangover, as I prepared a double espresso just
the way Madeleine liked it. How cruel of her to have me act
out the most menial of tasks before disposing of me, I thought.

Madeleine used her office for private phone calls and meetings
only. It felt more like a showroom than anything else – cold and
unlived-in. When I entered, she was sitting on the chaise longue
with her legs crossed tight, the screen of her iPhone inches away
from her Tom Ford spectacles.

'Sit down,' she said without looking up.

I placed the espresso in front of her and took a seat opposite,
feeling my sweaty thighs merge with the cold leather. It seemed
ages before she put down her phone and took off her spectacles.

'Okay. So, can you tell me why you're here so late every night?'

I paused for a second, confused. 'Just . . . to get all of my work done.'

'Are you slow?' she said sharply.

I wasn't sure what the right answer to that question was. 'I don't think so,' I tried.

'I know this job is a lot, but when people can't get their work done in normal hours, it makes me question how efficient they are.'

I said nothing for a few seconds, and then the hangover blurted the truth out for me: 'I can't afford to buy food, so I stay here for dinner.'

Madeleine blinked at me several times and then she laughed, like I'd just told her a dirty joke that she knew she shouldn't find amusing. 'Well, I've never heard that one before.'

I laughed as well, partly to cover my shame.

'Okay, now that I know you're not mentally challenged, how long have you been here exactly?'

'Three months.'

'And you like it?'

I nodded as I silently processed my relief that I wasn't being fired.

'Speak up!' she barked.

'Yes. I love it.'

'You want to continue in our industry?'

I nodded and then, taking on her previous correction: 'More than anything.'

'Okay. So, I asked the agents for feedback on you. They said your digitals aren't great, you're disorganized and messy, you put the wrong calls through and you forget to take messages.'

Maybe I'd be on a train back to Topsham by the end of the day after all.

Madeleine reached for the espresso as she spoke. 'But ... they said you've got big-dick energy. Which they know is all I care about.'

Was that a compliment?

'I need to know you're committed. It takes a lot to be an agent and I'm only interested in training people who are sure it's what they really want to do.'

'It is what I want,' I said quickly, as a guilt-ridden voice in my head whispered the words 'fashion school'.

'And you're willing to give me a hundred and fifty per cent?'

'More. I'll give two hundred per cent.'

'That's your whole life, you know?' She smiled. Her throat swelled as she threw back the espresso, then continued: 'Now, there are people who will continuously remind you that you're not saving lives. And you are gonna have to shut them out. Do you understand what I'm talking about?'

'Yeah.'

I didn't.

Madeleine read me. She sat forwards, resting her forearms on her thighs, and started kicking her leg back and forth, the sharp triangular tip of her Louis Vuitton shoe tapping the rim of the coffee table. 'Here's the thing about this job. You can do it half-heartedly and you'd be bored as hell and you'd suck at it. But if you treat what we do like it is the most important thing in the whole world, that's when you'll thrive.'

I nodded, hypnotized by the swinging Vuitton.

'What do you really want to do?' she said.

What a gargantuan question that was for a hungover Thursday morning.

What did I want?

I thought about it. I wanted to be repackaged, remarketed and sent out into the word afresh. I wanted to be free of Scizzle from Topsham. I wanted my life to reassemble into an artistically curated photobook of moments that looked like they'd been captured at Studio 54. I wanted London to scoop me up and place me onto a plain so high in vibrations that I would barely be able to breathe. I wanted people who had never met me to know my name and want to be my friend. I wanted to live my best life and be a part of something. Something fabulous.

I looked at Madeleine and said all of that in a single sentence: 'I want to be an agent.'

CHAPTER 6

Even now, the words 'fashion week' spark off my own personal brand of PTSD, which is basically a cocktail of exhaustion, misguided laughter, anxiety, tears and a shitload of adrenaline. It happens twice a year – September for Spring/Summer collections and February for Autumn/Winter collections – over four back-to-back weeks in four different markets: New York, London, Milan and Paris.

'You have the hardest job of fashion week,' Steph told me in early September, already razzed up by the anticipation of high stress and drama. 'It's a rite of passage. Every agent is a survivor of fashion week as an assistant.'

After a summer spent as the permanent fixture of the 'skeleton staff' taking messages while the entire fashion industry appeared to be in Ibiza or Mykonos, a challenge was welcome. I'd always known that fashion week happened and had followed hashtags like #LFW to salivate over the clothes on display, not even noticing that there was a model wearing them. It seemed surreal that I was about to become a miniscule part of the event itself.

In the run-up to New York Fashion Week, or NYFW as the cool cats called it, Lilah was 'out of shape' – meaning her hips were measuring 34 inches rather than 33 inches, which Madeleine noticed just by looking at her. The thing about Lilah was that there was a lot riding on her at that time. She was on the cusp of great success and it could go one way or the other. The agency were in desperate need of a rising star, and the hope was that Lilah could be that star. So there was a lengthy meeting about Lilah before she flew to New York, the main question of which was how to tell her to skinny down without upsetting her.

The Lilah meeting was an important moment for me because it was the first time in the six months I'd been working there that I was invited to sit at the grown-up table. Madeleine asked me to join, for no other reason than that Lilah and I had actually become what you'd call 'close friends' over the summer. It all began when she'd been gifted a complimentary room at the W Hotel, which I was instructed to tell her about, and she invited me to join. I'd been expecting a debauched night, rinsing the minibar and snorting lines of cocaine (or horse tranquilizer, or whatever) while her shiny friends came and went. But when I arrived, Lilah was in her pyjamas, her hair in an oily treatment mask, watching *Love Island*. I'd never seen it, but as it turned out, it wasn't a hard programme to follow. The next time I saw her, we went to a Bikram Yoga class. We met for lunch. We went out for coffee. We had dinner once when she was on a raw food cleanse.

The thing that had become clear to me was that Lilah and I wanted different things from each other. She wanted me to be her companion when she was doing 'ordinary' things, like watching TV in free hotel rooms, when her boyfriend was out of town. I wanted her to take me to the life of her Instagram feed. Parties in Room 39 at the Chiltern Firehouse, group hangs in someone's garden and a villa full of attractive beings overlooking Es Cubells. I wanted her to engulf me in her glittery network. But being her ordinary friend was certainly better than nothing.

Regardless of how I felt, the news of our budding friendship was spreading like a catchy hashtag. Everyone at the agency seemed a bit more interested in hearing my opinion. It was decided, in the Lilah meeting, that Steph should be the one to break the news about her oversized hips, and she did so in an undoubtedly awkward phone conversation. I was then sent over to her flat with a consolation cooler of raw pressed juices, which she would be living on for the next week. That's right: liquid only, please. *How bleak.*

Lilah's Primrose Hill flat was actually owned by Annabel's family, but it wasn't nearly as cutting-edge as the Camden affair. In fact, it was pretty soulless. Lilah had filled the place with photographs of herself, but other than that there wasn't much about it that felt like her.

I arrived with a smile on my face, ready to make her laugh about the ridiculousness of everyone fussing about the cir-cumference of her waistline, which I assumed she knew was a waistline to kill for. But as soon as she let me in, I could sense that she wasn't in the mood to laugh about it. In fact, her energy was completely different to how I'd known it to be. Rather than flitting between the bright, friendly Lilah that I'd fallen head over heels for and the distant, indifferent Lilah that made me want to please her, she was in a place that reminded me of the rumble you hear in the sky when a thunderstorm is about to start.

We sat on the sofa as she glugged at a dark crimson raw juice and angrily flicked through television channels, her jaw clenched tight. I asked questions that I thought were light-hearted – about the flat, about the weather in New York – and she answered them all with single, monosyllabic words. I then showed her a YouTube video of a Cocker Spaniel lip-syncing to a rap song and she burst into tears. I knew it had nothing to do with animal rights – she wore fur – so I asked her what was wrong. It turned out that the song the dog was lip-syncing to was by one of Zack's musicians. I asked her why that had made her cry and she snapped and told me that they'd broken up, again.

I truly felt like the shittest person on earth when I realized that the tiny flutter I was feeling in my stomach was excitement.

Obviously I hid that ugly reaction and moved closer to her on the sofa. 'Look, it can only be a good thing. I mean ... he represents a dog rapper.'

She frowned at me through teary eyes, and I thought, *That was a bad joke at the best of times.* Why would she have been in the mood for that? But then she let out a snorting sound as her face twisted into what I thought was a grimace, until I realized she was laughing.

I laughed too, relieved, and reached over to take her hand. 'Guys are shit. You are so lucky you get to be single now and do whatever you want. You can have as much fun as you want, without having to worry about what someone else is doing.'

'I do have more fun when he's not there,' she admitted, and something about the idea of having fun purely for and because of oneself, was a comforting thought.

'You'll be in New York, having way more fun than him,' I continued.

'Well, I *am* more fun than him,' she said, very seriously.

'Exactly. You're young, he's old. You're gorgeous, he's –' *gorgeous* '– got too many tattoos.'

She laughed again, scrunching up her nose, looking like a cute little rabbit. It was hard to believe she had been that icicle version of herself moments before.

My generic screw-all-men pep talk went on and by the end

we were both quoting Bridget Jones – 'I think a well-timed blow job's probably the best answer' – and Lilah was WhatsApping a selfie to her New York fuck buddy captioned 'Ready to ravage?' *Feminism at its best.*

Lilah left for New York the next morning, and I tracked her trip via Instagram like a devoted, envious fan. I felt a swell of FOMO every time I saw a photo of her at a party, or even just walking the streets of New York with a bunch of other models. The realization that Lilah's world could go on without me, while she was basically at the front and centre of mine, was starting to make me feel a tad anxious. I was also jealous of how great they all looked and decided to treat myself to a bit of a consolation rebrand, even though I was, as ever, nearly broke.

I booked myself into the Hoxton hair salon where we sent the models to, and handed the stylist a picture of Abbey Lee Kershaw, asking him to make me look like her, which was bold considering she was a supermodel with a bone structure that could carry a comb over. But he went for it and bleached my hair platinum blonde then expertly cut a choppy fringe.

I loved it, but I still cried when I walked out of the salon because I realized that I looked nothing like Abbey Lee Kershaw. I took a selfie and sent it to Billie, who returned it with a meme of Draco Malfoy, captioned: 'BABY WANNA WIDE MY BROOM?', which made me laugh a lot. Even after the news of her 'barren womb', as she called it, she was still so very Billie.

On the way home, I wandered into a tattoo parlour, remembering that promise I'd made to myself about getting one with my first pay cheque. Aside from the fact that I couldn't afford it, the real problem was that I just couldn't think of anything that I was sure I wanted inked on my skin for the rest of my life. After half an hour, I walked out again.

We had forty models arriving from New York and I was responsible for coordinating the movements of every single one of them. I was genuinely waking up in the middle of the night with my 'Models – Hotels' list jumping about behind my eyebrows, certain that I'd made a mistake somewhere. The new face models had been paired up and shoved into twin rooms at a cheap hotel near the agency. That was the easy part. The big models, however, had preferences. But, being fashion week, the hotels were fully booked, so I had to beg the booking managers to help me fulfil wishes, like the invisible fairy-fucking-godmother.

An even bigger minefield was getting them all in from New York. Under Steph's instruction, I'd had the flights on hold for weeks. But I couldn't confirm any of them until I got the go-ahead from their agents in New York, and those agents couldn't give that to me until they knew what shows the models were confirmed on over there – and the shows, it seemed, only confirmed models a day in advance. It blew my mind that the system for organizing a global, high-profile, four-week-long, multi-million-dollar event was about as efficient as a dial-up operated call centre run by Donald Duck.

Most of our models were taking the Thursday night flight from New York. But the last show of NYFW was Marc Jacobs, apparently the most prestigious because there was some top-dog stylist involved. Any girl confirmed on Marc Jacobs wouldn't be able to travel until Friday morning and would miss the first day of London shows. No one except London cared that much about London, needless to say. So, I had to have two sets of flights on hold for anyone on the Marc Jacobs option list. *Head spin.*

By Wednesday evening, I was still waiting for Marc Jacobs to confirm their damn line-up. The agents in New York were shouting at me because I kept bugging them for news. The travel agent was shouting me because he had prime flights on hold. Madeleine was shouting at me because she was Madeleine. And in the midst of it all, I had to go to The Edition, a celebrity-ridden hotel in Fitzrovia, to make sure all of our big models had the rooms of their dreams.

The booking manager of The Edition met me in the Punch Room, an intimate bar for hotel guests only. Both of us were sweating like bacon, thanks to the Indian summer we were having. I'd never have imagined that, working in an industry as glamorous as fashion, the people I'd speak to most frequently would be Addison Lee drivers, couriers, travel agents and hotel booking managers, but you learn something new every day. Without meaning to, I realized that I was behaving with an air of superiority as I went through each model and their require-ments, regardless of the fact the booking manager was twice my age and probably made double my salary. *Treat this job like it's the most important thing in the world*, said the Madeleine-inspired voice in my head.

When I'd gone through the list, she told me that none of it was a problem, that they'd dealt with hundreds of high-profile guests and that musicians were generally the most demanding. So, really, what she was saying was that I could pipe down with my snootiness and let her do her job.

After the meeting, I went to the bathroom and winced at the sight of myself in the floor-to-ceiling mirror. The plat-inum blonde and fringe was far harder to manage than I'd anticipated and most of the time I looked more Myra Hindley than Abbey Lee Kershaw. On the way out, I scrolled furiously through the hundreds of unread emails that were polluting my inbox. Still no word on Marc sodding Jacobs. My armpits were itching with sweat and the nylon lining of the floral dress that I'd bought from Portobello Market was sticking to my skin. I couldn't wait to get home, take it off and lie naked in front of the fan. I knew that it would be the last full night of sleep I'd get for the next few days, having been warned that sleep was a bonus during fashion week, not a given. Maybe I could even get some washing done if the ceramicist wasn't in a pissy mood. Maybe I could watch the final episode of *Stranger Things*. Maybe I could—

'There she is,' a familiar voice said, cutting through my thoughts of solitary domesticity.

I looked up – confused, exasperated, hot – and there he was, not quite smiling. An image flickered behind my eyes: the outline of his facial hair coming towards me in the dark. Now, he was clean shaven.

I was both enraptured and terrified to see him. Enraptured because I'd been dying to run into him for weeks. Terrified because I knew that that wasn't a good thing.

'Hey, what are you doing here?' I asked, thinking only of my sweaty underarms.

'Just settling in one of my acts,' said Zack. 'How are you?'

'Stressed!'

'Oh, of course, it's fashion week, *daaaarling*,' he said, mocking what I did, because clearly fashion was much less serious than music.

Needless to say, I didn't appreciate it. 'It's fucking too much! I've got fifteen flights on hold and they haven't confirmed Marc Jacobs and everyone is shouting at me!' I pressed a hand over one eye, scrunching up my face, like I had a migraine. It was a totally overdramatic reaction, but it was how I felt. I didn't tell him that I had no idea what I was doing half the time and that I was sure I would fuck up and get fired.

'You need a drink, missy,' he said.

'No, no. Definitely don't need a drink.'

Don't need one. But really want one.

'Yes, you do. Come on.'

I knew, for an array of obvious reasons, that I should have walked out into the hot September night and taken the bus home. But at that moment, a drink with the most alluring man I'd met to date sounded so much more desirable than my eggshell-blue, stuffy shoebox of a room.

'One drink,' I said, holding my index finger up in a straight line. I don't know if I ever believed that I meant it.

We sat down in the lobby bar, ornate with marble floors, pillars and – for reasons that were unclear – a giant silver egg hanging from the restored stucco ceiling. I ordered white wine. He ordered a beer. It seemed strange that something as ordinary as a beer could be consumed in a room that looked like something from a Baz Luhrmann film.

'So, how did you become an agent?' asked Zack, in an overly conversational manner, sliding his arm across the back of the sofa top.

I picked up a black napkin and used it to dab at my perspiring neckline, aware that I was probably sporting an attractive heat rash, which would likely soon become an even more attractive lash rash. 'I'm not an agent yet. I will be though.'

His eyes flitted over the napkin, and I realized that he might have thought I was doing it provocatively, rather than self-consciously. 'Have you always wanted to do that?'

'No, I wanted to be a designer,' I said, noticing the damp

patches that had appeared among the blooming floral print of my dress. I dreaded to think how I smelt.

'And what happened?'

'You need to go to fashion school.'

'So, why didn't you go?' he asked.

'I will,' I said. 'I'm just working at the agency to get experience. Learn more about the industry.'

And pay for fashion school.

'You should go to Parsons,' he said, which I knew from my research was in New York and was virtually triple the cost of any of the schools in London. He added, 'I've got loads of mates who went there.'

Of course he did.

'Maybe,' I said.

Maybe in another life, I meant.

Like he'd read my thoughts, he said, 'There's plenty of time. You're still young.'

'How old are you?' I asked.

'Thirty-four.'

He didn't ask my age in return, probably because he knew that I was too young for a 34-year-old.

We got through our drinks rapidly as he chatted away about his job, telling me, in great detail, how he scouted new musicians and nurtured them to success. In typical male fashion, he didn't ask much about what I did, but then again, he probably knew all about model agents. He ordered another round of drinks, and I didn't protest.

With a second glass of wine down me, I finally summoned the elephant in the room. 'I was sorry to hear about you and Lilah.'

He gave a tiny sigh of – was it relief? – as he said, 'You've heard.'

'Yeah, she told me.'

'Do you know her well then?' he said.

I felt a little put out that Lilah hadn't ever mentioned me. I did, after all, drop her name to Billie almost every time we spoke. But when it came to answering Zack's question, I shrugged and said, 'Quite well.' I was aware that it was not a good sign that I was playing down our friendship, but the wine had gone straight to my head and sense was starting to feel like a lost friend. I suddenly realized that I hadn't eaten since breakfast – that was a first.

'Another drink?' he said, presumably to help me forget that I knew his ex-girlfriend 'quite well'.

'I should go soon,' I said, and I hate to admit that I only said it so that he would urge me to stay. 'I've got a big few days coming up.'

'That's well behaved of you,' he said, shifting the tone of the conversation, so subtly, yet so clearly.

'I'm generally pretty well behaved,' I said, echoing that shift.

'You weren't very well behaved the last time I saw you.' He hooked his finger around the back of my knee.

I leant forward awkwardly, looking anywhere but at him, cautiously eyeing the other people in the room. Next to us, there was a table of middle-aged men in suits, drinking martinis. I realized that everyone who worked in fashion was in New York, which was probably why he wasn't panicking about someone seeing us and telling Lilah, like I was.

He called a member of staff over, and still I refused to look at him, even as he said, 'Can I get a room please, buddy?'

'Certainly, Mr Smith,' said the staff member, like a caricature of a butler, and then disappeared.

I didn't say anything about the room. I should have been

offended by the presumption, but the casualness and the virility of it turned me on.

'I've got a gram burning a hole in my pocket,' he said.

I sucked in a sharp line of breath and shook my head. 'I really should go home.'

'Yeah. You probably should.'

In the lift, I checked my emails. No news from Marc Jacobs.

Zack stood behind me, loud with silence, and slipped both hands around the base of my neck from behind, pressing his middle fingers into the dip at the centre of my collarbone.

The travel agent was threatening to release the flights.

I felt like I had stepped into my darkest, most exhilarating fantasy as I drew out lines of cocaine on the low, circular table using Zack's hard metal American Express card as he opened a bottle of red wine from the minibar. It was a room in the same price category as the one I had on hold for our top supermodel, Yulia Kuznetsova, the following night.

Zack poured two glasses of wine and joined me on the sofa. He handed me a rolled-up note. 'After you.'

'How chivalrous,' I said. I inched forward on the sofa and hinged from the waist. The floral dress lifted at the back.

He slid his hand over my knickers without hesitation. 'Fuck. You're. So. Fucking. Fit.'

I didn't know if he was lying, or if he'd just missed the feel of womanly flesh after years with a bag of bones. *Bitchy thought, I know.* I took a long, hard sniff, and the cocaine hit the space between my eyes. His hand was inside my pants by the time I surfaced, his fingers cold.

'I've thought about that night a lot,' he said. 'Have you?'

I nodded, still hovering over the table. I couldn't tell him that I'd played it over in my mind to the point where it was naturally coming up in my daily thought chains. I swallowed over the dry swell in my throat and sat up. We hadn't kissed yet and, for some reason, that made it all feel okay, as if kissing would have really been crossing a line. I slid over to the other side of the sofa, pressing him away with my foot. 'Let's try not to touch for a bit.' I don't know whether it was guilt, or nerves, but I felt the need to put some distance between us.

He took hold of my foot and bit the end of my toes, which made me jump. 'What are we doing then? If not touching?'

I stood up and stepped away from him. 'What do you want me to do?'

'Take off your dress.'

I was so flattered that he wanted to see me naked that I wasn't the slightest bit offended by the command. Obediently, I reached to gather the cotton fabric at the waist in tight fists, pulled the floral dress over my head and let it fall to the floor, like I was Margot fucking Robbie in *Wolf of Wall Street* or something. I felt self-conscious about the softness of my body, so I unhooked my bra, unprompted, and discarded that, in the hope that he'd be distracted by my large and – if I might say so myself – rather perky breasts. Surely he must have missed breasts?

As if he'd read my mind, he said, 'You've got great tits,' and an image of Lilah's flat chest appeared in my mind. Yet another thought I wasn't proud of having.

Remembering that he'd enjoyed my rear side a moment before, I did a full rotation, on tiptoes, practically begging him to desire me.

'In fact, the whole thing is great,' he said, which I sensed was a line he'd use on anyone.

I wasn't sure what to say, or do, so I racked my imagination for what I thought Lilah would do at that moment. For some reason, I thought she'd bend over.

He laughed a little and said, 'You're like a porn star.'

I quickly lifted myself up, completely embarrassed. Maybe I had learnt that from porn. I had no clue what the realms of normal were when it came to having sex. How did anyone know? No one sees anyone else having sex.

'You know, I wanked to your Facebook profile,' he said almost proudly.

'How did you find my Facebook?'

I felt a thrill charge through me at the thought of Zack Smith actively searching my name on social media.

'It's not hard,' he said.

'I didn't even think you knew my name, really.'

'Of course I know your name!' he said. 'Come here.'

I took a few steps towards him. He slid his hands around the back of my thighs and I stretched, like a large cat, towards him. I wanted him to lust over me. I wanted him to crave me, long after I'd left. His fingers were inside me again and I collapsed at the knees. Then I was lying on the floor and he was planked over me, fully clothed, while I was almost completely naked. I melted beneath the weight of him and muttered a sound like, 'Ohmygod'. He took a hot inhale, sated by his own power, gratified by the sight of me helpless.

'I feel like this is very slutty behaviour,' I whispered.

I wanted him to tell me that I needn't feel that way, that it was his fault, not mine. That he couldn't help it: he just wanted me.

Instead, he said, 'Yeah, you're a fucking slut,' and turned me over onto my stomach.

*

I reached for my iPhone as Zack shook a cigarette packet from his limp trousers. I watched him stand up, tall, ink-ridden, looking like a nude statue that had been vandalized. I opened my Pure Models inbox and started swiping through emails, with one eye closed and the other clouded in sticky wine fog. There it was, the email I'd been waiting for: Marc Jacobs confirmations. I read the list. We had six models confirmed on the show. Lilah was one of them.

'Lilah got Marc Jacobs,' I said, and then suddenly wished I hadn't. She had become, over the past few hours, like a distant, fictional figure for both of us.

Without looking at me, Zack brought the flame of a lighter to the end of his cigarette and held it there for a long time, as if he was trying to burn away his discomfort. The flame went out of its own accord and he said, 'She'll be really happy. She deserves it.'

The lilt in his voice as he said it sent a surge of jealousy through me. It made me think that he was longing for her. And why wouldn't he? *I* was longing for her.

I sighed as I forwarded the list to the travel agent. My mouth was parched.

'Tell me how you remember that night,' he said. 'When we kissed?'

I took a sip of red wine. It stuck to the roof of my mouth and I washed it down with water from a tiny, and probably extortionate, Evian bottle. 'Well, when I arrived at the Louis Vuitton party, you stood up to say hi to me. And . . . I sort of knew there was something in it. Because I didn't think you'd remember me from when we first met.'

'Of course I remembered you. In that little schoolgirl skirt.'

It made me laugh that he called it that. I wondered if the

skirt was what had caught his eye in the first place. And if so, did I have Steph to thank – or blame – for all this, since she had handed it to me? Clothes were, after all, a way to tell the world how you wanted to be perceived.

'Do you remember when I fell over?' I said.

He laughed. 'Yeah, it was cute.' And then: 'Carry on.'

'So, I went off to hang with Patrick. And then, when you were leaving, you said, "Come to my friend's house," and when we were walking to the off-licence, you kissed me. And immediately after that, you said, "Oh, by the way, I have a girlfriend!"'

'And you didn't care, which turned me on even more,' he said, planting himself next to me on the sofa.

'What do you mean, I didn't care? That makes me sound like a right bitch.'

'Well, you did let me kiss you again, didn't you?'

'Yeah, but at that point we'd already gone through everything you go through when you're going to get with someone. The flirting, leaving the party. I was in it by then. And I couldn't really believe it was happening, if I'm being honest.'

The possibility of honesty felt so much more available when we were just two people, naked, in a hotel room.

'I wasn't expecting it to happen,' he said, ashing his cigarette into an empty wine bottle, leaving little grey specks at the rim.

'You made it happen!'

'No, I was passive. *You* made it happen.'

'That's definitely not true,' I said, flabbergasted by the idea. 'How do you remember it?'

'I just remember you being all over me. And I found you so fucking sexy, I couldn't resist.'

I couldn't believe it. He'd just rewritten the night. Granted, I'd probably skewed some of the details, but I knew that his memory was wrong, because I'd never been forthcoming with anyone in my life. I was too scared of being rejected. I knew that there was no way I could convince him of that because everyone believed in their own memories, however fallible they were, so I just sat there, frustrated, until my iPhone vibrated on the table.

The travel agent had replied to my email:

Friday flight is now full.

CHAPTER 7

'You were too late,' said the travel agent. 'The Friday morning flights are booked up.'

I was outside Seven Sisters underground station, unable to get on the tube in case I lost signal. That meant I'd be late for work, and no one would be interested in hearing my excuse.

'You have to get the girls on that flight!' I shrieked, close to tears, the hangover not helping a thing. 'Just the six who are doing Marc Jacobs. The rest need to fly tonight!'

'I've confirmed the flights tonight. But tomorrow morning's trickier. Everyone wants to fly tomorrow. Even Anna Wintour's having trouble.'

The travel agent fancied himself a bit of a big cheese in the fashion industry.

'Please, just make it happen!' I said.

He said he'd see what he could do. I got on the tube with plugged nostrils, sticky sinuses and a stress-related stomach ache that I recognized from childhood. Of course, there were no free seats. With one hand looped into the ring above me and my temple resting on the inside of my arm, I opened WhatsApp and reread the messages between Zack and me, which had occurred around 1 a.m., when I was safely hidden in the eggshell room, having left the hotel in a panicked frenzy.

Me:
I left my bra in the hotel room 🐵

Zack:
I'll grab it for you but finders keepers . . .

Me:
In bed all alone. How sad.

Zack:
I should come.
That was so sexy

Me:
V hot

Zack:
Just what I needed
Are you happy?

Me:
Very
And horny

Zack:
Very horny
Nice tits
Good time to call it a night

Me:
Yes. Well behaved
Think I'm quite drunk

Zack:
You're so fun to hang out with

And then I'd fallen asleep.

I had three heavy balls of guilt weighing down inside of me: one in the base of my throat, one just behind my sternum, and the other at the pit of my stomach.

I typed out a reply with a single thumb as the tube rattled on.

Me:
Delete this conversation.

Then I looked up and realized that I'd arrived at Tottenham Hale, which meant that I was on the wrong fucking tube. Stellar start to fashion week.

When I finally got to the agency, Patrick was quick to shout, 'Oh, good afternoon, so nice of you to join us.'

I didn't even try to explain myself. I sat down at my computer with an oddly satisfying pain pinching at the inside of my vagina, reminding me exactly what I'd been doing the night before, and refreshed my inbox. The travel agent had sent me an email in his trademark overfamiliar style:

I've sorted out your Friday flights. Had to put
Christina Lima on British Airways which is
more $$, the rest of your girls are on Kuwait.
YOU OWE ME.

For the first time that morning, I took a full breath. Had it not been sorted, it would have been an epic disaster that I'd never have heard the end of. But I would get no congratulations or pats on the back for the stress I'd gone through to make it happen because no one really cared when you just did what you were supposed to. Why would they?

I'd been moved onto the booking table for fashion week, so that the agents could communicate with me – or shout at me – more effectively. I had the phone pressed to my ear, the tone of a holding line ringing through.

'Camala isn't getting any show requests,' said Drew, referring to our Jamaican new face model who was set to debut in Marc Jacobs later that day.

'Have you told them she's walking MJ?' said Madeleine, taking a swig of Diet Coke. She spent most of London Fashion Week out of the agency, chaperoning models, usually Yulia Kuznetsova, but every now and then she'd land herself upon us to make sure there were no major catastrophes.

'Yes, I've told them, Madeleine,' said Drew, the only person who could be irritable with her.

'Don't the shows have a diversity quota these days?' she said flippantly.

'The designers don't even take notice of government-imposed BMI regulations. You think they care about the Fashion Council's meek little quota?' said Drew, his voice getting more and more high-pitched.

I pressed a button on the phone to take the very important, very irate casting director off hold. 'Jonathan? Madeleine is still on the other line.'

Lies. They were a fundamental tool for model agents. The more you lied, the further you got, it seemed. I couldn't count the number of lies I'd told that day.

But the irate casting director seemed to know that I was lying.

He screamed, 'Tell her I've got Donatella Versace with me and she's not happy!'

I put him on hold again. 'Madeleine? He said he's with Donatella Versace and she's not happy.'

Madeleine rolled her eyes. 'Tell him I'm with Jesus and he's not happy either.'

I decided against passing that on. 'She'll call you back as soon as she can, Jonathan. She's dealing with a crisis.'

Jonathan's voice came hissing down the phone. 'Remind Madeleine that I've put at least seventy grand in commercial jobs through Pure Models in the last six months! If she doesn't give me the girls I want for my show, I won't ever include her in any of my deals again!'

That was about the fifth time I'd been screamed at and hung up on, and it was only Thursday.

The stress of the flights and hotels seemed pretty trivial compared to the mammoth job of fashion week cars. I had fifteen chauffeur-driven cars to micro-manage. They had to be shared between forty models, who were charged by the hour. If a car was empty, at any time, the agency had to swallow the cost. All of the models, it turned out, had different schedules for their fittings, castings and shows, so organizing which models to put in which cars was like trying to a complete a thousand-piece puzzle while sinking into quicksand.

If a model was running late for an appointment, I had to notify an agent so that they could tell the client. When they arrived at an appointment, I had to notify an agent so that they could hassle the client to see the model as fast as possible, so we could move her onto the next job. I had to keep on top of the minute-by-minute schedules of forty girls and fifteen drivers – not easy for someone who can't even keep on top of her washing. And all the while, I could not stop thinking about having sex with Zack. A tickling worm would travel down the front of my stomach every time I replayed even a fraction of that night.

Thursday went relatively smoothly, all things considered. We were out of the agency just after midnight. That may have been because there weren't actually any shows on Thursday, only castings and fittings for Friday's shows. On Thursday night, the girls who weren't on Marc Jacobs flew from New York, arriving Friday morning.

On Friday morning, the Marc Jacobs girls got onto their flight and were due to arrive Friday evening. They'd have to go straight to fittings for Saturday shows. The timings were already ambitious, so it caused a furore when the travel agent called to tell me that the flights had been delayed. The planes were circling in the sky because of a thunderstorm over south-east England. The agents informed the casting directors, who were waiting on the girls. The casting directors snapped at them, like it was their fault the weather was bad, and in turn, they snapped at me, but would always follow it with the phrase, 'Pozzy vibes!', which basically meant the same as 'no offence'.

It was almost 9 p.m. when the travel agent called to tell me that the plane was landing in Newcastle. I closed my eyes and asked him to repeat the information. He did so and, amazingly, nothing had changed – they were still landing in Newcastle. I asked him to hold, knowing that there would be a thousand questions, and stood up to talk to the agents. 'Guys?'

They were fighting about whether they should be prioritizing a casting director from the British *Vogue* show or one who was a big deal to our New York agency, the higher power.

I spoke louder: 'Guys!'

'What is it, darling?' said Drew impatiently.

'I'm scared to tell you this, but none of the flights are landing in London because of the weather.'

The agents all went silent and exchanged looks. You would've thought I'd just told them there'd been a nuclear attack on the capital.

Treat this job like it's the most important thing in the world.

'All of the girls, except Christina Lima, have landed in Newcastle,' I said with an apologetic grimace.

'Where's Christina Lima?' asked Steph.

'Still circling in the sky. She's on the same plane as Anna Wintour –' (the travel agent had made sure to tell me that) '– but they'll all be put on an overnight bus as soon as they land and will arrive in the morning.'

Heads went tumbling into hands and words like 'fucking', 'shitting' and 'cunting' were flying around the booking room like a cyclone.

'Okay, we'll just have to send them straight out when they get here. The casting directors will have to understand.'

'We can't do that, they'll be exhausted!' I said, aghast. 'Imagine spending the night on a bus, when you're sixteen years old, and having to go straight to work the next morning.'

'These are the hottest girls of the season – we need them on those runways,' said Patrick.

'Newcastle Airport! There's probably not even anywhere they can buy food at this time of night,' I said, and looked at Drew imploringly.

He sighed. 'Okay, disconnect all the phones. Let's have a meeting.'

I did as I'd been told to, feeling pretty anxious about all the drivers who would be trying to get hold of me, waiting for their next instructions. We went into the conference room, which had been turned into a 'chillout zone' dotted with huge bean bags and aromatherapy candles. It was where the agents took the models to break bad news to them. It was meant to be calming, but looked more like a VIP room in a regional club that sold Apple Sourz for a quid a pop. Many a model had sat in that room expelling their tears. A fail during fashion week was taken so much harder than a fail at any other point in their career. I slumped down into one of the bean bags, going from frenetic high energy to feeling like I could fall right to sleep in a second.

'Okay,' Drew began. 'The models will arrive on no sleep. They'll be tired. They'll be hungry. Some of them are children. And they're all underweight by government legal standards. I agree with Scarlett that, morally, the thing to do would be to pull them from all Saturday shows.'

'What?' said Patrick, with histrionic outrage.

'We can't do that,' said Steph. 'JW Anderson is on Saturday. That's one of the biggest shows!'

'Yeah, I know that, Steph, I've done this job for ten years longer than you, thanks,' said Drew, pressing his fingers into his temples. 'But I'm starting to feel uncomfortable with what we put these models through.'

So am I.

'I just feel we need to look out for them. Don't you agree?' he said, throwing his hands out to the sides.

Patrick and Steph both stared at him. Clearly, the thought hadn't crossed their minds. They weren't bad people – they were just so used to talking about the girls as non-human commodities that they'd started to view them that way as well.

'Guys, I need us all in agreement,' said Drew.

At that moment, I got a WhatsApp from Moffie bugging me about her damn end-of-LFW party on the Monday night for that rogue sunglasses client. She wanted me to send top models to the event. I took it as a compliment that she thought I had any authority to do that, but now I realize she simply thought I would be easy to manipulate, being as inexperienced as I was. I'd asked Steph several times if we could send anyone, but apparently it wasn't the kind of thing that our models should attend. I didn't think it was the time to ask again.

Instead, I said, 'Please, please don't send them out tomorrow,' imagining myself at sixteen, in a foreign country, with people I didn't know, being confronted by the likes of Pawel Dyk.

'Scarlett's right,' sighed Steph. 'It's not fair on them.'

'Fine,' said Patrick, standing up dramatically. He looked at Drew. 'You tell Madeleine.'

We exited the chillout room and I felt a little proud of myself for influencing such a big and controversial decision. Patrick, Steph and I went out for a cigarette, which was the first one I'd had time for all day. I had momentarily forgotten about the fifteen cars that were on standstill, the drivers frantically calling a disconnected phone number. Steph and I agreed that we felt a strange sense of personal elation at the idea that we were doing a moral deed in the middle of the fashion calendar's most vicious week. Patrick made fun of us for our virtuosity, but I could tell that even he had come round. The wind whipped at us, blowing a Tesco shopping bag past.

'There goes Christina Lima,' said Patrick, and we all laughed.

'Newcastle's in for a shock!' said Steph.

'Oh my god!' said Patrick. 'Those creatures crawling off the plane, all thin and pale!' He did an impression of thin models by making his hands into spiders and drawing his shoulders into the centre of his chest.

'Trust me, Newcastle's never seen anything like it!' said Steph.

We all laughed again. My conscience tugged at me for mocking the girls, whose wellbeing I'd just leapt to defend, but I just needed to laugh. When we went back inside, Drew was staring glumly at his computer screen.

'Did you talk to Madeleine?' asked Patrick.

'Yes.'

'What did she say?' I asked hopefully.

'She said get them off that bus and into fittings. We're not to cancel any model from any show.'

There was a nod of understanding from all as we put our moral compasses back into their boxes, where they belonged. I reached for the flailing wire of the telephone line and re-plugged it. Suddenly, red lights went flashing and missed calls from almost every single one of my drivers came flying up on the screen.

I took out my iPhone.

16 September 2016, 9.48 p.m.

Breathe breathe breathe breathe.
God you sound dramatic

I'd been sent to meet the girls at Victoria Station, where the overnight bus was arriving, at six in the morning. Steph had given me her credit card to buy fresh fruit and energy snacks. I'd also made a stop at Gail's – which by then I'd worked out was a large UK coffee chain that lured the unaware into consumerism by posing as a local, family-run bakery – to get Lilah an oat milk turmeric latte. That's what friends did for each other, after all. *Oh, and fucked each other's ex-boyfriends . . .*

Madeleine had pointed out that no other London agency would be pulling their models from the shows, so we'd be the only ones missing out. No one would write blog posts or fashion columns about the impressive morality of Pure Models. With our distinct lack of presence in the shows, they wouldn't even think about us, she said. They would only be talking about the models from other agencies who *were* walking down those cat-walks. So, we all swallowed whatever scruples we had and tried to sit comfortably with our discomfort.

A whole army of models arrived on one coach. I watched them disembark in single file, all from different countries, cultures and walks of life, being shuttled around the world, side by side. They grouped off by agency after hugging each other goodbye, and I noticed an unexpectedly strong sense of camaraderie. They'd all been thrown into this weird life that was worlds apart from what they knew, and they were the only ones who understood it. It seemed like a subcultural support group, a family of sorts. I have to say, shitty though fashion week was for them – four weeks of scrutiny, judgement, pres-sure and barely any food or sleep – I was a little envious of that team feeling.

Lilah came charging towards me and flung her arms over my shoulders. 'Babe! Oh my God, your hair!'

'O-M-G, don't even!' I laughed, sounding more like Steph – and less like myself – than ever. From the way Lilah held onto me, I got the feeling that she'd really missed me. My excitement about her return had been contaminated by nau-seating remorse. I didn't know how I'd react if she asked what

I'd been up to. Luckily, she was more interested in giving me a blow-by-blow account of her fuck-fest with a Puerto Rican photographer.

Once all six models found their way over to us, I led them out to the waiting Addison Lee car like the Pied Piper of Pure Models. When we were in the car, they all talked over one another, recounting the terrifying experience of the flight.

'We were flying out of our seats. People were vomiting,' said Breje, 'the scarecrow'.

'It was like God was trying to wipe out the evil of fashion,' said sixteen-year-old Kailey, who was from Alabama.

Lilah glanced sideways at Kailey, raising a mocking eyebrow, then looked at me and smiled. I smiled back.

'At least you had each other,' said Christina Lima, who had actually touched down in Glasgow in the end and come over on the sleeper train. 'I was all alone.'

'You had Anna Wintour,' teased Svetlana, a scrawny Russian girl who was very vocal on social media about her lesbianism. I remembered a selfie she'd posted that was captioned, 'Girls, suck my cervix'.

'In first class!' said Christina.

'Well, your plane would've been the first one to fall out the sky,' said Kailey, who I noticed was very pale. In fact, her features seemed to be sliding over to one side of her face.

'Kailey? Are you all right, darling?' I said. I no longer paused on the pet names.

She nodded weakly. She hadn't touched the fruit in her lap. I shifted my gaze to Camala, strikingly beautiful, from Jamaica, nibbling on a nut bar in silence.

'How are you, Camala?' I said.

'I'm fine.' She didn't look at me.

Suddenly, Breje made a loud wincing noise. I looked over and saw that she was holding a handful of fluffy blonde hair. Her own hair. 'Look at this,' she said, swivelling it in her hand. 'This always happens in show season.'

The other girls nodded sympathetically, and I suddenly felt like it was my fault they were all losing their hair from lack of sleep and sustenance. And it kind of was.

The car pulled up outside the agency and they all spilled out, collecting their suitcases from the overstuffed boot. Lilah took hold of my forearm and made me hang back as the others traipsed into the building. She gestured towards them and whispered, 'It's like being with the fucking Make a Wish Foundation.'

I pressed my lips together to stifle a snorting laugh. She squeezed my arm harder, her lips spreading into a smile, and both of us heaved with silent giggles. I knew how unkind it was, but I just loved how much we made each other laugh. Contritely, I wondered if she and Zack were still in touch.

When we got inside, the agents were already there, eating croissants and drinking coffee out of tall Starbucks cups.

'Oh, my poor girls,' said Steph, as the six tired models trawled in. Lilah was first to dive into her arms and Steph locked the hug by clasping her own forearms around Lilah's lower back. I felt the unreasonable dilation of jealousy that often arose when I witnessed a friendship that I wasn't involved in.

One by one, the girls were given their schedules. The agents carefully talked them through their days, explaining exactly who each casting director was, why they were important and whether they'd shown a specific interest. All six girls were 'fit-to-confirm' for JW Anderson. That meant the casting director already knew them from New York and was happy to fit them into the clothes without an official casting, even though it was only a few hours until the show. After the show, they'd be carted off to fittings for Sunday shows and castings for Monday. No rest for the tall and thin.

First was Svetlana – *JW Anderson FTC & show, Preen fitting, Mary Katrantzou fitting, Peter Pilotto fitting*. She looked a total mess. Her long hair was matted from the flight and she'd put together an outfit that was aiming for androgynous chic but had landed on butch pin-up girl.

'She looks homeless,' whispered Patrick as she walked off, schedule in hand. 'I can imagine her begging.'

'Begging for pussy,' muttered Drew.

The wannabe woke millennial in me knew that some of the agency banter was plain offensive, but when I was in the moment, I couldn't help but just laugh along.

After Svetlana left, Breje – *JW Anderson FTC & show, Preen fitting, Mary Katrantzou fitting, Burberry casting* – approached the booking table. She listened carefully as everything was explained to her, with Steph eyeing her up and down the whole time. When she walked away, Steph made a gesture with her hands that looked like she was holding a box, which meant that Breje's hips looked wide. Drew and Patrick conceded with anxious nods. I wondered if I'd ever get the hang of what was too big or too small in this industry.

Next was Christina – *JW Anderson FTC & show, Versus FTC & show, Roksanda casting (not on the list but shove her in there)* – the enigmatic, sultry Brazilian – the girl you'd expect to get into all the shows just by turning up and smiling but who was apparently 'too glamorous for the London market'. Too glamorous! Honestly.

Then Camala – *JW Anderson FTC, Burberry casting* – silent, strikingly beautiful and dead behind the eyes.

'I'm over her already,' said Drew when she was out of earshot. 'Dud personality.'

The girl had come all the way from Jamaica with hopes of a career that was about to be scuppered by one man who wanted a bit more 'va-va-voom' from her after a night of no sleep.

Next was Kailey – *JW Anderson FTC & show, Preen fitting, Mary Katrantzou fitting, Topshop fitting, Burberry casting* – whose features were still sliding questionably to one side of her face.

Drew leaned towards me, whispering in my ear, 'She looks like a piece of washing that's blown off a line. What's wrong with her face?'

I bit down on my lower lip and stared. Something wasn't right with her. When she'd gone, Patrick glanced over at Drew and me, and we must've looked worried.

'Oh, she just needs to have sex!' he said, seemingly out of the blue.

'What's that got to do with anything?' I asked.

'Trust me. You can spot the virgins a mile off. They become way better models once they've had sex. You'll see.'

I looked at Drew, who nodded and made a face like, 'Yeah, that is true, actually.'

'Why?' I asked, completely nonplussed.

Patrick shrugged. 'Opens them up? Makes them love themselves? I don't fucking know. You tell me, woman.'

I looked at Steph, but she was furiously typing an email. I guessed that it was a conversation she wasn't comfortable with and was deliberately not listening. I wondered what these men – gay men, sure, but still men – thought could possibly change so drastically in a girl once they'd done something that every member of the female sex will probably, at some point, do – unless they're part of some celibate cult. I thought about the first time I'd had sex, with Tim, who was too drunk to realize that I was a virgin – and, to be fair, how would he have known given that I'd never told him? The whole experience was uncomfortable, unemotional and, frankly, uneventful. How primitive, exactly, did they think women were that something as unextraordinary as having sex for the first time could advance us into the people we were meant to be? And what about men? Did they have this same kind of shift into themselves when they lost their virginity? I wondered if it was something they'd even considered.

As I was reeling over it all, in came Lilah, the last model to collect her schedule – *JW Anderson FTC & show, Versus FTC & show, Burberry casting, Topshop fitting, Preen FTC, Mary Katrantzou fitting* – and she was not happy about it. She was feeling pretty cocky about her Marc Jacobs win and was having a lazy diva moment.

'Can't they all just fit me at the show?' she whined.

I was nervous that Patrick or Drew wouldn't be able to curb their annoyance and might snap at her, so I felt it was my duty to step in. 'I'd just go, babe, it will be faster. The girls who are getting fitted at the shows are having to get there ridiculously early and not getting any time off in between each show. Honestly, this way is easier.'

Steph's eyes were darting nervously between Lilah and me. Lilah looked at me for a second and then shrugged like, 'Okay, whatever,' and off she went. Drew caught my eye and gave me a small smile of approval. It was such a minor thing, but I felt like I'd averted a potential catastrophe.

So, other than Camala and Christina – whom the agents were already calling the 'flops of the season' – all of the girls were looking at a 4 a.m. finish and 7 a.m. call times if they got confirmed on Preen. While they were in the bathroom, having what Billie and I called a 'babe bath' (which was basically just a wet wipe moment), I asked Steph about Moffie's party again.

'Darl, literally no one cares about that party,' she snapped, and swivelled her chair in the other direction.

Wondering how I was going to tell Moffie that her party was top of the list of things that people in fashion week didn't give a fuck about, I went to hurry the models up and herd them out of the door. I walked them to the car and they piled in, one by one, mustering whatever energy they had left in their lethargic small forms. I counted them in: one, two, three, four, five ... By the time I turned around, Kailey was on the floor, with passers-by sidestepping to avoid her. I leapt into a squat beside her and pressed my hand to her wonky pale grey face. Her skin reminded me of one of the stones I used to pick up on Exmouth beach on cold winter days.

'Help!' I shouted involuntarily.

I kept my hand on her face, though I don't know why I thought that was productive.

This girl is about to die, a dramatic voice rang in my head. *This girl is about to die and it's all your fault.* Fighting against that voice was a more rational one, one that should have had no place speaking in such a moment of crisis: *You're only a tiny cog in a big machine. There's nothing you could have done.*

The driver was out of the car, calling an ambulance.

And then, after a few seconds, I felt Kailey's hard, cold head stir beneath my hand.

Collapsed on one of the beanbags in the chillout zone, Kailey told us that she suffered from celiac disease. The agents in New York hadn't told me, which meant that I hadn't organized a gluten-free meal for her flight, so, basically, this clusterfuck *was* my goddamn fault after all.

When the girls landed in Newcastle, the only food on offer was a small sandwich, which Kailey shouldn't have eaten, but did so to stop herself from passing out from starvation, and as a result her immune system was attacking her small intestines.

We suggested sending her to hospital, but that made her panic, because she didn't have health insurance and in America that meant thousands of dollars. So we put her in a taxi back to the hotel and spent £200 on a call-out doctor, whom we sometimes paid to write fake sick notes when we had to cancel models from jobs last minute. I asked if Kailey would be charged for the doctor.

'I'll hide it in a booking,' muttered Drew.

By that point, however, Celiac-gate was old news, because the new drama was that Breje had been cancelled from JW Anderson. Apparently, she didn't fit the clothes.

'I said she looked big,' said Steph as she bit the tip off a stale croissant.

'We have to give a big girl to Marisa Velanquez,' said Steph, for the nine-hundredth time.

'It's a fucking accessories brand!' snapped Drew, which I had gathered, by then, meant that it was a third-rate show.

Steph reminded them, again for the nine-hundredth time, that the casting director and stylist were both loyal clients of the agency who needed to be kept happy.

'When Preen release girls, we'll find someone to give them,' said Patrick wearily.

There was a hierarchy of shows, I'd learnt, and some of them clashed on the schedule. The second- and third-rate shows spent their lives waiting for the bigger shows to 'release their options' so that they could mop up the sloppy seconds.

It was almost midnight on Saturday, during a lull in the madness, that Preen released their options.

Steph jumped up like a hungry, yet exhausted, terrier. 'Who can I give to Marisa Velanquez?'

Patrick rubbed his face with his palms, then looked down at his Preen list, tapping the paper with the end of his pen. 'Give them Lilah.'

Everyone was very tired by then.

The relentless car management was starting to make my anxious head spin. I hadn't slept more than more than four hours a night, was glued to my phone, had barely seen the light of day or breathed fresh air, had no time to eat, and with the tiredness starting to weigh me down, I was sure I was going to make a catastrophic mistake that would cost some poor model her whole career, not to mention my own. Among it all, I had to find time to complete the 'show round-up', which entailed copying and pasting images of our models walking in the shows and emailing them to the global network. I loved that task because it finally meant I got to look at the clothing collections, if only for a split second. It was easy to forget that this whole saga was actually about the craft of fashion design, when my role in it was so solely model-focused. And even easier to forget that I was meant to be using this as a stepping stone, getting ready to hop onto the next island.

I started the round-up of the Marisa Velanquez show minutes after it went live online. At first glance, it didn't look like such a third-rate show. It was at the Roundhouse, and they'd splashed out on a lavish set design and a fully celeb front row. The models didn't look half bad either. They were styled simplistically in black and white, with just a splash of colour when it came to the shoes and bags, which was what the show was really about. And then, with one click, it all changed.

Suddenly, out of nowhere, one of the models was dressed up as a bunch of grapes. And not in an artsy way, where her silhouette was a nod to the Merlot variety; she was wearing a full-on 3D grape suit, like she was promoting a new flavour of Fruitella at Westfield.

I clicked again. The next girl was a giant pineapple, which was no less bizarre. Another click and we had a watermelon. I clicked again and came face to face with Lilah, her head poking out of a metre-long felt banana skin. Beneath that she was balancing on a pair of rather fabulous Marisa Velanquez heels, but my God, even I knew that however fabulous those shoes were, a model of Lilah's level should not have been in a banana skin. Without saying anything, I turned my computer screen towards Drew.

His eyeballs rounded and popped. 'OH. MY. GOD!' And then he broke down into hysterical fits of laughter. I was relieved that he found the situation amusing, rather than catastrophic. He called Patrick over, who gasped at the sight of the image, his face full of glee.

'She's a banana!' shrieked Drew.

I hate to say it, but there was something quite satisfying about seeing Lilah, who had turned full diva the day before, reduced to the skin of a banana.

Drew called out for Steph. She slumped in, looking grey in the face, the beginning of a spot coming to life on her chin.

'Come and look at this,' said Drew.

Steph wandered over curiously. As soon as she saw the screen, her hands went flying up to cover her mouth. I wasn't sure if she was going to laugh or cry. I don't know if *she* was sure. She ended up laughing, through utter weariness and horror, with her fingers pressed into her tear ducts. We were all in fits.

'What the fuck is that?' she breathed.

'It's your show, doll face!' said Drew.

'Tell me that's not real?' she said.

'One hundred per cent real,' I said, clicking through the images to show her the entire fruit ensemble.

'I don't know what to say,' she rasped.

'I think this is your best hot mess moment yet,' laughed Drew teasingly.

'Did they not tell you about the fruit creative?' asked Patrick through his guffaws.

'Obviously not!' she said. 'The casting director should have told me. Right?'

'She should have flagged it for sure,' said Drew. 'I mean ... *JE* CANNOT!'

Steph laughed again, but I could see that she was starting to freak out. The phone rang. I reached for it, but Drew was there first.

'Hi, Madeleine?' he said.

Steph gave him a look of dread. Drew did a lot of umming and ahhing and, eventually, told Steph that Madeleine wanted to speak to her.

'Is she laughing?' she asked as she walked over to her desk.

Wishful thinking.

Drew gave a small shake of the head.

Steph took a dramatic breath and answered the phone. 'Madeleine?' She was silent for a long time while, I imagined, Madeleine ripped into her.

'Madeleine needs to chill,' Drew said quietly to me. 'It's been disaster after disaster that we couldn't control. First, the flights. Then Kailey arriving with a fucking lopsided face and a leaky gut. Who cares if Lilah Fox was dressed up as a blooming banana?'

I couldn't help but laugh again. But Steph wasn't laughing when she hung up the phone. She didn't look at any of us as she muttered, 'Apparently, Lilah's fuming at me.'

I felt for Steph, I really did, but I couldn't deny that little bit of nasty pleasure that had wiggled to the surface upon hearing that. Worse than that, a part of me hoped that Zack would see the image of Lilah and that it would dismantle the pedestal that I was convinced he must have her on, even though we'd barely spoken about her.

I hate to admit it, but I think I was actually glad the whole saga had happened.

CHAPTER 8

'I think we might be out of here before 7 p.m.!' said Drew with childlike excitement.

I hoped that meant me, too, because despite the fact that my eyelids were being dragged down and I felt like I was on an aeroplane, I really wanted to go to Moffie's party. I was pumping with fashion week adrenaline and needed to let off a bout of steam. Plus, Lilah would be there, as would all her friends, and it seemed like too good an opportunity to miss. I wondered if Zack would be there too, and just how awkward that would be.

We had finally reached the light at the end of the tunnel that was Monday. Many of the big shows happened that day: Christopher Kane, Roksanda, Erdem and − the doyenne of London shows − Burberry. Lilah had been confirmed for all of them except the doyenne, which apparently was a real slight for a British model. ('It's 'cus she's a scuzzy at heart and Burberry really like a lady,' said Drew when the list came through.)

I was in the midst of organizing travel plans to move all of the models onto Milan, where they would continue the madness of show season out of our hands.

Patrick was on the phone to the director of the Milan agency, with whom he'd had an 'erotic affair' (his words) a few years back. 'Milan don't want Breje,' he said once he'd hung up. 'She has no options, darling,' he continued in an overblown Italian accent, 'because she is mad, and she is ugly.'

Steph and Drew half laughed, half groaned in an exhausted way as I waited to hear what the hell I was meant to do with her. 'I guess you want me to have that conversation with her?' said Steph.

'Yes, darling,' said Patrick, still speaking in an Italian accent.

Breje arrived an hour later and disappeared into the chillout zone of doom with Steph. When she emerged, her cheeks were red, blotchy and stained with tears. I gave her a sympathetic but pretty unengaged smile, a bottle of water and instructions to make her own way back to the hotel. I was becoming immune to models' tears by that point.

'Breje needs accommodation. We're going to keep her on in London,' said Steph when I sat back down at my desk.

One more thing for me to think about.

'I'll put her in the model flat,' I said.

'No,' said Steph. 'She's in a bad way. I don't want her bitching to the other models about us. It'll get them all riled up.'

'They might revolt,' said Patrick.

'Like *Lord of the Flies*. Lord of the Duds,' I said, reproaching myself but feeling that familiar thrill at making everyone laugh.

'Put her in private accommodation,' instructed Steph.

We had a model flat near the agency, but if it was full, or if there was another reason I couldn't put a model in there, I'd reach out to one of the trusted landlords who let their rooms to us. Another one of my glamorous jobs. I booked Breje into a room in South London. Then I went on to confirm flights for the girls Milan *did* want for their shows.

By 7 p.m., the agents had completed all of their show bookings for the following day. They stood up in unison, cheering, shaking their hips, almost crying with excitement at the thought of crawling into their beds. We had a group hug and they told me not to stay too long before they all darted out the door.

I checked the Milan flights once more, making sure that every model who needed to be was booked onto a flight and had a car to the airport.

Then, finally, I went into the fashion cupboard to get ready for Moffie's party.

The cupboard was more crowded than usual, with all the bags of clothes – hand-beaded haute couture gowns, buttery silk slip dresses, the most perfectly structured tuxedo I'd ever seen – that the PRs had sent for 'influencers' to wear while they sat on front rows, doing shit all, and complaining about their busy schedules. Again, I failed to take the opportunity to get dressed to the nines, for fear of looking like an idiot. I opted for a black-and-red, fairly low-key Jonathan Saunders dress that hugged the lines of my figure in a way that was either alluring or grotesque. I couldn't quite tell.

The party was being held at a nightclub in Soho that no one had ever heard of (probably a struggling venue that gave the space up for free) and was one of many parties happening that night. The desirable one was the *Love* magazine party at 5 Hertford Street, but only the crème de la crème were welcome there. Lilah had told me earlier that she planned on going to the *Love* party for one drink and then onto Moffie's, so I expected she'd be there when I arrived.

A stressed-out iPad girl let me in immediately, for which I showed way too much gratitude and definitely too much enthusiasm about the event, given that it was bottom of the pile. The club was the kind of place in which I imagined people opened £500 bottles of champagne that arrived with sparklers accompanied by the *Star Wars* theme tune. Tables glowing with LED lights played stage to the ostentatious bottles of vodka from the brand that was sponsoring the party, and everyone was wearing sunglasses from the emporium we had to thank for it all. I did two laps of the club, and on the second lap I ran into the three models I'd secretly sent to the party. I hadn't told the agents, and I could suddenly understand why it wasn't the kind of party they should be seen at, particularly when I noticed the vape station staffed by silicone-stuffed, bodycon-clad promoters. *Good one, Scizzle.*

Lilah was nowhere in sight. Nor was Moffie, or any of their crowd. I thought there must be some sort of VIP room they were hiding in, drinking their own bottles of vodka and snorting drugs freely. I went outside and asked the iPad girl where Moffie was.

'She left,' said the girl, presumably her assistant.

'Did Lilah leave too?' I asked.

'Lilah never came,' she said, scrunching her nose up, which I thought was her way of implying that it was quite embarrassing for Moffie that Lilah hadn't shown.

I WhatsApped Lilah asking where she was. If she was still at the *Love* party, I didn't know what I'd do – a mere mortal like myself would never be allowed in. She responded with one word.

> Lilah:
> Chiltern.

Thanks for telling me! I thought, irritated, as I replied.

> Me:
> Shall I come?

I needed to know that she could get me in, given that the Chiltern Firehouse was another destination you needed some sort of golden ticket to get into. Granted, I probably should've said 'Can I' rather than 'Shall I', but I didn't want to sound desperado. 'Shall' implied that I was more bothered about whether it was fun or not than whether I was welcome. She replied a few seconds later.

Lilah:
Def come! It's fun

Despite the fact that she clearly hadn't thought about me until I texted her, I felt like my casual texting tactics had worked a treat and quietly applauded myself. I was learning. I immediately hailed a black taxi, even though I'd have to pay out of my own pocket, and asked to be taken to Chiltern Street.

There was a throng of photographers waiting outside the institution, which was too expensive even for our highest-earning models to justify staying at. I wondered if they'd take my picture just because I was arriving there, in case I was someone worth capturing, but they all lowered their cameras as I stepped out of the taxi.

'Don't get too excited,' I said to curb the feeling of diminishment, and a few of them grunted a laugh.

The woman at the door was puffed up and ready to turn me down, but when I said I was with Lilah she got on her walkie-talkie and whispered into it like she was part of MI6. Eventually she let me in and I was allowed upstairs, though not without being stopped by a member of staff almost every step of the way.

Chill out, guys, I wanted to say. *Do I look like a celebrity*

132

axe-murderer? Instead, I just said Lilah's name each time and they let me pass. I reached room number 39 – somewhere I'd seen people writing about all over Instagram – and knocked on the door. Annabel opened it wearing a silk Gucci printed pyjama set and high heels. She introduced herself to me.

'We met at your place,' I said, immediately wishing I'd just gone with it.

Annabel nodded with a doped-out smile that said, 'I'm not interested' and headed back into the room.

I followed her, wondering what I was about to be faced with in the famous Room 39.

At first, all I saw was a bunch of dubious-looking characters lounging on the bed, and I thought Lilah had only invited me to join because it was a dud night. Then, at the centre of the cluster, I saw Jade, and felt myself smile with relief. She was propped up on one elbow giving a fervent monologue about far-right nationalism to the hangers-on and stragglers that Lilah had told me she was prone to picking up. She briefly tossed her head back to see who had come in and said, 'Hey, sugar,' giving me just enough recognition to satisfy me that we were friends, and returned to her address, punctuating it with 'So that's why I'm with her' – 'her' being Hillary Clinton.

Lilah was nowhere to be seen, so I looked around the room searching for something Instagrammable. I couldn't leave without social media proof of being there. But there wasn't really anything lavish, or fabulous, about the room, which surprised me given it was *the* place. Something told me that the low-key décor was the *thing* about it – that and the mirror-surfaced tabletops practically shouting, 'Come party in here'.

Moffie appeared from nowhere with a cigarette between her teeth, wearing a Kappa tracksuit, looking like iconography for the working class. 'Oh, you!' she said, in a tone that could not be interpreted as friendly. 'Thanks for all your help.'

I knew she was being sarcastic, but pretended that I didn't and said, 'No worries, babe. Is this your room?'

'It's Rob's room,' she said.

Was I supposed to know who Rob was? I asked if Lilah was around and Moffie jabbed her thumb towards the bathroom door. I gave her a smile that was more loaded than polite and pushed the already ajar door open. When I stepped in, the first thing I saw was the sweep of Lilah's messy hair hanging obscenely over her face. She was up on the countertop with her legs wrapped around the waist of a man as he thrust in and out against her. All I noticed was that he had grey hair. I had just walked in on Lilah having countertop sex with a grey-haired man in Room 39.

'Sorry!' I said, whirling to leave, but the strap of my handbag caught on the door handle and before I knew it I was being flung back into the room.

'Babe, do you have a note?' Lilah asked. I was nervous to turn and look at them, so took an unnecessarily long time unlooping the bag strap. When I did turn around, the grey-haired man was only just removing himself from her to do up his pants.

I busied myself deep in my handbag, giving them time to fully disentangle. Miraculously, I found a crumpled ten-pound note in there. The grey-haired man turned around to take it from me. All I could look at were the prominent, pulsating veins running all along his temples. He wasn't even a silver fox. He was just old.

'Urgh, don't you have a fifty?' said Lilah, smiling at him, not at me.

I knew it was a joke, but I still felt slighted. The ageing man – who I'd decided must have been Rob – drew out three monster lines of cocaine and we snorted them through my sad tenner. Then Lilah said she had to pee, kissed him on the lips and he left us.

'Who is that?' I asked, trying my best not to sound too shocked.

She lifted the monochrome Marc Jacobs skirt that she'd been lent to wear to the *Love* party. It billowed around her like a throne as she planted herself on the loo seat. I loved the intimacy of it. We were loo friends now.

'Rob Halper. He's a sweetheart,' she said. And then: 'Been shagging him for like a year.'

'What, when you were with Zack?'

She shrugged, pulling a face like, 'Yeah, and what?'

'You cheated on him?' I asked, urging her to affirm it, because I knew it would bring me so much guilt-relief.

'We cheated on each other,' she said, like it was nothing.

I wiped my nose with the back of my hand. 'You mean, you were fine with him cheating on you?'

'Hell no! I'd have fucking killed him if I'd found out. I still would kill him if I found out he'd cheated on me. But I'm not stupid,' she said, reaching for loo roll to wipe between her legs.

'I don't get it?'

'Babe, when Zack and I first started going out, we were wild. We'd bring home girls and fuck them. We'd bring home boys and fuck them. We'd fuck in rooms with other couples. Do you really think, after that, we could go back to having some sort of monogamous, normal person's relationship?'

I felt a little tickle in my groin at the image of Zack and Lilah in a sordid orgy. But I had a more practical question to ask, 'Why weren't you just honest about it? You could've had, like, an open relationship or something?'

She pulled a face. 'Those are for calm middle-aged couples who need to spice up their marriage. We'd get way too jealous! Once, when we were fucking Annabel, I went off for a piss, came back in and she was sucking Zack's dick. Babe, I almost fucking killed her.'

'But you were midway through group sex?' I said, confused.

'Well, that's why I couldn't stay angry at her. It was my fault, wasn't it?' She stood up and let the skirt fall demurely back to her calves.

'Do you miss him?' I asked, dreading the answer, but also so perversely curious to know.

'What do you think?' she asked, turning her almond-shaped eyes on me, and for the first time I heard pain in her voice, not anger.

Nausea bubbled away in my stomach as I reached out to stroke her arm comfortingly. 'It's for the best.'

'Did you see the Marisa Velanquez show?' she said, quickly regaining her brash edge. 'That's why I didn't get Burberry.'

It wasn't. Burberry had actually confirmed their options before the fruit nightmare.

'It literally could have ruined my career,' she continued. 'Steph has lost her fucking mind.'

I should have told her that it wasn't Steph's fault. That the casting director really should have flagged up the niche creative decision. That it wasn't exactly something agents asked before each show: 'Will the models in any way resemble one giant fruit salad?' I should have reminded her that we'd all been working nineteen-hour days since Thursday, that mistakes happen, and told her to see the funny side, like the rest of us did. Instead, I nodded and rolled my eyes, because there was something seductive about the idea of Lilah and me in a little boat together, drifting away from Steph.

We joined the others in the bedroom, but I didn't stay long, since the conversation was a convulsion of random words that I couldn't follow and I wasn't drunk enough to pretend I could. But more than that, I felt a bit stupid being there, because really, I wasn't one of them. Lilah was all wrapped up in Rob the Old, Jade had enough outsiders on her hands and no one else was particularly interested in my presence, so it wasn't long before I booked a work car home with a sudden pang of longing to see Billie. I took out my iPhone in the car with the intention of texting her, but got distracted by that familiar rise of excitement that happened when I saw a new notification.

Patrick had tagged me in a photo on Facebook. It was a picture of the Muppets, captioned, 'Booking team at Pure Models really rocked this season'. Kermit had been tagged as Patrick, Drew was Miss Piggy and Steph was the hook-nosed Gonzo. The tiny dog at the bottom was me. I laughed to myself. Maybe it was the lack of sleep, but I found it truly hysterical. I just laughed and laughed, so much so that my stomach cramped up. And then, just as suddenly, my eyes started to dampen. I may not have been part of that crowd strewn over Room 39, but I was part of this one. Patrick cared about me enough to include me in their joke. He considered me part of a team that had rocked the season. I was part of their team. More than that, I was part of *something*.

I scrolled down to read the comments. Drew had left a line of laughing face emojis. Steph had written, 'What you sayin about my nose???' I wrote three letters: 'LOL'.

It made me feel terrible about not defending Steph to Lilah. It also made me feel even guiltier the next morning when I scrolled through the press photos from Moffie's party on the *Mail* online. All three of our models had been photographed and appeared on the story alongside the reality TV stars and second-rate presenters and vape promoters. When Steph asked me about it, I shrugged and said that they must have gone of their own accord, which she seemed to accept as an answer.

I was pretty used to lying by that point.

CHAPTER 9

I was back in the corner. Relegated, or at least it felt that way. Though my stint on the booking table was only ever meant to be for fashion week.

Madeleine came in with cash bonuses for all of us, which apparently didn't happen every season, only when she was in a particularly good mood with the team, so I felt it was special. After work, I walked into a nearby tattoo parlour. I could afford one, for the first time, and was feeling empowered after managing to survive fashion week as an assistant, so I barely even thought when I asked for the word 'London' on the inside of my wrist. The tattoo artist convinced me to do it in Chinese, which wasn't really the point. Anyway, I ended up with some Chinese symbols that were meant to say, 'Made in London', but could just as easily have said, 'Suck my Dick'. Still, I had a tattoo. I was a tattooed person.

On top of it all, Greek yoghurt had arbitrarily been added to the agency's weekly Tesco order and I'd discovered that it was actually incredibly filling. We'd also been sent a fridge of gazpacho from some food PR company, and combining the two saw me through the day nicely. I didn't even have to stay late to eat sushi scraps. The Greek yoghurt and gazpacho diet. Very continental. After only a few days, something started to happen. There was this breathing space between my skin and clothes, which had always been comfortably snug before. I kept rubbing my hand back and forth across my stomach and then wriggling my fingers up to my ribs like they were a foreign entity.

I was clicking through images of the Fendi show that had just happened in Milan, wondering how many weeks, months or years of Greek yoghurt and gazpacho it would take me to get close to the size of one of the models, when my desk phone rang.

'Hey, Carl,' I said ironically. I'd recently found out that Worm's real name was Carl. I found it hilarious to call him that, even though Worm was meant to be the funny name because he was so tall and worm-like in his spectacles.

'It's the landlord that Breje's staying with,' he said, and slammed down the phone.

'Hello?' I said. I got calls from landlords all day long and didn't think this one would be any different.

'Scarlett, it's Molly, from Pomerey Street.'

'Hi, Molly. Everything okay?'

'Unfortunately, it's not. I'm not sure Breje can stay here anymore.'

Oh for fuck's sakes, what this time? I thought. I was constantly having to move models from private accommodation for being messy, noisy, rude, drunk, kleptomaniacs.

'She's broken the bed,' said Molly.

Well, that was a new one.

'Okay . . . on purpose?'

'Not exactly,' she sighed down the phone. 'She's had a different bloke in here every night since she moved in, Scarlett.'

Definitely not what I was expecting.

'Honestly, I'm not exaggerating,' she continued. 'I wasn't going to say anything. I didn't want to get her into trouble. But the bed has fully collapsed.'

'I am so sorry,' was all I could say, holding back laughter.

I wondered how hard you'd have to be fucking someone to break a bed, or if Molly's place was really worth three hundred and fifty quid a week with such rickety furniture. I couldn't really be bothered to go into it, so I just told her we'd move Breje out by the end of the day, then eagerly wheeled my chair over to the booking table to recount the story, telling them an elaborated version of what Molly had told me, knowing that it would get a good laugh.

Drew spluttered through pursed lips.

Patrick made a frustrated 'uh' sound.

Steph dropped her forehead to the tips of her fingers and moaned, 'Even the scarecrow's getting it!'

And everyone laughed.

I didn't fully get the joke, so I smiled, a little confused, and asked, 'Has it been a while?'

She puffed air between her lips. 'Maybe, just over a year?'

'A year?' I cried, aghast. Not that I was burgeoning with sexual opportunity myself, but a year sounded like a hell of a long time to be inactive.

'Oh, honey, you'll get there too,' said Patrick, attempting to raise his eyebrows at me, but no crease would form. 'Just wait.'

'Oh God, why? What am I missing?' I said.

'Nature of the job,' said Drew. 'Models kill mojo. It's a fact.'

It may have been a fact, but it was one that made zero sense. Weren't we in the reckless, hedonistic world of no sexual boundaries?

'It's not the models!' said Steph. 'It's being around you queens all the time! That's what's zapped away the sexual energy I once had.'

'When do you think Madeleine last got boned?' asked Patrick.

'1984,' said Drew, and we all laughed.

Hyperbole or not, I was pretty surprised. I'd always imagined Madeleine to go home to some toy boy she kept locked up in her Holland Park mansion (I'd searched her address on Google Earth). I'd even gone as far as to fabricate a sex dungeon, thoroughly enjoying the idea of her as a female Christian Grey.

'I literally don't think I'll have sex ever again,' said Steph, laughing in a self-deprecating sort of way. I looked at her sitting there in her ultra-trendy outfit. Baggy trousers, shirt buttoned up to the collar, clunky shoes and a swampy jacket hanging on the back of her chair. I couldn't help but wonder if her style was a reaction to her sexless existence, or the cause of it. It made me think of the way I always opted for low-key when I went to a party that I found intimidating, like I was afraid to be looked at when I knew there were more beautiful, more interesting beings outshining me. I wondered if Steph, after years of being eclipsed and called a hot mess, had found an identity in her clothing that made her feel safe.

But I was definitely not up for a sexless existence. In fact, my sex drive had been off the chain ever since that night with Zack. I woke up every morning with some sleazy thought about him. And I couldn't stop myself from watching porn on the regular – something I'd never, ever admit to anyone. Looking at Steph tap away at her keyboard, half of me wanted to take her out to some cheesy nightclub and refuse to leave until she got laid, and the other half of me desperately wanted to be shrouded in a particular erotic mist myself.

Guess which half was more dominant?

I took out my iPhone and opened a message to Zack. It was amazing how easily I was able to stop any thoughts that resembled sensibility or guilt about Lilah from making their way into my consciousness. Everyone always wonders how good people can do terrible things, but bad behaviour is the easiest thing in the world, really. You just don't think about it.

> Me:
> Hey. Can I grab that bra from you at
> some point?

Within half a second, the double tick appeared, letting me know that the message had been delivered to his phone. I wondered where he was and if he'd seen it, but not opened it. I imagined him sitting in a meeting with some famous rap – or grime? – artist, talking confidently about the direction of his next album, noticing his phone vibrate, glancing at the screen, smiling and then having to explain to this made-up artist what the coy smile was for.

'Move Breje to the model flat,' Steph called out to me, cutting the scene short. 'I'll tell her to come in and pick up the keys.'

I opened the drawer that I kept all the keys in. None left. 'They're all gone. The models keep forgetting to return them.'

I glanced at my phone. The ticks had turned blue. Was the rap – or grime – artist helping him compose a response? Or was that something only twenty-something-year-old girls did?

'So, how's she gonna get in, hon?' said Steph, exaggerating her Northern accent on the last word.

'I'll give her the code for the main door. I think the girls leave the door to the flat unlocked most of the time anyway,' I said absentmindedly.

'Great. That sounds safe,' said Steph.

I glanced at my phone again. *Zack is typing . . .*

'A rapist's paradise,' said Patrick.

'A people smuggler could just walk in and take them all to sell,' said Drew.

'Think they'd fetch a high price?' I asked, twisting around in my chair to look at them.

'Some of them,' said Drew.

'Not many,' said Patrick.

'No, not many,' Drew repeated and we laughed. Any jokes about the fact that the models were not necessarily attractive got an easy giggle, which I knew was not good girl code.

My phone vibrated in my hand. I looked down.

Zack:
Yeah wanna come pick it up tonight?

Zack's flat was in Maida Vale. I took an Addison Lee car, courtesy of Pure Models, because there was no way I was going to navigate the tube in the outfit I'd assembled for the occasion. Finally, thanks to Greek yoghurt and gazpacho, I was dressed to kill – or, more accurately, to shag.

I was wearing a black lace and mesh Mulberry dress that I'd been eyeing up for weeks. Unlike the swampy clothes that Steph opted for, it was a piece of clothing that I understood had been specifically designed to enhance the female form, but still concealed enough to be considered modest, which I guessed meant it was alluring. The collar was high and chokingly tight, with transparent mesh running from the neckline, down my shoulders and over my chest, until it reached the top of my breasts, where the fabric became opaque. It was cinched tight at the waist and a multi-layered A-line skirt fell alongside the thighs, stopping just above the knee. I didn't even care that it had been baggy on one of the stick insects who wore it to a party the week before and was tight on me. I was a real woman – *yes, Pawel Dyk, that's right* – not a coat hanger, and I was certain that I looked better than I ever had before.

I knew I couldn't just turn up at Zack's in a dress like that out of nowhere, so I fabricated a story that I was coming from an event at the Saatchi Gallery. It wasn't a total lie; the event was actually happening, I just hadn't actually been invited.

I'd swapped the usual Charlotte Olympias for what I thought was a more feminine shoe, as if the concept of a heel wasn't quite submissive enough. I rang the doorbell and waited, balancing precariously, my pelvis refusing to do anything but jut out like an underbite. I tried to focus on the aggressive pinching at my toes rather than the image of Lilah – laughing with me, at her best – that was intermittently flashing between my eyebrows. Then his voice came rippling through the intercom – a pro-longed 'Hi!' – and the picture miraculously dissolved. With one loud buzz and a push of the door, there was no going back. Not that I wanted to.

I walked up to the first floor in the dark, clutching the banister, pretending to be the *femme fatale* of a film noir, until I saw a narrow opening of light, which I gathered was Zack's flat.

'Survived fashion week?' I heard his voice call out as I slipped in.

I shut the door gently and followed the voice into the living room. It was high-ceilinged with tall French windows. Everything about it – the large flat-screen television, surrounded by a state-of-the-art sound system, the stupidly large L-shaped sofa, the reclining armchair, the out-of-place Ottoman poufs – looked to me like a relic of his success and, in turn, his independence.

The man of the manor was sprawled on the sofa, watching a sports channel – not quite the romantic scene I'd hoped for. But he did stand up when I entered. 'You look lovely,' he said, drawing out the word 'lovely'. He kissed me on the cheek and then held me in what felt like a long, protective hug. When I caught sight of myself in a large oval mirror being embraced by him, I thought that it looked like a picture from someone else's life. He stepped back, looked me up and down and said, 'Heels really turn me on.'

No shit.

'Well, aren't you lucky then?' I said.

'Very lucky,' he said. He picked up the remote control and changed the channel from sports to music. 'How was the event?'

I shrugged. 'Oh, you know what these things are like. Boring!'

I had to admit, I was disappointed that he wasn't fawning over my appearance more. I don't know what I expected – to be swallowed whole?

'Do you want a drink?'

'Can I have a glass of wine, please?' I said.

'I've only got beer,' he said, unapologetically. I didn't think beer was in congruence with my *femme fatale* persona and my newly flat stomach, but accepted anyway.

When he disappeared off into the kitchen, I looked around to see what I could piece together of Zack Smith's existence. I'd always thought you could tell a lot about a guy by his bedroom, and there I was with a whole flat to contend with. Everything in the room was pretty nondescript except for the cluttered mantelpiece behind the sofa, which looked like an afterthought. I stepped closer to have a good look. There were handwritten thank-you letters from sponsorship brands, gig tickets, invitations to award ceremonies – Brits, Grammys, NMEs – all long passed, a wedding invitation that seemed out of place, a single generic candle. And then my eyes settled on a framed photograph of Zack and Lilah, on a boat, at what looked like sunrise. She was wearing a bikini, leaning against his chest, and he had his arms wrapped around her. They were both gazing moodily into the camera, hinting at a smile. Leaning against the frame was a mini-polaroid of Lilah backstage at a fashion show. My first thought was, *Why hasn't he binned these?* Surely the first thing you did when you broke up with someone was to erase all reminders of them? There was only one answer, and that was that he didn't really think it was over, but I didn't want to consider that option, so I moved to the other side of the mantelpiece.

There was another framed photo that looked like it was a good twenty years old, of a man and a woman in a music-recording studio. The man had his arm draped over the woman and they were laughing. She was holding her middle finger up by her hip, the gesture barely noticeable.

Zack walked in, holding two beers, as casually as if we were a couple. I pointed at the photograph and asked, 'Are these your parents?'

'Yeah. That's Mum and Dad,' he said, handing me a Stella Artois.

I closed my hand around the icy bottle and condensation seeped between my fingers. 'Are they in music too?'

'Well, they're retired now. But Mum used to be a record producer and Dad was a tour manager.'

'Is that how you got into your job?' I said.

'I like to think *why*, rather than *how*,' he said in a prickly manner.

I didn't mean it to sound disparaging but I guess he took it that way. *God, men could be oversensitive . . .*

'I do A&R, which is completely different,' he added. 'But yeah, they taught me to love music, I guess.'

'Do you see much of them?'

'Not loads. My mum moved to Ibiza when they split up, about ten years ago. She's gone all hippie, into Ayahuasca and shit.'

'Is that the plant that makes you hallucinate?' I asked. I'd read something about it in one of the newspaper supplements that I had to go through every Monday morning, and I have to say, I kind of loved the sound of it.

He nodded. 'Apparently you trip out for nine hours.'

'Fucking hell, that's a long trip!' I said.

'Yeah. She got herself off heroin and dived straight into hard-core psychedelics.'

'Did she find enlightenment?'

'If you can call him that,' he said and I laughed. He smiled and slid his arm over my shoulder. Was this all it took to form a relationship? Asking personal questions and getting truthful answers that you can both laugh over, though you both know that the reality is sad? Were they not about two people trying to impress each other? I suddenly thought that, maybe, I was in the first stage of forging a connection with someone. It filled me with both warmth and panic.

'And your dad?' I asked quickly, not wanting to break the rhythmic flow of our conversation.

'He lives in Kilburn,' he said curtly, and I could tell he was trying to end the conversation. He added, 'Never moved onto the psychedelics,' as he set his beer on the mantelpiece. Then he stepped behind me and placed his hands on either side of my waist, squeezing the skin between his fingers. I tipped my head back, leaning against his collarbone, similar to the way Lilah was doing in the photo. I could smell the stale stench of alcohol on his breath. He stroked his hand across my almost-flat stomach, the lace of the dress a barrier between his skin and mine. I thought of the night in the hotel room and how quickly I'd undressed, while he'd remained in his clothes up until the last moment. I suddenly understood the power of clothes and my ability to control him by keeping them on.

'Do you like my body?' I asked.

When I was a child, everyone had always told me how pretty I was, with my big blue eyes and my chubby cherub cheeks and my Dutch golden hair. Unfortunately, that made the ugly duckling years that followed a bitter pill to swallow. I was never sure whether I was going to grow into a swan or head the other way, so it was safer never to allow myself to feel beautiful again. But being wanted by Zack had started to make me feel that maybe, just maybe, there was something desirable about me after all.

'I like your body, a lot,' he said, brushing his lips against my ear.

I slipped away and leaned against the back of the sofa, trying to smile with my eyes, whatever that meant. 'What do you like about it?' I was hungering for more praise, silently begging him to take away my self-doubt and prop me up on that fantastical pedestal that I'd always longed for.

'Your perfect tits,' he said. He stepped towards me and ran the tips of his fingers over my collarbone, 'This.' Then he turned me around, quite roughly, and I grabbed the back of the sofa for stability as he took a handful of flesh from behind, 'This.' I let out a sticky breath. He slipped a hand inside my knickers and said, 'You're so wet,' instantly bringing me down from whatever throne I thought I was on. 'Is that for me?'

'Who else would it be for?' I said, trying to be cheeky, but actually just sounding rude.

He hooked his fingers around the gusset of my knickers and

pulled the fabric tight against me. From that one assured gesture, I melted into vulnerability. It wasn't long before the Mulberry dress was on the floor, abandoned in a heap like a fallen starlet. He carried me into his bedroom and spread me flat on top of his navy bedsheets, which smelt distinctly of man. Unwashed, uncared for. He took hold of my left foot and raised it, pressing my toes against his tongue, bit the end of a toe and then took the entire ball of my foot into his mouth and I gasped, somewhat shocked, but also enjoying it. Then he lifted both of my legs up above my head, holding onto my ankles, and started having sex with me like that. It hurt a little, but not enough for me to stop him, so I just listened to the heavy R&B track that was playing over us until he turned me around. I balanced on all fours, but every time he tried to vigorously go at me, his penis would pop out.

'Why's it doing that?' he asked, evidently frustrated.

Don't ask me, buddy. You're the expert.

'Have I got a small knob?' he said, which was ridiculous, because whatever his knob was, it certainly was not small.

'Definitely not!' I said overexuberantly. 'Maybe I've got a small vagina.' Clearly I felt the need to take the fall for whatever was going wrong, even though I was doing nothing but being pumped into.

He reached over to stroke the back of my head, like I was a dog. Then he said the words, 'A small little pussy.'

Pussy! There's the noun I'd been looking for.

'I love how tight you are,' he said, and I found it a little gross, but it also turned me on, and I hoped that he didn't realize it was because I'd never had regular enough sex to open up down there. He flipped me back over to face him and pressed his hand over my throat, closing his fingers around it. I could feel my windpipe closing up.

150

'Careful,' I rasped, because I wasn't wild enough not to be a little scared.

He moved his grip to my jaw. Then he whispered, 'I want to punch you in the face.'

As Romeo said to Juliet.

'Maybe don't do that,' I mumbled, thinking that if I was the person I wanted to be, I would have just let him punch me in the fucking face.

'I'm joking,' he said quickly, and I knew it was because he was embarrassed.

'No, you're not.'

'Of course I am!' he said, removing himself from me, but I couldn't quite believe that I had the ability to embarrass him.

'I don't care,' I said, trying so hard to be a Cool Girl. 'I just think . . . it's the kind of thing that could easily go wrong. And would be hard to explain.'

He laughed a little and muttered, 'Hard to explain.' The pad of his fingers moved over my cheekbone in circles. 'Your face looks so innocent sometimes.' He traced the shape of my eye socket. 'Then it has these flickers of complete filth.'

'Thank you,' I said, in a parody of a filthy voice.

I definitely knew that I should not take that as a compliment, but it left a loitering thrill.

He laughed, kissed me and got up to light a cigarette. I dragged myself off the bed, feeling hot and out of breath, lit one as well, pleased with the notion that I was now the kind of person who smoked cigarettes after sex, or, actually, in the middle of it.

Zack handed me his iPhone, which had the Spotify logo glowing on the screen. 'Here. Choose a song.'

Oh dear God, I thought. Music was where I'd always feared

151

I'd be caught out. Hands down, my worst question to be asked was, 'So, what kind of music are you into?' Did anyone actually have an answer to that question? It's not that I didn't like listening to music. I enjoyed the sound of it, I just had no idea who sung what, which genres were in or out, or what the names of the songs were. In the end, I decided to go for a classic – everyone liked a classic, didn't they? – and put on 'The Chain' by Fleetwood Mac, thinking that the sultry melody would be perfect as the soundtrack to a mid-coital fag.

It made him laugh.

'Not a good choice?' I said.

'It's good. Just . . . basic.'

'Oh, fuck off!' I said, light-heartedly, chucking the iPhone at him as my chest slowly went sinking to the depths of my stomach, where it turned to a heavy bag of sand. He'd said it flippantly. It wasn't meant to be an insult. How would he have known that he couldn't have chosen a more cutting word?

'Can I ask you a weird question?' I said, keen to take his and my mind off my evident lack of taste in music. 'Am I similar to other girls in the way I . . . have sex?'

Am I basic in bed, too?

'No, you're much naughtier that most girls,' he said.

I gave a thoughtful nod, wondering if that was a good thing or not.

'It's a good thing,' he added, reading my mind. Oh, how it scared me that he could do that. He continued: 'A lady in real life. And a slut in bed. The perfect combination.'

'Why is that the perfect combination?' I asked, with mixed feelings about whether I wanted to be called a slut or not.

'Well, everyone likes a lady.'

Sorry, I thought, *but what even* is *a lady?* And what, in his mind, quantified me as one? I wasn't exactly Grace Kelly. Was it my sudden bouts of anxiety that he could sense? Or maybe it was the fact that I'd not asked much of him, not called him out for kissing me when I knew he had a girlfriend – not called him out, in fact, on anything. The worst possibility was that he thought I was docile, having allowed myself to slip into his control so readily. I should have asked him why he thought I was a lady, but I just wanted to sit with the compliment, having spent most of my life being called 'feral', and not in a cute way.

Instead, I attacked the vulgar part of the statement. 'But does everyone like a slut, is the real question?'

'It's not meant to be derogatory by the way,' he said, which I felt was an almost robotic response, his way of reminding me that he was really a twenty-first-century media man, in full support of women's rights, and not the character who had been close to choking me to death a few minutes before. 'It's sexy. You wouldn't want to be awkward in bed, would you?'

I raised my eyebrows. 'Does that mean I'm awkward out of bed?'

'You're a little socially awkward, yeah,' he said, throwing it out there in a blasé manner.

'That's only with you,' I said. And then, 'I mean, with any guys I'm seeing. Not that we're seeing each other. I'm just not great with relationships. But this isn't a relationship or anything, so I don't really know what I'm trying to say.'

I've never sounded more socially awkward than I did then, scrambling for the right words, the words that wouldn't make him run to Timbuktu.

'Tell me about your exes,' he said. 'Since you know all about mine.'

I felt even more awkward then, not only because he was alluding to Lilah, but because I had no ex to speak of.

'Haven't been with anyone recently,' I mumbled.

'Is this conversation making you uncomfortable?' he said, coming over to where I was leaning against the open window to take my face in his hands, dropping cigarette ash on my shoulder. There he went again, reading my bloody mind. Was I really that transparent?

'I just don't fully understand relationships,' I said, which was an understatement, but not a lie at least. Again, I felt the sense that we might actually be connecting, socially awkward though I may have been.

'I don't either,' he said.

'You must. You were with Lilah for ... how many years?' I said, wincing internally as I said her name.

'Couple of years, on and off. But it's not been the healthiest of relationships, I'm sure you've heard. When we're both on good form it's great. The best you can ever imagine a relationship being. But when one of us takes a dip, there's no hope.'

I chose to ignore the fact that he was, technically, talking about their relationship in the present tense.

'What do you mean, a dip?' I asked.

'Everyone has dips. Things aren't great all the time. When things aren't going well for Lilah, she expresses it through anger, as you know. I don't like anger. I'm not an angry person. So I can't relate to her when she's like that.'

'Me too, I'm the same,' I said, which again was true. I was feeling closer and closer to him with every passing word.

'When things are bad for me, I sort of ... retreat,' he said. 'She thinks I'm pulling away from her, or that I just don't care about her. She doesn't realize that it might just be ... depression.'

154

And with that, he had me on my knees, figuratively speaking. I wanted to wrap him in the fluffiest cotton wool ever spun, hold him in my arms and make him feel all right. That's how all great romances start, don't they? *'You had me at . . . depression.'*

I reached out to stroke the side of his torso, soft, sinewy, with the ends of my fingers. He tugged my face towards his and kissed me, making a loud 'mmm' sound as he held his lips against mine. Then I was on my knees, literally that time, and he finished off inside my mouth, with one hand on the back of my head and the other still nursing that cigarette.

I stayed over that night, drifting in and out of sleep with my head on his chest and his arm draped over me, far too aware of his presence to properly shut off. I imagined what it would be like to be held by him, or anyone, every night. I turned over and pressed my back against his chest. He reached across me, half asleep, and covered my hand with his. I looked up at our hands, fitting each other like lock and key, and I wanted to stay there for ever.

I didn't ask for my bra when I left the next morning.

23 September 2016, 8.48 a.m.

It's just physical and sexual attraction! Don't confuse it for something else!!!!!!!!!

'Someone needs to go to Paris with Lilah,' said Madeleine.

I was retouching digitals of a model, stretching her legs to make them look longer – something I'd started doing to my personal photos – when she said it. Lilah had been booked for a Chanel exclusive. That meant Chanel was the only show she was allowed to walk in over Paris Fashion Week, and she was also contracted to attend the Chanel party and model in a few magazine editorials for them. Overall, not a bad deal.

'I can go with her,' said Steph.

'She might want a bit of distance from you after Fruit-gate,' said Madeleine.

I wasn't looking at Steph, but I knew she would be rising to the colour of my gazpacho – as she always did at any mention of the incident.

'She's fine with me now,' she said curtly. 'We've been texting all week.'

'I'm gonna ask her who she wants,' said Madeleine, being deliberately dismissive. 'I'd do it myself, but we have the director's meeting.'

The directors of Pure Models Worldwide were meeting in Paris to discuss strategy for the coming season. I imagined them at a long table, draped in expensive silks, smoking cigarettes, drinking vodka on the rocks and discussing the secrets of the trade like some sort of global fashion cartel. Madeleine, Drew told me when we got a drink after work one day, had previously been a senior agent at Pure Models New York, and was married to a hedge fund manager at the time. When she got divorced, the owners of Pure capitalized on it and moved her across the world to take over the London agency, since their director at the time had inconsiderately fallen pregnant. Technically, Madeleine was meant to be her maternity cover, but, amazingly, the pregnant predecessor was never seen again. Madeleine was constantly banging on about her agent days in New York and forever complaining about the crappy London budgets in comparison.

I vaguely overheard her phone conversation with Lilah vis-à-vis Paris. She started by telling her about a new kind of TRX workout she'd been to (which I made a mental note to try out), spilled some gossip about a photographer who'd been cheating on his husband with the Manny, laughed a few times, and then casually mentioned Paris at the end. After that she hung up and returned to her computer. I didn't hear her say anything else, so I assumed she'd given Steph the all-okay in a nod or gesture of some sort.

Then, ten minutes later, she suddenly called my name from across the room.

I left the mess of magazine cuttings on my desk and stood up to attention.

Madeleine raised her eyebrows above her spectacles. 'You're going to Paris.'

I will never forget the look on Steph's face.

'You may have noticed,' said Madeleine, briefing me in her office with Drew, 'that London is not exactly taken seriously by New York, or the other markets.'

'We practically have to beg them for options,' added Drew.

'Right. I mean, I get it. When I worked in New York, there was nothing more annoying than an email from some London agent asking for a first option for a job that's a month away, for two thousand pounds, on a girl who's working back to back in New York at ten grand a day.'

'Oh God,' Drew laughed, feigning embarrassment.

'So, not to be rude,' I said, 'but why do we have an agency here, if they don't take it seriously?'

Madeleine looked pleased that I'd asked the question. 'Because some of the biggest stylists, photographers and casting directors in the entire industry are based in London. Mert & Marcus, Tim Walker, Charlotte Stockdale,' she reeled off the names like they were her friends. 'The problem is, we're not in with those people. They still go straight to the New York agents when they want to book one of the big girls. Do you know why?'

I had no idea, so just shook my head.

'Because we don't have our own star,' she said. 'Yes, Yulia Kuznetsova swaggers in every few weeks and demands the shirt off my back and the bra off my tits, but New York still thinks she's their girl.'

'We've searched high and low, but British models are hard to come by,' said Drew. 'And when you find them, most of them are too lazy to want to work. Offer a Polish model a thousand-pound booking and she'll get on an eleven-hour flight before you've ended the conversation. Offer a British model a five-grand one, and she'll head to the pub for a WKD and a burger.'

'Lilah could be our star,' said Madeleine, ignoring Drew's comic rant. 'Now, it would help if she'd just get a famous boyfriend, but until then . . .'

'. . . a Chanel exclusive is the next best thing,' finished Drew. 'It's huge, in fact. It could be the making of her international career.'

'Unfortunately, Lilah knows how to play the nice game for about ten seconds, then she gets bored and wants to leave the job early to take blow, or blow her asshole boyfriend.'

'They've broken up,' I added far too hastily.

'Yeah, heard that one before,' said Madeleine, rolling her eyes at Drew.

'No, I think it's for real this time,' I said.

I so wanted to believe it.

But Madeleine had already lost interest in that thread of conversation. 'Your job in Paris,' she continued, 'is to make sure that Chanel are happy from the moment she gets there until the moment she leaves. But you have to make Lilah think that you're there to keep *her* happy. Does that make sense?'

I nodded uncertainly. It made sense, but that did not mean that I felt confident about it. Yes, I knew how to make Lilah laugh, but her moods were unpredictable and prone to fluctuation at the best of times. And an even larger pressure was Chanel. How the hell was I meant to know if and when a global entity like Chanel was happy?

'You sure it's fine for me to go?' I said, pre-empting what I was sure she and Drew were both thinking.

'I would send Drew or Patrick,' said Madeleine, giving Drew a knowing smile, 'but Lilah doesn't know what to do with men she can't fuck. And anyway, she asked for you.'

A wave of pride swelled inside me at being reminded of that. My girl crush was no less of a thing than it had been when we'd met on the Damien Stern shoot all those months ago – though it was undeniably more of a labyrinth now, given that I'd fucked her ex-boyfriend twice, and one of those times I'd totally known what I was doing.

'So, what exactly do I have to do, day to day?' I asked.

'Whatever she wants you to,' said Madeleine. 'Go out, go to parties, but don't get drunk. Make sure she's home at a reasonable hour, so she's not late for work, or a bitch when she gets there. Get her whatever she needs. Get the client whatever they need.'

'And don't take drugs,' Drew warned me.

I felt my face flush hot.

Madeleine ignored it. 'You're staying at the Bristol because

159

Madame doesn't want anything less, but Chanel are paying, so I don't care. I'll be there if there are any emergencies, but I'll be slammed with these director meetings.'

I tried to imagine what kind of emergencies she was talking about – a car crash, a drug overdose, or a pair of laddered tights?

'And remember – this is important,' said Madeleine, clicking her fingers at me like I was a highly strung dog, 'Lilah's your client. Not your friend.'

I nodded my understanding, though I preferred to think of us as friends. When I left the room, I called the travel agent extraordinaire and booked myself onto the 7 a.m. Eurostar the following day, so I could arrive ahead of Lilah, who was coming from Milan. I really wanted to ask Steph to help me put together a wardrobe for the trip – and to tell me exactly what to expect and that it would all be fine – but I knew that it would be like smearing salt over an open wound. She wasn't openly throwing me shade, and was still calling me things like 'honey' or 'dolly', but I thought she seemed to be avoiding direct eye contact. I felt a swoop in my gut every time I remembered that she knew about that first kiss with Zack. She could easily use it to put me right back in my place. What, I wondered, was stopping her?

I should've spent the afternoon writing a detailed handover list, but instead I spent almost two hours clicking through street style images for outfit inspo and trying to identify catwalk trends. The shows were full of bralettes, but I wasn't stupid enough to think that they could be carried from flat-chested models onto my big balls of flesh without looking totally obscene. There was a lot of fuchsia to speak of, but it was always on some dark stormy girl, and I had a feeling that pairing it with my platinum affair could only lead to trashy. So, I was left with shoulder pads, puff-ball sleeves, Victorian ruffles, slogan

T-shirts, tulle layered skirts, asymmetric necklines, uneven hemlines and deconstructed shirts.

Sexless dressing.

It was time to become an erratic silhouette.

I raided the fashion cupboard and found a few bits and bobs, but not enough to construct a whole outfit from. I consulted Worm, whose eyes almost popped through his Dennis Nilsen specs when I told him I was going to Paris. He wrote me a detailed list of East London vintage stores, and I left on the dot of six to make my way to Dalston. I'd always wanted to be a person who vintage-shopped, but frankly, I hated the smell. Putting that aside, I walked into musty store after musty store and waded through all the crap in the hope of finding a gem, but any gem I did find was way out of my budget. The whole thing was highly stressful, especially given the time pressure. Eventually, I ended up with a silk shirt from the eighties, clunky gold jewellery, brogue shoes, high-waisted cigarette pants, angular sunglasses – and that was my salary gone for the month. I believe the look I was going for was called 'kitsch'.

Later, in the eggshell room, I hacked and stitched away at my old Topshop A-line skirt – the skills I'd learnt while making Henrietta, all those years ago, still lingering in me – and turned it into a haphazard, uneven-hemmed creation. I must say, I felt hugely satisfied by my work, and even a little proud. I had basically just become a designer. Or a stylist at least. I laid my clothes out on the bed, planning entire outfits, making sure that I picked the accessories carefully and not just randomly. I wondered if Steph did that every night before work, and who exactly she was dressing for. Herself, or the industry?

When I finally got to bed, rushing with both excitement and nerves, I wrote a message to Zack. What I should have said was that I shouldn't have come over, that Lilah was my friend, that this wasn't the kind of girl I wanted to be and that it could never happen again.

Instead, I said:

Me:
Please don't ever tell anyone.

He sent back an emoji. A face with a zipper along the mouth line.

I thought about deleting our entire conversation history, but I just didn't want to.

CHAPTER 10

It wasn't until I was on the Eurostar that I remembered that pointless little story I'd told Lilah about having worked for a stylist in Paris. The good thing was that her brain was scattered to say the least, so she probably didn't remember. But then again, she sometimes surprised me with the things she did remember. I did a last-minute Google of Paris, just so I could feign a broadish knowledge of the city. I took note of restaurant names, like Café de Flore (Karl Lagerfeld's favourite, apparently), and a few pieces of buzzwordy trivia, like the fact that taxis were harder to come by than pelicans (though Uber had probably scuppered that one). All I needed were some sound bites. Lilah never asked that many questions.

I was wearing my new clothes: vintage shirt, high-waisted trousers, brogues and angular sunglasses, topped off with a Saint Laurent bag from the fashion cupboard. And I don't want to blow my own trumpet or anything, but I looked pretty damn lit.

I ran my eyes over the schedule one more time. It was relatively straightforward. Meet Lilah at hotel. Take her straight to Chanel fitting. Call time for show at 5 a.m. tomorrow. Party at 7 p.m. tomorrow. Two editorial shoots the following day. Odette at Paris agency arranging cars for all. And then, in big capital letters, it said, 'UNDER NO CIRCUMSTANCES IS

LILAH TO ATTEND ANY PARTIES ASSOCIATED WITH OTHER BRANDS'.

Piece of cake.

I'd been given five hundred euros in cash, so I took a taxi to the hotel, because why the hell not? At first, Madeleine had wanted me to share a room with Lilah, which was fine by me, but then she suddenly decided that it didn't look professional and told me to book my own room. Though it was the cheapest one at the Bristol, it was still the plushest place I'd ever seen. The first thing I did was go to the bathroom and look through all the free mini soaps and shampoos and cottons buds and shower caps. I opened every cupboard and drawer, had a good look at what was in the minibar, then read the menus for room service and the spa. I even opened the Bible for a second.

Even though I was there to be with Lilah, I kept imagining staying in that room with Zack, the two of us swathed in the hotel bathrobes, drinking from the mini bottles of champagne, me lying in the crook of his arm as we ordered room service and watched TV.

After a bit, I realized there wasn't really anything to do in that beautiful room – unpacking seemed like a waste of time – so I went downstairs to wait for Lilah in a lobby crawling with sartorial mastery. Every single person must have worked in fashion, and everyone was, by Parisian cliché, hyper-chic. Lilah finally traipsed in, looking as far from chic as one could be in tracksuit bottoms, a baggy jumper and completely extra Dior silver sunglasses, but she was still the most striking person in the room. I stood up and stretched my arms out with a big smile, urging her into a hug. She let me embrace her, only very briefly, before slumping into a chair, and my first thought was, *Oh God, she knows.*

But of course she didn't know, or she wouldn't have hugged me at all.

'I don't want to do the fitting,' she said, rubbing her eyes beneath the sunglasses.

I hadn't expected to be tested so early on.

'They need to fit you into your look, babe,' I said, dumbly stating the obvious.

'Why can't they fit me at the show?'

'Because they are Chanel. Everyone has to have a fitting.'

'Have you even asked?'

Of course I haven't fucking asked.

'Why don't you go up to the room and I'll call them,' I suggested lightly.

'Call them now.' She glared at me, daring me to admit that I had no authority.

'I need to call Madeleine first.'

'Fine. Call Madeleine. I'm going to have a bath.' She stood up in one fast motion and dragged her suitcase over to reception to get her room key.

Madeleine answered her phone abruptly when I called. 'Is it urgent? I'm getting off the Eurostar.'

'Lilah doesn't want to do the Chanel fitting,' I said.

'Well, she has to.'

'She asked if they can fit her at the show.'

'Does she look big?' she asked, sounding far calmer than I'd anticipated.

'Big?'

'If she doesn't want to fit, it's probably because she's gained weight.'

'I don't know. She's wearing baggy clothes.'

'Mm. You need to get her to that fitting. Karl's not gonna

make an exception for Lilah Fox.' Then she started shouting for her driver. 'I've gotta go. Just make her feel good about herself.' And she hung up on me.

I took the lift upstairs, wondering what it would be like to have people around who were being paid to make you feel good about yourself. I knocked on Lilah's door. She opened it, barely looking up from her iPhone, and I could tell which side of her personality was going to take precedence today.

I told her she had to do the fitting and she let out a long, agitated sigh.

'It won't take long,' I said. 'They're just really excited about you. It's your first time working with them and they want to make sure you feel comfortable in your look. Also, we want them to spend time with you because we know they'll fall in love. If you show up at the call time tomorrow, they won't get to know you, or see how fab you are.'

Blah, blah, blah.

'Can I at least have a shower?' she said. 'I smell like a fucking fish-gutter.'

'Sure. Go for it,' I said, even though we were already running late for the fitting. I felt like I needed to compromise somewhere. I waited, perched anxiously against the bathroom doorframe as Lilah stripped down to her slender natural form. I glanced furtively to see if she had gained weight, feeling ashamed that I had to care, and noticed that her stomach did look the slightest bit bloated.

She must have seen my – obviously not so furtive – glance, because she muttered, 'I'm on my period' as she stepped into the shower.

I felt even more ashamed that I had to wonder if she was telling the truth. My eyes flickered south and I saw that there was indeed a string hanging limp between her legs. I felt sorry for her then. I couldn't think of anything worse than having the eyes of fashion royalty raking over me when I was on my period. I also couldn't help but notice that her vagina wasn't as neat as I'd always envisioned it. I'd expected a tiny slit, like I'd seen on porn stars, but her labia hung out like everyone else's and the skin around it was speckled with dark hairs. Suddenly I wondered what kind of a wax she opted for. God, I can be weird.

I texted Odette, my Paris counterpart, to let her know that we'd be late. Then I texted Madeleine to let her know that all was in order. She texted back a quick 'well done' and I felt my lips curling into a smile, pleased that I'd managed to please her.

Lilah took a long time to dry her hair and an even longer time putting together an outfit. I guessed that she was thinking the more outlandish the outfit, the less anyone would notice the unbecoming qualities of her menstruation, because when she was done, she had everything but the kitchen sink on her person.

It wasn't until we were in the car that she looked at me and said, 'You look nice. Different.'

One thing was clear: she was not happy about it.

The Chanel head office was like Fort Knox. I had to stand outside, much to my chagrin. I had been dying to stand in a real design studio, watching Karl drape soft materials over Lilah like a wizard. Instead, I stood around with agents from other model agencies like we were a bunch of nannies waiting for the kids to finish school, smoking cigarettes and talking shop. I was definitely the most junior person there and had to do a lot of pretending I knew who and what they were talking about. I hoped word would get around about the assistant from Pure

Models who was so good at her job that they'd already sent her to Paris for fashion week.

After two whole hours, Lilah emerged, chewing gum noisily in an 'I don't give a fuck' way, which I took to be a reaction to feeling out of her depth. I hoped, for her sake and the agency's, that she'd been less of a twat with Karl Lagerfeld.

She wanted a drink, so we walked and sat down outside the first Parisian café we came across ('This reminds me of Café De Flore,' I said – *why?*). We ordered a bottle of wine and, on top of that, Lilah asked for a cranberry juice and a fresh mint tea. She had a habit of gluttonously over-ordering liquids. I hadn't eaten anything since my Greek yoghurt on the Eurostar and knew I should probably line my stomach if we were about to tuck into a bottle of Sauvignon, so I asked for olives. Nuts were calorific, but olives were fine, right?

When all the liquids arrived, she took out a transparent orange pot that had a prescription sticker on it and emptied two pills into her hand.

'What you taking?' I asked, snatching the pot and reading the prescription label. Adderall for a Mr Jacques De Fontaine. 'Who's Jacques?'

'My friend,' she said, throwing the pills back with a glug of wine.

'Why are you taking these?'

'To keep my weight down, darling,' she said irritably. I always wanted to say 'darling' like Lilah did – quickly, with a barely pronounced 'G' – but whenever I tried, it sounded like I was taking the piss.

'Babe, you do not need to be taking these! You're already so thin,' I said, even though I'd been silently critiquing her little period paunch earlier.

'I'm not fucking thin, Scarlett. You know that!'

The notion that Lilah was anything but thin was totally ridiculous, but we were in model world. And in model world, the truth of the matter was, she did need to keep an eye on her weight. So I handed the pot back to her and shrugged, wondering if I should get on the Adderall bus too.

'It's not easy for me, you know,' she continued in a softer tone. 'I don't have a parent who's a rock star or an aristocrat, or a family on some reality TV show.'

Neither do I, I thought. Or a coat-hanger figure and a face so beautiful that it made people gape. But everyone's problems were relative, I supposed.

'I have to fucking work to make my career happen,' she said, sounding very indignant about it.

'Could always get a famous boyfriend,' I offered.

At that, she laughed – and my God it was a relief!

'Yeah, that would really make Zack jealous,' she said. 'He's such a star fucker.'

I took two large gulps of wine, feeling conscience-stricken because she obviously wasn't over Zack if she was still thinking about making him jealous. But I also felt anxious about the idea that he was a star fucker, because I was sure as hell no star.

The wine started to lubricate Lilah and her mood lifted, thank God. After a while, Jade called, and Lilah told her to come meet us. I was worried that Jade's presence might send Lilah back into a slump, given that she was the model everyone wanted on their catwalk that season – and because the industry had yet to come round to the idea of diversity, it was that much more impressive, so every fashion journalist was talking about her. Thankfully, Lilah was drunk by the time she arrived and had a glint in her eye that I knew meant party time. Finally, some fun! I was so relieved by the idea of it that I wasn't even thinking about Madeleine's demand that Lilah be strictly my client, not my friend.

'Have you got anything on you?' Lilah asked straight out as she clung onto Jade's neck in a display of Girl Love that I wanted in on. Jade nodded and the two of them went off to the bathroom, promising to be quick. I knew that they wouldn't be, so I lit a cigarette, put on my angular sunglasses for a selfie and sent it to Billie. She replied almost immediately.

> Billie:
> All right Dame Edna?
>
> Me:
> Lol. Kisses from paris 💋
>
> Billie:
> You are a massive dick 👊
>
> Me:
> Do you still love me tho? 🙏
>
> Billie:
> If I must

Eventually, the other two returned and sat down. Within seconds, I felt a hand press into my inner thigh and I glanced down to see Jade's long fingers there. A familiar current went shooting up my leg, straight to my nether regions. Then I realized that there was something in between her skin and my new trousers. My face turned hot with embarrassment, because for a split second, I had thought she was coming on to me, and what's more, I'd been pleased about it. But actually, she was just trying to subtly pass me drugs. I placed my hand over hers, which she then slipped away, so that I could feel the piece of neatly wrapped card against my palm. Despite Drew's warning not to take drugs, I thought that taking cocaine in Paris was too glamorous an opportunity to turn down, so I went to the loo and did a line on my own. And yes, I knew that doing a line on your own was not a good sign, but again . . . when in Paris.

When I went back outside, Jade was standing in the middle of the pavement holding her iPhone steady in both hands, taking a picture like any old tourist. I looked at the subject of the picture: Lilah, wearing her Dior sunglasses even though the sky was nearly black, a cigarette balancing elegantly between her fingers.

I hung back, waiting for the flash to go off.

And then Jade looked at me and said, 'Get in there, sugar.'

I didn't need any more persuading. Immediately, I pounced into the seat next to Lilah and draped my arm over her shoulder.

'Very Parisian,' said Jade, pronouncing it 'pareejan' in her New Orleans accent, as I eagerly wondered when the right time was to ask her to send me the photo. When she sat down, she was typing on her phone. 'Should we go to the Balenciaga party?'

'Fuck yeah, let's go!' said Lilah, throwing her arms in the air.

'No, no, no, no!' I almost shrieked, realizing that I was going to have to stop being so laissez-faire and do my job.

They both looked at me like I was entirely mad.

'Lilah's under contract with Chanel,' I added hastily. 'She can't go to a Balenciaga party.'

'Oh, "under contract with Chanel", wow!' said Jade, teasing Lilah, but in my coke-paranoia, I felt like she was teasing me.

'Oh, whatevs. I just won't let anyone take pictures of me,' said Lilah, flapping her hands around.

'*UNDER NO CIRCUMSTANCES IS LILAH TO ATTEND ANY PARTIES ASSOCIATED WITH OTHER BRANDS.*' The words flashed in front of my eyes in showbiz light format.

'Doll, you've got a 5 a.m. call time tomorrow,' I reminded her.

'So have I,' said Jade, chilled as ever, even though the drugs were speedy.

'Come on,' said Lilah, draping both arms over my shoulders. 'You know you want to.'

Was this an emergency that warranted a call to Madeleine? Surely that would just make me look completely incompetent?

Your job in Paris is to make sure that Chanel are happy from the moment she gets there until the moment she leaves. But you have to make Lilah think that you're there to keep her happy.

I tried a different strategy: 'Guys. We've got rooms at the Bristol fucking Hotel. I've got hard cash from the agency. Let's just order a few more grams, go back to the hotel, get into those delicious bathrobes and raid the mini bar!'

I thought I sounded very like Steph when I said all that. I may have even said it in her accent.

Lilah looked unconvinced, but luckily, Jade seem to have been swayed by my little offer.

'That does sound kinda more fun, you know,' she said, giving me what I would call a flirtatious smile, which made me worry that she'd noticed my rise in colour during the leg-touch scenario.

There was a suspenseful pause. Then Lilah said, 'Fine!', feigning a sulk. 'Let's be boring then.'

I paid the bill with my hard cash, giving myself a silent pat on the back for averting that potential crisis with the promise of more illegal substances. Then the three of us got in a taxi to the Bristol, also courtesy of *moi*. We sat on Lilah's bed, drinking the welcome champagne and the mini bottles of spirits, smoking – first by the window, then directly from the bed – and doing lines of Jade's cocaine until it ran out, at which point I ventured into the street to meet a French drug dealer. I knew it wasn't professional, but what was I meant to do? Lilah wanted me there because we were friends and suddenly I had to become some sort of nanny to her, without losing our dynamic. It was impossible to get it right.

When I returned with the goods, we settled in and chatted the night away. Both Lilah and Jade were on a mission to prove that their life had been harder than the other's. Jade said we had no idea how difficult it was growing up as one of five kids, which sounded all too appealing to me, the lonesome only child, despite the fact that they'd lived in total poverty in the racist Deep South. Her automatic and acutely natural confidence now made sense, knowing that she'd grown up as part of a wolf pack.

Lilah told stories about her competitive mother, once a runner-up in the Miss England competition, her mentally ill sister and an alcoholic father, whom I guessed she was placing on an undeserved pedestal. I listened with total affection, doubt-lessly enhanced by the drugs, and in that moment I thought, *I am never seeing Zack Smith again*.

I could have participated in the conversation in my own way. I could have told them about my virtually estranged father and Ursula Andress. I could have told them that my mother thought I was a useless sack of lard, which I played up to because I knew I could never live up to her expectations, or her, for that matter. It would have been the perfect opportunity to connect to them both on a deeper level.

Instead, when there was a moment of silence and they looked at me, I said, 'My Labrador died last year. Henrietta. I really loved that dog.'

They acted like I hadn't said anything and continued.

We eventually went to bed at 3 a.m. – Lilah and Jade in one room, me alone in another – with two hours until we were all meant to be at the Grand Palais for the Chanel call time. I lay in between the cool sheets of the most comfortable bed I'd ever been in, twitching and sniffing, sleep showing no signs of arriving. I kept checking the time on my iPhone: 3.10 a.m., 3.45 a.m., 4.23 a.m. The next time I checked, my screen was crowded with a grid of rectangular notifications, all of them from Instagram. I sat up in bed, wondering what on earth was going on with my social media. Every few seconds a new notification would appear out of nowhere to let me know that someone I'd literally never heard of was now following me on Instagram. I scrolled down through hundreds of little rectangles, like I was working through a virtual Rolodex. When I got to the bottom, a single sentence shone up at me: 'JadeDeress tagged you in a post'.

I clicked on the photo of me and Lilah sitting outside the café. Technically, it wasn't my best. My eyes were droopy from the wine and my lipstick really could've done with a touch-up. But all I cared about was that I was in it. Little old me from Topsham, looking like a proper fashionista, in Paris with my arm around a model, on the Instagram feed of another model. I would be the object of envy for girls all over the world, sitting in their bedrooms, scrolling through Instagram and wishing their lives were more exciting. I would be someone that myself just six months ago would've looked at and thought, *Fucking unfair*.

I was relevant. And, dare I say it, maybe even bloggable.

There were 257 comments.

'This is amazing'

'HAHAH you guys having so much fun'

'OMG Lilah is so cool always'

'The blonde girl has awesome hair'

'Lovely and cute women'

'PLEEEEASE FOLLOW ME'

'Askim bu ne'

'Marry me?'

'I LOVE YOU ALL'

My heart was racing.

However, my excitement was cut short by the struggle I endured getting Lilah out of bed. At least she'd slept, I guessed, unlike myself. We were late for the call time and I had The Fear weighing down on me in the car. There was a frantic assistant at the door checking the models in and I was freaking out that she — and everyone else in my radius — would be able to see that I'd not had a wink of sleep. But as soon as we crossed the threshold, Lilah was whirled into hair and makeup and no one even gave me a second glance.

The Chanel show that season was appropriately tech themed, the catwalk imitating a data centre and clutch bags decorated with sparkling circuit boards. While Lilah waited to be dressed, her hair and makeup done to perfection, I took a photo of her and posted it on Instagram for all my new followers and captioned it: 'This ain't no robot #backstage #models #PFW #aw17 #chanel'. I thought that was quite a clever one.

Within an hour, it had over two hundred likes.

I couldn't stop checking my phone.

*

The Chanel party was, hands down, the most stylish party I had ever been – or will ever go – to in my life.

It was held at their ultra-exclusive couture salon, which is basically a shop that only does business with the super-rich or the right kind of famous.

Lilah had been dressed in head-to-toe Chanel. A razor-sharp, black sequin-embellished tuxedo, which cut a low V down her chest, stiletto heels and a Perspex bag shaped like the Chanel fragrance bottle. I wore a Sonia Rykiel mini dress from the fashion cupboard which had a modest neckline and luxurious fringes and moved in a way that, I thought, told everyone I was playful. When the makeup artist who'd been sent to Lilah's room by Chanel had finished on her, she asked if I wanted my makeup done too. Of course I accepted. When I looked in the mirror, I kind of felt like a clown, but overall, I was pleased, because I looked *fashion*. I just wished that I'd had more than a brief afternoon nap and four cups of coffee, which had sent me trembling.

The second Lilah emerged from the car outside the store, cameras were flashing at her like strobe lights at a nightclub and clicking away like disapproving tongues.

'Lilah! Lilah! Lilah!' was all you could hear.

I walked a few steps behind her, feeling a rush of blood to the head. I remember seeing the white light in front of us and imagining it was like being caught in front of moving traffic. We walked cautiously through and the press parted like the Red Sea as we strode into the building. On the other side of the threshold there was a more civilized photo call, where Lilah posed in front of an enormous rose-filled urn, one leg out and the opposite hip jutting to the side. She was over-posing, but it totally worked in that tux.

Dare you to try and fuck me, I felt she was saying.

She stepped aside and I fell in stride with her, trying not to gawk at the movie star, who had taken her place by the urn. The room was a squeeze of sophisticated beings poised like figures in fashion design sketches. Lilah was immediately engulfed by various well-known individuals.

I spotted Madeleine in the crowd standing with a French style icon and a silver fox of a man. She was wearing a heavy silk crimson dress which swept down the lines of her body in one elegant movement, with a high neck, an open back and a tie that cascaded down the length of her spine. Both she and the silver fox were laughing at something the style icon was saying. I made my way over and stopped by Madeleine's shoulder. She turned to me, still holding her smile from the previous conversation, and said, 'You look great!'

She may as well have handed me the Nobel fucking Peace Prize.

'Ralph?' she said, placing her hand on the arm of the silver fox, who was Ralph Edelman, the owner of Pure Models Worldwide – a.k.a. her boss. 'This is Scarlett. Part of my London team.' She took a handful of my hair and twirled it around her fingers. I suddenly wondered what it would be like to have Madeleine as a mother.

'Hello, Scarlett, great to meet you,' he said in an even heavier New York accent than Madeleine's, shaking my hand firmly. Before I could say anything, he was being hugged by another French icon.

I smiled at Madeleine and let out a loud sigh, as if to say, 'Is this really all happening?'

'You're doing a great job,' she said briefly, before slipping off to join Ralph and all the icons.

I spent the rest of the evening with Lilah, drinking champagne and introducing myself to everyone as her agent, which she didn't ever dispute. I had a sense that people whom I'd met a number of times before were suddenly greeting me with more enthusiasm than they ever had before. I don't know if I was imagining it, or if that really was the case, but it didn't matter.

For the first time, I had an identity that I was proud of. I was a hard-working Londoner, in a Sonia Rykiel dress, with a job in the fashion industry and 2,153 followers on Instagram. People who had never met me knew my name and wanted to be my friend.

I was, I thought, making something of my life.

4 October 2016, 11.38 p.m.

The next day, on the Eurostar, I responded to the barrage of messages that I'd received. The photos of Lilah arriving at the Chanel party were on the *Daily Mail,* and I was in them. Not just the corner of my hand, but my whole face and body. Never, even in my wildest dreams, had I imagined that I would end up on the same page as movie stars and fashion royalty. I was the colour of Casper the Friendly Ghost and my legs were a little chunky, but other than that, I didn't look terrible.

The first message I read was from my mother, who had been brought up to speed by her gossip-hungry sister.

Mum:
Margot sent me the pictures from the DM.
Ashamedly, she still reads middle-market
tabloids. Hope you're not getting swept up
by the theatre of it all, but good to know that
someone in the world is having fun, given its
current state. Visit home soon. Love, Mum.

My father had messaged too, saying that he hoped I'd enjoyed
Paris and that it was one of his favourite cities. Not that I would
have known that. The last message I'd received from him before
that was a Happy Birthday message back in February. I wondered
if he'd been the one to see the *Daily Mail* pictures or if someone
had sent them to him and whether he'd shown them to Ursula
Andress. I wondered if it had stirred any emotion in him, or if, like
me, he felt nothing but an empty hole where the feeling should be.

I had a WhatsApp from Billie ('You're a celeb, Draco!') and
countless messages from girls that I hadn't seen since my school
days. I even had a message from Tim, joking about a kiss and
tell, which was very unexpected. I screenshotted that one and
sent it to Billie along with a line of exclamation marks.

In the midst of it all, a message from Madeleine slid down
my screen.

Madeleine:
Are you on this train? Come talk to me.

I stood up and made my way down the wobbling aisle of the
carriage, grabbing onto the heads of seats for support. I arrived
at a set of glass sliding doors marked 'First Class Only', pressed
a button and the doors slid open, as easy as that.

The dark gloss of Madeleine's hair was visible above the line of seats, which were only a bit wider than the ones on the rest of the train. As I got closer, she raised her hand and waved, 'Come. Sit.' There were two plastic flutes of champagne on the table between us. Madeleine picked one up and said, 'Here. Cheers.'

I took a seat, picked up the other glass and clinked her, though it was more of a tap than a clink.

Then she asked, 'How long have you been working for me?'

'It's been just over six months,' I said, eyeing her Cartier love bracelet, a solid gold circle hanging around her bony wrist. I wondered if she'd bought it for herself, or if it was a remnant of her failed marriage.

'Oh, I feel like it was just yesterday that I terrified you with that pussy joke!' she said humorously.

I laughed, going hot at the thought of it, but also flattered that she remembered, and that she was joking about it like we were just a pair of pals. 'I know, time flies.'

'When you're having fun!' she said and smiled in a way that made me feel uneasy. 'Well, I threw you in at the deep end with this trip. And it looks like you swam.'

I conceded with a vigorous nod. 'I really loved it. I learnt so much about the industry.'

'I'm moving you onto the booking table. We'll shuffle people around so that you can sit next to Steph and she can help you. You'll still be an assistant, but I'm going to give you a few clients to start booking jobs with. E-commerce clients, testing photographers, some of the smaller magazines. That's the way you'll learn. If you do a good job and you keep on top of your assistant duties, you'll be a junior agent pretty soon.'

'Thank you so much,' was all I could say.

'You have any questions?'

I shifted uncomfortably. 'My salary ...' I hated talking about money.

'Twenty grand a year,' she said. 'And believe me, it's not standard to get a pay rise. Some people actually get a pay drop.'

'Thank you. I really appreciate that, Madeleine.'

It would make no difference month to month, but it still felt like validation and, for that, I was obscenely grateful.

'You're welcome. Now get out of first class, before someone figures you out.'

I laughed at the very appropriate analogy, picked up the plastic champagne flute and returned to my seat, overwhelmed by the feeling that life was finally happening for me.

The train rushed through the Channel Tunnel and pressure flooded my ears. I took a sip of champagne, letting the dry fizz go flat on my tongue.

It was happening. I was succeeding at life.

The pressure dropped around me as the train emerged at the other end.

Don't fuck this up, Scizzle.

'Come here,' said Zack. He was sitting on one of his Ottoman poufs in front of the oval mirror.

I planted myself on his lap, slipping into the crease of him. He draped a sculpted, tattooed arm over me. We were both looking in the mirror, our hearts beating with cocaine.

'Look at us,' he said. 'Look at how hot we look.'

He was actually looking at himself.

When I said nothing, he added, 'Don't you think so?'

I gazed at our two naked figures in the reflection. He wasn't wrong. My body fitted perfectly into the groove of his, since I'd dropped almost two dress sizes, and his swarthy complexion was the perfect contrast to my milky skin. I thought at the time we could have been one of those couples that you see on Instagram accounts like @HumanLovers. (Needless to say, we'd have actually been much better suited to @ketflixandpills.)

'We do look good,' I agreed.

'We make a hot couple.'

'Shame we'll never be a couple,' I said, full of sass.

'How do you know we'll never be a couple?' he asked, sounding almost offended.

I looked at his reflection. I knew, in the part of my brain that was still in possession of logic, that he didn't mean anything by it. But the damage had still been done.

I didn't want to answer his question because I was scared it would end in him admitting that of course we could never be a couple. So I stood up, put on my filthy voice and said, 'D'you still wank to my Facebook?'

He laughed. 'I do sometimes, yeah.'

'Really?' I said, so very pleased to know that I still retained some erotic mystery for him.

'I'd like something new to wank to,' he said, pulling me towards him and kissing the hollow beneath my ribcage.

I glanced down at him to see if he meant what I thought he meant. 'That would be very naughty,' I said, rubbing his earlobes between my fingers, because Barbra Streisand in *Meet the Fockers* had convinced me that it was a legitimate arousal technique.

'But you are very naughty, aren't you?' he said, tapping his hands against the backs of my thighs. He leant over to reach for the discarded pair of high heels that I'd arrived in – because I knew that heels turned him on – and helped me step into them.

Then he picked up his iPhone.

And even though he told me, loud and clear, that he was recording me, I wasn't thinking about whether I should do it or not. I wasn't thinking about the promise I'd made to myself, days ago, that I'd never see Zack Smith again. I wasn't thinking about Lilah. I wasn't thinking about the fact that what he called a 'naughty little video' was, in simple terms, a sex tape. I was just thinking, *He wants me.*

CHAPTER 11

Two weeks on the booking table and I made my first model booking. It came relatively easily. Drew was off sick, so I took a phone call from his online luxury retail client. They needed a model to shoot an editorial, one day only, in London for a fee of two thousand pounds, plus the twenty per cent agency fee. Personally, I would've loved to make two grand in a day, but apparently, that was a measly fee for a modelling job.

Still, it was money, and Madeleine always drummed it into us that any fee was better than no fee. I put together a digital package of model portfolios, including all the girls who were in town, even if they didn't necessarily fit the brief. The client requested to option three models from the pack. I checked that they were free on the date and gave her a first option on all the girls. Two hours later, she confirmed Breje.

And that's all that it was.

I felt a sense of pride when I called Breje, as if I was really doing something to help her, not least because she'd been trawling into the agency, day after day, complaining that she hadn't worked for weeks and was running out of money. Weren't we all! It was only once the agents started congratulating me that I suddenly thought, *What do I have to be proud of?* I didn't draw her face. I didn't pull any major strings to make the booking happen. I just responded to a client's request for a package and entered some details into the chart. Yet Madeleine was happy, so shouldn't I have been happy too? Sometimes I wondered whether it would ever be possible to feel satisfaction as deeply as I felt the lack of it.

Despite having taken what was, technically, the first step towards the shit-hot agent career that I so wanted, all I could think about that week was Zack. And not just about having sex with him. The day after I'd inadvertently become the star of a secret sex video was a Sunday, the day that I usually found the hardest to fill. Most Sundays, I'd wake up late, usually hungover, and watch something on Netflix. Then around lunch time I'd take a long walk to Finsbury Park, treat myself to an overpriced cappuccino from a hipster coffee joint called Fink's and smoke my first cigarette of the day, after which I'd always lose count. I'd walk around for as long as I could, getting exercise, letting the buzz of London set into my bones and basically just killing time. Eventually I'd go home and do some much-needed laundry, tidy my room, choose my clothes for the week ahead and, finally, open a bottle of wine. The ceramicist, as far as I could tell, didn't drink, but she said nothing about my drinking two to three glasses of Merlot as we watched *Strictly Come Dancing*, followed by the *Antiques Road Show*, like a pair of strangers.

But that last Sunday I had woken up in Maida Vale. Granted, the hangover was about three times as bad as usual, given that I'd put away two bottles of wine and taken all the cocaine in London, but at least I wasn't alone. Zack made coffee in his expensive machine, which we drank in bed. We deliberated over going to Tesco's to buy eggs, as there was nothing in his fridge, but eventually I'd had to admit that I couldn't really cook and it turned out neither could he, so we went out for breakfast. I'd taken the end of the meal to be my cue to go home, but he'd put his arm around me and led me back to his flat, where we spent the afternoon entangled in the corner of his L-shaped sofa watching Sunday TV.

It was unusual for me to want to spend an entire day with someone after sex. Normally I'd scramble off, feeling like I needed to physically rid myself of their weight. I'd breathe a sigh of relief when I was finally alone, but didn't feel truly free of it until I'd had a shower. But on that Sunday with Zack, I'd had no desire to leave. For the first time, I had a feeling that I could get used to coexistence.

I was thinking about him so much the following week that when Steph told me to look at her new Facebook profile photo, I started typing in the search bar and the letters that instinctively came out were, 'Z-A-C-K-S-M'.

'*My* Facebook!' squawked Steph over my shoulder.

My hands flew off the keyboard and landed over my eyes in a fit of embarrassment. 'Shit!'

'Something on your mind, hon?' she said, looking at me with wide blue-grey eyes and a tiny half-smile.

'I was just thinking about him,' I said, lowering my voice so as not to attract the attention of anyone else on the booking table. Madeleine – who had extendable ears – was, thankfully, in a meeting.

'Has it happened again?' she asked, matching my tone.

I thought about lying, but I was truly dying to tell someone about it. And Steph could've already used the kiss against me if that was her intention, so I decided that I could trust her and gave a very sheepish nod.

'Right. How many times?'

'A couple. I'm just thinking about him because ... we were meant to have dinner tonight,' I said, a lie that just slipped out, as easily as any other. I don't know why I pretended that we were having dinner. To try and convince her that I was capable of connecting to a human being on an intimate level, like everyone else?

'You need to get him out of your head,' she said.

'Who're you getting out of your head?' Drew piped up, popping up above his screen like a nosy emu.

'Just some loser she's been seeing,' said Steph.

I loved the idea that people now thought I'd been 'seeing' someone, even if he hypothetically was a 'loser'. I just wished she'd said, 'A very cool, attractive loser.'

'Tell me more!' said Drew, like a schoolgirl in a juicy round of Never Have I Ever.

'No one you know,' said Steph. 'But she's got to get over him, because he's a serial womanizer who's still completely in love with his ex-girlfriend.' She looked at me pointedly there. And then, with a wildly excited glint in her eye, she grabbed her phone and said, 'Actually, I'm going to set you up with my friend Jason. He's good at dates. That'll get your mind off him.'

'Who's Jason? What does he do?' I asked, like I was Anna fucking Wintour and would take no less than a global CEO.

'He's a teacher,' said Steph.

My mouth involuntarily lifted at the side, a gesture that Drew mirrored. Not only did it seem boring next to a high-flying music executive, but no matter how many years I'd been out of school, there was something about a date with a teacher that still didn't sit right with me.

'Don't be closed-minded!' said Steph, furiously typing away on her iPhone. 'Give him a chance.'

'Yeah, give him a chance,' said Drew teasingly. 'Open your mind, open your heart, open your legs.'

'I've been opening my legs my whole life. That's the problem!' I said, which made them both laugh.

'You don't have to have sex with him,' said Steph. 'Just go for drinks. Have some fun.'

I'd never been on a date that didn't end in sex, but before I could chime in with that, my iPhone let me know that I was now on a group WhatsApp with Steph and this Jason character.

> Steph:
> J meet my good friend Scarlett. Think you two would get on like a house on fire. She's AWESOME! Take it from here xxx

> *Steph Conway left the conversation.*

J did not hold back.

'He's already typing!' I said, alarmed – repulsed even.

'He's prolific!' said Steph. 'You're probably too used to being ghosted by the last one.'

Ouch! But fair.

I looked down at my phone. I already had four lines of conversation from a teacher I'd never met, culminating with a request to take me to dinner on Thursday. Whirlwind.

I managed to muster some excitement for my date after a Facebook search told me that Jason the Teacher was actually quite a looker. But I still felt the need to go completely anti-teacher vibes and decided to rock a baggy ripped jean with an oversized army jacket and clunky heels. I mean, really, who did I think I was?

I arrived at the bar in Soho, which was serving Happy Hour cocktails, and my first thought was, *He's basic.* Sure, less than a year ago I'd been drinking the Co-Op's finest straight from the bottle on the Topsham quayside, but now I'd had a taste of Le Bristol Paris and fancied myself some sort of connoisseur of the high life. Still, I managed to put on an exuberant front when I spotted Jason standing up to greet me, mainly because it would have been awkward to do anything but mirror his own enthusiastic mania.

'I'm so happy we're meeting!' he said, in a voice that was both posh and Northern. 'I have a good feeling about this. Steph never gets it wrong!'

'Pressure!' I said, shaking the army jacket away from my arms. 'Has she set you up before?'

'Well, I've known her for a long time. We're friends from back home,' he said, which definitely was not an answer to my question, but I let it slide. His hair was longer than in the photos I'd seen and flopped over his circular glasses. He wasn't bad looking at all, but I did wish he'd lose the specs.

'So, Steph tells me you have a tattoo?' he said. 'So do I!' He rolled back his sleeve to reveal a line drawing of some sort of sea-shell. It looked like a turd. 'Already got something in common!'

'Yeah . . .' I said.

Doesn't virtually everyone in London have a tattoo these days?

'Do you want to eat?' he asked.

'I had a really late lunch,' I lied, because for some reason something about eating on dates cringed me out. So we drank and drank and drank and after God knows how many vodka sodas, Jason the Teacher's enthusiasm seemed endearing and his Harry Potter glasses nothing short of erotically stimulating. When we went outside for a cigarette, he kissed me, or maybe

I kissed him. Who knows? Who cares? All I know is that we were in an Uber before I could give it a second thought, belting it out to a Whitney tune on Magic FM.

I don't remember what we chatted about, but I do remember that when we got out of the car, he said, 'Do you know why I like you, Scarlett? Because you're so down-to-earth!'

Oh, buddy, I thought. *Oh, bud, you don't know me at all.*

I can't quite describe how much being called down-to-earth annoyed me. Maybe it was because he'd totally misread me, and therefore couldn't have been that interested. Down-to-earth people were practical, realistic, level-headed. I was none of those things. Or maybe I was annoyed at myself for giving off the impression of being something I didn't want to be. In my mind, no down-to-earth person had ever set the world on fire. The ones who lived on the edge, from extreme high to extreme low, who thought too little and fell in love too fast – they were the ones who got to swallow the ecstasy of life.

In Jason the Teacher's flat, I suggested we watch a movie, because the down-to-earth comment had sent me off the idea of kissing him. He flicked through channels, with an arm around my shoulders, and eventually I told him to stop on *The Darjeeling Limited.*

'I love this film so much,' I said.

'Me too! Another thing we have in common: we love Wes Anderson,' he said excitedly, taking my hand and twisting my fingers around his, like you might do to someone's hair. It irritated me that he was forcing all these connections on us. Sure, we both loved Wes Anderson, but honestly, who didn't?

Jason continuously insisted on kissing my temple and doing that weird twisty thing with my hand, over and over, and all I could think was, *Please can you fucking stop?*

I immediately recognized the feeling I was having.

It was 'The ICK' – that monster infliction made up of repulsion, cringey-ness and a little bit of anger that spread faster than wildfire. I was a frequent sufferer. I never knew exactly what it was that brought The ICK on, but there was one thing I could always be sure of: The ICK was there to stick.

It wrapped its claws around me and consumed me as Jason the Teacher planted tiny bird kisses all the way down my neck and then suckled my nipple like a baby pig. It roared as he slid his hand into my knickers and started fiddling around like a hungry pescatarian trying to get the last anchovy out of the jar. I wanted to scream at him to get off me. But how could I? I was there because *I'd* kissed him, *I'd* agreed to go back to his. *I* might have even suggested it. I had got myself into it and he was doing nothing wrong. There was no way I could leave without making it very awkward. Plus, it was marginally better than being alone in the eggshell room. So, when he led me to the bedroom and started clumsily undressing me, I didn't stop him. I reasoned with myself that I had fancied him an hour ago, so maybe I just needed to reignite that sexual fire. And what better way to do that than by having sex with the man?

As it turns out, having sex on The ICK is the worst. I felt like I was having non-consensual sex, except I'd consented to it, so really, it was all my fault. I squeezed my eyes shut and prayed that he was one of those guys who came after a minute when they were drunk. For once in my life, I wished that I was using a condom. He hadn't asked whether we should use one, or if I was on the pill (I wasn't). Zack had never asked either, but he always pulled out just in time. After a few minutes, I couldn't deal with the scent of Jason or his body on top of me for any longer.

'Can I turn over?' I said.

'If you want to,' he rasped, panting away.

I lay flat on my stomach and tried to pretend that Zack was behind me as Jason the Teacher mounted me, although that was impossible. He started thrusting backwards and forwards, making loud sex noises. But the thing was, he wasn't inside me at all. He appeared to be fucking the air between my thighs. Fed up, I wormed my hand behind my back and tossed him off until he came on my back – at last!

I retrieved my hand, my shoulder aching from the awkward position, and lay dead-still on my stomach. He went off to the bathroom to ... what do men do when they go off to the bathroom after sex? I closed my eyes and willed sleep to come before he got back. It didn't. But I pretended it had.

The next morning, Jason brought me tea in bed – *Can't he tell I'm a coffee girl?* I thought – and invited me to a gig the following night. I smiled and told him I had friends in town from abroad, but that we should definitely meet up next week. I couldn't wait to get out of that flat.

He gave me a long hug and kiss before I left.

I desperately wanted a piping hot shower to rinse Jason the Teacher, and The ICK, from my body, but I had to get to work. I knew I'd be teased about arriving in yesterday's clothes and really couldn't be bothered because I didn't want to talk about it. I didn't want to have to explain my sudden hatred for poor Jason either, who had done nothing wrong, or why I'd slept with him. The more I thought about the conversation, the more icky the feeling grew, so I stopped off at Zara and bought a new outfit, though I had barely any money to my name. When I felt my phone vibrating in my pocket, I thought, aghast, that it must be him. But it was Billie.

Billie:
How was the date?

I rapidly searched #theick on Instagram – feeling deflated when I noticed that I'd lost nearly twenty followers since the day before – and found a meme posted by @reasonswerenotdating of Margot Robbie sticking her tongue out, captioned, 'I had an overwhelming feeling of ickyness'. I knew Billie would understand.

Billie:
Lol. Least you cleared away the
cobwebs I guess

I was unreasonably affronted by her comment, since I'd been burgeoning with sexual energy only a week earlier. But I'd withheld the Zack scenario from Billie, given that all I ever told her was how close Lilah and I were, so the presumption of cobwebs was fair enough.

Of course, everyone at work asked about the date, despite my fresh outfit. My answer was to pull my lips up like I'd just had a very bitter sip of coffee and shake my head. I couldn't lie about having slept with him, because I knew Steph would ask him, so I turned it into a comical and rather cruel anecdote about how he was literally fucking my thigh gap while I glanced back, confused, and muttered, 'You all right, hon?' Steph was mildly defensive, but even she couldn't help roar along laughing with the others. Poor Jason.

As the day went on, I tried to forget about the whole incident. It had made one thing completely clear though: I wanted to be with Zack. No one else could compare. Not when I'd experienced what I had with him. I knew that he wasn't the ideal candidate for a boyfriend, given his fidelity history, lothario qualities and intermittent drug problem. I knew the whole thing was destined to be a total disaster, but I felt it was a disaster that I had to let happen in order to ever move on. I also knew that there was a problem called Lilah, but I kept pushing that to the back of my mind, thinking that I'd cross that bridge when, and if, I came to it. First things first, I needed to tell Zack how I felt.

I'd never in my life been honest with a guy about how I felt because I never wanted to come across as needy or desperate. I was Cool Girl, up for anything, making no demands. But Cool Girl had got me nowhere, while the girls who screamed and cried and gave ultimatums all seemed to get what they want. I wasn't about to go full-blown *Fatal Attraction* on Zack, but I was going to feel it out.

14 October 2016, 4.19 p.m.

Hi. Want to do something this weekend? x
Hi, how are you? Want to do something this weekend? Love to see you again x
Hey. What your plans this weekend? X
Hey babe. What your plans this weekend?
Hey how are you? Plans for the weekend?
Hey. Shall we hang out this weekend?x

I don't know why I felt the order of words made such a difference, but I changed them around for about fifteen minutes, adding commas and kisses until, eventually, I randomly decided on one and sent the damn message.

Me:
Hey. Do you want to hang out again this
weekend? X

Then Patrick appeared at my shoulder shouting, 'It's Prosexy Friday, bitch!'

I put my phone in my drawer and locked it, knowing that I'd drive myself crazy checking for blue ticks otherwise.

'Is it time yet?' I asked, glancing at the clock on my computer monitor. It was only four-thirty and Prosecco didn't usually happen until five.

'Time is an abstract concept. Prosecco is not!' said Patrick.

'Roger that,' I said and got up immediately. A drink certainly sounded appealing. I walked down to the corner shop, which we called 'the free shop' because we put everything from magazines and sweets to Prosecco and cigarettes on the Pure Models account, knowing that no one ever looked at an itemized bill.

When I got back to the agency, laden with bottles, I went straight to my drawer. My stomach leapt when I saw his name on my screen.

Zack:
Was just about to suggest the same.
Let's do that x

A smile spread from one side of my face to the other and I felt a warmth creep up the front of my body. I popped open a bottle of Prosecco and poured glasses for everyone, silently celebrating. I sipped it while finishing off my work for the week. Then I went to the pub with the other agents, which inevitably turned into a long night out. And for reasons I will never be able to figure out, I didn't reply to Zack's message.

My anxiety levels were no joke on Monday morning. I'd given up locking my phone in a drawer to save myself from losing my mind and was fully letting it happen. I kept the device on the desk, right by my elbow, and snatched it up every time it shook with a vibration, but every time it was just a work email that I'd already received on my computer, coming through a few seconds delayed.

I had eventually messaged Zack on Saturday night. I was at the pub for Liz's birthday. I thought it was about time I showed up to thank her for taking me in for all those weeks when I'd been homeless, but there was also an element of wanting to show off about my new life too. At about 9 p.m. I took out my phone.

Me:
Hey, what are you up to?

I'd waited and waited for a reply, but the double ticks didn't even turn blue, despite the fact that he was constantly 'online'. So, as it happened, Liz and Tim got more than they bargained for by inviting me and were stuck with a white-girl-wasted gooseberry until the early hours of the morning. When I woke up on Sunday, the ticks were blue, but there was still no reply. My hangover seemed to fuel my determination when I thought of how great it would be to have someone to cuddle me through the day. Plus, I generally gave less of a shit about things like playing it cool on a hangover. So I sent another message.

Me:

Hi. Want to hang out tonight maybe?

Nothing.

So, there I was, on a Monday morning, staring at two read-but-not-replied-to messages, wondering if I'd done something to offend the silent recipient.

'Scarlett?' said Drew lightly, and I swivelled in my chair to look at him. 'You have the infectious *joie de vivre* of . . . Camala.'

Oh, this game again. It was an agency favourite.

Despite my sour mood, I dived in with a rebuttal: 'You have the bounteous sex appeal of . . . Svetlana.'

He howled with laughter, as did everyone else at the table. It felt like an elixir, lifting me from my slump.

Drew went in for round two. 'You have the healthy, radiant glow of . . . Kailey.'

There were a few winces at that one, but more cackles.

My turn. 'You have the relevance and career trajectory of . . . Christina Lima.'

Another swell of laughter filled the room, another shot of that elixir. I don't know why we found the game so funny, given that we were the people responsible for making the careers of all these models, but it truly was hysterical, every time.

'You have . . . ' Drew squinted, thinking hard, ' . . . the grace and finesse of . . . Lilah Fox.'

That one really sent the room off, and within seconds everyone was talking in Lilah's accent about cum and other filth. We were so into it that we hardly noticed when she walked through the door and said, 'Fuck me, it's loud in here, guys!'

*

It's not clear whether the meeting that Steph and I had with Lilah following her inopportune entrance was a response to hearing our insulting impressions of her, or whether it had been planned. Either way, she wasn't fucking around.

The Chanel exclusive had gone to her head like a shot of flaming absinthe. Her first demand was that we reduce her agency commission. It was kind of ironic that her agents had worked so hard to get her that exclusive in the first place, and in doing so they had, basically, handed the power baton over to her. She also reeled off a list of clients that she wanted to work with – Katie Grand, Tim Walker, Edward Enninful, Burberry – as if it had never crossed the agents' minds to suggest her to those people, as if she needed to tell them how the industry worked. Her final point was that she expected to make a casual two million quid in the next twelve months. Even by top model standards, that was ridiculous.

'I don't know if two mil is realistic,' I began, because I was outraged that she thought she deserved that much. For the first time, I wasn't sure if I felt like her agent or her friend. She certainly wasn't acting like we were friends.

'It's doable. I'll tell all the agents that we need to push on the money jobs,' said Steph quickly, taking the beating of that power baton like a helpless animal. 'We'll get you a great contract. And definitely, we'll set up meetings with all those people you mentioned. And others. I have loads of ideas of other people for you to meet.'

'And the commission?' said Lilah.

'I have to ask Madeleine,' said Steph, running her fingers along the inside of her turtle neck as blood flooded visibly to her face.

'Where is Madeleine?' asked Lilah.

'She's on a shoot with Yulia Kuznetsova today, darling,' said Steph apologetically.

'Okay, well, get back to me about that tomorrow,' said Lilah, completely business-like. 'So I can make my decisions.'

What she meant was: '*There are other agencies in London who would kill for me now that you've made me so famous.*'

'Will do, honey. Any fun plans for this week?' asked Steph, desperately trying to go back to the amiable relationship she was used to having with Lilah.

'Going down to Soho Farmhouse with Zack,' said Lilah. 'We got back together on Friday night.'

My face slipped into a wobbly sideways smile as disappointment weighed down on me and an ache crept up my sternum. There was no shock there, because she was telling me something that, somewhere in the back of my mind, I must have expected.

Steph gave a small sigh of, 'Ah, good for you.' Then she reached for my hand under the table and gave my index finger the tiniest squeeze.

17 October 2016, 2.12 p.m.

You were never really mine but why was I not
enough for you?

CHAPTER 12

I moved out of the ceramicist's place at the end of October. An assistant at *Elle* magazine, whom I regularly hounded for go-sees ('Who cares if she's an assistant? As long as the model gets through the door, she could be meeting the tea lady for all we care!' was Patrick's motto), reposted her friend Chloe's Facebook status: 'Room in my Ladbroke Grove flat available to rent. Slip into my DM for details.'

I didn't wait around to slip into Chloe's direct messages and she was fast to invite me over to 'view the crib'. The crib, it turned out, was above a chicken shop on the top end of the very noisy Ladbroke Grove. The interior of the flat had been what I'd describe as 'gentrified', much like the neighbourhood, with parquet floors, True Grace candles and a velvet Habitat sofa bursting with ethnic cushions. It was in the heart of London, on the outskirts of the very desirable Notting Hill, so I knew it must be worth a fortune, regardless of the chicken odour that wafted up through the front window and the passengers on the top deck of the bus who you could basically high-five as they went by.

Chloe was a 27-year-old lifestyle PR who had a posh accent and a seriously deep voice. Her parents had paid for the deposit on the flat when she graduated from university and she let the second room out to pay the mortgage. She'd had, it sounded, a string of best friends living there, all of whom she'd lost to their boyfriends or job promotions in other countries, and thought it would be healthy to live with someone who 'wasn't her bezzie' for once. Chloe was friendly, if a little manic, and followed everything she told me about the flat with a self-deprecating comment: 'There's only one bathroom but, literally, I hardly ever wash, as you can probably see,' or, 'The walls are quite thin but, literally, I never get any action, so do not worry about that.' That and the fact that she seemed to have an extensive friendship group that I might be able to hop onto instantly made me want to move in.

Chloe asked me what I did for a living and I told her that I worked at a model agency.

'That's so cool! So glamorous!' she said.

So, she was the one with the million-pound flat and the posh accent, but I was the cool and glamorous one. How the perception of my life had changed.

When we got to the tiny sliver of a kitchen, Chloe opened the fridge, grabbed a half-empty wine bottle by the neck and poured two glasses. That was the deciding factor for me. Yes, the rent was a bit beyond my budget and there was a mould situation in the bathroom, but I would finally have someone to drink my nights away with. *See ya, ceramicist.*

Aside from moving, my work life had become pretty hectic. For one thing, I was the person at the agency whom Lilah called daily. Sometimes it was because she wanted to know what was on her chart, or whether she had any money to be transferred. Other times she told me how great things were with Zack and went into details about some hot weekend away, which made it hard to push him out of my head, as I was so emphatically trying to do. Often she wanted me to book her a hair appointment, or find a way for her to get a free facial, or colonic, or Burberry handbag. I had to admit, her requests were getting a bit much, especially because I was going above and beyond the duties of an agent and was acting more like her PA. But I never complained, because I was under no illusions about the career ladder I was climbing. I knew that my relationship with Lilah was my USP and that I needed to keep it strong. In other industries, I imagined, you fucked straight male executives to get a leg up, but in fashion, you befriended the hot-property women. I wasn't sure which was more depraved.

The time I put in with Lilah also paid off in my social life when she invited me to her birthday celebrations at Annabel's family's place in Marrakech. Madeleine was thrilled that I'd been invited, like it was testament to her judgement. But the question on everyone's lips was whether Steph was going. The other agents cornered me in the kitchen and muttered the question under their breath, like it was a hugely scandalous issue, and I always just shrugged in a way that I hoped implied that I didn't think it was important, though really, I felt too awkward to ask her. Finally, when Patrick, Steph and I were alone in the kitchen one day, Patrick dropped the question casually, but it still landed between us like a hornet's nest. Without looking up from the toast she was buttering, Steph mumbled that she had a family engagement she couldn't miss. I knew then that she hadn't been invited.

'That sounds way better,' said Patrick, and he meant it, but it still came out completely patronizing. 'Who would wanna spend a weekend with all those rabid, coked-up hags? Or with models in general?' And then he turned to me and added, 'No offence, babes,' before spinning off and leaving the two of us alone with that swarming nest.

I was about to say something, but Steph turned to me first and said, 'Do you not find it awkward that Zack will be there?'

I felt my heart beat a little faster. It wasn't in Steph's nature to make passive-aggressive comments, so I knew how upset she must have been.

'I've tried to forget about that whole thing with Zack,' I lied. 'It was nothing really.'

'True that,' she said, which felt like an even harsher sting.

'That's a nice jumper,' I said, pinching the fabric of her new turtle neck between my fingers, hoping that we could re-bond over clothes, something we both loved.

And we could, it seemed. Steph's face lit up and she held both her arms out to fully, proudly display the item. 'Thanks! Maje sale!'

'Love!' I said, amazed at how fast a dynamic could change over something so trivial as a turtle neck.

Even though we seemed to be buddies, I didn't forget what Steph had said about Zack. Was it meant to be a threat? A warning? A judgement? Or just a fair question? Of course I found it awkward as hell that Zack would be there, but it was in a strangely thrilling kind of way. Part of the thrill was rooted in pride. I thought he'd see me in a different light when I was part of the inner circle, one of the select few people that Lilah had included. But mainly I was glad for an opportunity to see him. Sometimes just being in the same room as him felt like enough. There had been times that I'd gone to parties with Lilah, thinking that he might be there and glancing around like a creepy gossip writer while my stomach bubbled with nerves, and then I'd hear her tell someone else that he was away and I'd feel both relieved and disappointed. Once, I ran into Johnny and Lolly, who told me that he was at another party. I leapt into a taxi, with a heart beating so fast that I had to take deep breaths to stop myself from hyperventilating, and the driver asked if I needed to go to A&E. Then, by the time I got there, he'd already left. Yes, I felt like an idiot, and yes, I did the same sort of thing time and time again anyway.

The saddest part about it was that when I did run into him, I'd pretty much ignore him. I'd mill around, acutely aware of his presence, but too ashamed to speak to him, or even look at him. I'd stick close to Lilah, thinking that he would appear at her side eventually. But usually they were independent at parties. She'd say things like, 'I really should go find Zack, but I can't be arsed,' an apathy that I envied given that I was so eager to find him. I was always so excited to see him, but it did beg the question: *What exactly was I excited about?*

I spent the days in the run-up to the Marrakech trip scouring travel sites and Pinterest boards for outfit inspo, then calling various PR companies and asking them to send their best resort-wear, which I had to make out was for Lilah. I also managed to persuade the hairdresser to touch up my roots for free, promising I'd tweet about him from the Pure Models account (which I wasn't really allowed to do), and got my nails done on the same pretence. By the end of it all, I imagined, I'd look just like Anita Pallenberg basking on a Moroccan rooftop in the seventies.

The day before I left, while I was having a bikini wax – everything off – I started writing a text to Billie asking if she wanted to come to London when I was back. Before I sent the message, my mother interrupted with a call. Her voice sounded bright when I answered the phone, and within thirty seconds she told me that she was 'seeing a man', which brought rise to a very complicated tangle of emotions.

'What? Who?' I squawked, my eyes darting around the tiny torture chamber.

'Oh, just someone. He gave a guest talk at the university. On dream theory. Turns out we share a penchant for deconstructing Freud *in vino veritas.*'

Sounded like a barrel of laughs.

'Have you seen him since?' I asked, watching a thick layer of mint green gunk being lathered over my pubic bone with a lollypop stick.

'Oh yes, he's been staying at the house with me for the past week,' she said.

At our house?

'It's nice to be able to reconcile my brain and anatomy after so many years,' she said.

'Oh God, Mum, please!' I groaned as I tried to dispel a disturbingly vivid picture that had entered my head.

She laughed. 'He really is a fascinating man. I think I might adore him, you know.'

I knew that I should be happy for her, and shouldn't I also be relieved? If she found a companion it would take the pressure off both of us. Yet the child in my head selfishly cried out, *But what about me?*

I changed the subject and told her I was going to Marrakech. I expected her to scoff at the idea that a birthday warranted a trip abroad, but instead she went off on a long tangent about *Casablanca* and some Edith Wharton novel. I couldn't remember the last time I'd heard her so animated, unless it was in an indignant, angry way, yet still I struggled to just be happy for her.

I flew to Marrakech on EasyJet. Lilah and Zack were already there, with Annabel and her new boyfriend. I imagined Jade and Moffie to be in first class on some upper-echelon airline, but it turned out they were on the same flight as me. We ran into each other on the way into the terminal and checked in together, like good friends heading off on a girls' weekend. I'd never spent time with either of them without Lilah and it felt utterly bizarre to be doing so in Gatwick Airport, where Billie and I had once managed to barter down two tickets to Amsterdam and then missed the bloody flight on account of wine and risotto at Jamie's Italian.

Moffie chatted away on the phone, her accent flitting between West London and an imitation of Lilah's Essex one, depending on who she was talking to, right up until take-off, when the air hostess told her off and Moffie retorted that she should 'get a fucking life'. Then she closed her eyes and went to sleep. That was totally fine by me, as I thought it was a great opportunity to bond with Jade. I'd had a sense, after Paris, that we'd moved beyond the acquaintance stage, but I hadn't seen her since to build on it.

At first, I buckled under the pressure and acted kind of like I did around guys: a bit too eager to please. But thankfully she was pretty easy to talk to without all the glittering beings and hangers-on surrounding her. She was also politically intrigued, in a woke, millennial sort of way, and I spent a good portion of the flight regurgitating anti-Trump trivia, which – thanks to my vociferous, intellectual mother and unhealthy meme addiction – I had plenty of.

When we landed, Annabel's driver was there to take us to the house. It was a huge assortment of neatly arranged ochre-coloured blocks surrounded by clusters of cacti and bougainvillea creeping up the walls. Jade told me that Annabel's family had bought it in the eighties, when it was rumoured to have been a brothel, and converted it into one of their many holiday homes. Apparently, they'd hosted the wildest of parties there over the years. Jade told me all about Annabel's sister's wedding – it had gone on for four days, during which time no one slept. Listening to her, I felt a rising panic that I recognized as FOMO, which was ridiculous given that I hadn't even known any of them back then.

We walked through a very opulent front door into the circular dome of an entrance hall, and Moffie shouted, 'Oi, oi!', her voice reverberating off the mosaic ceiling.

'Finally!' We heard Annabel's voice and traced it into the kitchen. It was a long narrow room that felt like the underside of a bridge and was the kind of kitchen that I imagined was usually inhabited by an army of staff. But the only person in there now was Annabel. She was standing at the stove with her bare, bony, milk-white back to us, the skin on her buttocks slack beneath tiny bikini bottoms.

Moffie wrapped her arms around her from behind. 'Dinner?' she asked, peering into the frying pan.

I craned my neck and saw a brown-white substance forming on the surface of the pan, like sugar. I was almost certain that it wasn't sugar, but I still had to ask exactly what it was. Up for a good time though I always was, there were still places I wouldn't go, and heroin was one of them.

'It's K,' said Annabel, turning around to point her nipples at me, barely a bump beneath them. She held a ketamine-crusted spatula up between us, like a weapon, to stop me from hugging her. She hated being touched, I'd noticed, and only endured it from her closest friends. 'The others are at the pool. I'll be out in a sec.'

Between the blocks of the house there was a magnificent

courtyard lined with palm trees framing a dark blue swimming pool. Lilah, Zack and a long-haired man were at the far side of the courtyard, their bodies crowded hungrily into the last patch of sun. Lilah was topless, leaning towards Zack so that he could light her cigarette. I felt a tug of frustration that he was not leaning over my naked breasts – that were bigger and better than hers – to light a cigarette, which was superseded by the thought of what a hot picture the two of them would make for my Instagram against that setting. But how weird would I have to be to post a picture of Zack and Lilah?

Moffie started her inevitable over-the-top hollering, Jade called out, 'What up, bitches?', and I waved both arms above my head excitedly, my voice caught at the back of my throat at the sight of Zack's torso glistening in the sunlight. Lilah jumped up and dived into a hug with Jade, which Moffie somehow forced her way into, so I made a bee-line for the suspect-looking long-haired man, in a clumsy attempt to avoid Zack. The long-haired creature enthusiastically introduced himself as Travis, in an Australian accent even heavier than Patrick's, and I could instantly tell that he was the sort of person who would sleep in a hammock under the stars to be 'at one' with the universe. I gathered Travis to be Annabel's new squeeze. Unexpected choice, but apparently she never stayed with anyone for that long because she always came to the paranoid conclusion that they were only with her for her famous family. At least that was one thing I'd never, *ever* have to worry about.

When I eventually dared to turn to Zack, my heart started to flutter in what felt like my throat. He wrapped his strong arm around my neck, the same arm that had once held me through the night and all day on his L-shaped sofa. He planted a hard kiss on my cheekbone and I felt him all over me. I held my breath until we separated, then an awkward few seconds passed during which we weren't sure whether to talk to each other or not. Lilah came over and threw her own long arms around me, pulling me against her warm, sticky skin. I inhaled her – coconut oil, sweat, vodka, cigarettes, cumin – and I loved the feeling of being loved by her at the same time as wanting Zack to see her loving me.

'I'm so fucking happy you're here, babe,' she said.

'Me too!'

Can you feel my crazy heartbeat?

Lilah kept one arm around me and I felt very heavily clothed when she was so exposed. I thought I saw Zack's eyes flicker at me behind his sunglasses, though they were completely black, and I couldn't help but think, *Yes, you know what's under this.*

At that moment, Annabel emerged from the house holding the frying pan of freshly cooked equine pharmaceutical. Delicious.

'Here comes Nigella Lawson,' said Travis, which should have fallen flat since there was nothing about Annabel that resembled the buxom brunette of a chef except the frying pan, but they were all drunk, so it got a good laugh.

'Ah, all my gals together!' said Moffie. Then she thrust her iPhone into Zack's hand. 'Take a picture for us, babe.' She squashed her way between Lilah and Jade, who were photo-ready, as ever, and Annabel scuttled over to join, looking like a malnourished child.

For some reason I got the impression that I'd not been invited into that particular photo, though it may not have been an invitation-only thing. I lay my hand flat along my eyebrow line to shield my eyes from the sun and pretended to be looking out at the mountains, dappled in smoky pink light. They were all completely silent while the picture was being taken and then spent ages scrolling through the images, pointing and commenting on the ones they liked and the ones that should be deleted, until they finally settled on a winner.

I suddenly had an image of Moffie's Instagram likes appearing in her eyeballs like dollar signs.

Maybe I was projecting, but I couldn't see that at the time.

So, there were staff, it turned out, but not an army of them. Just a charming English married couple who had been working there for twenty years and served us a feast in the candlelit courtyard, with soft music playing overhead. No big deal.

Without even surreptitiously orchestrating it, I was sitting next to Zack.

Jade started a hypothetical conversation about having one night to live and being able to have sex with anyone in the world, but it couldn't be with someone you'd already slept with.

'Freja Beha,' said Zack, cleverly choosing someone who looked a lot like Lilah.

'Oh, dude, come on!' said Jade. 'Your final fuck and you'd pick a skinny white chick?'

'A white *girl*, Jade,' he corrected her, with a light smile. 'Chicks are small helpless animals. Girls are not.'

'Someone's been reading *Feminism for Dummies*,' said Jade, and I laughed quite emphatically. She caught my eye and gave me the same smile that I'd interpreted as flirtatious in Paris.

I thought Zack would ignore my laughter, but he tapped my forearm playfully. 'Why are you laughing? I am a feminist.'

Sure you are, Zack. I mean, you cheated on your girlfriend, called me a slut and asked if you could punch me in the face during sex, but sure, you're the male Oprah Winfrey.

'Whatever,' said Jade, before I could answer. 'I don't believe you'd pick her if you really knew it was your last.'

I thought she glanced at me then, but I may well have imagined it.

'What about you?' asked Zack, briefly touching his knuckles to mine. 'What's your type?'

You.

Obviously, I couldn't say that, so I threw my mind back to the days when I'd been absorbed by the lives of strangers on Instagram. I realized then that my obsessions had been rooted in female idolatry, or life envy, and that I hadn't really had any boy crushes until my dark sexual urges kicked in. Suddenly I felt a passing wistfulness for the idea of being able to idolize in the blissful knowledge that the subject was entirely unobtainable and that I was safe from judgement or rejection. I shrugged my shoulders and said, 'I don't have a type, hon.'

'Good to know,' said Jade, and out came The Smile again.

That time I didn't dwell on whether she might have been flirting with me because my thoughts were with Zack. I glanced sideways at him and quickly looked away, as I always did, but that time, he saw me. Our eyes locked for no more than a second, yet I felt that second rush through my whole body. I got up and muttered that I was going to the bathroom. I don't know what I thought. That in asking me what my type was, he was trying to tell me something, rather than just including me in the conversation? Did I think that by touching my arm he was clawing for physical contact, and not just treating me like he treated all of Lilah's friends?

I went upstairs to the bathroom at the far end of the open-air corridor and I really, really thought he would follow me. I waited a few moments, standing in the middle of the room,

211

unmoving and highly sensitive to sound. After a while I got bored and went to the loo, even though I didn't need to. And then, as I was washing my hands, I heard someone say my name. I held my breath, checked myself briefly in the mirror, and opened the door.

And guess what?

No one was there. Fucking no one.

I had actually imagined it. I had convinced myself that I'd heard a voice because I so needed to believe that I was a feature of his psyche. I felt like a crazy person. Realistically, why would he come find me? He had his supermodel girlfriend right there next to him. He didn't need to risk his whole relationship for a quick fumble in the bathroom. And it would be nothing more than a fumble for him. For me, on the other hand, it would be so much more.

When I went back downstairs, there he was, still sitting at the table, but next to Lilah, his arm draped possessively over the back of her chair. A flicker of anger towards Lilah morphed into a surge of disgust at myself. She had done nothing wrong. I had. If Zack had come to the bathroom to find me, I really would've let him. I couldn't bear to look at them for a second longer, so I glanced at Jade, hoping she would catch my eye and smile again. She didn't. I sat down beside her anyway, thinking that I really might have been going gaga with a need for love.

'Where's that magic box, baby?' said Lilah, reaching over her shoulder to tickle his hand with the end of her fingers. Zack reached under the table and pulled out a Tupperware box. Lilah handed it to Moffie. 'Look, you'll like this.' Zack pinched his fingers at the back of Lilah's neck and she melted against him. I felt a claw scrape along my gut.

Moffie opened the box, full of mini plastic bags and little

apothecary bottles. 'Fuck me, it's a pharmacy!' she said. 'What is it all?'

Zack massaged Lilah's neck in small circular movements, which I actually felt in my vagina and had to draw my legs tight together.

Annabel started plucking contents from the box, lining them up on the table. She named each one, very seriously, 'Coke. K. MDMA. CK. GHB. CBD. THC . . .'

'What, no QRSTUV?' said Jade.

I burst out laughing. Jade glanced at me and laughed too. Then she grabbed hold of my thigh and squeezed it. I continued laughing to hide the fact that I didn't know whether she was into me or just being friendly.

From the Tupperware box, Annabel retrieved a bag of innocent-looking chocolates. 'We should take these tonight.'

'Yes, let's get all mushy!' said Lilah excitedly.

Zack turned her face towards him and they kissed. For a second, I wondered if he was doing it for my sake, then I realized how stupid that was. They were two highly charged, beautiful people, who were in a relationship with one another. Of course they kissed at inappropriate moments!

And anyway, Jade still had her hand on my thigh.

The mushroom chocolates were passed around the table. Everyone started checking their doses with one another, discussing the strength of different strains of mushroom and reminiscing about times they'd taken them in the past.

'I've never taken them,' I said.

You'd think I'd just told them I'd never had a sip of water, the way they all gasped and shook their heads in disbelief.

'You're in for the time of your life, babe!' said Zack.

'I'm so excited to de-virginize you! I wish it was my first

time,' said Lilah, looking at Zack seductively. How ironic, I thought, that she was using my mushroom virginity to arouse him.

'How much should I take?' I asked, holding the lump of chocolate on my flat open palm, inspecting it like a foreign specimen.

'Here,' said Zack, taking it from me. He broke off a small piece. 'About that much.'

I smiled, silently thanking him for that protective gesture, feeling that we were sharing a secret moment.

Then he did the same for Travis.

Lilah and I were compressed in a tunnel, by which I mean an armchair, and the others were far, far away, by which I mean two metres across the room. We were shrieking with laughter about the phallic-shaped lanterns hanging from the ceiling in the drawing room. We kept enacting scenarios of Annabel's mother coming home with the lanterns, exclaiming how perfect they would be for that room, and every scenario was funnier than the last.

Suddenly, Jade crawled across the floor in front of us and I felt a little creeped out, because every time I looked at her she metamorphosed into a Rastafarian man. Then Lilah pointed at Moffie, dancing to the music, swinging her head from side to side, her blonde hair flying all over the place, and that set us off again.

'She's like the Dulux dog,' I said.

At that, Lilah keeled over the side of the chair, heaving in silent hysterics. 'The Dulux dog!'

For the next ten minutes, all either of us could see was the shaggy animal from the Dulux TV commercials, dancing across the room.

The music got louder.

'I'm gonna get up,' said Lilah.

'No, don't get up,' I said urgently.

I really did not want her to get up.

'I'm going to.'

'Don't do it!'

For some reason, the thought of either of us leaving that armchair made me feel incredibly anxious.

Lilah launched herself out and tumbled far, far away from me. I couldn't be alone there, so I stood up too and walked slowly to the other side of the room, feeling like there was something metaphysical between my feet and the marble floor. I reached the others and joined them in long swinging movements, throwing my limbs light years away from my body. It was just the seven of us, but I felt like I was in a burrow of a thousand people.

The living-room door thrust itself at me menacingly. 'What's that door doing?' I said, and everyone ignored me. The door flared angrily. 'We need to keep the doors closed!'

'Chill out about the doors,' said Lilah.

I realized that I was killing her vibe, so I shut the hell up. Next thing I knew, we were all outside in the courtyard, and then naked, and then in the swimming pool. Jade was still a Rastafarian man.

I stared down at my bare breasts glowing beneath the water like two crystal balls. I tipped my head back and it formed a soft crown around my skull as the trees breathed down on me. I could see Annabel and Travis at the other end of the swimming pool, which looked like another world, and they may well have been fucking. Then I turned around and saw Lilah and Zack, right next to me, embracing. I smiled, full of nothing but love for them both.

Lilah reached out to gently tug me towards them and I floated through the water, completely weightless. Zack folded his arm around me, his fingers resting on the space between my shoulder blades. There was nothing erotic in it. Not at that moment. It was pure psychedelic love. I felt no jealousy or longing then. I was right where I wanted to be. I was part of their unit.

I looked up at the sky, a rich navy with a freckling of luminous stars, and said, 'I think we're in heaven.'

Their laughter rippled across the water. Lilah's voice came out soft and sweet, 'No, we're in hell. This is what hell will be like. Really warm. All of our friends there.'

I heard 'warm' and 'friends'.

It was four in the morning and I was craving something. The fuzzy feeling of the mushrooms had long disappeared. We'd cut the trip short when we started taking cocaine. A part of me was relieved, because although I'd felt happy on the mushrooms, I'd been on the constant cusp of anxiety.

We were sitting in a semi-circle, lock-jawed, by the wood burner in the atrium-style drawing room, all of us trying to talk over one another. I was craving something but I didn't know what it was. I thought maybe it was a cigarette, so I lit a Marlboro Light, but no matter how deeply I inhaled, it didn't sate me. I sipped on the heavy red wine, thinking that might do it, but it hardly touched the sides. Then I saw Zack drawing out thick lines of cocaine on a plate and I knew that was what I wanted. I was craving drugs. In that instant, I had a sense of how people became drug addicts. Was I a drug addict?

From then on, I honestly must have taken a line every five minutes. I waited for the few moments of elation that I knew were coming, but didn't even enjoy them because I was too busy dreading the mood dip that followed. I silently willed the sun not to come up, but, of course, it did. Suddenly, all I wanted was to be folded up, foetal.

I did the old Irish goodbye and went upstairs without telling anyone, thinking of nothing but the bed that awaited me. I took off all my makeup, brushed my teeth, did everything to make it seem like a normal night. Then I lay on top of the sheets, staring up at the white specks of light on the alcove ceiling while my eyeballs spun around in their sockets, moving light from one corner of the room to the other. There were no two ways about it – I was wide awake. I wanted to reach for a glass of water to dampen my parched throat, but my body felt like it was melting into the mattress. So I just lay there, heavy and dry, my mind spinning. Sometimes, I couldn't tell if I'd actually been asleep or not.

I was in a dense place between sleep and awake when Lilah's voice came screeching through the wall: 'You're fucking sleeping!'

I opened my eyes. The bright sunlight was leaking through the blinds.

'You always do this!' I heard her shout. 'Every time we fight, you fucking go to sleep!'

Then I heard his muffled voice: 'It's ten in the morning, Lilah.'

'Oh, as if you wouldn't usually be the last fucking person hanging off a twenty-pound note!' The wall shook as she shouted, 'Don't you dare go back to sleep!'

'Babe, I'm tired,' he whined. 'Just chill out. Come to bed.'

A few seconds of silence passed. And then I heard a dull smacking sound and realized that she was hitting him. I could hear him telling her to stop as she hissed words I couldn't make out. I got out of bed and pressed my ear against the wall,

217

knowing that I was a complete weirdo for doing so, but totally envying her connection to her rage. I visualized the scene on the other side of the wall: Lilah perched above him, like a vulture, gangly but strong, swatting at him violently; him grabbing her wrists, stronger, holding her off. Then I imagined he would pin her onto her back and put a hand around her throat. They would stare at each other, hot with lust and then they'd kiss, ravenously.

But the last thing I heard was Lilah shouting, 'Go on the fucking sofa if you want to sleep!'

And then the slamming of their bedroom door.

5 November 2016, 10.37 a.m.

I don't need anything from him and it's wrong for me to expect anything. Even if they break up I can't be with him because she is my friend. Stupid mess to get yourself into in the first place.

CHAPTER 13

I gave up on sleep and went downstairs just after 1 p.m. The divine married couple had laid out breakfast in the courtyard, with newspapers, which I guessed there was slim chance of anyone reading. Annabel, Moffie and Travis were still up from the night before. They were spread out on the poolside divan, sweating in the sun, talking gibberish. I piled up a plate with mini pastries – diet momentarily forgotten – and sat on the floor next to them, listening to their nonsensical chat while I filled the empty pit of my stomach. I couldn't be bothered to even try to get involved.

Lilah came down soon after wearing an embroidered kaftan with small tassels at the neckline, looking like she perfectly belonged to the setting, which made me feel self-conscious about my crappy pyjama shorts and T-shirt. She poured herself a cup of coffee and climbed onto the divan with the others.

'You've not slept, have you?' she said, and I could instantly tell that she was in a shitty mood.

They all confirmed that no, they had not, in fact, slept, while reaching out to touch her in a way that I could see was highly annoying.

'Where's Zack?' she asked.

'Conked out on the sofa,' said Moffie, squeezing Lilah's tiny breast in her hand, as if that wasn't completely invasive.

'Well, if he's not awake by the time the minibus comes, we're fucking leaving him here,' she said and slurped a loud sip of coffee. Definitely in a bad mood.

'Where's the minibus taking us?' I asked brightly, trying to lighten her up.

'Atlas Mountains,' she said, then prodded Annabel with her foot. 'What time is it coming?'

Annabel snatched up her iPhone to look at the time and giggled stupidly. She held up ten fingers.

'Ten minutes?' said Lilah.

Annabel nodded, grinning, and rubbed at the red skin around her nose. She flopped over and pressed her head against Travis's shin. 'We're going to be a bit late for that!'

Lilah slurped her coffee even louder. I felt like her patience was about to become a thing of the past.

Then Zack emerged from the house, yawning, his linen trousers hanging low around his waist. 'Morning, all!' He bent over to wrap his arms around Lilah, kissing her cheek.

She shoved him away and spilled coffee all over her own arm. Shaking it off angrily, she got up and said, 'We're leaving in ten minutes. If anyone's late, you're not coming!' Then she tapped me on the shoulder: 'Come up with me, babe.'

I may as well have said, 'At your service, my lady' and curtsied.

Lilah and I sat in the front two seats of the minibus. For once, I was pleased about her bad mood because I was golden child. Not that she was much fun to be with. She sat stiff and livid, glaring out the window for most of the journey, tapping her lips with the end of her finger. Zack sat behind us, spread over two seats, taking bumps of coke with Moffie, Annabel and Travis, while a freshly arisen Jade smoked a joint out the tiny crack of the open window.

Every now and again, Zack would reach over to touch Lilah and she'd roll her shoulder back in a fast motion to shake him off.

After an hour's drive, we arrived at a shack in the rocky desert of the Atlas Mountains. There were four quad bikes parked outside. My mind suddenly went flinging back to one of the last memories I had from before my parents split up: a motorcycle ride through the English countryside with my father that my mother had absolutely forbidden me to go on, but my father had taken me anyway. I remember having a sense that my mother must have forbidden it for a reason and that something bad was going to happen to me. The next thing I remember is thinking that my enraged mother looked nothing like the mother I knew as she screamed the words 'I hate you' at my father, while he held her by the wrists to stop her from hitting him.

I felt a little sick as everyone started mounting the quad bikes, but was too embarrassed to express my fears because it didn't really suit the overall vibe I'd constructed to be afraid of something so carefree. Annabel got on the back of Travis's bike and I realized that someone was going to have to go alone. I darted over to Lilah, even though I didn't exactly have confidence in her as a driver. I wished I could go with Zack – because he was a man? Because he was Zack? – but I knew that that wouldn't go down well. My stomach turned over in slow, heavy somersaults as I slipped my head into the warmth of the helmet and clipped it under my chin, pulling it tighter than was necessary, lest my brain explode. I said a silent prayer – to whom, I don't know – as I climbed onto the bike behind Lilah, straddling her and wrapping my arms around her tiny, solid middle.

'Ready?' she said.

'Born ready, hon,' I just about managed, and squeezed my eyes shut.

She pulled on the handlebar lever and off we went, speeding down the dirt path. Zack went soaring past us and Lilah upped the speed. *Oh God.* Were we about to get into some dangerous ego race? I really wished I hadn't put my life in her hands. Dust came flying up from the ground into our faces, and I tightened my grip on Lilah. She kept taking her hand off the handlebar to wipe her face, which was making me very nervous. Ahead of us, I saw Annabel and Travis bobbing up and down over the dunes and I couldn't help but imagine the most gruesome of scenes when I thought about the fact that they were on no sleep and a cocktail of narcotics. I tried to take a deep breath but it got stuck in my throat. Then, luckily, we pulled to a stop.

I breathed a sigh of relief as I climbed off the bike, my hands light and quivering, my legs itchy with dust.

'Oh my God, this is insane!' I heard Lilah say.

Coming to, I looked around. We were at a clearing among the rocky landscape, scattered with greenery, punctuated by a lavish picnic. There were Moroccan rugs, low circular tables, oversized cushions, lanterns, a delicious-looking feast and an arrogant-looking camel nearby. I'd never seen anything quite so charming in my life.

'Happy birthday!' said Annabel, spreading herself into a star-fish shape in front of Lilah. They had a long hug – even though Annabel hated physical contact – the hug of best, best friends. I guessed that I was no longer golden child.

I took a three-sixty video for Instagram stories, which I also WhatsApped to Billie, because I knew she hardly ever looked at stories and I wanted to show her how fabulous my new life was. I realized then that I'd never sent the message inviting her to London and felt a tug of guilt.

A team of waiters in traditional Moroccan dress appeared,

seemingly out of nowhere, to serve us lamb tagine with cous-cous, labneh and a pale blush rosé wine. I thought about my life seven months ago, in Topsham, pulling pints at the pub, sketching away in my amateur design book and making the odd trip down to Exeter. I wanted to bring my former self into the present moment and say, 'Look. It'll all be fine. Better than fine.'

But despite everything around me being completely perfect, I didn't feel that comfortable, and I wasn't having nearly as much fun as I did on, say, Prosexy Friday (though my Instagram feed would beg to differ). That said, I was grateful just to be there.

Over lunch, Lilah and Zack were not exactly speaking, but bit by bit her steely exterior started to fall away. She even forgot she was angry at one point and laughed at a joke he made. When it was time to leave, I thought she might be ready to ride with him, but as she mounted the quad bike, she beckoned me over. I was less terrified that time because I'd had enough wine to placate my rationality. I even thought it was quite fun as we jumped up and down over rocks and bumps. The nerves kicked in when we started traversing across a narrow path of the mountain and I stole a glance down at the menacingly steep hill beside me. Even Lilah must have been aware of it because she drove slowly at that point.

Then, suddenly, the front wheel lurched into what must have been a deep hole in the ground. The bike tipped over in one fast motion, catapulting us off the side. I remember hitting the ground and instantly rolling down the steep, pebbly slope at an alarming speed. I dug my fingers into the surface of the land, clutching on until, finally, I stopped rolling.

I lay there, in a silent panic, but with an understanding that I was intact. Whoever I had prayed to before, I was now thanking.

And then I saw the zig-zag outline of Zack's dreadlocks appear at the top of the hill, rays of light reflecting from his sunglasses. He charged down the hill towards me, frantic, truly terrified. As he got closer, I focused on his arms, winged either side of his torso to maintain balance, and imagined them reaching down to pull me up from the ground. Then I felt a gust of air as he ran straight past me. I turned my head and saw Lilah, a few metres down the hill, already half up, while I heaved pathetically on my back. Zack crouched by her. She dropped her head into his chest, looking the most powerless I'd ever seen her, and he wrapped his arms around her, holding her tight.

What I would have done to have been held like that.

I sat up. My knees were bloody and there was a graze along my forearm. Other than that, I was unscathed, on the outside at least. I stood up and started the trek up the hill.

'Are you all right, Scarlett?' I eventually heard him call out.

I nodded without looking back.

We left the bike lying on its side. I rode back with Jade, who was touchingly concerned when I reached the top of the hill, and Moffie, who had zero shits to give. Lilah went with Zack. They drove ahead of us and I watched them the whole way, feeling the least relevant I'd ever felt in my life. Of course Zack had ran to Lilah. He loved her. They loved each other. Sure, he had a problem with the way she expressed anger, and yes, she got frustrated by his impassivity, but it was that very anger and that impassivity that gave them both a sense of their own consequence. I, on the other hand, had no concept of my own consequence. That's why I managed to sleep with a friend's ex-boyfriend, easy as anything; that's why I continued to lust after him as if it were nothing. I didn't think it was affecting anyone, because my behaviour, as far as I could tell, had never had any significant bearing on another person.

I felt desperate to talk to someone about how I was feeling. I wished I could call Steph, but I felt too awkward, given that she'd not been invited on the trip. I would have loved, more than anything, to speak to Billie, but I couldn't tell her the truth about Zack just after I'd sent her a braggart video, which she hadn't even replied to.

When we got back to the Riad, the married couple weren't there, but there was a birthday cake waiting for Lilah. So we sung 'Happy Birthday' and she blew out the candles.

'I need a photo!' she said, as we were all clapping. She turned her head from one side to the other, as if reminding herself who was there. And then she handed her iPhone to me.

She wanted me to take the photo.

I accepted the phone in silence. Everyone else huddled in, surrounding the cake, posing, arms around one another. I stared at them on the screen, processing the thought that Lilah didn't want me in the picture. She had no regard for the fact that she'd just taken me over a cliff with her and that I'd lain there, with no one rushing to my side.

I tapped the bottom of the screen with my thumbnail, which still had the dirt of the mountain underneath it, and the image froze. Then the phone started vibrating in my hand and a picture of a brown-haired woman flashed up on the screen with the words 'Mum mobile' written across it. I turned the phone around and thrust it towards Lilah. She glanced at the screen, then looked at Zack. I saw a brief smile appear on both their faces and they shook their heads lightly in unison. I thought of what Zack had told me about his addict of a mother and the vitriolic picture Lilah had painted of hers, and for the first time

I recognized them as two people who viscerally understood each other, after so many years together, rather than just two beautiful creatures fucking each other to within an inch of their lives.

Would anyone ever understand me like that? Would anyone ever feel so instinctually connected to me that they would want to know more and more about me, want to know my very bones and the foundations of my emotional makeup? I just didn't believe that anyone would.

We picked at the cake, had another drink, and soon after, Zack and Lilah went to bed. Once they'd left, everyone started to get languid and lethargic. Annabel and Travis fell asleep on the divan, while Moffie sat cross-legged next to them, still taking cocaine. Jade went up to her room. I had no desire to stay up with Moffie, but I really wasn't in the mood to be alone.

That's why the glow of light spilling from Jade's open bedroom door felt so appealing when I passed it. That's why I didn't think twice about slipping in and joining her in bed to watch *Keeping Up with the Kardashians*. It was such a relief to be able to do something universally relatable with her that I wasn't even concerned about how the night would unfold. At some point I dozed off to Khloe Kardashian moaning about her 'somewhat decent-sized boobs'. When I woke up, Jade was closing the laptop and turning off the lights. Suddenly, I was very awake and very aware of her presence.

'G'night, sugar,' she said.

'Night.'

I could have stayed still and we would have woken in the morning as only slightly better friends than we were the night before, having shared the intimacy of sleep. But instead I slid a leg out, closer to hers, to test the water. She moved her leg an inch and took a loud breath in as we touched. Sure, I'd had the odd softcore lesbian fantasy before – didn't all women? – but I'd never considered it something I'd actually foray into. Yet I edged my hand along the gap between us, just far enough for her to know that it was there. Her hand found mine and we interlaced fingers in a way that felt so innocent, like two little girls at a sleepover. Then she pushed her bony leg in between my more cushiony ones and let it rest there for a while. There was a pounding in my head that was really coming from my chest. Jade was probably waiting for me to make the next move, but suddenly I wasn't feeling so sure if I wanted to. I was satisfied enough by the touch of skin and the feeling of her fingers between mine. Maybe that's all I'd ever wanted. But she was in it, and propped herself up to look down at me, nothing more than a silhouette. My heart was literally about to burst through my sternum. Her hand flattened against my cheek and my fingers gripped her wrist uncertainly. She kissed me. I only barely reciprocated because my jaw was frozen.

'You okay, dude?' she said.

I nodded and swallowed over the dry swell of my throat. 'Yeah. Sorry.'

'Why are you sorry?'

'I . . . I don't know.'

It was dark, but I could feel her smiling. 'You ever done it with a girl before?'

I laughed then, probably because I was nervous, and shook my head. Loosened by her gentle concern, I lifted my head from the pillow, reaching out my neck to kiss her. Then I clumsily grabbed her breast.

My hypothetical lesbian fantasies had always involved off-the-chain libido, sensuality and, finally, orgasm. But the reality felt clunky and unfamiliar. I didn't know what to do with my hands. I could barely touch my own vagina, let alone some-one else's. Once, I'd read that if you'd never had an orgasm, you should get to know your vagina by looking at it in a hand mirror. I'd been able to do so for all of three seconds. I even masturbated over thick cotton knickers. Jade must have sensed my reticence because she held back. I felt anxious about what she must have thought. What was wrong with me? I loved women. I was a girl's girl. I was open-minded and free-spirited. Or so I thought, at least.

Eventually Jade sighed, turned on the light and reached for her little tin of weed.

'How was that for you, sugar?' she asked, lying on her side and opening the box.

I laughed a little and lied, 'It was great.' And then, 'Have you always been into . . .'

'Women? Yeah, I really hate dick,' she said, plucking a Rizla from its pocket and laying it flat on the bed.

I laughed again. I was suddenly very concerned about the next morning. Would it be awkward? Would we pretend that nothing had happened, or would she go downstairs and simply say, 'Scarlett and I fucked last night.' Did we even fuck?

'Have you ever slept with a guy?' I asked.

'Oh yeah, of course,' she said, sprinkling tobacco into the groove of the paper, spreading it out evenly. 'When I started out modelling, I was always off on location with male photographers and art directors and I guess I was too young to know how to say no.' She pinched a bud of weed and sniffed it. 'I was so freaking angry at the world. Stereotype, right? The angry black chick. My agents used to call it my "trailer park armour". I've never even lived in a fucking trailer park. They didn't get that I was just angry because I fucking hated myself for what I was doing. God, people are weird about women's rage.'

'Were they nice to you? The men you slept with, I mean?' I asked.

'For like a second, until they worked out that I wasn't into them because I was fucking gay. Then they made me suffer for it,' she said. 'And it's not like I could turn to the women in the industry for help. They're just as bad! Once, I was shooting nude for an American magazine. There was this freakish smell, like something had died, and it was coming from my vagina. Everyone knew. It was so embarrassing. The photographer couldn't take it anymore. He wanted to stop shooting. Then the stylist, this crazy anorexic woman, took me into the bathroom, opened my legs and pulled out a tampon that must have been there for ages. It looked like a black olive. Guess what she did? She took it out and threw it into the middle of the room.'

'Are you fucking serious?' I said, sitting up in shock, boiling with anger at the thought of her humiliation. 'Did you tell your agents?'

She shook her head, ripping tiny pieces off the weed and dotting them among the tobacco. 'Either they'd do nothing or they'd complain and then I'd never work with that stylist or photographer again. I wasn't gonna ruin my career because of some bitch on a power trip. I don't even blame her. I blame the industry. There's this hierarchical power structure that puts women in competition with each other. There's no sisterhood.'

I thought of my underlying competitive attitude towards Steph, and felt instantly guilty. I was part of the dysfunctional power structure. I might even, one day, be as bad as that anorexic stylist.

'Anyway, it's boring to talk about. Tell me about you, sugar,' she said.

I got a little uneasy then because I didn't feel I had anything interesting enough to tell. I told her about Topsham, about how I had never fitted in and had been yearning to escape. I explained that I had wanted to design clothes, but had fallen into being an agent when I desperately needed a job, mainly because I didn't want her to judge me for being part of the evil nexus that had made her suffer.

'You ever had a boyfriend?' she asked.

'Nope, not really.' I was longing to tell her about Zack, but of course, I couldn't. 'There've been guys that I've had flings with, but never anything serious.'

'Maybe that's 'cause you're into girls,' she said, almost whispering.

I said nothing for a long time. Was that what it was? A long-repressed and unreachable sexuality complex that was barring me from intimate connection? Surely that couldn't be possible when I craved sex with men – or certain men – so often, and had been largely unable to engage with our encounter? I told her I needed the loo and slipped out of bed. I looked around for my knickers, careful not to take hers, wrapped myself in a muslin sarong that was on the floor and slipped out. I thought of Lilah and Zack on the floor above, having wild, penetrative make-up sex, and I knew that I wanted that. When I returned from the bathroom, Jade was dozing off. I moved the ashtray from the bed and slid under the covers, lying flat and rigid on my back.

Out of the blue, I asked her, 'Have you slept with Lilah?'

'Not for ages,' she yawned. 'She gets so weirded out every time, so I won't do it anymore.'

We fell asleep after that.

*

Zack and I happened to be going downstairs at the same moment the next morning. It was the first time that we'd been alone together all weekend. He placed his hand on my shoulder blade, digging his thumb beneath the bone.

'You okay?' he said.

No, I wanted to say. *You started this whole thing. It was meant to be fun for both of us. It wasn't meant to be you getting what you want, when you want it and ignoring me as soon as your girlfriend takes you back.*

Instead, I smiled, showing gratitude that he'd even asked, and nodded.

I flew back to London on my own – being the only person who didn't have the autonomy or money to stay on an extra day, as everyone else had decided to – feeling like a heart monitor that was displaying a flat line, which no one had noticed yet. My adrenaline levels had gone from one hundred to minus one thousand and all I could do was stare ahead.

The cosiness of my new flat was, at least, a comfort, even if it did smell like chicken. Chloe wasn't in, but there was a bottle of wine in the fridge. I drank three quarters of it, watching TV, but really more focused on refreshing my Instagram feed to see the like count on my Marrakech photos ticking up (at a slower rate than I would have expected for such deliciously plush images, I'll admit). I couldn't understand why the trip hadn't earned me more followers. Eventually, I fell asleep on the sofa.

When I woke up in the morning, I was covered in an Indian blanket, with my iPhone face down on my chest. I lifted it and read the sentences on my Notes application.

9 November 2016, 9.18 p.m.

I feel so desperately sad I can't stop crying. Whenever I think
of being alone I cry more. The very thought of how lonely I
sometimes feel devastates me. When I think about the fact
that I may never find anyone to connect with I cry.

Not even recognizing the words as my own, I deleted the
whole note, got up and dressed myself in the most extra outfit –
metallic blue pinstripe shirt, silver-sequined skirt, leopard print
coat, hat, boots, fishnets, *how do you like me now?* – and went
off to work.

Of course, I told everyone that Marrakech had been utterly
fabulous from start to finish.

Just look at my Instagram if you don't believe me.

CHAPTER 14

The Marrakech trip had been like a torrent of fuel, propelling me into wild, flapping motion. I didn't want to have to rely on Lilah, or anyone, to bring me into their world for a day out, like a competition winner. I wanted to be at the centre of my own world, leading a crusade. I wanted to be like Zack, ultra-independent with his French windows and flat-screen TV, so that the party would come to me. In other words, I wanted that promotion that Madeleine had dangled in front of me more urgently than ever. If I became an agent, I could start creating the life that I wanted, and then I would become someone. If I could prove that I was worth something by rising through the ranks, I would become respected and I would never be left lying on a hillside, alone, ever again. The agency was no longer a stepping stone to fashion school. It was my lifeline.

But despite my determination, the months that followed the trip sat on the shelves of my brain as hazy fragments, in no chronological order:

A bellboy following a crawling Lilah through the lobby of Claridge's.

Lying naked in bed, wondering if I should vomit in the bin, or make a dash for the loo.

Watching the opening scene of *The Americans* and wishing I looked that good giving a blow job.

Paying for a week-long juice cleanse and drinking white wine on the first night.

#followforfollow

Taking a nap in the fashion cupboard.

Overdue rent.

3,000 followers!

Waking up in the middle of the night to a posho house party at least once a week.

Drinks with an average-looking photographer's assistant, followed by average sex, after which he turned over and slept with his pale back to me all night.

#like4like

Fashion-induced heart palpitations.

Wanking over thoughts of Zack and still no orgasm.

Eating takeaway in bed.

Asking for a cash advance until the end of the month.

4,000 followers!

Being in a K hole and reminding myself that other people had done much worse and lived through it.

Trying to recall emails.

#fashionjunkie

Pretending I'd been to New York.

#fashioninsider

Pretending I did Pilates.

#topmodelphotos

Longing to see Zack.

5,000 followers!

Saying '*Je* cannot' all the time.

Models responding to messages entirely in emojis.

'Pawel Dyk started following you.'

The quick rise and swoop of an adrenaline rush.

The throbbing monster beneath my eye, tapping away at the underside of my skin like a warning sign.

Me and Chloe half asleep, half drunk, in front of the TV, our female worlds turning grey as Donald Trump becomes the forty-fifth president of the United States.

Sending emails around the agency of heinous cartoon characters that looked like the models.

The agency getting fined for price fixing.

'Send her home. She ate her whole family.'

'She's not relevant in our market.'

'Her nose is off-centre.'

'She looks like scarecrow after a stroke and a really hot curry.'

Judgement, judgement, judgement.

Feeling like there was a civil war going on inside my body.

Feeling like I could not go on without seeing Zack.

'I cannot believe it's nearly Christmas!'

Wishing Christmas would never come.

It was a week before we closed for Christmas when I got a text message from someone called Alana. Alana ran another model agency. Alana wondered if I wanted to meet her for a chat. I understood what that meant: Alana wanted to poach me.

A very arrogant sense of self-importance swelled inside me after receiving the message. People in the industry knew who I was. I was a step towards being 'in demand'.

It came at the end of a crazy stint where I'd been darting around with a different plan every night, evading loneliness, jumping on Lilah's plans, or Chloe's, or Steph's, attending any old fashion event and posting my whole 'fabulous' life on Instagram. I was convinced that it was my continuous presence at the opening of an envelope and my 5,000 followers that got me noticed by this other agency.

Alana and I met at a nondescript pub, one that was too random for us to run into anyone from the industry there. I knew it was disloyal to go behind Madeleine's back, but she was still taking out her anger on us over the large fine she'd had to pay for price fixing, even though it had fuck all to do with anyone but her, so my guilt diminished. The story was, Pure Models had been part of an association of model agencies that were pre-discussing rates, so that clients couldn't negotiate lower than a certain figure, which, it turns out, is illegal. Investigators had turned up at the agency like a SWAT team and dramatically seized all our iPhones and hard drives while we all frantically flushed grams down the loo. After the investigation, the agency received a six-figure fine, and Madeleine was under huge pressure from New York to make up the cost in bookings. She was constantly losing her temper, telling us we were lazy and that we should be booking money not editorial. The other agents were worried that we were risking the trust of the models by booking them on jobs that were clearly below them, just because we needed to cash in, but they never said anything to Madeleine.

Alana was nothing like Madeleine. In fact, she seemed like an older version of Steph. Although it was the first time we'd met, the conversation was as fluid as it would have been between two old friends. Just by being part of the same industry, a small industry, we had so much in common. As we got to the end of our beers — Madeleine would never drink beer — Alana explained that there was a junior booker's role going for twenty-five grand a year and that they'd heard great things about me.

'From who?' I asked eagerly, taking a sip of the warm, flat liquid.

'Oh, you know. Couple of photographers. Couple of e-commerce bookers. Trusted clients, of course.'

I felt proud and a tad smug. There was no denying the fact that I did most of my job hungover, or drunk, and there was a part of me that always felt like I was failing. That's why I'd assumed the meeting was to do with my social life rather than my work merit.

'That's really flattering. I'm really interested, but I'm going to have to think about it,' I said. I wanted her to think that I was interested because I didn't want to lose the attention she was giving me, but I already knew that I didn't want to leave the agency. Leaving Pure would mean leaving Lilah, and leaving Madeleine, and truthfully, I didn't believe I could get anywhere without them both. Despite my apparent prestige among the up-and-coming photographers and low-rate e-commerce bookers, the reality was that people knew who I was because of Lilah. Being attached to her made me desirable by proxy, and I knew that without her, I was just any old junior agent. I also knew that, as nice as Alana was, she was no Madeleine. She would never become invested in me the way Madeleine was, or send me to Paris. She was, I could tell, too professional.

I called my mother from the Baker Street platform to tell her about the meeting, even though she had few shits to give about the ins and outs of my job. I wanted her to know that I was good at it. Good at something.

'More money?' was the first thing she said. 'You should take it, obviously.'

'I don't want to leave Pure. I've got a good thing going with Madeleine.'

'Well then she should give you more money.'

'Yeah . . . I guess.' I knew I should use the situation to leverage more money for myself, but the thought of asking for more made me feel instantly apologetic. 'She did give me a raise two months ago.'

'Tough,' said my mother. 'Someone else wants you. She'll have to give you more.'

I sighed down the phone. 'I guess so.'

'Don't ask her yet though. I'll compose something for you. Wait until I send it.'

A bubbling sensation rippled along the front of my body and I recognized it as anger. There she went again, implying my total incompetence to do anything for myself. 'Do not email me anything,' I snapped. 'You don't even know Madeleine. I'll ask her.'

'Fine. You ask her,' she said, and I knew then that I had to make it happen.

I changed the subject and asked how her man friend was.

'He's okay,' she said curtly.

I could immediately tell that something was wrong. 'Just okay?'

'He's spending Christmas with the ex-wife in Cornwall. Doesn't want to be away from the children.'

A distant siren went off in my head at the realization that we'd been here before. The 20-year-old Italian poet she'd gone off with for three weeks when I was six and left me with my Aunt Margot. The literary critic, who never left his wife. Philip, the closeted homosexual. Always unrealistic choices.

'Are you all right with that?' I asked.

'Well, I have to be, don't I?'

My tube was arriving, so I told her that I loved her and that I'd let her know how it went with Madeleine.

When I got into work the next morning, I crossed my fingers that Madeleine would call in sick, though she was never sick. Worm had taken it upon himself to decorate the office for Christmas in a style that he said was 'kitsch', but was actually just heinous. There was a string of bright red and gold tinsel stretching from one corner of the booking room to the other and strings of glittery dangling baubles, which Drew said looked like anal beads.

When Madeleine strode in, dressed all in black, she stopped in her tracks and shouted, 'What happened in here? It looks like the Rovers Return!', prompting a howling laugh from everyone. I was surprised that she knew what the Rovers Return was. She'd never struck me as a British soap fan. She rapidly removed a layer of clothing and sat down at her desk.

Setting an espresso by her elbow, I forced myself to say, 'Can I speak to you, when you have a moment?' It felt like that moment you press 'send' and wish you hadn't.

'Let's do it now, before it gets busy,' she said, standing up sharply.

I picked up the espresso and followed her into her office, prickling with guilt. She thought I was going to tell her something constructive, and instead I was about to take up her valuable time attempting to manipulate her. And on top of that, she'd just made such a funny joke about the Rovers Return.

Be strong, Scarlett, don't disappoint your mother.

I wiped my sweaty palms along my jeans and said, 'So, I just wanted to let you know that another agency have contacted me.' I watched the lines at the side of her mouth twitch. 'I went to meet them. They'd heard about me through some clients . . . and offered me a job. But I said no, because I love working for you so much. But they did offer me more money. And it just made me think . . . about my value . . .' I trailed off.

Madeleine looked at me like, 'Are you done?'

I gave a tight little smile and sat on my hands.

She cleared her throat, frowning, and sat back. 'Okay. First of all, Scarlett, that is not how you negotiate. You don't tell me, from the beginning, that you've already said no. Because if you've said no, why the hell do I care?'

'I didn't want you to think I was being disloyal.'

'Then why did you meet them?'

'I just ... thought ... I just wanted to see what they were going to say.'

'Listen. This industry is small. There is not a single agent in here, or anywhere, who hasn't received a call from another agency. I get them almost every day. It doesn't mean you're special.'

I nodded as my ego deflated swiftly.

'If you want a raise, I'd rather you just asked me.'

Of course. Why hadn't I just done that?

She continued: 'In fact, if you had asked me, I would've given it to you. But now you've pissed me off and I'm not going to.' And then: 'Yulia's arriving tomorrow. She'll need a full day of go-sees and a car from the airport.'

14 December 2016, 11.01 a.m.

I should never have listened to you. You're always
ruining things.

Madeleine took a cold stance with me after our conversation, even though I was doing some next-level arse-licking. I laughed at all her jokes, made extra espressos, hated on models that she hated. She knew what I was doing, and the more I did it, the friendlier she was to Steph. *Oh, to be a master manipulator*, I thought. I felt like total dirt.

My thoughts, as they often did when I felt powerless, turned to images of Zack. Generally, the more helpless I felt, the more coercive the fantasy. No one in the office would ever have believed that while I was frowning intently at an email, I was actually picturing myself on all fours being pulled roughly by the hair. There was a strange mixture of frustration and comfort in knowing that the fantasy was only that. It wasn't like I could sleep with him again.

Instead, I decided to cope with the situation by texting a drug dealer, politely requesting that he meet me by the agency. It was Moffie's Christmas party for the *W Magazine Style* that night and what better opportunity to trash myself?

As I stood on the corner of Leicester Square, clutching my iPhone, waiting for the guy to arrive, a call came through from Billie. I rejected it, realizing as I did so that I couldn't even remember the last time I'd spoken to her. I'd sent her a video from Marrakech, I remembered that, but couldn't recall a response, or any messages since. Could it have been so long? Another call came through, this time from Coke Man.

After meeting him, I walked back to the agency with the gram safely tucked in the pocket of my jeans. As I opened the door, I caught sight of a bomber jacket that I knew so very well. Confused, my eyes went darting up to the blood-red hair, short and messy, above it. The bomber jacket whirled around.

Billie was standing in the reception of my office.

'Surprise,' she said, in a not-so-friendly tone, raising her eyebrows like, 'Thanks for rejecting my call.'

Steph was with her, as was Worm. It was a trippy moment.

I almost didn't recognize her out of context, even though she'd been my best friend for almost ten years and looked exactly as she always did.

'What are you doing here?' I asked.

'Come to be a model,' she said sarcastically. 'Here to see you obviously, you div.'

'Oh my God,' I said, in an attempt to express what I knew should be total happiness, even though I was feeling oddly uncomfortable that Billie was in my new world – the world that I'd been so eager to boast about from a distance. We hugged and I told her how busy I'd been, apologized for not being in touch.

'What happened to the rest of you?' she asked, grabbing my muffin tops, which were still there, if a lot smaller.

'Oh. Too poor to buy food,' I said, suddenly embarrassed about my weight loss, even though I loved being thinner. 'How long you in town for?'

'Dunno. Just the night I guess,' she said.

'So annoying, we've got this thing tonight,' I said, thinking of Moffie's party, which I was not keen to miss.

'She should come along with us,' said Steph. 'To the party.'

'What party's that?' said Billie, and I thought her accent seemed more Devonian than usual.

'It's the *W Magazine Style* Christmas party. It's a real banger every year!' said Steph.

'Sounds well trendy!' said Billie.

'What about the list?' I said anxiously.

'It's fine. It's Moffie,' said Steph, waving her heavily ringed hand around in the air.

As she said it, I imagined Moffie sweeping a judgmental glare over Billie and the bomber jacket that I'd decorated for her, then clocking me and putting the two of us together. I hated myself for caring what she thought.

'She said the list was full,' I said.

'She won't even be at the door,' said Steph. 'Her girls know us. We'll just walk in.'

I saw something bleak inside me, a monster of sorts, squawking that it really didn't want Billie to come to the party. I felt disappointed in myself that I couldn't be the person who laughed and told Billie that it wouldn't be her scene, that I'd sack it off and go for a curry with her. Instead, I forced an entirely fake smile and offered her a new jacket from the fashion cupboard. She didn't accept it.

Steph and Patrick chatted animatedly to Billie as we all lined up outside Tramp, an elite member's club that was big in the nineties. I was in the midst of dealing with a fashion catastrophe involving a bag of Dior clothing that was meant to have arrived at Yulia Kuznetsova's hotel, and was glued to my iPhone, showing off by acting more frantic than I needed to.

'I used to come here when I was a model and take acid,' I heard Patrick say. 'I'm pretty sure I took blow of Madeleine's nipple behind the coat check one time, but she won't admit that it was her.'

'Scizzle and I once took some cocaine we found on the floor. Remember that?' said Billie.

I smiled briefly and nodded, without looking up from my phone.

'Yeah, she's only ever done it once, haven't you, Scizzle?' said Patrick, nudging me.

'Oh, shut up,' I muttered as a message from my mother slid down the screen, telling me to donate to a Syrian rescue charity.

With one swipe of my thumb, I hid the message and continued dealing with my fashion drama.

Billie tapped my Stella McCartney shoe with the end of her trainer and said, 'What the hell is that?'

I looked down at the shoes that Steph had lent me. Granted, anyone had every right to think they looked ridiculous, given that they were made from shiny, bronze faux-leather, covered in big stars and balanced on a three-inch wooden platform, but the industry was going crazy for them that season.

'Stella McCartney,' I said tersely.

'They're like orthopaedic shoes for clowns,' said Billie, which was a fair description.

Steph and Patrick laughed, even though they knew, like I did, that the shoes were fucking stylish.

'Like my big bird coat?' said Steph, referring to the big, fluffy, yellow and green Shrimps coat she was wearing.

'Yeah! Feel like I'm at bloody Disneyland,' said Billie.

I glanced at Steph and she winked to remind me that we weren't dressing for the world – we were dressing for fashion. Only we understood the trends we followed and everyone else thought we looked like lunatics. My ten-month-ago self wouldn't have understood them, however much of a fashion junkie she'd thought she was. But she had evolved since then, and understood the secret code: appreciating the Stella McCartney shoes, or the Shrimps coat, was a sign of being an insider. Anyone who didn't understand them was clearly not in our sphere, which meant that their opinion didn't matter, or at least that's what we silently told ourselves, holding an invisible middle finger up to the 'outsider' – in other words, the old me.

We got to the front of the queue and, as Steph had anticipated,

Moffie's girls let us walk straight in. Moffie was standing at the bottom of the stairs. My stomach tightened.

'Looks wicked in here,' said Billie, gazing up at the bushy twinkling garlands and silver foil banners. Unlike Worm, Moffie knew how to do kitsch.

I agreed with her, keeping a good bit of distance between us.

Moffie greeted us with so little interest that I felt embarrassed for having been worried that she cared enough to pass judgement. When Steph asked where everyone was, she muttered something about a table by the dancefloor and turned to the next, more important guest. We shared an eye roll and headed into the main room, where we found Lilah, Jade, Annabel and Travis, among other fashion people, at the table in question.

No sign of Zack.

My heart sank.

But maybe he'll still come.

That's what I always told myself.

It was the first time I'd seen Jade since Marrakech, as she'd spent every second she wasn't modelling working with a black female activist group in New York. We greeted each other with a lengthy hug, and the scent of her – coconut hair oil, Chanel No. 5 and weed – ignited a vivid memory of the night I'd slept with her. Having that thought when I was in such close proximity to Billie made me feel anxious. I'd always had a sense that she could read my mind. I glanced at Lilah. She was dancing in a lackadaisical way, seemingly in her own world, and wouldn't meet my eyes.

Billie leaned into me and said, 'Got something to tell you.'

'Okay, just a sec. Get a drink with Steph,' I said dismissively and stepped towards Lilah. I kissed her on both cheeks, which she barely seemed to notice. 'You okay?' I asked, genuinely thinking that her offish behaviour was something to do with Billie being there, even though I knew she was apt to a mood swing and that the very idea was completely ridiculous.

She shook her head. 'Just had another fight with Zack. I'm really worried about him,' she said, over the music. 'He's in a bad way.'

'What do you mean?' I said, excited by the opportunity to talk about him.

'He's always on coke.'

Who isn't?

'I know we all take it,' she added. 'But he's lost control. He takes it at work, in the day.'

I had definitely done that too on occasion but said, 'Shit, that's bad. Do you think he's okay?'

'No, babe, he's on a downward spiral.'

Suddenly I felt a desperate co-dependent desire to call Zack. I wanted to tell him that I was also spiralling, and couldn't we spiral together in filthy, drug-clouded obscurity?

I asked Lilah if she wanted a line. She nodded, with an ironic laugh, and off to the bathroom we went. We successfully evaded the attendant and squeezed into a cubicle together. Lilah crouched by the loo and I handed her the gram from Coke Man with my oyster card. She unfolded the wrap, like tiny origami. Without looking up she said, 'So, Jade told me what happened in Marrakech.'

A rubber band snapped sharply in my stomach, but I tried to sound very nonchalant. 'Oh, yeah. It was kind of weird. Random. And weird.'

'You enjoyed it, didn't you?' she said, finely cutting up the powder in her anal way.

'I don't know.'

That was the truth. I didn't know.

She wiped the end of the card with two swipes of her finger and licked it. 'Just be careful, yeah?'

I drew my chin back against my neck to look down at her. Not an attractive angle, I imagined, especially as my face was the only part of me that wasn't getting thinner, thanks to the constant wine bloat. 'What do you mean?'

'I'm just saying, I know Jade. She'll pull you in.'

I took the rolled-up note from her, unfurled it, then started to re-roll it. 'It was just a one-time thing. We were both really drunk.'

'No. She's had her eye on you for a while. I've seen it.'

I suddenly had a thought – and what a thrilling thought it was – that Lilah could have been a little bit jealous. 'I'll be fine, babe. Really, it was just for fun.' I said, feeling the usual power imbalance between us shifting slightly. I crouched awkwardly, trying to find an angle in the small cubicle where I could reach the toilet seat with my nose.

'And by the way, she'll try to turn you off me,' she said acerbically.

'Why would she do that?' I stuck the end of the note up my nostril and inhaled.

'Because she always does that. Secretly. She's always done it.'

I surfaced and most of the line was still on the loo seat. I wiped the end of the note. It was wet. 'She loves you. She only has good things to say about you. I think she really gets you.'

At that, Lilah looked irritated. 'She doesn't get me and whatever she's told you is not true. She's jealous that you and I are friends. That's why she's into you. Why do you think she told me about you two?'

A banging sounded on the door. 'Only one at a time!'

We finished up quickly and slipped out. The attendant pointed at the silver plate by the sink. I reached into my wallet and took out a handful of twenty-pence coins, apologizing that I didn't have any more change. Lilah was already gone.

When I emerged from the bathroom, she was right outside waiting for me. She pulled me into a hug and said, 'I love you, babe. You know that?'

What she actually meant was, *'I love how you think I love you'*, but I didn't know that at the time, and instantly loathed myself for being a terrible, vitriolic human who would rather be fucking her boyfriend than in that hug with her.

When we got back to the table, everyone was on the dancefloor undulating to a remix of 'No More Tears'. We weaved our way through the familiar fashion faces to join them. Immediately, Jade planted herself right in front of me and placed her palms on either side of my neck. She went straight in for the kiss and I jerked my head aside, offering my cheek. She looked surprised, so I took hold of her hands and kept them in mine, not wanting to offend her, but also not wanting to kiss her in front of Billie, or any of my colleagues for that matter. She raised my hands to her lips and pressed against them quickly. I smiled and carried on dancing, gradually edging towards the others.

Billie was jumping up and down like a maniac, dancing how we both used to dance on all those nights out in Exeter and Bristol. She took hold of my arms and tried to get me to join in, which stressed me out. I took a few steps away from the group, prompting a look from Billie. She knew me unsettlingly well. Jade whirled around to join me. She pulled me towards her and I felt suddenly claustrophobic. Something resembling anger rattled inside me, as if she was purposefully trying to make me feel defenceless with her lack of respect for physical boundaries when

I'd been the one who'd crawled into bed with *her*. I took hold of her hands and set her away from me. She raised her palms up like, 'Okay, I get it' and spun in the other direction. Guess she wasn't familiar with rejection ...

I glanced at Billie to see if she had noticed what happened. She wasn't looking at me, but I sensed that that was almost deliberate, like she was giving me privacy. The idea that she would feed the story back to anyone in Topsham filled me with a sense of shame that I was even more ashamed of feeling. How could my supposed worldviews and emotional reactions be so unsynchronized? I was a wannabe metropolitan liberal, I couldn't even hear the first word in a sentence about social injustice without getting furious, yet I was embarrassed about kissing a girl?

I could tell that Billie was getting bored of the party since Steph and Patrick had lost interest in her and were off talking to other people. I clearly wasn't going to enjoy it either, so I suggested we leave and she agreed. When we stepped outside, I linked my arm through hers and said, 'Do you want to go for a drink somewhere?', putting on a warm front to make up for the chilliness that I knew I'd shown her all evening. I still couldn't completely relax into our old friendship, which felt odd, like I was an imposter.

'Let's just get the bus,' she muttered, fiddling around with her Lucky Strikes.

'It's okay, we can get a work car home,' I said, maybe a little smugly, and she smirked. I tried to ignore the tension and asked, 'What was it you wanted to tell me before?'

'Forget it. You're not interested, clearly.'

I knew I couldn't ignore that one, so I tried to play dumb. 'Are you okay?'

'Take a guess, Sciz,' she said, unweaving her arm from mine and shaking it out.

'I don't really get called Scizzle anymore,' I said, to avert the conversation more than anything else.

'Oh well, pardon me!' she said aggressively, stopping to light a cigarette.

'Look, I don't know what I've done to upset you, babe?'

I knew full well.

'*Babe?*' she cried. 'You won't let me call you Scizzle but you expect me to be okay with "babe"? And since when did you start dressing like you're Kylie fucking Jenner?'

'Since Paris Fashion Week.'

That time, I was being deliberately affected and annoying.

'Oh my God, who *are* you?' she said, exasperated.

'It's perfectly normal to change when you leave home and grow up a bit. You can't be angry at me for that.'

'I don't care if you change your *clothes!*'

'Then what is it? That I didn't stay in arse-fucking Topsham with you, pulling pints?'

'No, as a matter of fact, it's not. I'm angry because I came all the way to arse-fucking London to see my arse-fucking best friend, because her mum's worried about her, and she was so busy arse-fucking a bunch of vacuous dicks that she acted like she didn't arse-fucking know me!'

'I didn't act like I don't know you!'

I did.

My mother was worried about me?

'Yes, you did!' she said.

'I didn't mean to.' *I did.* 'I was just surprised. Why didn't you call me? I would've told you it wasn't a good night to come.'

'Why, because you didn't want all your fucking nobody friends to see where you came from?'

'They're the nobodies, are they?'

That was the monster talking.

'Hard to see when you're so far up their shit-holes, isn't it? Hope you're not suffocating in there.'

We were still too close to Tramp to be talking so loud, so I started to walk on.

'Are you honestly walking away?' she said.

'No, I'm not. Let's walk and talk,' I said, without turning back. 'Say whatever you want to say.'

'Why do you care so much what all these wankers think of you?' she shouted, walking at her own pace behind me.

'I don't care what anyone thinks of me!' I lied. 'But these "wankers" are my friends, Bill. I'm sorry if you don't like them.'

'Really? Half of them hardly seemed to know you were alive.'

I smirked, or maybe laughed – embarrassed, hurt and furious at her for pointing out such a thing. 'That was a big party, full of people who know each other. You wouldn't understand that, because all you've ever done is hang out in Topsham pubs with a bunch of basic bitches.'

'*Basic bitches?*'

'Yes!'

She looked at me like I was mad, or vile, for a few seconds longer, then she lowered her voice to its normal volume, which was still pretty loud. 'Just tell me, honestly. Please don't lie. Are you happy?'

I spun around and glared at her furiously.

'I've never been happier in my life,' I spat like a spoilt child.

'Liar.'

The anger rose up further inside me. I sputtered, 'The world finally gives a shit about who I am. And if that doesn't suit you, sorry not sorry about it!'

She shook her head in disbelief. 'You've forgotten who you are.'

'You're right. I have. Because I wanted to! What I'm wondering is, why don't you want to forget who you are?'

It was a low blow and I felt instantly sorry, but she'd really inched her way under my skin and I hadn't released any anger for such a long time. Billie looked as shocked as if I'd physically slapped her.

'You've met your match in these people,' she said. 'I don't know what you're looking for, Scizzle, but whatever it is, you probably don't deserve it.'

And then she left me there. I watched her go, thinking of the time at school that she'd taken the blame for the fag ends that were mine, so that I wouldn't be banned from going on the art trip, and the time she'd slept next to me on the bathroom floor because I was convinced I'd choke on my own vomit, and the way she looked at Tim like he was a piece of shit when she came to visit me at university. I thought of the way she'd taught me to smoke properly when I was fifteen. I thought of the fact that she could never have children.

I don't know where she slept that night.

16 December 2016, 3.17 a.m.

I feel hopeless and helpless and completely unlovable.

Delete note.

CHAPTER 15

Christmas came around far too soon, like it always did.

Lilah and Zack were off to Ibiza to stay with his reborn hippie mother. I imagined Lilah arriving full of charm, babbling away about Ayurvedic medicine and guided meditation, until she flipped into one of her moods, when she'd probably retreat into her iPhone and not lift a finger. Jade had gone home to New Orleans. Annabel was at her family's house in St Barths, which Moffie had invited herself along to. Steph was at home, in Manchester, with her family. Drew was in the Midlands. Patrick and Madeleine were spending Christmas together at a spa in Thailand, which everyone at the agency found hysterically amusing.

And I was in arse-fucking Topsham.

I'd never been a fan of Christmas. It always looked better from the outside. The thought of a wood fire crackling next to a twinkling Christmas tree and mulled wine bubbling on the stove warmed my heart, but when I stepped over the threshold I was bored, irritated and basically pissed off that I hadn't been born into a better family. Maybe it was a hangover from childhood.

That Christmas was particularly grim. My mother's dream theory man friend had disappeared. He hadn't called, or texted, or taken her out to dinner to explain why he was ending things. He'd just plain ghosted her, like a teenager. The worst part was, Philip was in India, so she had no one to discuss it with. I could see the pain sitting inside her, like wet sand in a sealed glass bottle, but I didn't feel comfortable talking to her about it. We seemed to operate by the silent agreement that if you didn't talk about difficult subjects, they had a better chance of evaporating.

On Christmas Eve, I decided to go to the pub to find Billie. We hadn't spoken since our blowout by Tramp, but surely a familiar setting would relax us both into our old ways. Wouldn't it? I sashayed in, wearing an utterly ridiculous outfit for Christmas Eve in Topsham: conker-brown faux fur jacket, tweed blazer, ombre turtle neck, high-waisted jeans, second-hand Gucci belt and orange silk scarf hanging futile around my neck. I'd spent almost an hour putting it together, more concerned than ever about how I wanted my old world to perceive me. I never even got that stressed about dressing for a fashion party.

The pub was heaving with Topsham locals. There were no obliterated uni students – they'd all gone home for Christmas. I pushed my way through the crowd and leant on the bar. Billie had one hand on the ale tap and her ear pressed close to the mouth of an old bloke in a cap as he belted his order at her. I knew she'd seen me but she was deliberately avoiding eye contact. I waited, listening to a local boy describe an 'epic night out' in Yeovil, to which he and his friends had gone dressed as Smurfs, and I thought, *I only ever want to be around people who are alive,* which I guess meant that I thought I was more alive than he was, even though I'd never be free or confident enough to dress up as a Smurf. Eventually, Billie turned to face me with an impatient look on her face.

I decided that the easiest thing was to completely glaze over it. How long could she really stay angry? 'Merry Christmas!' I said brightly, trying to reach over the bar to kiss her.

She stepped backwards. 'We're not mates anymore.'

I sighed almost irritably. 'Ten years of friendship and you're dropping me after one shitty night out in London?'

'Don't play the victim – no one will buy it. You know you've been a twatty friend. Never invited me up, never came back down to see me, even though you knew I was having a hard time.'

Did I know she was having a hard time? We'd spoken about her ovary problem plenty. It wasn't like I'd ignored it. I had just thought she seemed so fine. But then, I always seemed fine to everyone too.

Billie continued: 'You only ever texted me bollocks, to be honest, which I pretended to care about, until I couldn't be arsed anymore. Then you never got in touch again!'

'I'm sorry, Billie. I've just been busy—'

'Busy being a drugged-up mess with your fake friends. Yeah, I know you have!'

'Okay, enough with the "fake friend" crap. It's actually really offensive!' I almost shouted. 'You think they're fake because you're not in touch with the real world. You don't fit in here, which is fine – neither did I. But the difference is I've found somewhere that I do. And you hate that because it makes you look pathetic.' I wasn't certain I'd exactly hit the nail on the head, but thought I must have been pretty close.

Billie glared at me with a look that I interpreted as total disgust. 'Have you got anything else to say? I'm pretty busy,' she said briskly, though I knew she didn't give a damn about all the Johnsons waiting to be served.

'Yes, I do.'

'What?'

'Can I have two shots of tequila, please?' I said, every word dripping with acid.

Billie smirked. 'I don't think that's a good idea, for you.'

'Well, I'm the customer,' I said, taking a ten-pound note from my borrowed Mulberry bag and sliding it across the bar. I might as well have said, 'Keep the change.'

Billie looked at the money, looked at me, and then made a real show of filling two tequila glasses to the brim. I had intended one of the shots to be for her, as some sort of power-trippy gesture of goodwill, but I ended up throwing both of them down my throat, one after the other. A burning sensation ripped through to the centre of my chest. I whirled around and charged outside, where a smattering of drunk people by the quay were singing 'Fairytale of New York' in an out-of-tune bellow.

And then I heard a flat voice behind me say, 'Is that Scarlett Willems?'

Oh God, I thought. *Who's this going to be?*

I turned around to see two girls I'd gone to school with, both of whom had been too cool – by Topsham High standards – to hang out with me. They were wearing padded anoraks and holding pints of dark ale between icy purple fingers.

'It *is* Scarlett!' said the ex-Captain of the school lacrosse team, who was sporting the same wholesome ponytail she'd always had. 'Look at you!'

'We saw you in the *Daily Mail*,' said the Captain's sidekick, as the bellowers in the background sang something about an old slut on junk.

I smiled, pretending to be embarrassed, but relishing in the news, and said, 'Nice to see you, guys.'

'That's an interesting outfit,' said the Captain, with an ironic smile that took me right back to sixth form.

Basic bitch.

'What you doing hanging out with all these celebrities?' asked the Captain's sidekick, a little mockingly.

'Oh, well, I'm a model agent. So it's mainly work stuff,' I said casually, thinking how unfair it was that they were both thinner than me.

'A model *agent*?' said the Captain, like it was something entirely unheard of. 'So you go around town looking for fit people to sign?'

'No, we have freelance scouts for that,' I said tersely. And then, in case that made me sound like I had no power, 'Though if we happen to see girls who could be models we can sign them ourselves. But, basically, agents are the people who look after the models day-to-day, get them booked on jobs and see the deal through to the end.'

'Don't you want to sign us up?' said the Sidekick, jokingly framing her face with her hands.

At that, I excused myself from their company, which sounds harsh, but it was a joke that I'd heard from every non-fashion person that I'd ever told I was a model agent and, frankly, I was bored of it. I also felt like I'd failed to make them think that I'd become utterly fabulous – which, after all, was the point of the Inappropriate for Surroundings outfit – and I was irritated with myself for that.

'Cheer up, love!' yelled one of the bellowers, mid-song. I gave him the finger. I knew it was Christmas and all, but I just couldn't help it.

My mother's sister Margot, who was basically a less intelligent version of her, arrived for Christmas lunch. Margot lived in

Surrey and made money by selling beauty products to friends in some sort of pyramid scheme that my mother said was a Ponzi. She was recently divorced, and her two adult sons had chosen to spend Christmas with their father, which was a relief to me. Every time I saw her eldest son, George, I remembered the time he stuck his tongue in my mouth and wagged it about, then threatened to kill me when I wouldn't stop following him around. I'd always had a sense that the story might have been more sinister than I gave it credit for – given that I was five and he was thirteen – but it seemed best not to delve into it, or mention it out loud, ever.

My mother didn't want to cook, so we'd booked lunch at a farm restaurant in Taunton. There's hardly a sight as sad as a table in a Taunton restaurant laid with three crackers. I had a sticky feeling in my head from the tequila shots and half-bottle of wine I'd drunk at home, and my stomach churned every time I thought of my altercation with Billie. I knew I should just text her an apology, but that would be admitting that I was wrong, and I wasn't up for that.

'It's been rather a good year, I'd say,' said Margot, ever an enthusiast of lying to make life bearable.

'Has it?' said my mother, sawing into a piece of dry turkey that was making me consider vegetarianism. 'You got divorced!'

Whenever she was with her family, she took on an abrasive manner, and usually threw her intellectualism around in an aggressive way, since it was her upper hand on them.

'Other than that,' said Margot, tight-lipped.

'It's been a terrible year!' said my mother. 'Brexit, Trump, UKIP, Jo Cox, Aleppo!'

'Killer clowns,' I added, and my mother laughed for the first time since I'd arrived home. Oh, how happy I was to have made her laugh, even though killer clowns were fucking terrifying.

Margot turned to me and changed the subject. 'How's London treating you?'

'Pretty well, so far,' I said.

'Any glamour boys?' said Margot.

'What are glamour boys?' I asked.

'Oh, you know,' she said, 'boyfriends?'

'No, no one ever wants to go out with me,' I said, which was my passive-aggressive way of telling my mother that I blamed her for that.

'Nonsense!' said Margot. 'Haven't you met any lads at work?'

I shook my head, shoving an undercooked parsnip into my mouth. Maybe vegetarianism was no better after all. Trendier though. 'It's fashion. They're all gay.'

'I'm sure there's the odd straight one?' said Margot.

'I wouldn't trust a straight man working in fashion,' my mother piped up, her mouth turning down at the sides.

'Why not?' I said, ready for an argument.

'They've chosen to be in the most misogynistic industry in the world and that's not a coincidence,' she said, taking a sip of her wine, glancing away.

'It's not the most misogynistic industry in the world!' I said irritably, with a mouth full of food.

'It is,' she said.

'What about porn?' I said, and Margot flushed.

My mother looked a bit amused. 'Men working in the porn industry are either greedy for money or looking to fulfil a perverted fantasy. Fashion is different. Everyone knows that the fashion industry promotes unrealistic notions of beauty. Now that women are gaining financial power, body shaming is the patriarchy's strongest currency. Men working in fashion are just sublimating their fear of puissant women, by seizing an opportunity to exacerbate the beauty myth.'

'I don't know what you just said,' said Margot.

'Bullshit, basically,' I said, though really, her point made perfect sense.

'Excuse me?' said my mother, fury rising to the top within a millisecond. 'Don't speak to me like that!'

'Do you have anything to say about women working in fashion?' I said, cutting her anger short.

'Either they feel threatened by other women, or they dislike themselves,' she said with finality, truly believing that there was no answer other than her dogmatic theory.

'When you say "they", you mean "me"?' I challenged.

'I'm speaking hypothetically,' she said, wiping a watermark from the edge of her wine glass.

'You know, modelling is pretty much the only job where women out-earn men, by a fortune?' I said.

'I know. Because they're selling clothes to other women, to be worn for the gratification of men.'

'That is not true. Women dress for other women!' I said, pushing away an image of the Mulberry dress I'd worn for Zack and trying to think of those imaginary clothes that I'd pledged to make for 'real women' almost a year earlier.

'That's true. My boys haven't a clue about women's clothing,' said Margot.

The waiter came over to ask if we were all done. My mother snapped her knife and fork together, though she definitely wasn't all done. She was just done with the conversation. He took away our plates and replaced them with bowls of Christmas pudding. At that point, Margot insisted that we pull our crackers. My mother and I did so half-heartedly, with limp wrists, so Margot won the tiny tats of landfill on both sides. I had a tight pain in my throat.

On the way home, I sat in the back of the car, scrolling through Instagram. Everyone's Christmases looked so fucking dreamy. I couldn't have even faked it for a post. There I'd been, pulling a Poundland cracker, while Annabel and Moffie were having Christmas lunch on a private beach. Annabel had a big family, lots of brothers and sisters and aunts and uncles and cousins. They were wearing bikinis and trunks, looking every bit the rock-and-roll family they were, and I thought, *Why can't they be mine?* Even Steph's Instagram story of her big, rowdy Northern family singing along to 'Come on Eileen' made my chest flutter with envy. And then I saw a picture that Zack had posted. A mish-mash of eccentric-looking people at a long table, him and Lilah embracing at the centre of it, not a trace of a bad mood on her beautiful face. The caption was 'Family Figures'.

That's what I needed. *Family figures.*

Why hadn't my mother thought of that? Why hadn't she created a network of vibrant people to fill my lonely world rather than saving all her energy for her students, who disappeared after three years anyway? I don't think I'd ever seen her laugh more than when she'd told a story about one of them writing 'meta' on every single dormitory door. And then she was baffled that I chose to see life through a social media prism. Suddenly, I wondered what my life would have been like if Madeleine had been my mother. I didn't consider the fact that Madeleine was basically my mother's critical nature amplified by a hundred. All I thought about was how much more exciting things would have been.

It was dark when we got home. My mother went up to

her room, and I sat in the living room with Margot watching *Call the Midwife* followed by a nineties adaptation of *Great Expectations*. She fell asleep halfway through the film, so I turned off the TV and left her there, snoring away, with her back turned to the television.

Upstairs, my mother's bedroom door was closed. I stopped outside, thinking that I wanted to go in and curl up to her, like I did when I was a child. But then I heard her crying. She was crying because she was alone. Did she know that I cried too, out of a deep-rooted belief that I would be alone for ever? I stood outside her door, my eyes welling up, wanting her happiness even more than I wanted my own. And at the same time, that child inside me repeated the same question that it had been asking since the day my father left: *Why aren't I enough to make you happy?*

Over the next few days, I felt my mother's pain attaching to me like wet mud. I didn't speak to her about it. Instead, I went back to London, thinking that it would fall away from me, shedding bit by bit like an extra layer of skin.

Of course, that's not what happened.

CHAPTER 16

The first of January came round again, and for the first time, it didn't feel like *déjà vu*. I wasn't on a bathroom floor in Topsham, hugging a stranger's toilet basin. I was sitting in my London flat, in a Markus Lupfer jumper, with a steady income, a lesser-than-usual hangover (mainly due to an alcohol tolerance increased from months of non-stop partying) and over five thousand followers on Instagram. So why was I still picturing myself, a year in the future, as a person who was miraculously transformed? Why did I still feel like I was only half cooked?

Lilah had ditched me on New Year's Eve. She'd invited me to a party and then decided she was going to stay home and have a fuck-fest with Zack. And why would she bother going out on a freezing cold night when she and Zack could just lie in the bliss of each other's perfect arms? She didn't need anyone else to make her feel alive. She had him.

Thankfully, Chloe came to the rescue and invited me to a dinner party at her posh friend's house in Kensal Rise. Everyone was in their late twenties and most of them were couples. The role that Chloe played in the friendship group was clear. She was the party girl. The single gal about town that they invited to tell tales of drunken mischief and bring them wayward moments in the midst of marital security.

We ate the most succulent roast lamb I'd ever had at their

Graham & Greene dining table, then saw in midnight with bottles
of Veuve Clicquot – whom the hostess worked for – watching
fireworks over the Thames on their Apple TV. Then we danced to
eighties and nineties classics, slipping off to the loo intermittently
for lines. It turns out that posh people take a shit load of cocaine
too, but they're more polite about it. They discreetly ask if you'd
like to join them in the bathroom, rather than shoving a key up
your nose in the middle of a crowded room.

They weren't famous, or particularly fashionable. They didn't
have trendy haircuts, or vintage garb, or neon 'cunt' signs, or
talk about cum all the time. But they partied and went to nice
restaurants and took lavish holidays. They were wild in their
own way. Maybe it didn't have to be all or nothing.

A new mum, on her first night out since giving birth to her
baby – whom she referred to as 'The Fun Sponge' – became
my best friend after a trip to the loo where we sat in the free-
standing bathtub talking about everything from our untameable
sex drive to insecurities about the state of our vaginas. I told her
how Lilah's vagina wasn't perfect, even though every other part
of her physical being was of supermodel standard. I didn't tell
her about Jade's because that felt disrespectful, like something a
loutish guy would do. I even told her about Zack and she told
me all about the affair she'd had while she was pregnant. We
were virtually joined at the hip for the rest of the night.

When the new mum's husband was dragging her off at 4 a.m.,
she gave me the biggest hug, knowing that's we'd probably never
see each other again, and said, 'You are FABULOUS!'

I'd almost forgotten.

I had been so preoccupied with trying to dress a certain way,
act a certain way, fit in with the right people, that I had forgotten about that fabulous spirit deep down inside of me. The new

mum had picked up on it because I'd put on no pretensions that night. I was just doing me. Lilah had picked up on it too, when we first met, which is why we became friends, but it had fizzled to the point where I hardly featured in her world at all. I was like some sort of passive bystander, lurking in the shadows just to be somewhere near her relevant, bloggable circle. It wasn't me. I didn't want to be a person who watched life happen from the peripheries. I wanted my own life to take off.

Sitting on the Habitat sofa, smoking a cigarette, as the bus passed the upstairs window, I typed out yet another set of resolutions.

1 January 2017, 1.07 p.m.

NY RESOLUTIONS
Get promoted (and get a raise)
Spend less time with fashion people, more time
with Chloe etc
Stop envying or trying to ignite envy
Join a dating app
Find my G spot (or some other way to orgasm)
Limit drinking to 3 times a week
Stop taking drugs
Sign up to gym
Open savings account & save at least £100 a month
Spend less on clothes
Get up to 10K insta followers

I started a hashtag: #SecondRowAgent.

I decided that satirizing my role in the shadows was going to be my way of blowing up.

Previously, my followers had only cared about images of Lilah, or Jade, or other models. I ditched the carefully curated images with catchy captions and just went for content, content, content. I used widely searched hashtags to entice people onto my profile. I went to every fashion event, however small or big, just to get a picture, tagging locations and celebrities. I snapped a shot of every model who passed through the agency. I took selfies with them at parties, or in taxis. I uploaded models' digitals as Instagram stories with funky overlays and took Boomerangs of models' portfolios being flicked through. I found myself in the background of *Daily Mail* pictures and uploaded those with ironic hashtags. I took a selfie with Lilah whenever I was with her, regardless of how private the circumstance was, or how she was looking. I knew that it irritated her but, somehow, I had become shameless, at least in the social media spectrum.

Sure, I was still appropriating the lives of the models that my followers were so interested in, but I had found a way to bring myself into the picture.

I was thinking like an influencer.

And it was working.

I might've even been eligible for a blue tick if I kept it up.

Two weeks after we opened in January, Madeleine's smug bright mood over the killer body she'd secured in Thailand (Patrick had gained weight) turned dark. Something had happened, which I realized was the worst possible thing for her.

Yulia Kuznetsova had left Pure Models.

Yulia was the biggest model we'd represented. She was thirty years old and had been with Pure for ten years. She had shot with every major photographer, appeared on over a hundred magazine covers, fronted campaigns for high-end luxury brands and didn't even need to do the shows anymore. She brought in millions of pounds for the agency every year, and was ranked as an industry icon on Models.com. She was so important that only Madeleine was allowed to deal with her, so she couldn't even blame anyone else when she left.

Yulia had been poached by a bigger, better agency and had probably been offered a deal on commission. She announced her departure in an email to Ralph, which she merely copied Madeleine into, like she was an afterthought. She thanked Pure Models for all their hard work and wished them the best. That was it. No phone call to Madeleine. No acknowledgement of the ten years they'd spent talking on the phone every day, travelling the world, drinking champagne at Claridge's until the early hours of the morning. She'd just discarded her in an email that wasn't even addressed to her.

Yulia's swift exit unhinged Madeleine, though she wouldn't admit it, and her nickname changed from 'Crazy' to 'Hannibal Lecter'. She snapped at anyone who broke her chain of thought by speaking at the wrong time. She caused an epic furore over the smallest mistake. She decided, one day, that we should get rid of all the model portfolios and switch to iPads. I dismantled every one of them and sent the empty folders to a local art school to be reused. A few days later, she asked me for a portfolio, and when I reminded her that I'd done away with them, she denied that it was her idea and flew off the handle, calling me sloppy and useless. I really hated her that day. But at least I had 6,000 Instagram followers.

Then, in the middle of January, Madeleine called the whole women's division into a meeting and announced that, 'We need some new fucking models.'

'We just met with fourteen girls that were scouted over the Christmas holidays,' said Drew quickly.

'I'm not talking about new faces!' she barked.

'Oh, well forgive me for thinking the obvious!' he snapped back. It was always a relief to see that at least *someone* was unfazed by her.

'We need to be stealing from other agencies,' she said, banging the fingers of one hand against the palm of the other. 'They all do it and we get left behind!'

'We're up to our eyeballs in lawsuits already,' said Patrick.

'Doesn't matter. We can afford it!' Madeleine almost shouted. 'I want Jade Deress.'

Steph jumped immediately, 'I'll give her a call this week.'

Madeleine leapt down her throat: 'You've been fucking telling us for the past three years that you're going to get Jade for us. It's clearly not happening!' And then she looked at me, rubbing her fingers roughly at the side of her nose. 'Scarlett?'

I noticed that she had bags under her eyes and looked a little like I did after a bender.

'Yup?' I said.

'Can you get her for us?' said Madeleine.

'Jade?' I said. 'I can try. I think she's pretty happy with her agents though.'

'Well, talk her against them! That's what a good agent does. Tell her we'll give her whatever commission deal she wants,' she said, reeking of desperation. 'If we can get Jade, others will follow. And then that over-the-hill, trashy hag can suck my dick.'

Woke-millennial-me shuddered inside, but model-agent-me laughed along with the others. Everyone loved it when Madeleine slagged off the models.

'We don't need her, Madeleine! She looks like Salad Fingers,'
said Drew, to egg her on, which it did, and we all spent the rest
of the meeting bitching about Yulia.

When we left Madeleine's office, I sent a message to Jade.

> Me:
> Hey babe. Haven't seen you for so long.
> Happy new year! What you doing tonight?
> Want to hang out? X

It was so easy when there was an agenda at play. She replied
almost immediately, inviting me to 'hang' at hers, which I
guessed meant to smoke weed. I'd discovered on the occasions
I'd tried to smoke with Lilah that I wasn't much of a stoner. I
guessed that I was someone who liked my energy to be brought
up, not down, but I could pretend.

I went to her place after work, a Hackney warehouse that she
shared with two other models. We lay on her bed, a floating
structure suspended from the ceiling by metal ropes, and, as
I'd predicted, smoked joint after joint, filled with potent weed,
which made my eyelids droop halfway down my face. She told
me all about her Christmas in New Orleans and I fabricated a
story about mine. I even managed to snap a picture of her ironically showing off the Yeezy hat she'd been sent for Christmas
to post on my Instagram ('Yeezus Christ! @JadeDeress
#nomorejanuaryblues for #secondrowagent 😂 #girls #models
#kanyewest').

My intention, initially, had been to hang out with her as
a friend, and then broach the agency issue. But in reality, I
should have known that she wouldn't read it that way. I should
have considered how I would read it if it were me and Zack,

and how it would make me feel if I'd known what he was really thinking.

There was a moment when we fell silent simultaneously, like it had been planned. Funny how something as uneventful as a silence can be so loaded. We both knew what that silence meant and what was coming next. Jade reached over and took hold of my chin softly with her ringed thumb and skinny forefinger. In all honesty, I was just thankful for an opportunity to let my tired, stoned eyes close as she kissed me.

When we parted, she said, 'I didn't think you were into me anymore, after that Christmas party.'

I winced, the memory of my monstrous self from that night creeping into my head, with a blurry image of Billie shaking her head from the sidelines. 'Sorry. I was so stressed out that night. Another agency tried to poach me, and Madeleine found out and threw a shitter at me for meeting them. It was all a lot.'

'I'm glad that's all it was, sugar,' she said and kissed me again.

We tossed and fumbled, like eels with hands, until we were interrupted by the ringing of her iPhone. She reached over to glance at the screen, then answered to her agent. I listened to the short conversation that I could tell was based around formulating a lie to tell a client. Once the lie was settled on, she said a friendly goodbye, hung up and rolled back over to me.

'What was that about?' I asked, trying to sound as nonchalant as possible.

'I have to cancel on this Mulberry shoot on Friday,' she said.

'How come?'

'I got a bigger job in New York. But we're gonna tell the casting director that I'm sick, so don't say anything to anyone.'

'I won't,' I said, turning the information over in my brain. If Jade's agent was going to cancel her from the shoot, that meant they would need a replacement girl. I mentally shuffled through our talent board for someone with similar attributes to Jade. Camala wouldn't be right if they wanted someone of Jade's level, but I thought of another model that the agency had recently signed. Delphine. She wasn't quite the superstar that Jade was, but she was definitely on the hot list. She was based in New York and Madeleine had been pressuring the agents to book her on a London job so that we could get her into town.

'You okay?' said Jade.

I realized that I must have looked distracted, so I kissed her to cover my scheming thoughts.

I spent the night with Jade and went straight to the agency the next morning, full of excitement to relay the information I'd uncovered. I knew that Mulberry was Drew's client, but I waited until Madeleine arrived to share it, because I didn't want him to take the credit.

'So, I saw Jade last night,' I began, like it was the first line of a thrilling book.

They all looked at me – Madeleine, Steph, Drew, Patrick. Even the agents from other divisions seemed to be waiting to hear what I had to say.

'I didn't think it was the time to ask her about switching agencies, but I did find out that she's cancelling Mulberry tomorrow for another job.'

Drew twisted his face into a strange sideways smile, or grimace, obviously wondering why I hadn't already told him, given that we'd had a whole conversation earlier about his cat.

I continued: 'She told me not to tell anyone, but I thought we should try to push one of our models as a replacement. Maybe Delphine?'

'Good idea,' said Drew. 'I'll call Emma. She's casting it.'

'Hold on,' said Madeleine. She whirled around to look at Drew. 'You mean she hasn't contacted you about the cancellation?'

'Well, no,' said Drew. 'It just happened, clearly.' He looked at me to confirm that fact, but I said nothing.

'I want Scarlett to handle it,' said Madeleine, flicking her eyes between us like she was watching a game of ping-pong.

I glanced at Drew to see if he was going to object, but it was clear that he was waiting for me to do so. I spoke up, albeit weakly, 'It's Drew's client.'

'I know it's Drew's client,' said Madeleine, her eyes darting even more madly between the two of us. 'But he obviously hasn't got much of a relationship with Emma, have you, Drew?'

'We've got a great relationship!' said Drew. 'We talk every day.'

'If you talked every day, you'd know that she'd had a top model cancel from her shoot. I want Scarlett to deal with it.'

Drew almost laughed. 'Fine. Whatever. I've got a million other jobs to book.' He and Steph shared a loaded glance, and my heart sunk as I realized that I had taken the first step towards ostracizing myself.

'Good. Send her the details,' said Madeleine, before starting to type away furiously on her keyboard.

I tried to give Drew an apologetic look, but he wasn't interested. He forwarded me Emma's contact details and the original Mulberry brief. I called her, introduced myself, and told her that I'd heard Jade had been cancelled.

At first, she sounded a little angry and asked how I knew.

'She's a really good friend of mine,' I said proudly, tracing over a doodle of a chunky 3D arrow on my notepad. I quickly added, 'She told me she was sick.'

'Oh, okay,' she said in a notably friendlier tone.

I suggested Delphine as a replacement. She asked for up-to-date digitals and said she'd check with the designer. When I told her Delphine was in New York, she moaned that they had no extra travel budget, so I went off on a confident sales pitch – 'She's just shot Italian *Vogue* with Willy Vanderperre and, honestly, she's the nicest girl. She's so great to have on set. She really knows how to move' – even though I'd never met Delphine. Emma said she'd see what she could do. I hung up the phone and emailed her the digital sheet that I'd received from New York a week earlier, along with a list of all the shows Delphine walked in back in September, copying Madeleine into the email.

She immediately squawked at me across the table. 'Have you checked she's even free?'

My cheeks started to burn. 'No ... she didn't ask to option her. She has to check with the designer. New York aren't open yet.'

'But she might assume you're offering her the first option! That's how you've made it sound,' she said in a voice that made me feel utterly stupid.

Drew cut in: 'Call her up, tell her you've sent the digitals and that if she wants to option her, she needs to let you know before New York opens, so we can request the time.'

I gave him a grateful nod and called Emma. She'd already spoken to the designer and definitely wanted to option Delphine. They'd confirm her immediately if I gave them the first option. I quickly sent an email to Delphine's agent in New York.

Dear Ron,
    Please can I urgently have an option on

Delphine for the following job?
MULBERRY Lookbook shoot
Date: 13th January
Location: London (studio)
Rate: £20,000+20% plus travel expenses
Usage: Online, instore and social media 6
months only
They are ready to confirm and she would
need to fly tonight. Please let me know ASAP.
Best,
Scarlett

It was only 5 a.m. in New York, so I knew I'd have to wait a few hours for a response, but kept refreshing my inbox anyway. I was determined to book the job. I knew that if I could pull it off, Madeleine would let me take on other big clients, and that it would be the lever I needed to catapult me into the next stage of my career as an agent. The idea that I'd ever wanted anything other than this career felt almost unbelievable.

Ron replied by 11 a.m., which I calculated was six in the morning for him, saying that he'd 'circle back' to me 'pronto'.

'Ron's up early!' I remarked to Steph.

'He's probably in the gym,' she muttered.

'At 6 a.m.?'

'He's a New Yorker.'

'Oh yeah, true,' I said, as if I knew exactly what New Yorkers were like.

I waited for Ron's follow-up email, doing very little but staring at my inbox. When it arrived, I jerked up with excitement, reading the single line:

Take the time for Mulberry

I emailed Emma to give her the first option. She thanked me three times in one sentence and confirmed the job.

'Delphine's confirmed for Mulberry,' I said curtly, casually, but racing inside.

Steph let out an exaggerated gasp and stretched out her arm to squeeze me around the shoulders.

Madeleine glanced at me briefly across the table through her Tom Ford specs. She gave a quick, tight smile and said, 'Well done.'

Drew rolled his eyes, but even that didn't quash my joy.

In that moment, I understood where the reward in being an agent came from. It didn't come when you responded blindly to client requests, with a package of any models that happened to be available. It came when you went out and made shit happen. I didn't dwell on the fact that I'd basically pimped myself out to even hear about the booking.

I emailed the travel agent for Delphine's flights, organized a hotel for the following night, and wrote myself a reminder to book the cars. Madeleine told me I should pop by the shoot to meet Emma. I took that to mean that Emma had become my client.

My first important client.

I was basically a senior agent.

Towards the end of the day, Steph answered a phone call.

'Lilah?' she said to Worm on the other end of the line. 'Put her through.' A pause. And then, 'Hi, babe!'

I listened as Steph went over Lilah's schedule and finances, wondering why she hadn't asked for me. Steph was quiet for a long time, as Lilah talked at her, I imagined, and only occasionally said, 'Mmm'. Then she wished her a safe flight to Madrid, where she was shooting Spanish *Vogue* – I knew that because I'd booked the flight – and said goodbye.

I waited a few seconds before saying, 'All good?'

'Yeah ...' she said, without looking at me. 'She just wanted to check her chart.' Then she stood up and lifted a heavy coat from the back of her chair. 'I'm going for a ciggie if you want to join?'

Madeleine hated us taking cigarette breaks, but I had a feeling that Steph had something to tell me, so I followed her out.

As we lit up, she said, 'Well done on that Mulberry booking, babe. It's super exciting.'

I saw a red herring.

'I hope Drew's not angry,' I said.

She waved her hand. 'It's not your fault. It's typical Crazy. He'll get over it.'

'Hope so. I feel bad,' I said.

Then, very casually, she said, 'Babe, just quickly. I would just be a little bit careful with Lilah, and Jade, and whatever.'

Thanks for that, hon. Could you be a little vaguer, please?

'What do you mean?'

'Like, I know they're your friends. And you're free to do what you like. But just remember that Lilah's your client, and you need to maintain a little bit of professionalism. I know it's a fine line and all. But just be aware of it.'

'Did she say something to you?'

Steph shook her head, blowing out a line of smoke, then flapping it away with her hand. 'Hardly.'

'What do you mean "hardly"?'

'Well, she mentioned you and Jade.'

276

I felt heat rise all the way to the top of my head, despite the fact that it was three degrees and spitting rain.

Steph continued, very awkwardly: 'And she said something about your Instagram. But it was just a passing comment – like, she didn't sound angry. I don't think it's a big deal. Just maybe take a step or two back.'

'Why wouldn't she say something to me?' I said.

'You know what she's like. She just says stuff to whoever she's talking to at the time. I just don't want it to be Madeleine next time, you know?'

I said nothing. I suddenly became distracted by a fantasy of Zack pinning me down at the wrists and fucking me.

Steph changed the subject by telling me how much she was dreading fashion week. We finished our cigarettes and went inside. The rational part of my brain knew that Steph was a good person, that she was trying to protect me. But that horrible little devil child was shouting louder, convincing me that this was some wicked plan for sabotage. It was the same one who had burst out of me and attacked Billie, the same one who turned away from the Captain and her sidekick. I slipped into the kitchen and dialled Lilah's number.

She answered abruptly: 'I'm about to board the flight, what's up?'

'Oh. I just wanted to check if everything's all right?'

'Everything's fine.'

'Are you angry with me, babe?'

A brief pause. And then, 'No.'

'Steph said you were.'

Another pause. 'I'm not angry.'

I so wanted to believe her, but I could tell that she wasn't totally perplexed by the idea. She just couldn't be bothered to speak about it. I pressed her: 'Please just tell me if there's something wrong, okay? I never want to upset you.'

'Okay. I have to go now.'

I sighed. She cared so little, really. 'Have a safe flight.'

'Love ya,' she said and hung up.

I felt something like anger rush down the front of my body as I thought about her total dismissal of me. I had wanted her to say that Steph had had no right to tell me. That she wasn't angry with me, she couldn't ask for a better agent, and that she didn't know what she'd do without me. But no, I got none of that.

I returned to my desk, distracted and totally unable to think about what I needed to do next. Again, Zack forced his way into my mind, completely involuntarily. The craving was worse than ever. I flattened three fingers across the screen of my iPhone and stared at them. Lilah was away for the next few days. He was a free agent. But not really. It would be wrong. So, so wrong. And anyway, what was to say that he'd want to see me?

Madeleine announced that she was going home. I watched as she stood up and put on her coat. It was a new one, from Dries Van Noten, a bulbous silhouette made of magenta- and grey-panelled wool. She asked Drew to walk her out in what I gathered was an attempt to make up for having forced him to hand his client over to me. As they departed, I picked up my iPhone, squeezing it tight between my fingers, and opened WhatsApp. I typed out the message that I knew I shouldn't, but my fingers and my brain seemed unconnected at that point.

Me:
Still need to get that bra off you.

As soon as I pressed send, I literally chucked the phone away, feeling like there were creepy crawlies all over my skin. I had crossed a treacherous line. I knew I had. But I wasn't even kidding myself that I was about to step back. Crossing that line was as easy as having a bump of coke when you were meant to be off drugs.

And, he responded almost immediately.

Zack:
Oh yeah? Do you want to come over naughty?

I sent a 'thumbs up' emoji. It looked so positive, so happy-go-lucky. No one would have been able to tell that there was a lifetime of pain in that little emoji.

I quickly sent an email to Delphine, attaching her call sheet, flight confirmation and airport transfer details. Then I switched off my computer and left without saying goodbye to anyone. I didn't put on a designer dress, or high heels, or any special underwear. I went as I was, with bad root regrowth, an unwaxed fanny and sensible pants that weren't being involuntarily swallowed up by my vagina – I mean, my *pussy* – every time I moved, with the image of him pounding into me playing on repeat for the whole tube journey.

Arriving at Zack's building, I felt a strange combination of numbness and a sense that I would scream if I did not see him within the next ten seconds. I went upstairs to find him already in bed, with Boy Better Know playing from the speakers. The duvet was crumpled on top of him and the whole room smelt of man sweat and cigarettes. There wasn't even a window open. Suddenly, the flat that I'd always viewed as a symbol of his independence had the unkempt look of addiction and demise. What a turn on.

'All right, my love?' he said.

Don't call me your love, not unless you mean it.

'Fucking had the shittest day. I can't tell you how busy I am,' I said, using my shit day to excuse why I'd contacted him and 'busy' to suggest that I was very important. Only important people could be busy, obviously. I climbed onto the bed next to him, above duvet level. He reached over for an iPad covered in ready-cut lines of cocaine and balanced it carefully in front of me. 'Lilah thinks you have a coke problem,' I said, in a real snitchy manner, as I dipped over to snort two lines in one go.

'Pot, kettle,' he said, resting the iPad on his lap to cut up another.

My throat immediately started to go numb. 'Do you think I have one?'

'I mean, we all do, don't we?' he said nonchalantly, like I'd asked him if I ate too much chocolate.

'Do you think I have a sex problem?' I said. I don't know why I asked it, but evidently it was something I was worried about.

'What's a sex problem?' he said, making light of it, though it was a serious question.

A bad excuse for sleeping with your friend's boyfriend.

I shrugged. I was pretty sure that if I had a sex problem, Zack definitely did, too.

He did a line, set the iPad aside, and pulled my face roughly towards him, compressing it between his fingers like an empty plastic bottle. We kissed in a way that felt carnal, grasping at each other's body parts. I clambered on top of him. His large hands moved up and down the back of my jumper and I let out a slightly desperate-sounding whimper. He drew one elbow back and reached down in between my legs. Grabbing onto the crotch of my jeans, he said, 'Are you getting wet under there?', laughing – a little derisively I thought.

'Yes, but I haven't had a wax,' I said apologetically, feeling the coarse sprouting hairs niggling between skin and knicker.

'I don't care about that,' he said, like the idea that he would was completely ridiculous.

Of course you don't. You're older, you're worldly, you've been in a long-term relationship, you've probably been with women your own age and not only sycophantic young girls like me.

Yes, that really is what I was thinking.

I stripped down to my underwear perfunctorily, then crawled under the duvet and nestled into him, like we were a couple. All the months I'd spent feeling immobilized by the thought of him, and there he was, holding me in the sinewy shape of his arm, kissing me, pressing his whole weight over me and staring into my eyes. He took it slow, guiding himself into me gently, holding my jaw tight between his fingers and repeatedly laying soft kisses on my dry, cracked lips.

I couldn't imagine him showing the same passion to anyone as he was showing me in that moment. Suddenly, I wondered if he had other bits on the side. He had been so easily willing to let me come over, like it was nothing. I knew it was totally unreasonable, but the thought of him cheating on Lilah with anyone else made me furious.

'Do you fuck other girls like you fuck me?' I said, as he worked his tongue around the inside of my ear.

'Yeah,' he said. Then, in a filth-charged whisper, 'Who do you wanna see me fuck?', clearly thinking that my question was to do with a kinky fantasy rather than a desperate need to be told I was special. After a few seconds of silence, he repeated the question. I said nothing. He repeated it again and I slammed my fingers over his mouth.

'Just fuck me,' I said, and he did, but not for long, because he'd taken too much coke and kept going soft inside of me, which was a disappointing sensation. *Hurt me if you want to*, I was dying to say, *just don't stop*. Eventually he gave up and we lay facing each other, his arm flopped over me like a dead weight.

'Did you miss me?' I said, still hook, line and sinker for a compliment.

'Of course.'

Of course. Like it was so obvious. Like he ever gave me any inclination that he thought about me, other than when I was legs-open in front of him.

'What did you miss about me?' I pushed.

'Your perfect tits,' he said, cupping his hand around one of them. 'Your sexy body.'

I pressed my lips tight. 'What else?

'I missed the dirty way you suck my cock.'

A part of me died inside.

'So, what you're saying is, you missed having sex with me?' I said in a voice that was only vaguely frosty.

He tilted his head down to look at me and I could see he wasn't sure if I was angry or if I was trying to talk dirty. I untangled myself from him and got out of bed.

'Do you ever think about me in a non-sexual way?' I asked, stark naked in the middle of his bedroom. 'Do you ever wonder where I am, how I am, or what I'm doing? Do you hope you'll run into me sometimes, just so you can give me a hug?'

'Do you ever think about me in a non-sexual way?' he said, sitting up and sliding to the edge of the bed.

'Of course!' I said, and it was far more convincing than his 'of course'. I thought I saw a flicker of fear on his face and hurried to assuage it by ambiguously adding, 'I don't expect anything from you, by the way.'

'I don't expect anything from you either.'

'Why didn't you tell me you were back with Lilah?'

'I knew you'd find out anyway. I didn't think you'd want to hear it from me,' he said, which made no sense at all.

'Why are you still with her?' I word-vomited. 'Why do you do it to each other?'

He gave me a look that bordered on pity, or maybe ridicule, and said, 'Because we love each other.'

'You don't love her!' I said accusingly. 'If you loved her, you wouldn't be here with me.'

He laughed a little, shaking his head. 'You understand so little about love.'

My eyes flickered from Zack, to the lines of coke on his iPad, to my knickers on the floor, as I realized that it was the first real thing he had ever said to me and it was what he thought of me.

I curbed my emotions, turning very serious, and said, 'It's an abstract concept. There's nothing to understand,' aware that I was aggressively over-intellectualizing it, like my mother would have.

'Meaning?'

'When people talk about love, they're talking about pain, or fear, or desire. Maybe even happiness. But love itself isn't an emotion. Not a real one, anyway.'

Sure, I've never been in love, but I can deconstruct language.

'So, when I say I love Lilah, what do you think I really mean?' he said.

'You mean you want excitement.'

'Right. Well. Thanks for explaining that to me.' He was wandering around the room looking for something. A packet of cigarettes. He offered me one. It made a papery swishing sound as I plucked it out. He leaned in close to light it for me and, suddenly, I felt connected to him, as I always did when he made silly little gestures like that.

'Do you fuck other girls?' I asked again, imploring him to say no. 'Other than me and Lilah?'

No answer to that one.

I gathered the worst from his silence and my heart sank in between my legs. I was just one of his fuck dolls. Just another stupid girl who had toppled head first into filthy lust and understood so little about love.

Suddenly, I noticed that he was dressed – when did that happen? – and I was still completely naked. I leaned against the windowsill and crossed one leg over the other, covering my burgeoning bush in an attempt to preserve some decency, but why didn't I just get dressed?

'Don't you fuck other people?' he said, frowning as he took a swift drag of his cigarette.

An average-looking photographer's assistant, who came after five minutes and slept with his back to me all night. I left that one out, but admitted, 'I fucked Jade.'

'There you go!' he said, like it was great news. What he meant was, he really did not give a damn who I fucked.

'That's all though.' I flicked cigarette ash through an open crack in the window. 'It's not that I wouldn't. I just never meet anyone I'm attracted to like I'm attracted to you. I can't imagine having the kind of sex that we have with anyone else.'

'You *will*, babe,' he said, like he was a close friend trying to convince me that I would, one day, be happy. *You will be successful, you will be worthy of someone's love.*

It wasn't the answer I wanted.

'Can I have my bra, please?' I said with finality, although I was still naked.

He opened a drawer stuffed to the brim with socks and crumpled boxer shorts. He rummaged for a few seconds and then pulled out the black lacy H&M number that I'd been using, all this time, as a metaphor for wanting to see him.

'What would you have done if Lilah had found it?' I asked, shaking it out.

'I'd have told her it was hers,' he said, sitting down on the edge of the bed again.

'Girls know their own underwear, Zack.'

'Lilah doesn't.'

'Well, she knows she'd never have to buy anything this cheap,' I said, instantly aware of how bitter I sounded.

'Do you need money?' he asked uncertainly.

I felt my chest tighten. 'Not from you.'

'What do you want from me, then, Scarlett?'

What did I want from him? To be loved, cuddled, admired and looked after, or bent over and fucked and called a slut? I couldn't put my feelings into words. I could never put my feelings into words.

I climbed onto him, wedging his legs between mine and clung on like a koala bear. He lifted his hands to my back, and I could feel the confusion in his grip. I couldn't bring myself to tell him that I just needed to be held. I thought of the moment that he'd touched my spine at the Louis Vuitton party, and the thrill that had run through me, just because he remembered who I was. And then I thought of the first time we kissed, before I knew that he had Lilah, or any girlfriend, before I understood the situation I was in. I wanted to go back to that kiss and stay there.

I slept over that night because I knew it was the last time, and I couldn't bear to be alone with that knowledge. I woke up early, when it was still dark out. I knew that Zack wasn't asleep because he wasn't snoring loudly as he usually did. I slid my hand under the cover and crept it over his thigh, to rest on his dozing penis. My fingers worked their way underneath the doughy mound of flesh and I massaged his hairy ball-sack in circular motions. He reached for my hand and gently dislodged it. Then he turned away from me, sniffed a few times and began snoring. I lay there, basking in the humiliation, feeling hurt that he didn't even want me for sex anymore.

At 6.30 a.m., I awoke from a broken sleep to the sound of my phone ringing. It was an unfamiliar number. I answered, groggily.

'Hello, is that Scarlett?' the dim female voice at the end of the phone said.

'Yes?'

'Hello there, I'm calling from immigration at Heathrow Airport.'

Fuck.

CHAPTER 17

Agents were responsible for organizing visas for models whenever they booked them on jobs. It wasn't something that could be heaved off to assistants, like me, because it was too important. I'd never booked a job with travel before, so I'd never done a visa. But I knew that they were meant to be done.

I stumbled over my words as I tried to convince the immigration officer that Delphine was not coming into London to work, while my stomach weaved its way into an intricate knot. But she'd already had that conversation with Delphine and the poor girl was being detained.

I called Steph as I hurriedly got dressed, with Zack snoring away in the background. She suggested that I go online and quickly organize a visa. But it was too late for that.

I called Emma to let her know that Delphine was running late.

'How late?' she asked, in a voice that told me she had just woken up.

'Hopefully not too long,' I said, unsure of where I was going with the lie. 'She's just having some trouble at immigration.'

Emma said it was fine and thanked me for keeping her updated.

I glanced over at Zack. I had spent half the night thinking about what I would say to him in the morning, and whether we would kiss goodbye. But I had no time for anything. I gathered my things and left his flat.

Charging down the wide Maida Vale avenue that felt never-ending, I called Madeleine. She listened in silence as I explained what was happening, with no other choice than to admit that I'd fucked up.

She sighed down the phone. 'They won't let her through.'

'Surely if we just do a visa now?' I suggested unhelpfully.

'No, it's too late. Call immigration and tell them to put her on a flight back home. Save the poor girl a five-hour interrogation with some racist border officer.'

Her calmness was scaring me.

'What about the client?' I said.

'I'll deal with Emma.'

Well, that was that client gone. The client I'd been so exhilarated at achieving had literally just raced down through the cracks of my sweaty fingers.

'I'm so sorry,' I said, close to tears, but she'd hung up already. Off to swoop in and clean up my mess, if it was even cleanable.

When I got into the agency, the news of my epic cock-up had reached every corner of the booking room. I supposed that Madeleine had called Drew, as she always did, and that he'd told the others. I expected him to revel in my mess, but both he and Steph seemed genuinely sympathetic as I stood in the kitchen with them, shaking over a coffee in yesterday's clothes and makeup.

'What will happen?' I asked.

'The agency will have to absorb the travel costs,' said Drew.

'That's a fortune!' I said.

'They can afford it,' said Steph.

'The only thing is, if the client sues, we might be liable for the cost of the shoot,' Drew added.

'You think they'll sue us?' I asked, horrified at the idea.

'I doubt it. They just won't work with us for a really long time,' he said.

Blinking away tears, I returned to my desk and to the duties that I was actually capable of: magazine tears, portfolios, retouching fucking digitals. Madeleine had opened a door for me when she let me handle that booking, and I had stumbled through it, then straight out the back for an empty fuck. The worst part was, I still couldn't stop thinking about Zack. I knew that it was the end, but I didn't think it was possible for me to ever stop wanting him. The shame billowed over me like a chiffon layered skirt in a wind tunnel and all I wanted was for him to hold me down and do whatever he wanted to me, however he wanted, so that I felt truly powerless. I knew that it was all shades of wrong that my reaction to a work fuck-up was so filthily twisted. But it was all I had.

I went to the loo and, despite being desperate for a wee, nothing came out. Eventually, there was a tiny dribble that felt like a sharp blade. There was no ambiguity to the pain: I had cystitis. All thanks to a night of rough sex, which wasn't even satisfying. *How unfair our anatomy is*, I thought. He could wake up and feel nothing of me and there I was with a bladder infection and a bruised vagina.

When I emerged from the bathroom, Drew was there waiting for me. 'Darling, Madeleine's here. Why don't you go talk to her?'

'Where is she?'

'She's on the phone in her office. Just take her a coffee and have a chat,' he said kindly.

Grateful for the heads up, I went into the kitchen to make Madeleine's espresso, but the damn machine was broken. That alone made me well up with tears.

The door to her office was open slightly, and I could hear her shouting, 'Don't yell at me, Ralph!'

My heart sank. Ralph was her boss, the only person she answered to, and he was yelling at her – because of me.

She continued: 'She was taking initiative. She got the model booked on the job!'

My chest tightened with emotion and shame when I realized that she was defending me.

'Ralph, it's too much! My agents have too much on their plates because you won't raise the damn budget. That is why mistakes happen! You have an entire department in New York just for visas. You have entire departments, and assistants, running around in circles so that your agents can sit on their asses, eating their two-million-dollar salaries and partying with Lindsay Lohan. I can't even give my staff Christmas bonuses!'

I heard the scrape of a chair. She was up. I knocked quickly on the open door, and there she was, still wearing her coat. I guessed that she'd hung up on Ralph, which seemed like a very bold move.

'Where's my coffee?' she said sharply.

'Espresso machine's broken,' I said, sounding more apologetic for that than for anything else.

She rolled her eyes. 'Come on.'

I followed her out into the cold, even though I didn't have a coat on, and across the street to Starbucks. It felt strange standing with Madeleine in something so ordinary as the Starbucks queue. We were silent for what felt like a very long time.

'Madeleine—'

She turned to me and raised a hand to cut me off. 'Listen to me. I know all about having a good time. Having so much fun that you feel like you're swinging from the ceiling and nothing can bring you down. And then you push it so far that it's not a good time anymore. You realize the sun's up and you have to work. And then you hate yourself for having ever thought you deserved to have such a good time.'

We were at the front of the queue. She ordered a double espresso and looked at me. I ordered a cappuccino. She paid on her American Express and we moved down to the end of the counter to wait.

'I get it,' she continued. 'But it won't get you anywhere. Hard work, dedication, understanding the business. That's what will get you respected and sought after and, most importantly, well paid. That's when you'll be able to go back to the controlling parent, or the friend who thought she was better than you, or whoever, and say, "Fuck you. I don't need you. I've made a life for myself and it's a lot better than yours." Until then, everything can be gone in an instant.'

I nodded, with complete understanding, and ran my middle finger pads over the puffiness beneath my eyes, dusting away remnants of mascara. I understood what she was telling me: the party animal look was not cute on me; it was destructive. Some people could get away with it; I couldn't. Things had to change. And it was up to me, and me alone, to make those changes. My future was in my hands. What a terrifying thought that was.

And if I couldn't make my mother proud, at least I could make Madeleine proud.

I *had* to make her proud.

14 January 2017, 11.42 p.m.

Going forward:
Stop drinking until fashion week

No more drugs until a big party
No casual sex
No contacting Z
Exercise instead of going out
Organize bedroom/clothes
Organize desk
Clear flagged items
Clear overdraft
Do all washing
Shower daily

CHAPTER 18

I hadn't realized, until I made the decision to stop, how big a part of my life drinking was. Everything from work events, to my social life, to my rare nights home alone revolved around alcohol. All that darting around I'd done from plan to plan – I'd basically been darting from drink to drink. I'd actually forgotten what it felt like to be sober without a hangover. In fact, I'd gotten so used to the feeling of it that it didn't feel like a hangover as much as it did a thickness clouding my everyday life.

After the Madeleine-Starbucks conversation, I'd committed to pausing my love affair with alcohol, at least until fashion week was over. It seemed like the obvious initial step to take. For the first few days, I felt like my body was half asleep. Then I spiralled into an emotional abyss and couldn't stop crying, even though I had no idea what I was crying about. It went on and on, and all I wanted was a drink. So I turned to my dutiful Notes application to try and figure out the reason.

17 January 2017, 6.19 p.m.

Why do I want to drink: to numb the fact that I can't get a hold of my real feelings. To numb the frustration over Z. To reverse the boredom of the week. To numb the panic over my career. Because I feel I've lost control of things.

But, despite the temptation – the promise of joy trickling chemically through my body; the certainty that the undulating waves of anxiety would settle for at least a night; the twinkle of naughtiness that felt so innocent, so right, until the next morning – I didn't cave and, miraculously, I came out the other end.

Suddenly, I could wake up in the mornings without hitting snooze on my alarm for an hour and rushing into work unshowered. I started going to yoga classes, where I felt like I was breathing properly for the first time in my life. The bags under my eyes had almost completely disappeared, and I looked a lot better naked. Now I really *could* have been on @HumanLovers (if I had a lover, that was) rather than @ketflixandpills.

I knew that Prosexy Friday was going to be a struggle, so I booked myself into a life-drawing class on Chloe's recommendation. She was always cutting out alcohol then taking it up again a week later, but she said that life drawing helped her stay calm on a sober stint. When the bottles arrived at 5 p.m., I kept my eyes firmly on my computer, focusing on the upcoming fashion week schedule and not the clinking, swishing, fizzing and excitement that was going on around me.

'Off the bottle, are we?' asked Patrick, selfishly taking a delicious-looking swig from his flute right in front of me.

'Just until fashion week,' I muttered. I hated the idea of anyone thinking me teetotal. It felt off-brand.

'Oh, that's why you're suddenly in shape,' he said, making the hand gesture that he usually made to signify out-of-shape models.

'I never knew I wasn't,' I said a little resentfully. 'Anyway, I haven't stopped eating. Just drinking.'

'Honey, alcohol is the gateway drug,' he said, twinkling mischievously, and I could tell that he was ready for a real night of it. 'One glass and you want to eat every burger in town, get on the schnoz then wake up to a fry-up.'

'Booze, burger, schnoz, fry-up,' said Steph rhythmically, which made me laugh. I'd forgotten that she was once the one we'd all called a hot mess, when I'd gone so far down that path myself.

At six o'clock they all left for the pub and I felt a little sad that I'd be missing out on it all: the humorous teasing, the deep meaningfuls that were always centred around work, the one-on-ones in the loo, the laughter, the togetherness. But I reminded myself that it would be nothing new.

The life-drawing class was at a studio near Shepherd's Bush. There were two models, a man and a woman. The woman was old, probably close to eighty. She was very slight, and her aged skin hung from her frame like melting wax. The man was younger, and large – so large that his stomach almost concealed his dinky little penis. I started by measuring the proportions of the two figures against the length of the charcoal, mapping them out on the page, and then attempted to replicate the lines of their bodies in long, hard strokes. I was concentrating so hard that I didn't even have time to be judgemental. I realized that, for the first time, I was looking at a body for what it was, not what I thought it should be. What a contrast to my usual day's work that was.

I could see why Chloe went to calm her sober nerves. The forty minutes felt almost meditative. It must have been the longest period I'd gone, for months, without a thousand thoughts of Zack, Lilah, Madeleine, fashion, drugs, parties, conversations past and future tossing over in my head like clothes in a washing machine. I was there, in the moment, present.

I bought a sketchbook and pencils to take home, since I'd

thoughtlessly chucked my old ones out when I'd moved from the ceramicist's, like they were remnants of some phase long-passed. I sat on the living-room floor, using soft pencil lines to copy a picture that I'd always loved of Grace Jones in a purple wrap bodysuit. She had her arms in the air, a drink in her hand, and was bearing her teeth like a lion. Her nipple was unashamedly on show, and it was so different to the way that Pawel's subjects had their nipples hanging limply out, like they were too dumb to realize. I went over the drawing, harder, with my own lines, turning the iconic number into a more Autumn/Winter 2017 creation, with angular shoulder pads, a sweeping asymmetric neckline, a belted waist, a modern ruffled skirt with a skewed hemline and a choker at the neck, bringing that little stick figure to life. It may not have looked like a *real* woman, but it was a *fabulous* woman.

Chloe came in just after midnight to change her shoes before going out again. 'Oh my God! That's insane!' she said, breathing white wine over my shoulder. 'Scarl, seriously. That's, like, next-level amazing. You should be a designer.'

'Oh, shut up,' I said, laughing it off, but feeling a little flutter in my throat. Did I actually have talent? The thought of it made me incredibly anxious because it meant that I was on the wrong path. I wanted to reach success as soon as possible, and I didn't have time to fanny around doing the wrong thing. Chloe was drunk, and had a tendency to hyperbolize, so maybe I shouldn't take it seriously. But looking at the dress I'd just imagined up, I could see that she wasn't completely wrong. There was something about it. Certainly, there was a clear difference between that drawing and the ones that I used to produce, before I had the benefit of understanding real fashion.

'Do you want to come to the Globe?' said Chloe, her voice

sounding even deeper and posher than usual. 'I'm literally going to have one dance and I'll be home in half an hour.'

Sure you will. It sounded like something I would have said a few weeks earlier, and having to reject the invitation made me feel glum, rather than triumphant – like I was crushing a part of my spirit. Yes, I felt better for not drinking, but sometimes I kind of loved the jangling party girl in me, and I was starting to feel like she was dead.

'Have a dance for me,' I said.

'God, you're so good! I'm so jealous,' she said, but I knew that she wasn't really. After changing from high heels into trainers, she gave me a kiss on the cheek and left, shouting, 'Literally, see you in half an hour!'

I stared down at the modern-day Grace Jones.

Was it too late for fashion school? And did I really want to leave the high-octane world I'd popped myself into for the life of a student? There would be no glamorous parties, or fashion cupboards, or expense accounts, or trips to Paris. I wouldn't be able to rely on my surroundings to pump life into me and keep my cogs turning. It would all be down to me.

I looked at the drawing again. Maybe it wasn't such a work of art. Who can be objective about their own talent, anyway? The image of a wine glass – one of the long-stemmed, thin-rimmed ones, filled with a crisp white – floated into the space behind my eyes and I could actually taste it. Just one wouldn't be a problem, would it? It's not like I'd be drunk or hungover from one glass. I'd just be there, on my own, contemplating my potential talent or lack thereof, perusing Instagram, feeling lonelier with every like, every new follower, and dipping in and out of the TV.

I went into the kitchen and opened the fridge. There was a bottle, about two-thirds full. I imagined it growing jazz hands and shaking itself at me like a flamboyant dancer. Just one glass seemed so harmless given that I'd drunk entire vineyards in the past, but I'd promised myself that I wouldn't drink until after fashion week, and something told me that there was a word for someone who says they won't have something but ends up having it anyway. A word that begins with 'A' and ends with 'dict'. And would it really be just one glass? Chloe was only a stone's throw away, drinking rum cocktails and dancing in that funny little hole in the wall that she and her posh friends loved so much. Would one glass bring out that voice that told me it was fine to go out for just half an hour?

I grabbed the wine bottle by the neck, unscrewed it and turned it upside down over the sink, feeling both triumphant and disappointed as I watched it trickle away.

I'd have to buy another one for Chloe.

2 February 2017, 6.55 a.m.

I'm optimistic. It's fine to be alone. I don't need anyone. I'm calm and serene. But I still feel like crying all the time.

Another season, another fashion week.

That time, I didn't have Steph talking me through every step of the preparation. I'd had my teething season and I was a big girl now.

I was determined to prove myself. I had a clear head and would start fashion week like that, without inches of Zack inside me, clouding my focus, without the thought of Moffie's stupid party at the end of it all.

I made endless lists, charts and spreadsheets. I devised a new system for keeping up with the cars, which involved hourly check-ins with every single driver.

When we had our team meeting, I showed everyone what I'd been working on. They were impressed and doused me in compliments for a few seconds, and then they moved onto the important issues, like which casting directors should be prioritized, which girls should be aiming for which shows, whether there were any exclusives in the pipeline, what food we needed to order and the logistics of the chillout room.

When the meeting ended, I stood up and followed the agents out of the office.

'Scarlett?' said Madeleine as I reached the door.

I turned to her.

When the others had disappeared, she said, 'You keep this up and I promise I'll make you an agent by summer.'

I smiled, and my insides turned gooey with love for her. That was all I needed to hear: Madeleine rewarding me for hard work, not for being friends with Lilah. 'Thank you.'

She nodded curtly, gave a tight smile, and said, 'And don't forget to get Jade.'

Shit.

I had to break my sobriety to even begin to think about how I was going to 'get Jade', like she was a suitcase of dirty cash that I was employed to steal, rather than a supposed friend. I found a bottle of vodka in the agency freezer left over from when Patrick and I had come back after the pub closed one Prosexy Friday and yapped each other's ears off. I downed it with a bit of soda water, for courage, then messaged Jade to suggest an after-work drink, even though I knew that was outside her orbit, given that she didn't work a nine-to-five job and that she was a stoner. Inevitably, she told me she didn't want to leave her flat, but that I could come over if I wanted to. I didn't want to, because I knew what would happen, and teetering on the fringes of morality, I didn't want to be a person who manipulated someone into a business deal while lying naked in their bed.

But I went anyway, because I had to do it, for Madeleine.

There were a load of dodgy-looking people there – her flat-mates, two American skater dudes, a weed dealer – and they were all stoned. I sat on the sofa next to Jade, breaking my drug-free stint for a joint and hating every moment of it. Stoner life really was *not* my bag.

I knew it wasn't an appropriate time to ask, but really, when was an appropriate time?

'How are your fashion week options looking?' I asked.

She ignored the question – because who wants to talk about work when they're getting stoned? – and laughed at something one of the American guys said.

I was too tired and too desperate to sit it out any longer. So, I swallowed the last bit of virtue I had left in me, took her hand and led her into her own bedroom.

There was the usual kiss and fumble, more vigorous from my side than usual. Jade pulled her T-shirt down to reveal a nipple and it reminded me of Grace Jones in that picture I'd copied, which sent a sudden spasm of *Oh fuck, I'm pursuing the wrong life* through me. Then her nipple was in my mouth and I remember thinking that it was the texture of spinach. Through that mouthful of tit, I asked her when she was going to New York for fashion week, with a breathless air of 'Because I want to see you again before you do.'

'I'm not,' she said. 'Burberry exclusive, baby.'

I unsuckled the breast to congratulate her, but then I remembered something I'd heard in the meeting earlier that day: Burberry only booked British girls for their campaign, so there was no point in booking anyone on a Burberry exclusive unless they were pure Brit.

I repeated that information to her in a critical way, regurgitating knowledge way beyond my understanding.

She smiled a little, shaking her head, and let the T-shirt slide back into place. 'It's an exclusive with the casting director. Means I'll get all their shows: Burberry, Gucci, Saint Laurent. Then I don't have to bother with the other shit.'

I stumbled over my words a few times and eventually said, 'But what about Chanel?'

She shrugged. 'I already have a relationship with Chanel, but I don't have one with Gucci or Saint Laurent. It was a strategic decision.'

'Is there a campaign attached?' I asked, sounding far too invested.

Jade squinted at me, and I knew that she knew I was skirting around something.

I went for it, far too eager: 'Would you ever think of switching agencies?'

'You mean to Pure?'

'Yeah ... would you?'

'No. I wouldn't.' She slid off the bed and zipped up her jeans.

'Why not?'

'I think Madeleine's kinda crazy, to be honest. And I like my agents. Also, I wouldn't wanna be at the same agency as Lilah.'

'Don't worry about Lilah,' I said.

Jade looked up sharply and then smirked.

'I mean ... that's my job to ... worry about Lilah. Is what I mean,' I said uncertainly.

'Yeah, you keep worrying about her, sugar.' She gave me a hostile look and left the room. Embarrassed and saturated in disgust at my own momentary brazenness, I got dressed. I rejoined everyone in the living room, knowing that I'd failed to do what I'd come to do and had only managed to piss off someone who had never been anything but kind to me. Jade was squeezed into an armchair with one of the American guys and did not look at me again.

I left soon after that, self-reproachful and a little panicked.

The next morning, I was a little late to work because of a signal failure on the tube. I was dreading telling Madeleine that Jade would never move to Pure, and of course I wouldn't be able to say that it was anything to do with the fact that she thought Madeleine was 'kinda crazy'. At least I could blame it on the fact that she didn't want to be at the same agency as Lilah, but I knew that a good agent would have been able to talk her around that.

As soon as I entered the booking room, Drew stood up and rushed over to me. 'Madeleine needs to talk to you.'

'Is she in already?' I said.

'No. But wait in her office.'

'Let me just take my coat off and get through some emails.'

'Darling, go straight to her office. She needs to talk to you as soon as she gets in,' he said in a voice that told me he was not fucking around.

It was serious.

I could have vomited.

CHAPTER 19

'Madeleine will want an espresso,' I said as Drew sat me down in her office.

'I'll make it,' he said in an unusually soft voice.

But that's my job.

'Okay, what the hell is going on?' I implored, with evident panic in my voice.

'I don't know, sweetheart.'

'That is a lie, Drew! Of course you know.'

He shook his head. 'You'll have to wait for Crazy.'

I appreciated that, even in that moment, he'd tried to lighten the mood by calling her Crazy, which made me think that everything would be fine. And then he left me in there, like it was a holding cell. I took off my coat and waited. I checked my phone. Nothing from Madeleine. Only a bunch of rectangles telling me that a load more randoms had followed me on Instagram. I was too anxious to feel any frisson of excitement.

When she eventually arrived, she was calm. That really terrified me. She sat down, pinched the bridge of her nose between perfectly manicured fingers, and said, 'Lilah is suing the agency.'

For a few seconds, I felt a sense of relief. This dramatic meeting was nothing to do with me. Lilah was suing the agency over a rogue booking, or a financial matter, and Madeleine wanted my help placating her.

Then, she continued: 'She's suing us for putting her in the hands of an employee she deems unfit. She said she has proof that you two have taken drugs together. And that she felt pressured to take them, in order to please you.'

My jaw dropped, astonished, genuinely thinking that Lilah had gone mad. 'You know that's ridiculous!'

'She knows about you and Zack, Scarlett!'

A hot tingle rippled all over my body, inside and out. I felt like my thoughts were bubbling away at the front of my brain, but I couldn't quite hear or see them. At first, I couldn't draw any breath at all, and then I drew too much. Of course, I'd always known, somewhere in the back of my mind, that this moment would come. But still, I wasn't prepared for it.

'And why did you tell her that your mother was a friend of mine?' said Madeleine, sounding more outraged by that idea than anything else. 'I don't know your mother.'

My heart quickened and my neck burnt hot. 'I didn't tell her that. I don't know where she's got that,' I lied, hoping she'd just let that one slip away.

Madeleine sighed. 'Scarlett. You know that if Lilah leaves us, others will follow. I can't afford that.'

I blinked, trying to comprehend what was happening. 'Are you firing me?'

'I really hope not.'

I was silent for a few seconds, desperately hoping that she was about to offer me a solution.

But she didn't.

'You want me to resign?'

She threw her arms out like, 'What do you think?'

'What about fashion week?' was all I could say, as if I was indispensable to them.

Madeleine just pressed her lips together and shook her head.

'Madeleine, please give me a chance to fix things.'

'How are you gonna fix things, Scarlett?' she said, suddenly losing her cool.

'I'll talk to her. He came after me. He didn't tell me he had a girlfriend—'

She cut me off: 'She's not going to give a shit about any of that. You know that! She'll believe what she wants to about him.'

'But it's not fair that I lose my job over it!' I said indignantly, feeling like I wanted to appeal to some governing body of elicit affairs.

There was a pause. And then, without looking at me, she said, 'Lilah's coming in to hear our appeal. I need you out by then.' She said it with such finality that I knew she wasn't going to change her mind, not ever.

A sharp pain shot down my throat. 'I'm so sorry.'

Madeleine sighed and then, to my surprise, she said, 'It's my fault. I gave you more than you could handle.'

I thought of my mother, who didn't even think I could handle an onion. Madeleine had believed in me. She had given me a chance. And I'd disappointed her, just like I knew I'd always disappoint my mother. I wanted to blame someone, but there was no denying that I had totally and utterly fucked this one up myself.

'How did she find out?' I asked, suddenly and horrifyingly remembering that video I'd let Zack make of me. I'd always assumed he'd deleted it when he got back with Lilah. Isn't that what you'd do?

'Someone told her,' said Madeleine.

'Steph?'

'Not Steph.'

I didn't believe her. Who else could it have been? I felt hurt that

Steph, who was meant to be my friend, would betray me like that. Hurt, but not surprised. I'd always wondered why she hadn't used it against me. My expression must have given away my thoughts.

Madeleine said, 'Don't you dare try and blame Steph for this!'

Hearing her fierce loyalty towards Steph made my throat tighten, knowing that she would never fight my corner again like that. I imagined the conversation she'd had with Lilah about me. Had she defended me for a few seconds, before realizing that what Lilah was saying was true?

'Can you help me get another job?' I asked helplessly, begging her to make things better.

'In fashion?' she said, and I nodded. She laughed a little. 'No one will employ you after this, Scarlett. Lilah will make sure of that.'

'What am I going to do?' I said with desperation, feeling like I was shrinking under my own vulnerability.

Madeleine just shook her head and said, 'Go home and start over,' with no idea of how horrendous that sounded to me. She stood up. 'I'll walk you to the door.'

'Can I say goodbye to everyone?'

'You really want to go out there and explain this to them?'

I shook my head, as the last year of my life reeled off in my mind and I thought, *This is what it's like to die.* Dramatic, sure, but it really was how I felt.

Madeleine frog-marched me out of the building as Worm watched curiously through his thick-rimmed glasses. On the other side of the door, she said, 'Send me a resignation letter, so I don't have to issue a dismissal.' Then she gave me a look that made me want to cry. It was a look of regret. She didn't want me to go, but she had no choice. She squeezed my arm briefly and went back inside.

306

I stared at the door as it swung shut behind her. I would never walk through that door again. I'd never say, 'Morning, Worm.' I'd never walk into the booking room with unwashed hair and hear Patrick say, 'Babe, come on, you work in a model agency, not a library.' I'd never stand in the kitchen gossiping. I'd never hear Drew say, 'Are Tesco's hiring?' when Madeleine was giving him a hard time. I'd never play 'You have the . . .' game. I'd never spend a day hungover at work, arguing about who would pick up the fish and chips. I'd never fall asleep in the fashion cupboard, or knock twice on the door when someone else was asleep in there and Madeleine was looking for them. I'd never have another Prosexy Friday. I'd never cheer along with the rest of the agency when we got an email saying Madeleine was not coming into work. I'd never get to do fashion week again. I'd never get to make Madeleine proud.

I stumbled to the corner of the street and then stood there, with a paper-dry mouth, not knowing what to do next. I reached into my handbag, which suddenly felt exceptionally heavy, and grasped around for my iPhone. I almost cried with frustration at how deep that fucking bag went, but finally pulled out the phone and called Zack.

A generic, patronizing voice told me that the person I was trying to reach was unavailable. I knew that meant that he'd blocked me. The fucker had actually blocked me!

I wanted to scream. He was half of this situation. How could he leave me out to dry on my own? Not even a text to warn me that she'd found out. I'd always known he was a bit of a prick, but I hadn't been aware until that moment that he was a colossal fucking arsehole!

An Addison Lee car stopped at the curb and I stared through the blackened window. I'd never book another Addison Lee for a model, or take another work car home. The black glass slid down. I saw Dior silver sunglasses, the chocolate brown fringe, the gap in her teeth.

'Don't choke on basic bitch life.' Lilah spat the words at me like poisonous bullets.

The window slid up and the car moved on. In the distance, I saw her gangly body fly wildly from car to agency. She didn't look at me once. She didn't beg me to tell her that it wasn't true. She wasn't interested in salvaging one single part of our relationship.

I arrived at the cross-section of Covent Garden streets, feeling like it was the first time I was seeing them, like I was a stranger in my own body. I felt so desperately alone despite the busyness of the streets. People passed by, but no one looked at me.

What was I going to do?

I wrote a string of crazy messages to Zack, slumped on the sofa, smoking my hundredth cigarette, a bottle of cheap white wine already down me.

I never sent any of them. He probably wouldn't get them anyway, considering he'd blocked me. I so wanted to be the girl who turned up drunk at his front door and forced him to take responsibility for me. But instead, I was the girl who lay down on the floor and fantasized that he'd come and put his arm over my body, stroke my hair and make me feel safe.

I switched my WhatsApp thread from Zack to Steph, and typed with one finger.

Me:
Why did you tell her

I hit send then pressed my forehead into the dusty kilim rug, resting my hand limply on the phone. Almost immediately, it started vibrating beneath my fingertips. Steph was calling.

'What?' I said, exhausted.

'I didn't tell her, Scarl.'

'Yes, you did.'

'No, I didn't.'

'No one else knows!'

'Jade told her.'

I paused for a few seconds, computing the information. 'Jade doesn't know.'

'When Lilah came in today, she made it clear that Jade was the one who told her. I swear on my family's life it wasn't me.'

I hung up and pressed my face into the rug, finally letting the tears slip out.

I'd polished off two bottles of wine by the time I arrived at Jade's flat and can only imagine what a state I looked. Chloe had arrived home as I was on my way out and tried to talk me out of going, but I was on an unstoppable rampage. I rang the doorbell several times, something I remembered Lilah doing all those months ago and thinking, *There's a girl who's certain people want her around!* But I was certain that no one wanted to see me then.

Jade opened the door, wearing jeans and a T-shirt, as per usual, smoking a joint, as per fucking usual. She didn't look surprised to see me.

'You have ruined my life!' I cried dramatically.

She stepped aside and said, 'Come on in.'

'I don't want to be anywhere near you!'

'Then why are you at my apartment?'

I let out an angry laugh, but she had a point.

'If you wanna talk about it, come on in,' she said, and walked away coolly, leaving the door open.

I stood there, breathing heavily, anger pumping out of my nostrils in hot little puffs. Then I stormed into the flat. There was a strong smell of incense burning and a cold air that sent a chill through my body.

'It's fucking freezing in here!' I shouted, as if that was a personal insult.

'Can't feel it,' said Jade, falling back onto the sofa and throwing her heels onto the trunk that mimicked a coffee table.

I'd come ready for a fight, but her calmness was throwing me. 'Why did you do it?' I asked.

'Because she's my best friend.'

'He's slept with loads of girls! What difference did it make if it was me or someone else?'

'Just listen to yourself and think how that sounds.'

'She's cheated on him too!' I said childishly, like that had anything to do with me.

Jade shrugged and folded her torso over her legs with impressive flexibility to flick ash into a coffee cup.

'How did you even know?' I asked.

'I've known since Marrakech.'

'How?'

She sighed and tipped her head back, as if it was a real drag to tell the story. 'After you crawled into my bed and fucked me, for whatever reason that was, you went to the bathroom.' She stopped there, like it was the punchline.

'And?'

'You left your phone. Zack sent you a message.'

I threw myself back to that desperate moment after the quad

bike accident. I pressed my fingers against my aching throat. 'What did it say?'

'Can't remember.'

'What did it say, Jade?' I shouted, and my throat muscles rippled aggressively beneath my fingers.

She sighed again. 'Something like, "I really do hope you're okay babe".' She put on a deep and sarcastic tone for Zack's voice.

'You knew, just from that?'

'No. But I thought it was weird. So I read all the other messages between you two. Those ones were pretty black and white. Just like the two of you!'

I didn't know if she was talking literally or metaphorically.

'Did you delete the message?' I said.

'Yeah, well, I didn't want you to know I'd seen it.'

How badly I had needed to see that message back then. To have known that he had even the smallest iota of concern for me would have meant so much more than it was actually worth.

'Why now? Why did you tell her now?' I said.

'Because I realized you weren't a nice person and didn't know why I was covering for you,' she said, and I could tell that she really meant it.

'What, asking you to switch agencies makes me a not-nice person?'

'If that's the only reason you slept with me, then yeah, it does,' she said.

'It's not the only reason!'

'Oh, not the *only* reason? You mean it was *a* reason?'

I went silent. I felt like I couldn't tell another lie. Weakly, I muttered, 'Not the first time.'

She raised her hands in a way that said, 'I rest my case', and took a drag of her joint.

I fell into an armchair and hinged forward from the waist, laying both arms across my abdomen. 'It's not like you were in love with me or anything. You just wanted sex.'

'How do you know? You never fucking asked.'

'Why did it have to be me who asked?' I cried, which wasn't fair, given all the shitty ways I'd tried to use her. 'You never called me, or said you wanted to see me, or even asked me how I was doing. Are you just so used to people coming after you that you thought I'd be exactly the same and you didn't have to put anything into it?'

'I didn't put anything into it because I didn't believe you wanted it,' she said, discarding her joint and reaching for the equipment to roll another one. I wondered if she would have managed to remain so chilled with all the shit that went on around her if she didn't have her weed.

'That's not how relationships work!' said I, the guru. 'You couldn't bear not being wanted, could you? Is that why you told Lilah? To get rid of me, so you wouldn't have to be reminded that not everyone in the world will fall to their knees for you?'

She laughed at that. 'God! You are so self-centred!'

'*I'm* self-centred?' I cried, truly incredulous. 'You are some of the most self-obsessed people I've ever come across in my life! You spend all day trawling the internet for pictures of yourself, reading the comments. And your Instagrams—'

'Your Instagram is weirder than any of ours, sugar!' she cut me off. 'I told Lilah because she deserved to know. She may cheat on him from time to time, sure. But she loves him. You don't.'

'How can she love him if she cheats on him?'

You understand so little about love.

'You claim to love her, don't you? So, how can you cheat on

her?' she asked, and I went silent. She added, 'Of all the men in London, why him?'

'Zack came after me, not the other way around!' I said, close to tears by that point. 'And I bet they're still together, fucking it out, pretending to love each other, and I'm getting all the shit for it! I don't believe that you told her because you care about her. None of you care about anyone but yourselves. It's all you talk about! And you know what? You're not going to be beautiful for ever. One day you'll end up shrivelled and old and bitter just like everyone else!'

She'd probably always look like God's gift to the eye, but in my fury, I felt like attacking her assets. I stood up and whirled off, feeling like a truly unrecognizable version of myself. One of her flatmates was on her way in and barely batted an eyelid at the sight of my tear-streamed, fury-stricken face. When I was out in the street, I took out my iPhone. The screen was flooded with little rectangular-box notifications. Some from Instagram, some from Twitter, most of them with a YouTube link. Feeling sick, I clicked on it.

The title of the video sent a shockwave through my chest: 'SCARLETT WILLEMS CAN'T GET A FRONT ROW SEAT NO MATTER HOW MANY DICKS SHE SUCKS #SECONDROWAGENT'.

And there, online and available to the public, was my 'naughty little video'.

It was coming up to a thousand views.

CHAPTER 20

I was back in arse-fucking Topsham.

What else could I have done? Losing all sense of possibility happens in a matter of seconds. I no longer thought anything in the world was left for me.

Everyone had seen the video. Lilah had made sure of that. It had probably become a legendary piece of gossip in the fashion industry, but I wouldn't have known because no one was talking to me. Not that I'd tried to get in touch with anyone. It's a strange thing to know that not only random perverts and voyeuristic teenagers have seen you at your most intimate, but also people you know. I kept thinking of individuals – Jason the Teacher, the school lacrosse captain and her sidekick, the new mum, Liz and Tim – and wondering if they'd seen me careering around in nothing but a pair of stiletto heels before allowing an anonymous penis into my mouth.

That was the most infuriating thing about the video: no one would have been able to tell that it was Zack, unless they knew his dick – or his flat, I suppose – particularly well. And even if I named and shamed him, what difference would it make? Men were supposed to have perverted fantasies, everyone knew that. For a woman, though, *it wasn't natural*. We weren't allowed to get fat or die single, so why on earth would we be allowed to feel and act on our desires? We were only meant to want sex if it was going to lead us down the road to a suburban house with an Aga and a crib. I must have had a shamefully unnatural sex drive which had ruined my life because I couldn't keep it on a leash. Other women, *better* women, could manage emotional intercourse, while all I could do was sexualize any emotions I had. All those times I'd felt at my most helpless, I'd allowed my erotic mind to wreak havoc, thinking I could replace pain with pleasure so easily, turning to the most destructive fantasies when my self-esteem was at its lowest. I'd submitted to Zack, or, rather, the illusion of him, with a sense that I was gaining control of those difficult emotions, but actually, I was doing the opposite.

Every time I watched the video I felt more ashamed, not only because I'd let it happen, but because something about the utter humiliation still turned me on. That was something that I could never ever admit to anyone, but the realization was eating me up.

Obviously, I didn't tell my mother the full story. In fact, I didn't even tell her half the story. I just said I'd been made redundant. I couldn't tell her what I'd done to Lilah because I knew that there was no excuse for it, especially when she'd never actually done anything that terrible to me. I almost wished she had. At least that would let me off the hook.

My mother was appalled that I didn't receive a redundancy package, which made me think that Madeleine had duped me into resigning. She also asked me why I didn't contact the agency who had tried to poach me before. I had no answer to that one. It annoyed me that the career she'd been so disparaging of was something she was now making out I couldn't afford to lose.

The days were long. Chloe sent me a link to an anti-slut-shaming podcast called 'Guys We F**ked', but I couldn't bring myself to listen to it. Instead, I watched hours of murder documentaries on Netflix and listened to LBC, just to depress myself even more. The thought of trying to draw sent me into a panic, because I felt like that was a lost dream. Fashion was over for me.

I'd deleted my social media accounts, along with the 7,000 Instagram followers that I'd worked so hard to get, because the comments were too much to take – 'cum-guzzling slag', 'turn around and shove it in your beefy blown out balloon knot', 'white privileged bitch'– but I set up a nondescript account so that I could still view other people's. It was my only telescope into the life that I'd lost. I spent hours scrolling through images, ending up looking at photos of people I didn't even know half the time. I checked Zack's every day, but he didn't post much, or if he did, it was just some rap – or grime – artist that he represented. I went years back on his feed, looking at all the pictures of him and Lilah. I hated him. I had fantasies about running into him, only to find that he'd lost his job, his money, his flat, Lilah. I dreamt up scenarios in which some force of internet feminism had rallied behind me and brought him down. But then I would suddenly conjure up an image of him apologizing, telling me he couldn't bear to think of me hurt and then kissing my tired body from head to toe, healing the thousands of invisible wounds that were scratched across it.

I desperately wanted to see Billie, but I couldn't stand the thought of having to face up to the fact that she'd been right about everything. In the evenings, my mother and I would share a bottle of wine and watch TV. One day, two weeks after I returned home, I opened the fridge and the usual bottle of Picpoul was nowhere to be seen. I huffed like a grumpy old drunk and carried myself to the living room, stiff-legged from too many hours in bed. My mother was sitting against the arm of the sofa, knees up, staring down at a hefty book that was resting against her thighs. I could tell she wasn't really reading.

'Mum, do we have any wine?'

'I threw it away,' she said, particularly pointedly.

'Why?'

Without speaking, she reached into her pocket and pulled out a little bag of white powder and laid it out on her flat open palm. It was so unlike her not to speak.

'What is that?' I said.

'You know what it is.'

'That's not mine.'

'It was in your wallet.'

I tried to think of an excuse. I tried to think of anything at all. It wasn't coming naturally, so I turned away.

'Don't walk away from me!' she said.

I stopped in the doorway. 'Why were you looking in my wallet?'

'I thought your behaviour was strange.'

'What were you expecting to find?'

'Exactly what I found!'

'Then why didn't you just ask me?'

'Because I can tell when you're lying to me. And I knew you were lying about your dismissal from work, so what was the point in asking for the truth?'

'It wasn't anything to do with that!' I said, pointing at the drugs in her hand, truly outraged that she thought I'd been fired for taking drugs. I added, 'Everyone does that!'

'Everyone does drugs?' she said, looking at me like I was mad.

'Yes!'

'I don't know what world you're living in, Scarlett, but let me tell you that, in the real world, most people – successful people – do *not* take drugs!'

I glared at her, furious that she couldn't fix things, outraged that she hadn't ever been able to make me happy. I said, 'Successful people? Is that all you care about?'

Because it's all I seem to care about.

'I'm not going to apologize for wanting you to be successful after all I've done for you!' she said.

'You don't really want me to be successful though, do you? You just want me to tick all the boxes, so that you can feel like a good mother. But you don't want me to be so successful that I don't need you anymore.'

'What are you talking about? You're talking nonsense. No surprise,' she said, shaking the little bag of drugs in her hand.

'If you wanted me to be successful, why did you bring me up here?' I shouted.

Her face disassembled and she threw the drugs across the room. 'I've done *everything* for you!' she screamed at the ground. I looked from her face, blotchy with anger, to the drugs on the ground and back to my mother, who was trying not to cry. I scrambled to the floor, snatched up the drugs and charged out, taking only my wallet and phone with me. I didn't even put on a coat.

My heart was pounding into my chest as I sped through the cold. I didn't want to take the bus because I knew that I couldn't sit still. The cold air was getting caught in my throat, turning into an icy pain. I ran all the way to the pub and hurtled in, red-faced, like a mad woman.

The large, bearded man behind the bar looked put off by the sight of me. Fair enough.

'Where's Billie?' I gasped at him.

'Billie? She's been gone for weeks.'

I frowned. 'Gone where?'

'To Berlin.'

'On holiday?'

'To live.'

'*What?*'

'With her girlfriend.'

Girlfriend?

I tried to make sense of the information. It had only been two months since I'd seen Billie, and she'd already rediscovered her sexual orientation, met a girl and moved to a new country? But then I realized it must have all happened before I'd seen her. It must have been what she wanted to tell me at Tramp, when I'd turned away from her. It was why she'd come all the way to London. And I hadn't asked her a single question about herself. I'd been so resentful of her for bringing out my most hideous side and so critical that she was stuck in Topsham, but actually, she wasn't stuck at all. I was.

'Can I get you anything?' said the bearded barman.

'Two tequila shots and a bottle of Sauvignon Blanc.'

He poured the drinks without blinking an eye, probably used to drunks. I downed both the shots at the bar. Then I took the wine to a table tucked away at the corner of the pub and poured a large glass. I set my phone in front of me and hunched over it, my face close to the screen, my cold, stiff thumbs moving over it rapidly to open Instagram.

Fashion week was going on without me. I was nothing to the fashion world except a sex scandal to laugh at. I felt as if I was locked in a permanently sealed cage in the middle of a party, while all the fun went on around me.

I scrolled through a myriad of pictures. I saw all our

models – *their* models – walking in top shows. *Who booked the cars to get them there?* I saw the *Love* party, which I wouldn't have been invited to anyway. I saw a picture of Madeleine and Ralph, and I gathered that he had come to London to help mop up my epic mess. I wondered how much grief he'd given Madeleine for having employed me in the first place and whether she'd spoken a single positive word in my defence. I saw a picture of Jade walking out of Somerset House, wearing a hat and crop top combo, with some overpriced streetwear brand tagged. I wasn't tempted to click through to the shopping page now that I knew about product placement. I knew that the brand would have paid her to take that shot and that it was all just a fucking lie. I thought of young girls all over the world, sitting unaware in their bedrooms, clicking onto a shopping page that was way overpriced, and begging their mothers to buy them a hat and crop top that would never suit them, just because a model called Jade Deress was wearing them on Instagram.

Lilah had uploaded a story of herself, Annabel, Moffie, Jade and Steph all piled into the bathtub at Annabel's house with the words, 'All aboard the pussy express @JadeDeress @ AskAnnabel @StephConwayPureModels @theMoffieDunn' floating above them. Again, I thought of all the girls, just like me a year ago, sitting in their own bathtubs, which looked nothing like Annabel's, and wishing they had a crew like that one splashing around in the water with them. *It's a façade*, I wanted to tell them all. *They may be having more fun than you, but don't be fooled into thinking that it's anything deeper than that.*

Steph had also uploaded an Instagram story. It was a video of Patrick taping Drew to a chair and spinning him around, while the rest of the agents laughed hysterically. My eyes filled with tears as I realized that Pure was the only place, in my life, that I'd felt I fitted into. A misfit among misfits.

I had been doing well in that job. I had been a good assistant, moved up the ladder, and was on the road to becoming a good agent. If I hadn't been such a sex-crazed idiot, I'd have been an agent of Steph's level within a few months, and eventually I'd be like Drew, Patrick, and then Madeleine. I'd have still been part of the team who had tagged me as a Muppet on Facebook and drank Prosecco together on Fridays. But my stupid desperate need for validation had thrown me wildly off the tracks. I thought that my affair with Zack would validate me, because he was desirable, and having sex with him meant that he wanted me, and that, in turn, meant that I must have been desirable. I thought that I would gain validation by being invited to the most coveted parties, by walking alongside the upper echelons of the social media world, by surrounding myself with beautiful people. But Steph had been right, all that time ago, when she said, 'People will pretend to want us, but in the end it's always them they want. Not us.'

Why hadn't I listened to her?

I gulped wolfishly at my wine, then reached into my pocket for the little bag that my mother had been so upset by. I snatched the wine bottle roughly by the neck and stomped into the bathroom, the very same bathroom where I'd found my first-ever bag of cocaine.

22 February 2017, 4.44 p.m.

I feel scared of sounding patheric or depreesed but I feel truly desperate I don't know what do do

*

It wasn't until I was slumped against the cold brick wall of the bridge by the quay, watching the landscape undulate like a choppy ocean, that I realized I must have snorted three cocaine-sized lines of ketamine.

I wasn't just high.

I was white girl wasted.

A whirring sound went off in my head, like an alarm. I felt as if I'd been trapped in a never-ending laughing gas trip. I wondered, if I died then and there, who would come to my funeral? Madeleine would feel guilty, wouldn't she? Maybe not. Maybe she'd try to distance herself from me as much as possible and not even turn up. Would Lilah come? Or Zack? What about Jade? Would they cry? Would they even care? Maybe none of them would come. My mother would, in all likeliness, hold the funeral in Topsham, and no one from London would bother travelling that far. Maybe Steph, Drew and Patrick if the trains were running smoothly, but that's it. I felt embarrassed at the idea of the girls from school, who had seen me in the *Daily Mail*, standing by my dead body, looking around and noticing that not one of the people I so constantly posted about had bothered to turn up.

The whirring drifted into the distance and my ears were filled with deafening silence, which was even worse. I picked up my iPhone in slow motion. I wanted to play music, but somehow, I ended up on podcasts, so I clicked on the first thing I saw: 'Guys We F**cked'.

'Welcome to our anti-slut shaming podcast,' a strong American female voice rang out.

I melted further against the wall, lit a cigarette and listened to Krystyna and Corinne, feeling like they were right there with me.

'I was sexting a lot today,' said Krystyna or Corinne.

I felt both corners of my mouth lift towards my cheekbones. Was I smiling? Sexting was just such a funny word.

'This is a fuck I've been looking forward to for over a year,' Krystyna or Corinne continued.

I could look forward to fucking Zack for a year, even though he'd sliced me open and hung me upside down to bleed to death.

'He'll tell me things like, "You have a great pussy," which is my kind of romance,' one of them said.

Was that my kind of romance, too? And, if so, was there shame in that, or was it just something that no one ever fucking talked about?

'That's what happens when someone pops your anal cherry.'

All I could see were cherries dancing over the quay.

'If the dick is good, the pic is good.'

Men can send dick pics. Women can't. Because we have no dicks.

'I send nude pics all the time. From me, to me.'

God, I love you Krystyna or Corinne.

'But if the pussy's in it, no face. Face and pussy don't appear in the same frame. I'm not an idiot.'

But I was an idiot. Face and pussy and everything else had appeared in the same frame. *Total fucking idiot.*

'We're saying, have a lot of sex and be proud of it,' they said in unison, and that was that.

Those cherries just wouldn't stop dancing.

I listened to more Krystyna and Corinne on the train to London.

I had a plan to carry out because I felt it was my right. Sure, I'd fucked up, but I was forced to quit and I'd been left with nothing, while Zack, I imagined, was getting on with his life as normal.

I deserved *something* at least. Didn't I?

I was off to get something.

And, my God, the drugs were taking a long time to wear off.

I got off at Holland Park Station and walked five minutes to the house I'd Googled so many times, feeling like the pavement was a cloud. It wasn't far from Ladbroke Grove and I wondered why I'd never done a casual walk-by before. It hardly would've been more stalkerish than plenty of the stuff I'd done. I rang the doorbell, one time only.

An old-ish man from the Philippines opened the door. Not quite the toy-boy sex slave I'd pictured. I was about to demand Madeleine, but he smiled and stepped aside to let me in before I said anything.

'You have no jacket?' he said, rubbing his hands up and down his own arms. 'It's too cold!'

'I left it on the train,' I said, another futile lie.

He led me down a corridor and my trainers squeaked on the black and white Victorian marble tiles. I glanced up at an undoubtedly extortionate Mario Sorrenti print on the stairwell. I imagined grabbing it off the wall and running away with it. Then I heard a murmur of voices, which got louder and louder. Hearing Madeleine's cackle, I realized that I was undoubtedly about to walk into a soirée, but I was too high to think about what that meant, or to panic.

I stepped into the dining room, which looked like the private space of an expensive restaurant. The first person I saw was Patrick. He caught my eye, and even though he couldn't move his face, his expression said, 'Really?' Madeleine was at the centre of the table and looked completely calm. Next to her, there was a man who – if I remembered correctly from my

Google stalk – was her ex-husband. Damien Stern was there, and so were other members of the fashion mafia, and from the way they exchanged amused glances, it was obvious they'd all seen the video. In that moment, I truly knew what it felt like to be famous. To walk into a room and have everyone, even very important people, know me intimately. To be instantly, and completely, open to judgement. Until then, I didn't know true vulnerability.

I wished they would all stop looking at me, even though I'd stepped into the middle of their dinner party, uninvited, looking like the subject of a trashy magazine breakdown story.

Patrick stood up, preparing to jump in subserviently for Madeleine, but she stopped him.

'Excuse me a minute,' she said to her guests. I'd never heard her be so polite. Was she nervous?

I followed her out into the corridor, hearing a murmur of breathy whispers from the others, and into what seemed to be a cosy TV room. It was so different from the dining room and not at all how I'd pictured Casa Madeleine. She sat down in a velvet armchair by the fireplace and gestured for me to do the same.

I remained standing and announced, 'I want a redundancy package.'

She gave me a confused look, which I knew was contrived, and said, 'But you weren't made redundant?'

'No, you made me resign! I left with nothing,' I said righteously.

'Because I didn't want to fire you. Being fired for misconduct is not the same as resigning.'

'How can I get fired for misconduct in my personal life?'

I supposed, really, that I probably could get fired for what I'd done, but I wanted to know for sure.

'You signed your personal life away, remember? When you promised me you'd give the job two hundred percent.'

I heard what she meant: I had failed her.

She had put her faith in me and now she had to go around listening to everyone tell her that I was a slut. Suddenly, I boiled with anger at the thought of being called a slut, by anyone.

'It's not fair that I'm getting blamed for this and he's not!' I almost roared. 'He came after me!'

'Can you stop saying that? Unless you're trying to tell me that he raped you, in which case this is a whole different conversation, you were at least fifty per cent responsible for whatever happened. Do yourself a favour and own that fifty per cent.'

'He kissed me first!' I said stroppily, like a teenager.

'You don't lose all self-command at a kiss, Scarlett!' said Madeleine. And then, with an air of total despair, 'Why would you make a sex tape for him?'

I felt my throat go dry. The idea that Madeleine might have seen the video made me feel nauseous. I prayed that she'd only heard about it. Would she have really sat through the whole thing?

'I trusted him!' I cried out in response.

'Why would you ever, *ever* trust someone like that?' she said, totally aghast.

She was right. I'd never had any reason to trust Zack, other than the desperate need to believe that I could.

'Why am I the one getting slut-shamed?' I said indignantly, with Krystyna or Corinne in my head.

'Because you're a woman,' said Madeleine, almost rolling her eyes.

'You're a woman too!' I said. 'Why aren't you on my side? Women shouldn't slut-shame other women.'

Thanks again, Krystyna or Corinne.

'What do you want me to do?' said Madeleine, impatient now. 'Go over and yell at him? Call his boss? Nothing will make a difference. You did something stupid and you got caught. Deal with the consequences.'

'He's done this so many times,' I said with exasperation. 'I'm not the only one. He told me that! I bet there are tons of other girls. And he just keeps getting away with it and everyone still loves him. Why does he get to have that?'

'Scarlett, he's a sad case,' she said unexpectedly, in a softer voice. 'I've known him for years. He's a drowning man who grabs onto whatever he can to stop himself from sinking – drugs, expensive cars, vulnerable women. Why do you think it's always the young ones? Women his own age just think he's pathetic.'

'It doesn't seem to bring him down. He's so successful!' I said like a doe-eyed idiot.

'He's got charm and a good ear for R&B, but it won't last for ever. He'll never, ever get his shit together. Men like that never do.'

I finally fell back into the forest green sofa and let my cheek fall helplessly against the ball of my hand. 'Great. So I ruined my life for a drowning man.'

'Oh, you're being dramatic,' she said and stood up. 'You're not the first woman to get publicly shamed, so stop being so narcissistic. You're not even the first woman in fashion. The industry's like quicksand for lost souls. Some people can handle it, others can't. It's one industry, it's not life. Get over it.'

Again, all I heard was that I had failed.

'What am I going to do now?' I said, imploring her to give me a solution to the mountainous problem that was my life.

'I'm going to send you my therapist's number. Book a consultation and I'll have her bill me directly for that and all further sessions. Consider it your redundancy package,' she said, offering a small ironic smile.

'You see a therapist?' I asked. I couldn't imagine Madeleine sitting in a quiet room, talking calmly about her feelings and listening to some soft-spoken therapist tell her about herself.

'I'm from New York. Everyone sees a therapist.'

'Oh yeah,' I said, accepting the cliché.

'Take the time to figure out what you want to do. Not because of the lifestyle it will bring you, or the people it will impress. But because you really want to do it.'

I was surprised at how much she could see into me, or behind my façade.

'Was that your ex-husband in there?' I asked, out of the blue.

'I call him my best friend, but yeah, we were married once.'

'Why did you get divorced?' I asked, incredulous. Wasn't it everyone's dream to be married to their best friend?

'Not everyone in the world is made to coexist, you know.'

I nodded thoughtfully, wondering if therapy had helped her reach that conclusion. A spasm of light shot from the solid gold of her bracelet as she ran her hand through her hair. I remembered thinking that the bracelet might have been a souvenir from her marriage, locked to her arm as a constant reminder of her failure. But actually, her marriage hadn't failed at all. *She* hadn't failed at all; she'd just decided to do life differently.

'I have to get back to my guests,' she said.

I stood up immediately, suddenly feeling like we were boss and employee again.

'You'll be fine, you know?' she said. 'You've got big-dick energy.'

I couldn't help but smile then and also well up with tears.

'Thanks,' I said. 'So do you.'

We looked at each other for a moment. She headed towards the door, then turned back to me and said, 'Oh, and lay off the special K. Or whatever you kids call it.'

I suddenly felt acutely sober standing in the cold outside Madeleine's house. Had I actually just turned up there? I must've been crazy. Or just high. But even high people would usually draw the line way before embarking on a two-hour train journey and turning up at their ex-boss's house to demand a redundancy package that they know they're not entitled to. What time was it? The sky was black and the street silent. Some of the houses had their lights on, but the only other sign of life was a woman sitting on a doorstep across the road. It took me a good few seconds to realize that the woman was my mother.

I wobbled across the street and she lifted a hand like, 'I'm here', as if it were the most normal thing in the world.

'How did you know where I was?' I asked, squinting down at her. She looked absolutely miniscule, hunched in a ball shape like that, her bones draping towards the ground. Slowly, she turned her iPhone around so that the screen was glaring at me. Find My Friends. Of course. She had known where I was every second of the entire year. I wondered if she'd been watching as I darted all over London like a lunatic, crossing the city up to three times in one night and staggering home in the early hours of the morning. I sat down next to her.

'How often do you take drugs?' she asked, and for once, she didn't sound like her usual holier-than-thou self.

I took the change in tone as an invitation to tell the truth. 'Often.'

My 'often' sat between us like a gulf, spreading until she said, 'Your father had a drug problem, you know.'

I looked at her sharply. It was the first I'd ever heard of it, and I felt like she was fabricating to make a point. 'Did he?'

She nodded. 'It started when I was pregnant. He was going out to watch live music all the time because apparently I was chronically boring to stay home with. And then he discovered South London rave culture. We had absolutely no money and he was spending whatever we had on partying while I was dying of prenatal depression. I thought he'd stop when you were born, but it got worse. I'd wake up to the sound of your crying. You were always, always crying. And I thought he'd be there, next to me. But he never was. He was out all night.'

'You've never told me any of this.'

'I thought it was the one thing I could protect you from. I whisked you out of London, thinking that I could keep you from all that and that you'd be oblivious. But I fear it did the opposite. And anyway, children are intuitive. You were especially so. You probably knew what was going on.'

I thought back to the few memories I had of my father. Had I known what was going on? Had I imprinted it somewhere on my psyche and chosen it as a destructive path to follow? I suddenly remembered something and said, 'When he took me out on the motorbike that time . . .'

She gasped and pressed her hands to her throat. 'I can't believe you remember that. He was high, out of his mind. Oh my God, I've never been so furious in my entire life. That was it. That was when I told him to leave.'

'I thought he left when he met Ursula Andress?' I asked.

'Andrea? Oh no, he'd known her for years. She was part of that rave scene too, I take it. No, he wanted to stay with us. But I couldn't, for you – I couldn't allow him to.'

'Would you have stayed with him if it wasn't for me?'

'God, I hope not. But who knows? Even the strongest women do the stupidest things for men they love.'

I looked over at Madeleine's house, buzzing with the in-crowd, as I comprehended all this new information. My constant need for madness, excitement and adrenaline suddenly made so much sense, given that it had been my whole life in those early years, and had then been roughly pulled away from me, leaving me in the dark, abandoned, with no understanding of what was happening.

'He wants to speak to you, by the way,' she said, all of a sudden. 'When you're feeling up to it.'

'You talked to him?'

'I called him. I looked for you at the pub and someone told me you'd been passed out by the bridge.'

'I wasn't passed out,' I said, tutting with sudden outrage, like it was the most ridiculous suggestion.

'Well, I was worried. I didn't know what to do. So I called him.'

'Is he coming to see me?' I asked.

She looked at me for a few seconds and it was obvious she was trying to stop her face from caving in. Eventually, she shook her head and slid her tiny waif-like arm around across my shoulders. I collapsed against her, the top of my head fitting perfecting into the groove of her neck.

'Why did you lose your job?' she asked.

'I slept with a client's boyfriend and he videoed it and now the video's up online and everyone's seen it.'

God, it felt a relief to tell the truth. Utterly shameful, but a relief nonetheless.

She drew in a sharp breath. 'How bad is it?'

'Pretty bad. I wouldn't recommend watching it.'

'No, God no, of course I won't!' she said. She took my hand and rubbed it between her fingers. I squeezed her tiny wrist, desperately grasping for the invisible thread that tied us together. *Don't ever let me go.*

When she spoke again, she sounded very close to tears. 'You know that I would do anything in the world for you?'

I nodded because I did know that. I knew that she would do anything within her means. I also knew that what I wanted from her was not in her means. I wanted her to make me endlessly happy. I expected it of her. But it was a totally unreasonable, unrealistic thing to ask. I was always hoping others would give me something that they couldn't. I had wanted Lilah to give me life, Zack to give me a sense of connection, Madeleine to give me success, the fashion world to hand me an identity. It was like I had all these empty slots that were being filled up by external entities, with a life of their own. As soon as any one of those entities slipped away, I was left with nothing. That's why I continuously felt half cooked.

It had to change. Madeleine was right: I had to own the responsibility for myself. I'd survived before. I would survive again and rise through the flames of my own mess. And I knew that I would do it. I owed me.

CHAPTER 21

It was exactly a year after my ketamine-fuelled Madeleine confrontation that a brief stop at a news-stand sent my mind reeling, and it was freakily fortuitous that it was on the one day I happened to be in London.

I'd just handed my portfolio into Central Saint Martins, where I was applying for a foundation diploma in art and design. I had a jam-packed day ahead of me and, my God, I was thrilled to be back in that city. Even working on the portfolio for eight hours a day, and waitressing for the rest, I'd been in Topsham for too long.

I was buying a packet of cigarettes – yes, I knew I should quit, but no, I wasn't quite ready to – by King's Cross Station. As I waited in line, I skim-read a *Guardian* news story. Another Weinstein victim had come forward, another glimmer of hope that made me wonder when it would be the fashion industry's turn to take a hit. Then the front page of the *Sun* crept into my peripherals – and started to undo a whole year of mental development.

**SUPERMODEL SEVERELY WOUNDED IN
FATAL CAR ACCIDENT
8 February 2018**

Below was a photograph of Lilah, in a leopard-print coat.

British supermodel, Lilah Fox, was in a critical condition after a head-on collision in West London. The 22-year-old is photographed above leaving Laylow (newly opened member's club on Goldborne Road) with well-known DJ James Frampton. According to an eyewitness, the pair had been drinking endless amounts of Casamigos Tequila for several hours before getting into his Tesla, which collided with another car on the Westway just after midnight, sending both vehicles crashing into the central reservation. Fox and Frampton were both rushed to the Chelsea & Westminster Hospital, where Frampton's wife arrived soon after with their two-year-old daughter and no doubt a lot of questions. The driver of the other vehicle was left with a broken wrist. A close friend of Fox

Moffie? Annabel? Jade?

told us that she has been discharged, with potentially life-altering injuries. Her representation were not available to give a statement. Fox is the face of Saint Laurent, H&M and Just Cavalli. Her best friend is fellow supermodel Jade Deress. Police said the accident was caused by one of the vehicles switching lanes too fast, but given Fox's reputation and lifestyle (she has been photographed at parties every night this week), it would not be far-fetched to assume that alcohol and drug abuse may have played a part in this incident.

I'd long ditched the *Daily Mail*, and Instagram, and any other form of social media, because they were what I now recognized as 'triggers'. My therapist, whom Madeleine so generously paid for week after week, had taught me to understand that when I had a feeling, it wasn't really anything to do with what was going on in that moment. It was an old feeling, something from childhood, brought on by a trigger. The front page of the *Sun* was most definitely a trigger. *Bang*.

I immediately called Steph. She wasn't surprised to be hearing from me, which I guessed meant I was still as predictable as ever, but I didn't care about that.

'Is she all right?' I asked, picturing us all congregating at Lilah's funeral.

'She's okay,' she said. 'I mean, she's pretty distraught, but she's alive.'

'How bad is it?' I asked, allowing the funeral image to dissolve.

She paused for a second, and it sounded like she was eating. 'Both of her hips are broken. They're gonna operate next week. She'll be in a wheelchair for a bit. Patrick says he'll push her around Westfield.' She laughed a little, which made me feel relieved. 'I think she's more worried about her face. You should see what she looks like. It's devastating. She was meant to be shooting British *Vogue* today.'

'Where is she now?'

'At her flat. Her mum's supposed to be coming, but she just moved to the Costa del Sol and she doesn't want to fly over. Honestly, that woman does not give a shit about her daughter.'

'Is anyone with her?'

'I think Jade's with her now. I've been there a lot, so has Madeleine. We're taking it in turns.'

No mention of Zack, I noticed, though I knew I absolutely should not be thinking about him. Not ever, but especially with what had happened to Lilah.

'Should I come see her?' I said.

Steph sighed down the phone. 'I don't know, babe. Let me ask her.'

'Okay, let me know. I'm in London all day.'

Steph promised to call me back, and I knew she would, because she was Steph.

Placated by the news that Lilah wasn't at death's door, I bought a Frappuccino and carried on with my day. I had a list of galleries to get around. The one I really wanted to go to was the Trump and Brexit exhibition at the Design Museum in Kensington, but I thought I'd better stay around the north end of London, in case Lilah did want to see me. God, how familiar that feeling was, after a whole year. So, instead, I ended up at the 'Super Sharp' exhibition at Camden's Fashion Space Gallery, which was about the appropriation of Italian designers in the underground music scene.

I was listening to some know-it-all – probably a student – explain the ins and outs of jungle and garage music and how much sense it made that they'd embraced Versace and Moschino, when my phone rang. There was a slight tug at my gut as I answered. 'Hi, Steph?'

'She wants to see you.'

Lilah, it turned out, had moved to a flat in a mansion block in Knightsbridge, which meant that I could have made the Design Museum after all. I thought Knightsbridge was a strange move for her and could almost guarantee, before I got there, that she was living with someone.

Jade opened the door of the flat. She didn't kiss me, or hug me, or even turn a cold shoulder on me. She just greeted me like someone she vaguely knew and whom she had nothing but Lilah in common with. She explained Lilah's condition like I was a nurse, taking over her shift, 'She just took her painkillers, so she'll get kinda drowsy. She should probably eat before she sleeps again though.'

We were in one small room that felt like a hotel suite. Functional, but not particularly warm or lived-in. I glanced at the mail on the table. It was all addressed to Rob Halper. So, I had been right. Jade paused at the bedroom door, looked me up and down like she was deciding whether I was fit to be seen by the patient, then opened it.

Lilah was in bed, propped against a mountain of pillows, and she was unrecognizable. One side of her face was completely swollen, bulging out like an infected growth. She had blood-purple circles underneath both of her eyes and the tousle of her hair was greasy and matted. I stepped towards her cautiously. I'd never seen a badly injured person before. Not in real life. Her eyes followed me and she breathed heavily through her mouth.

'Hi. How are you feeling?' I said, knowing that my face screamed pity, knowing how much she'd hate that, but truly unable to change it.

'How do you think?' the words came wispily out of her mouth.

'Is it okay that I'm here?' I asked, scrunching up my face apologetically.

She stared at me through the bloodshot slits of her eyes and I waited for an acidic remark to eject itself from her swollen lips. But she just nodded and asked, 'Do you think everything happens for a reason?'

I nodded. 'Yes, definitely.'

'Guess I was wank at walking the shows anyway,' she said, a glint of her old crass humour shining through the pain.

'I'm a hundred per cent sure there will be a better reason than that,' I said. Instinctively, I took her hand, perching on the bed next to her.

A single tear crept down the bulge of her cheek as she rasped, 'It was my fault.'

'What was?'

'The accident.'

'Of course it wasn't your fault, Lilah.'

'Yes, it was! I knew he was drunk and I was giving him head. While he was fucking driving! He didn't want me to. He's married! He didn't fucking want me at all!' she faltered, gasping for air. 'I needed to know that I could have him. And now, look at my face! I look like Shrek!'

I couldn't help but laugh a little, sad though that laugh may have been. I knew why she was telling me: because I would understand. She knew that I would get what it was like to need validation so much that you'd morally debase yourself to achieve it. She knew that I could relate to believing that being wanted could make you happy and going to extreme measures to prove it to yourself.

'Lilah,' I said, looking down at her hands, the only part of her that was undestroyed, limp on top of the duvet. 'I'm really, really sorry. About everything. I should've told you before, but I just couldn't face it.'

'Yeah, I didn't think you'd disappear as easily as you did, to be honest,' she said.

'I didn't really have a choice,' I said. And then, in case she thought I was about to play the victim, I jumped in with, 'Which is fair enough! I don't blame you for that. I probably would've done the same.'

'Sorry if I ruined your life, but you're a stupid fucking bitch for making him a sex tape.'

I shuddered at the memory. 'It wasn't really intentional ... it just happened. How did you find it, by the way?'

338

'I took his phone as soon as Jade told me and locked myself in the bathroom with it. I didn't believe her, to be honest. I needed to see some proof. He'd deleted all the messages, so I went through his photos. I was only looking for a tit pic or something. Not a whole video.'

'Never doing that for anyone again,' I said glumly.

'Did you ever really want him, or did you just hate me?' she asked, which surprised me.

'I didn't hate you! I adored you. I wanted to be you,' I said.

'Did you think I was happy?' Her mouth spread out at the corners and then fell lethargically back into place.

I shrugged. I had never thought about whether Lilah was happy or not. Happy seemed too simple an emotion to attach to her. 'It wasn't about happiness. You just seemed so . . . alive. You didn't care what people thought of you, or whether you were liked or not. You just lived. I always thought I was like that, but then it turned out that I wasn't, at all. So, I guess I resented you for it.'

'You were jealous?'

I nodded. 'Yes. I was jealous of you.'

'How could you not have seen that it was all fake?'

'It seemed so real,' I said. 'I really am sorry, Lilah. I know I did a shitty thing.'

She lifted her hand from the bed, as if she was trying to wave it, but it quickly fell back into place. I wondered if she was saying, 'I've done worse,' but she didn't speak. The painkillers were kicking in.

'Can I get you anything?' I asked. She shook her head lightly as her eyes fluttered closed. I guessed it was my cue to leave, so I stood up, holding my breath, and rubbed the top of my thighs. 'I'll let you sleep, then.'

'Wait till I fall asleep,' she muttered.

I sat back down obediently – *trigger!* – and waited until she was lightly snoring. Then I blew out the Bella Freud candle that was burning next to the bed and dimmed the light. Before I left, I turned to look at her lying there in the half-gloom, broken. I thought it could be the last time I ever saw her.

In the hyper-functional living room, Jade sat at one end of the sofa, talking on the phone – seemingly to her agent – and smoking a joint, as if frozen in time. On the other end was Steph. She spread her mouth into a wide smile and stood up.

'Hi, chicken,' she said, opening her arms. I thought it was funny of her to call me something she'd never called me before, but then it was probably a new name she was using for everyone, perhaps even a new agency word. If I was still there, I'd have probably been calling everyone a chicken. When we hugged, she held onto me, genuinely delighted to see me, and said, 'Oh, I have missed you!'

'Why?' I said humorously.

Steph laughed, hugging me again, and I knew that she understood what I meant. She understood that I was trying to say I was sorry that I'd had no regard for her feelings, although she'd only ever been an angel. That I envied her for all her grace. That I was sorry I accused her of revealing my exploits to Lilah, when I was the one who'd made a fucking sex tape. That I was sorry I'd never apologized for that. That I couldn't have gotten through that year without her.

'How's Madeleine?' I asked.

'Oh, you know, crazy as ever. Hates the new assistant, so demoted her to receptionist and has brought Worm onto the women's division. I mean, *je* cannot!'

'Secretly, quite happy about that,' I said jokingly, but not really joking. I couldn't deny being pleased that Madeleine hadn't seen the new assistant as a narcissistic extension of her being, like she'd seen me. Also, good for Worm – finally!

We had a quick catch-up. I told her about Central Saint Martins; she told me that she was about to move to New York to head up Pure's new face division over there. I gasped happily, proud, excited and, of course, a tad wistful. *Could have been me.* She told me I looked well. I told her she looked better. She flicked her hair in jest, and I laughed. Then it was time for me to leave. Jade smiled, not a flirtatious smile but a distant one, and made a V sign with her long fingers, still talking on the phone. I left the two of them there, getting on with their lives, the lives that I was no longer a part of, and feeling oddly content about it.

Outside the building, I plopped myself down on the doorstep, closed my eyes and started rubbing the tips of my fingers in circular motions against my thumb – a technique I'd learnt in therapy – to bring myself into the present moment. I'd learnt that if you live in the present, everything really does seem okay. It's easier said than done, but on the occasions you manage it, it's worth the effort. If you've got one leg in the future and one leg in the past, your legs are open and you're fucked.

I let my eyelids peel apart and the glare of the streetlight shot through to my brain, making me light-headed. I was about to get up when I noticed a familiar silhouette approaching, and froze. For a moment, I felt like I'd conjured him.

He didn't give me that big charming smile, or greet me with casual familiarity, like there was nothing between us. Instead, he gave a smile that looked something like gritted teeth, and I remembered him doing that when we were sitting in the bathroom at the Louis Vuitton party, when he was still trying to make the decision about whether or not to kiss me. If only I could say that I wish he hadn't, but I didn't wish that at all.

I returned his gritted smile with a wonky one and stood up. He was holding a bunch of orange tulips wrapped in brown paper, without any extra foliage, which looked like they'd been freshly bought from a flower stand. An afterthought.

'How are you?' he said, stretching his neck awkwardly over the flowers.

'Yeah, I'm fine, thanks,' I said coldly, with a pointed hint of 'Like you care' in my voice. I remained stiff as he brushed my cheek with his and made an overstated kissing sound.

'Did you see Lilah?' he asked.

'Yup.'

'Was it okay?'

'Yeah, luckily she'd just taken her painkillers,' I said, pointedly, with a touch of humour.

He laughed and winced at the same time, as if to say, 'Yeah, thank God for that!'

'I didn't know if you two were still together,' I said, trying not to let onto the fact that I'd been wondering all day.

'We're not. We broke up about six months ago.'

'How long do you think that will last?'

'For good.'

'Yeah, sure.'

'No, really. It has to this time. There's too much we can't forget.' He picked a perfectly good petal from one of the tulips and let it fall to the ground.

I paused. I'd built that conversation in my mind so many times, but every takedown I'd carefully constructed was evading me. Instead, I said, 'It's been a while, Zack. Stupidly, I thought you might call at some point.'

'I'm so sorry. I know I should've.'

'At the very least, you should've warned me when she found the video.'

'I know. You're so right.'

I hated him so much, at that moment, for his compliance. It was an insight into the rage that must have built in Lilah for all those years they were together. I wanted to lay into him and make him see what he'd put me through. But how can you possibly lay into someone who tells you how right you are? How can you tell an arsehole that he's an arsehole when he's doing such a good job of pretending to be a decent guy?

'So, that's all you have to say?' I said.

I saw panic in his eyes as he searched for the words that would put a cork in me. 'I should have deleted that video as soon as we weren't drunk anymore.'

Frustrated by his feeble attempt to admit responsibility, I was ready to jump down his throat and rip it open. Then I heard Madeleine.

Do yourself a favour and own that fifty per cent.

'And I should never have let you take it,' I said curtly.

'Don't say that. Makes me feel like some arsehole old guy who forced a young girl to make a sex tape.'

Doesn't sound far off.

'Well. It's over now,' I said, although it would never really be over for me, not as long as the internet lived on.

'Was it really shit for you?' he asked.

'What the hell do you think?' I said breathily. 'Imagine the most shaming thing that could happen to a person. That was it.'

'Can I ask you a question?' he said. 'If there hadn't been the whole Lilah thing, would you have, like, properly gone out with me?'

I was taken aback because it sounded like something a 21-year-old girl would ask, not a 36-year-old, high-flying, seemingly self-assured man. Was he making like me and fishing for a compliment?

I answered him honestly. 'I don't know. I always thought I wanted to. Like I really, *really* wanted it. But maybe that was because I knew it couldn't happen. So it was safe to want it.'

'You always seemed half in, half out. So I never really thought of it as an option either. Can you hold these for a sec?' He handed me the tulips and I cradled them as he reached into his pocket for cigarettes. He continued: 'There's one thing I've been wanting to tell you though. Remember when you asked me if I slept with other girls, apart from you and Lilah? Well, I did sleep with other girls. But never the same girl more than once. Only you.'

I let out a snorty laugh, shifting the tulips from one arm to the other. 'I'm flattered.'

'Sorry. I'm just trying to give you what I didn't back then. I thought that would be important for you to hear.'

I watched as he lit a cigarette and awkwardly bit on his lower lip. Then I asked the question I'd been dying to ask since the first time we kissed: 'Why me?'

Because you're fish and chips.

He was silent for a few seconds as he took the flowers back. 'At first, I just thought you were fucking sexy. In a really unassuming way. But then, I really loved hanging out with you. There was something comforting about it. I thought I could have all the benefits of that, without having to emotionally engage. But that's not how it works, is it?'

'Isn't it? You never seemed emotionally engaged,' I said.

'I was. I didn't think *you* were. You seemed shut off, but you weren't shut off with your friends, so I thought it must've been something to do with me. That's why I didn't always treat you that well.'

It was all I could do not to jump in and take the blame, thanks to that poison story society told that said you were treated as well as you made out you want to be treated. I'd absorbed it and retold it so many times. But that time, I managed to bat it away.

'You've never treated anyone well. Not Lilah. Not even yourself.'

He laughed slightly, perhaps embarrassed, but more likely trying to trivialize my observation. Then, out of the blue, he said, 'We did have good sex though, didn't we?'

'Did we?' I asked incredulously.

'I thought we did?'

'I thought so, too, at the time. But we were coked to the nines! You barely ever came. I certainly never did,' I said. I knew that it was an inflammatory comment, but I didn't want him to go on believing he was some kind of gift to sex-hungry women, when clearly all he'd ever cared about was his own pleasure.

'I feel like I need to take you home now, just to change your memory of that,' he said.

I laughed a little and shook my head, though I couldn't deny that small part of me that would have loved to go home with him, even after everything that had happened.

'Are you living in London?' he asked, quickly switching to a more pedestrian tone of conversation.

'No. I was in town today for an interview.'

'Interview for what?'

'Central Saint Martins.'

'That's great!' he said. 'You don't want to go to Parsons anymore?'

I felt a tingle along the front of my body as he said that,

realizing that he remembered something I'd told him so long ago. I knew the feeling I was having. It was the feeling of common sense leaving my body.

'Yes, but that's still a pipe dream. Saint Martins could be a reality. And it's a fab school.'

'I know it is,' he said. 'Well done, babe. I'm happy you're doing well.'

I stepped down from the doorstep. 'Well, I would say keep in touch, but you've probably deleted my number.'

'As a matter of fact, I haven't.'

'Well, you blocked me.'

He stuck the cigarette in between his teeth and took out his iPhone. 'You're right, sorry about that,' he said. His thumb darted back and forth over the screen, and then he said, 'Unblocked', like it was nothing at all. And to him, it probably was nothing at all, and never had been.

'I'm joking,' I said. 'I don't think we should keep in touch.'

'Don't you?'

I looked at him and I knew that the conversation was on the cusp of moving into flirtation. The cusp was always a dangerous place to be.

Don't do it, Scizzle. It's regressive.

'Go and give Lilah her flowers,' I said pointedly.

He gave me a look that was a little sad, a little manipulative.

'Bye, Zack,' I said.

I turned away from him and headed out into the world. The real world, that is.

8 February 2018, 8.41 p.m.

Don't look back. We're all over this, hon.

CHAPTER 22

Reminiscence is a real fucker. There's no cure for it. After that trip to London, I couldn't stop my thoughts from bringing up memories that unravelled into fantasy.

He was in my head again, suffocating me. I was thinking of him when I woke up in the mornings. Not in full form, but a smothering fragment of him, sometimes plowing into me, sometimes closing his fingers around my neck, other times holding onto to me as he slept. And the really problematic part of it all was that he was reachable. All I had to do was pick up the phone and text him, now that I was unblocked. He'd tell me to come over, I'd send an emoji and get on the train down to London, we'd take cocaine and have highly charged, vulgar sex, burning through my entire year of personal growth, and then I would leave the next morning and I would feel the way I so dreaded feeling. Returning to him would be returning to a situation that I already knew the outcome of, thinking it would be different, believing it could bring me something that time round. Just like an addict.

I continued drawing and making scrapbooks, even though I'd already submitted my portfolio, and kept doing all the things that people who are trying to better themselves do. I went to yoga classes daily. I listened to my guided meditation app morning and night, though it was a struggle to sit still for so long. I repeated daily affirmations, such as, 'I am adequate at all times and I approve of myself', 'I am capable of creating happiness for myself from within' or, my personal favourite, 'Life is ordinary'.

One day, a few weeks after my trip to London, I felt the vibration of my iPhone against my bum cheek while I was waitressing at a local café. I didn't usually keep it so close to me, but that day, it was there. The customer I was serving was taking a hell of a long time to decide which of the three options on the menu she wanted, and she seemed to be visually impaired — judging by the way she was holding it about a millimetre away from her nose — so I reached for my phone and stole a glance. I nearly dropped the dirty plate I was holding.

> Zack:
> Hey! Can you send me your banks details?

'Can you give me a discount on the carrot cake if I only have half a slice?' said the partially sighted woman.

I looked up and quickly slid the phone back into my pocket. I told her I couldn't change any of the costs and she chewed on the side of her lip, staring at me, then went back to the mammoth question of what to order. I was dying to get back to my phone, utterly confused, almost believing that I'd imagined the message. Eventually she ordered a piece of carrot cake at full cost. I slipped behind the counter and quickly typed a reply to Zack.

> Me:
> Why?

I kept my phone in my back pocket all day, waiting for a reply, wondering why he could possibly need my bank details. Did he want to give me some sort of apology settlement? And would it be hookerish to accept it?

It wasn't until I was closing the café at the end of the day that I finally felt a vibrating sensation against the same bum cheek. I snatched the phone urgently, as if someone was about to beat me to it. All he'd sent me was this:

> Zack:
> Got an in with Parsons. Want to transfer
> you the fees

I stared at the message. *'An in'?*

> Me:
> ?

The brevity of my message was indicative of how I was feeling: too taken aback to string a sentence together. I leant against the wall and stared down at the screen, my tongue moving nervously around my mouth.

The three dots appeared. He was typing.

I waited.

The dots disappeared.

And then ...

> Zack:
> Friend of a friend is a benefactor
> Got her some epic gig tix in return 😊
> Just send an application or whatev and will
> be accepted.

I paused and read over the messages a few times. What was the winky face supposed to mean?

I replied with the same brevity as before.

Me:
Why?

For a while, I didn't think he was going to answer. It would have been so like him to leave me in ambiguity, under his power. But then the dots appeared . . .

Zack:
Want you to be happy
And have everything you deserve

I tried to mentally unpack both of those sentences. I appreciated that he'd used the word 'happy', but was really struggling with the meaning of 'deserve'. Did I deserve a place at Parsons? And if I did, why did he have to bribe a friend of a friend for me to have it? I knew it was probably stupid to think like that – life didn't always work in ways that were fair – but I couldn't help feeling that if I were to take him up on his offer, that's all I'd ever be able to think about.

The other thing I kept wondering was, *Why the hell is he doing it?* He didn't want to be with me, that was for sure. I didn't want to be with him either. I knew that he wasn't the person for me as much as he knew that I wasn't for him. So why couldn't we both just let go of the damn fantasy? Was he doing this to sweep away his residual guilt, or because he cared about me? Surely not the latter. If he cared about me, he would never have allowed Lilah to do what she did. At the very least, he would have called to see if I was alright. Zack Smith did not give two shits or a piss about me. Suddenly I thought of the way he'd called me 'basic' when I'd played a Fleetwood Mac song. Had he known what he was doing when he'd said that?

The three dots appeared. Zack was typing. I stared down at the phone, waiting.

For a moment, I let myself imagine what would happen if I sent him my bank details and accepted the offer. I thought of my teenage years when I'd spent all the hours of the day dreaming of a life in New York, looking flame, surrounded by all things fabulous, living at the highest pitch.

But I was no longer that girl who could happily dream the hours away. I'd made that mistake. I had been captivated by the idea of working at Pure from the moment I heard that ridiculous window argument, knowing that I would be surrounded by madness. After living such a solitary life for so long, physically close to my mother but emotionally disconnected, a noisy setting to cover the silence seemed so attractive that I had become utterly attached to a career that was entirely wrong for me, thinking that it could bring me something, just as I'd attached myself to Zack, who was not only wrong for me, but not mine to have.

The phone vibrated in my hand.

> Zack:
> I could come and visit you 😉

There was no question about the meaning of that winky face. I imagined what I would have done if he – or anyone – had made such an offer to me when I'd erratically jumped on that first train to London, with nothing to my name. I shuddered at the thought of the path I would've taken, and a sudden hailstorm of anger erupted inside me. I was angry with Zack, but more so, I was angry for all the women who received similarly demeaning propositions and who didn't have the luxury to say no because it was a matter of their survival. It was thanks to that fury that common sense came trickling back through my body. I dialled Zack's number.

He answered, with a voice drenched in sex. 'Hey, gorgeous.'

'I'm done with all that,' I said.

'Done with what?'

'Bad sex. Bad chat. Being nothing but another name on the fuck list. Basically, I'm done with you.'

'I'm just trying to do something nice for you, Scarlett.'

'I don't need it. And it's not *nice*. Look after yourself, Zack, but please don't contact me again. Ever.'

I hung up the phone, waves of adrenaline pumping through me. I deleted our WhatsApp conversation history and, finally, I felt the memory of him unwrap itself from my cerebrum. Funny, I thought, how you could do everything in the world to try and get someone out of your head – berate yourself for allowing them to be there in the first place, visualize the cords that bind you being cut and burnt, consciously push thoughts of them into an abyss – but they continued to lurk in the peripheries. And then one thing they do, seemingly random in its relation to all the other things that should have forced you to forget about them, is suddenly one thing too many, and you're done.

That is where I was. I was done with Zack Smith. I could forgive him for being an emotional fuckwit, for not telling me when he got back with Lilah, for treating me like a sex object, for blocking me when he couldn't face my emotions. But I could not forgive him for belittling me.

I was too fucking fabulous for that.

Three dots. Zack was typing again. I stabbed his name with my thumb and scrolled down to tap the alarmingly red words 'Block Contact', just like he had done to me.

And then I deleted 'Zack Smith' from my life.

That night, something happened. It started off normally: I did a yoga class, then went home and sat in the kitchen for hours, drawing.

I was still hyper from my phone call to Zack, so eventually I went for my old entire-bag-of-sweets trick to send me off to sleep. I don't remember what I dreamt of – I really don't – but all I know is that I woke up fully saturated by a sensation that was entirely alien to me.

The first thing I thought was that I was about to – or had already – wet the bed. But I was okay with it. I felt a gentle wave of ecstasy lapping through me. Then, as I opened my eyes, a spasm shot from my pelvic bone, all the way down to my vagina, and the whole area started contracting over and over, like it was rasping for air.

I parted my sweaty legs. The inside of my knickers was sticky and warm.

I had just woken up to my first ever orgasm.

I was inclined to stay still and let it be, in case it went away, but instinct took over. I slid my arm under the duvet and edged my fingers beneath the elastic of my knickers. For the first time ever, I allowed my fingers to explore the whole area. The pad of my middle finger found my clitoris and I started to move it round and round in circles, feeling it in my legs, my stomach, in my throat, until that trembling spasm returned. *It had happened again.*

It was absolutely nothing like I'd imagined it to be. I wasn't writhing around like a small animal trying to break out of a trap. Nor was I emanating rays of light. I didn't feel like I'd undergone some kind of life-changing awakening, or defied the patriarchy and stepped into my true feminist, orgasmic self, with a new outlook on love, life and autonomy. But as I lay there, drenched in sweat, my legs aching slightly, I felt a sense of relief. The wiring was in place. I might even be fully equipped with a G spot.

And the best part was that I hadn't even needed anyone else to get there for me. It was, I felt, my body's way of telling me, *We've got this.*

CHAPTER 23

Apparently, it was called a 'nocturnal orgasm'. That's what Google told me when I asked, 'Can women orgasm in sleep?', worried that the answer would be negative and that I'd imagined it all.

But as it turned out, it was a thing, though every article seemed to state that 'Women's orgasms during sleep have not been widely studied'. Shocker.

This led me down a rabbit hole of vagina literature, and I made another discovery: not every woman has a G spot. I smiled as I read on, thinking of that New Year's Eve when I was moaning to Billie about the non-existence of mine.

'What if I don't have one at all?' I'd cried, already too drunk.

'Everyone has one, you div!' she'd said, pouring another round of tequila shots.

I so badly wanted to call her up and tell her about this. She was the only person who would truly understand the gravity of it. But I knew that I owed her a far less trivial call than that.

I abandoned my vagina readathon and opened WhatsApp.

> Me:
> Hey

I had to remind myself that there was every chance she wouldn't reply. She was a strong character and I thought she would be unlikely to roll over for anyone who had treated her the way I had. But, to my surprise, the three dots appeared almost instantly.

Billie:
Hey. Everything ok?

Me:
Yep. All good
How's Berlin?

Billie:
Wicked thanks
How's London?

Me:
Back in topsham 😵

Billie:
I'm sorry

Me:
Lol
Was thinking I could come visit you out there?
If you don't mind
Or hate me
Understandable if you do

Billie started typing. And then she stopped. I waited, watching the phone screen hopefully. She started again. And then stopped immediately. She didn't want me to come. She had her own life, one that I'd refused to let her tell me about when she'd tried, even though she'd been my best friend for years, even though she'd never wanted anything but the best for me. Why would she want me to be a part of it?

But then she started typing again:

> Billie:
> Come this weekend?

I didn't pack much for Berlin. Clean knickers, about which my iPhone had been buzzing with reminders all week. An over-stuffed sketchbook, with a birthday card from Chloe taped to the front saying, 'Well-behaved women seldom make history'. *Truth.* A thrift store – and still fabulous – jumper I'd bought after selling all my designer bits on eBay. And a copy of Caitlin Moran's latest *How To Be Famous* (if only it had been written three years earlier, but actually, would it have made a difference to me then?).

I took the bus from the airport as Billie had told me to. When I got off, she was there waiting. Her hair, still blood-red, was the longest I'd ever seen it and tied in a short ponytail. She was wearing the bomber jacket I'd customized for her – oh, how pleased I was to see that jacket! – and smoking a rollie.

For the first few seconds, neither of us said anything, and I thought, *This is going to be an awkward weekend.*

Then she nodded at the canvas bag slung over my shoulder and asked, 'Where's the kitchen sink?'

Inwardly I cringed a little, knowing that she was referring to the me who wore 'orthopaedic shoes for clowns'. But outwardly I laughed and said, 'Sold it to get a piece of my soul back!'

Billie smiled and offered me her rollie. 'It's a ten-minute walk to the flat.'

'Cool. Excited to see it.'

We walked the wide and surprisingly low-key streets of Berlin, making small talk about the architecture and the night-life as the elephant in the room danced around us. Eventually the conversation dwindled and I knew that it was up to me to speak out, to say something real. And not about my orgasm. Not yet, anyway.

'Billie,' I said in a weighty tone. 'I'm so—'

'I know you are.' She turned her eyes on me and I knew that she meant it. She knew how sorry I was. Of course she did. She knew me better than anyone. She was Billie. 'I am too,' she continued.

'You? What for?' I asked with astonishment.

'Well, you did your time. Like, big time. And I wasn't there for you when it happened.'

'You saw the video then?'

She pulled a face and shook her head. 'No offence, Scizzle, but there are a few things in life that I'm a hundred per cent sure I never need to see. And one of them is you noshing off some idiot.'

I let out a sputter of laughter then. She laughed too. And just like that, the elephant went bouncing off into the distance. She held out her arms to me. Even when we were best friends, we hadn't been huggers, but at that moment I dived into her arms and held onto her for a long time.

'So, tell me why you're back in arse-fucking Topsham? You do still bloody hate it, don't you?' she said, suddenly sounding just like her old self.

'Oh yeah, absolutely!' I laughed. 'But I'm starting an art and design foundation in September.'

'No way! Where?'

'Central Saint Martins!' I said excitedly, truly proud of myself for what felt like the first time ever. After deleting Zack and his vaguely well-meaning but entirely offensive and outright controlling helping hand from my life, the real offer came so naturally, so strategically. It came like proof that life does have its ways of reaching out to us.

'Shut up!' said Billie, and stopped in the street to turn to me. 'Sciz, that's amazing!'

We got to the flat soon after that, a studio on the top floor of a new build. When we arrived, Billie's girlfriend, Mirjam, was putting the finishing touches on the adorably neat bed she'd made up for me on their little sofa. She came straight over to hug me. 'Scarlett, I'm so pleased to finally meet you! Billie talked about you so much!' I was very pleased to hear she had a Dutch accent, feeling like Billie was living with a part of me, even though I'd never been to Holland. As if she read my thoughts, Mirjam said, 'I hear you're Dutch also?'

'*Voor de helft,*' I said, one of the few phrases I'd ever learnt, meaning 'half'. And then, 'You've got the best hair.' She really did.

'Sciz just got into a top design school,' said Billie, leaning sideways to nudge her arm into Mirjam's, and I had a moment of acute awareness that they were girlfriend and girlfriend.

'Ah, my goodness. We have to celebrate!' said Mirjam.

'Of course, any excuse!' I said, content in the feeling that I was among people who wanted to celebrate my achievements.

We agreed that heavy carbs and cold alcoholic beverages would be a great way to celebrate and headed off to some trendy district. The signs of spring were just starting to show, and there was that feeling of a city that was coming out of hibernation. I thought of how much I had loved those days in London and of how lucky I was that I had a chance to restart a life there, in the city I loved so much.

We stopped at a lively street food market. Billie and I sat down at a long table with boxes of bratwurst, while Mirjam went off to get beers.

'She's alright, isn't she?' said Billie, smiling over at her girl-friend in a way I'd never seen her do to anyone.

'She is ... heaven!' I said, and I meant it. Then I casually asked, 'How long have you known?'

'Since the day that lacrosse stick with a ponytail dubbed me the school dyke. The twat did me a favour really.'

'How come you never told me?'

She shrugged. 'I guess I wanted to be sure, before it became a thing.'

I conceded with a nod, thinking about my fling with Jade that I'd so desperately wanted to hide from Billie, when actually she'd been trying to tell me about Mirjam. I made a mental note to explain what had been going on, but not then. That moment, I wanted to be with her in real time, not in the past.

'Anyway, it's not serious, I just want her for her ovaries,' said Billie as Mirjam returned to the table, and we all laughed.

After we'd eaten, Billie suggested a walk along the canal to their favourite bar. Moments after we'd started down the path, we heard the ripple of jazz music. We turned a corner and a full band came into view underneath the bridge. *A full jazz band*. They even had colourful lights sweeping over them and smoke wafting along their feet. We squawked with excitement, talking animatedly about how we felt like we were in a different era, until an angry director shouted at us to get out of his music video. That just made us laugh even louder.

I felt a warm sensation settle over me. It suddenly became clear that instead of chasing a thrill you could never find, life was about finding joy in the small moments. In randomly coming across a jazz band playing underneath a bridge. In the teenage girls on the canal bank, sharing a mini bottle of champagne and reading Margaret Atwood aloud to each other. In the explosion of colour in the form of graffiti on the brick walls. In the text from Chloe: *I really don't think there's anything better than cheese*. In the disgruntled-looking pug at the canalside bar we ended up at. In the caricature of a German barmaid, wearing a dirndl. In sitting outside with friends, sipping beer, thankful for the warm weather, thankful to be in a place like that.

While we were there, a girl walked by with a tangle of chocolate brown hair and a fringe, and for a moment, I thought of Lilah. I wondered if she ever found joy in the small moments, or if anything truly excited her at all anymore.

'Don't choke on basic bitch life.'

How could something as gargantuan as life ever be basic?

I smiled directly at the dwindling light of the sky and thought about the identity that I'd been chasing for so long, one which I knew would be ever-changing. I was a waitress from Topsham, a lover of London, a design-student-to-be, with belongings that I could fit into one bag. I had zero followers on Instagram and a sex tape somewhere in the depths of the internet. I was visiting my best friend in Berlin. I was exactly where I needed to be. Life really was happening, and I was in it.

I suddenly caught Billie's eye and realized that she was laughing at me.

'Sorry,' I said. 'Were you talking to me?'

'Yeah, mate, I was rabbiting on and you were just staring at me,' she said. And then, 'Are you a million miles away?'

I took a small sip of beer (I tried to only take small sips now). 'No, babe,' I said – old habits die hard – 'No, I'm right here.'

Acknowledgements

I am forever grateful and indebted to those who gave me a buoyant career in fashion, without which there would be no words on these pages. I will never forget the vibrancy of those years.

Huge thanks to my astute early readers who gave me confidence at the first draft: Claudia Costa, Olivia Marquis, Eve McQuiston, Xenobe Purvis and Polly West.

I am continuously grateful for my brilliant, committed agent, Holly Faulks, and to all at Greene & Heaton. And many thanks to Eleanor Teasdale, who believed in it from the beginning. Hugest thanks to my editor Bethan Jones, for taking a chance on material that was not an easy swallow, and for elevating it into what it is. And to the formidable team at Simon & Schuster UK, for getting behind us.

Many, many thanks to Jason Richman, for championing the book across the ocean. And great appreciation to Charles Finch, for enveloping me in the Finch & Partners family, whilst allowing me the freedom to write my next book.

For their wholehearted love, laughter, support and sofas to sleep on: Ruby Boglione, Hallie Bonnar, Amy Croxford, Theo De Gunzburg, Melita Gedye, Gala Gordon, Annie Green, Oli Henry, Sophie Humphrey, Becky Levett, Polly Lovelady, Lucy McGinn, Lottie Neil, Rifat Ozbek, Amy Pelham, Jerome Porritt, Phil Rage, Caspar Smyth and Niamh Watmore. And especially, Anna Bingemann and Gabriella Wall, for sharing everything in their life with me, unconditionally, and always.

Love and gratitude to my family all over the world. But above all, to my parents, for being astonishingly patient and full of belief, even when I was not.